Daydream Believer

About the author

Mike Burke has spent 20 years in leadership of a number of different churches. He has worked for Oasis Trust and now works at Church Mission Society. He is interested in exploring new ways of being Church and has researched how Fresh Expressions of Church operate across the country. He has been involved in forms of church that meet in a school, nightclub, pub or cafe as well local networks of new mission practice. He is passionate about finding new models of church community that are not based on a model of Sunday attendance as well as exploring how the gospel relates to popular culture.

Mike lives in Gloucester where he still helps in the leadership of his local church. He is married to Jacky and has two grown up children.

Daydream
Believer

a vicar's ministry goes parabolic

Mike Burke

Highland Books

Highland Books, Godalming Surrey

First published in 2010 by Highland Books,
Two High Pines, Knoll Road, Godalming, Surrey. GU7 2EP.

ISBN-13: 978 1897913 86 4
ISBN-10: 1-897913-86-9

Cover design by Inspiration-by-Design, Goring-by-Sea, Sussex.

Printed in Great Britain by CPI Mackays, Chatham ME5 8TD

Dedication

I would like to acknowledge and thank all those people who have provided encouragement, inspiration and guidance to me in developing the story of 'Daydream Believer'. In particular I would like to thank Dave Kelly, Tina and Les Timms, Simon Harkin, John Witcombe, Lindy Moat, Emma Burke and of course Jacky for all their help and affirmation. Without their help this story could never be told and Kevin's life would have remained just the figment of my over-active imagination.

Prologue

Struggling out
of the chair

Duty called. Obligation whispered in my reluctant ear. Responsibility beckoned me to overcome the inertia and safety of a particularly comfortable and inviting armchair. Every fibre in my body resisted this movement and struggled to overcome the pull of gravity that wanted to envelop me in the reckless indolence of a warm, familiar room and a quiet night in. From somewhere deep within me the gently disturbing thought entered my mind that this was not what I had signed up for. This was not how my life was meant to be.

Where had my drive and energy gone? It had already been a long and demanding day and the thought of going out to spend another evening doing something I would rather not be doing, in the presence of an eclectic group of people with whom I had little in common irritated me profoundly, draining me of any remaining enthusiasm and positivity. Quiet unexpressed resentment rose within me as I left the security of the living room for the formality of my study to collect numerous dog-eared files, my personal organiser and a rather battered looking *A to Z Street Map*. The words of *Pink Floyd* – 'hanging on in quiet desperation is the English way' [1] floated into my mind and refused to leave, providing the internal musical accompaniment for the activities that followed.

The distance between the two rooms was negligible yet in terms of the different worlds of work and leisure, duty and recreation, public persona and the real 'me', such a journey represented stepping across a huge void. The distance between the two seemed to grow with each passing day, presenting a formidable chasm which I had grown accustomed to breaching with regular weariness.

I collected my car keys from the hook by the door. Pointed and squirted them at my ageing Rover 45 diesel with a fish badge that rested wearily on the rain-soaked driveway outside. This fading iconic emblem of the now moribund British motor vehicle industry appeared emblematic of my life and aspirations - so many new starts and tantalising possibilities, yet so many promising breakthroughs that turned into disappointing outcomes before finally succumbing to global economic forces which only celebrated the strong and the successful.

I flattened what remained of my hair, slotted in a rather grubby work collar and paused in front of a familiar photograph which illuminated the dark and draughty entrance hall. The woman staring back in the photo always seemed to gaze out with penetrating recognition as if she understood my troubled mind and reluctant spirit, whilst imploring, me to move on and haul myself out of the well of my self pity. With that reassuring smile, I closed the door and stepped into the embrace of a dark and windswept winter evening. The night seemed to close in around me penetrating even my most optimistic thoughts and sapping my positive energies with a deep sense of foreboding and cheerlessness.

Twenty minutes later I was negotiating a series of pot holes in a crowded and inadequately lit car park. Trying not to scrape my

1   'Time' written by Mason, Waters, Wright and
       Gilmour in album 'Dark Side of the Moon', 1973

car against a Mini Metro parked so badly that it resembled a vehicle hurriedly abandoned in a snow storm rather than one whose elderly owner had arrived ten minutes earlier, when numerous car parking options had presented more choices than they were able to accommodate. I stepped out and immediately sank into a puddle soaking my new, slightly quirky leather shoes purchased earlier that month in the hope that they would make me appear more self confident and in touch with modern tastes, less like a Morris dancing Geography teacher. I squelched my way across the pot-holed car park.

The landscape of puddles gave way to a 1950s wooden framed pre-fabricated building where I was greeted with the smell of wet floorboards, weak coffee, dusty books and disinfectant. My thinning cranium was assaulted by the blast of a gas heater, creaking and pinging overhead. I paused briefly to wonder where else such ancient heating systems were still deployed in twenty first century Britain, but drew a blank. This was a unique environment, locked in time not because it couldn't change but rather because it didn't see why it should.

The room was furnished with those steel tubular stacking chairs with green, faded upholstery that were banished from polite society somewhere towards the end of the 1960s when public participation in communal activities was surrendered in favour of spending an evening watching the *Forsyth Saga* on television. They were arranged in jumbled rows in order to allow each occupant the opportunity to stare meaningfully into the back of the head of those late arrivals who were accordingly punished by the indignity of having to sit at the front.

An inviting semi-circle might have made a welcome alternative, but this was not a venue particularly acquainted with bold experimentation or informality. I reflected briefly on the fact that this was probably the last remaining public building in England that still retained such seating without ever being troubled by the thought of its immediate replacement.

Familiar faces looked up enquiringly over duck-egg blue crockery cup and saucers. Many were already engaged in intense one-to-one conversations, few seemed to notice my squelching arrival nor were they willing to offer a smile or a greeting. I secretly longed for one of those brightly lit and funkily decorated hotel conference suites that you enter wearing a company badge, a business suit and carrying complementary stationary and the mandatory laptop. Instead a charming grey haired lady in fleece jacket and black leggings, retained from the first time around rather than the result of any current retrospective fashion choice, caught my eye and with her best efforts at cheeriness asked if I had signed in by the door and whether I was bringing any apologies. I briefly considered apologising for my whole life which up to that point had probably been a bit of a disappointment to myself, but thought better of any attempt at wit or irony, a precaution that was supported by the fact that similar attempts at humour had seldom been understood or appreciated on previous occasions.

I was pointed in the direction of a low hatch in the prefabricated wall where I struggled to stoop in order to request a coffee, white, two sugars. My request was soon answered by the offer of duck-egg blue crockery and a plastic spoon, which subsequently buckled and bent upon immersion. The brown indeterminate liquid both failed to revive or stimulate my energy levels and also fell short of the market standard that it purported to be challenging by its fair-traded status.

I grabbed a broken custard cream, more out of habit than enthusiasm and laid it down in the brown liquid now occupying the saucer, the result of an earlier collision with a late arrival who likewise had struggled to stoop under the serving hatch in the wall.

I straightened myself up, took a deep breath and gazed around the room. A group of apparent strangers with little in common, waiting to go home. The reason for their assembly appeared about as pointless as a snooze button on a smoke alarm. I breathed in the mustiness of the atmosphere, the murmur of polite conversations and heroic attempts at forced humour, accompaniment by the rattling noise of people scraping their shins on green tubular steel stacking chairs whilst being lightly grilled by pinging overhead convection heaters. I took a sip of the brown liquid. It tasted of mediocrity and missed opportunities.

Welcome to the Church of England!

Chapter One

Arguing in the car park

"What did you think Kevin?"

But I wasn't listening.

I had switched off some time earlier. My attention had taken a side turning into the land of day dream during an earlier presentation on parish share allocations and Deanery indices of multiple social deprivation. My concentration hadn't been enhanced by a throbbing headache brought on by extreme temperature contrasts afflicting my tired body, due to the top half of my body being vertically assaulted by intense, radiating heat emanating from the ancient overhead heating system, whilst my feet had passed into unconsciousness by the numbing cold and incessant drafts throughout the two hour meeting. I recalled something I felt sure I had been taught in school many years before about how thermocouples work. Apparently it is possible to generate electrical energy through the application of extreme temperatures to opposite ends of metal conductor rods. I irreverently wondered if the creation of such temperature differentials was all part of a sinister Church of England plan to turn all Deanery Synod members into living batteries, capable of generating their own energy supplies in order to heat their drafty church halls and church buildings...

This thought caused me to drift off further into recalling one of my favourite films, *The Matrix* in which the mysterious and enigmatic Morpheus seeks to explain the alternative reality cloaked from the view of the inquisitive Neo, played by Keanu Reeves. In this strange film noir reality, Neo discovers that all humans are held in captivity by a huge conspiratorial computer programme - the Matrix. This system relies upon human batteries providing the electrical energy required to serve its needs. All humans were effectively slaves, held in unwitting, unconscious compliance that could only be broken when they dare to summon up sufficient faith to question the reality they lived under and to release themselves from the power of the Matrix[2].

(Across the room, a DARK FIGURE stares out the tall windows veiled with decaying lace. He turns and his smile lights up the room)

MORPHEUS: At last.

(He wears a long black coat and his eyes are invisible behind circular mirrored glasses. He strides to Neo and they shake hands)

MORPHEUS: Welcome, Neo. As you no doubt have guessed, I am Morpheus.

NEO: It's an honor.

MORPHEUS: No, the honor is mine. Please. Come. Sit.

(He nods to Trinity)

MORPHEUS: Thank you, Trinity.

(She bows her head sharply and exits through a door to an adjacent room. They sit across from one another in cracked, burgundy-leather chairs)

2   Written by Larry and Andy Wachowski (Shooting
     Script 3/9/98) Warner Brothers 1999

MORPHEUS: I imagine, right now, you must be feeling a bit like Alice, tumbling down the rabbit hole?

NEO: You could say that.

MORPHEUS: I can see it in your eyes. You have the look of a man who accepts what he sees because he is expecting to wake up.

(A smile, razor-thin, curls the corner of his lips)

MORPHEUS: Ironically, this is not far from the truth. But I'm getting ahead of myself. Can you tell me, Neo, why are you here?

NEO: You're Morpheus, you're a legend. Most hackers would die to meet you.

MORPHEUS: Yes. Thank you. But I think we both know there's more to it than that. Do you believe in fate, Neo?

NEO: No.

MORPHEUS: Why not?

NEO: Because I don't like the idea that I'm not in control of my life.

MORPHEUS: I know exactly what you mean.

(Again, that smile that could cut glass)

MORPHEUS: Let me tell you why you are here. You have come because you know something. What you know you can't explain but you feel it. You've felt it your whole life, felt that something is wrong with the world. You don't know what, but it's there like a splinter in your mind, driving you mad. It is this feeling that brought you to me. Do you know what I'm talking about?

NEO: The Matrix?

MORPHEUS: Do you want to know what it is?

(Neo swallows hard and nods)

MORPHEUS: The Matrix is everywhere, it's all around us, here even in this room. You can see it out your window or on your television. You feel it when you go to work, or go to church or pay your taxes. It is the world that has been pulled over your eyes to blind you from the truth.

NEO: What truth?

MORPHEUS: That you are a slave, Neo. Like everyone else, you were born into bondage, kept inside a prison that you cannot smell, taste, or touch. A prison for your mind.

(The LEATHER CREAKS as he leans back)

MORPHEUS: Unfortunately, no one can be told what the Matrix is. You have to see it for yourself.

(Morpheus opens his hands. In the right is a red pill. In the left, a blue pill.)

MORPHEUS: This is your last chance. After this, there is no going back. You take the blue pill and the story ends. You wake in your bed and you believe whatever you want to believe.

(The pills in his open hands are reflected in the glasses)

MORPHEUS: You take the red pill and you stay in Wonderland and I show you how deep the rabbit hole goes.

(Neo feels the smooth skin of the capsules, the moisture growing in his palms)

MORPHEUS: Remember that all I am offering is the truth. Nothing more.

(Neo opens his mouth and swallows the red pill. The Cheshire smile returns)(1)

I enjoyed the opportunity to indulge my imagination and allow my mind to roam freely over such evocative concepts. What was the connection between discovering the alternative reality beyond *the Matrix* and discovering an alternative reality beyond the familiar model of Church as served up and rolled out each Sunday morning? What faith choice did those red and blue pills represent that Morpheus offered to Neo when he wanted to find out what the Matrix was?

I also speculated on why Neo appeared to be wearing a black cassock in the later, somewhat disappointing sequels? Why aren't there any Kung Fu-kicking, black leather-clad 'babes' in evidence beating up the forces of control and complacency within General Synod? Where can you buy those trendy sunglasses and why was such a great role as Neo wasted on Keanu Reeves...?

"KEVIN. What do YOU think?"

All of a sudden the cold hand of reality descended upon my fantasy world. "Ask me another, less direct question." I replied, trying to bring myself out of what was increasingly becoming my grumpy old man default mode and into a more caring, responsive and spiritual mode instead. As I thought better of adopting such an abrupt and negative demeanour, I decided to change tack.

"I'm sorry Marjorie. It's been a long day and a long meeting."

"Well, you're not the only one who's tired. Some of us have worked a full school day before coming here, but I thought that it went quite well really, although there were some contrary views."

"Really," I replied, trying to coax myself back into a positive mindset whilst re-entering my well worn and more polite social persona. Gradually I was restored to the solid reality of my real identity as Reverend Kevin Trevor Birley, vicar of St Ebbs Moretown, Sheffield.

"Yes. I thought that at least everyone was able to have their say." Marjorie continued. "Ordinary people as well as clergy. If you know what I mean? So often these meetings get dominated by the clergy and the loudest voices among them...."

Marjorie was a wonderful person. She really was. She deserved a better response from me, even if it was after the end of a marathon Deanery Synod. She was in her late fifties, a former churchwarden, a teacher approaching retirement and stalwart of her parish church. She was always the first person to arrive at any meeting and the last to leave. She had amazing spiritual and emotional strength which she invested in all the people she came into contact with and most of all, she was reliable. The kind of person who would take a bullet for you. Without her and people like her, there would be no such thing as local church serving its local community. I had learnt that the effectiveness and indeed long term viability of St Ebbs if not the wider Church rested on the shoulders of people just like Marjorie. She truly deserved greater respect and reverence than I was showing her at ten fifteen on a wet January evening as the church meeting finally broke up and tired bodies hauled tubular steel chairs around a damp, wooden church hall floor in search of stacking possibilities. As those same bodies started to decant into the church car park, various conversations continued as lights were extinguished in the tired church hall and the car park was lit by car headlights, drivers anxious to get home for some relaxation in what remained of the day.

"Sorry Marjorie." I apologised once again, not wishing to appear distracted or unappreciative and guided Marjorie towards her car and away from the worst pot holes and puddles which littered the church car park. "Yes it was good that so many people were able to have their say and to start to engage with the issues of mission today."

I considered whether I wanted to continue my discussion with Marjorie or whether I should make an excuse and head off home. I nursed a secret ambition for a doner kebab on my way home for some reason. I had been salivating over the prospect during the meeting, the longer it dragged on, the greater the appeal of reconstituted, badly cooked dead sheep, salad and extra chilli sauce. Whilst musing over these options I made my way outside into the dark inky embrace of a poorly lit northern post industrial conurbation. It had started to rain, the street lights illuminating the pock marked car park whose numerous puddles had greeted my earlier arrival. It resembled an urban battlefield scarred by various water filled craters around which dispersing members of the Deanery Synod were now cautiously tiptoeing as they made their weary way home to more civilised surroundings. Across the car park I observed a rather heated exchange of views occurring in front on a battered Volvo estate. A smart, younger man in business suit and sharp designer spectacles was berating a somewhat large elderly clergyman weighed down with a bundle of lever arch files. I recognised the man in the suit from similar previous meetings but couldn't recall his name – an experience not uncommon in parish ministry.

"It's all right for you," the man in the suit protested, "your parish has its own vicar, but how are we going to manage sharing a priest with St Agnes? The two parishes just happen to live alongside each other, but we don't have anything in common. They're up the candle and we're Low Church. People just won't have it. I tell you they won't tolerate it. We're tired of being pushed around by the bullies in the Diocese. At least they should have the common decency to come here tonight to explain their thinking, rather than leave you, the Rural Dean, sorry Area Dean to explain it all."

"First of all let me explain that there are *no* 'them' and 'us'. It's all 'us'." The overweight, elderly clergyman explained. "We are a family. A Christian family. I have to declare an interest that those 'bullies in the Diocese' you refer to are my friends. They're not…"

"That's bollocks and you know it," injected the man in the suit, suddenly raising the heat of the discussion. "The Diocese forgets that it's the parishes that keep them going. We're at the sharp end of mission, while they sit in their offices and stare at their budgets and quota figures. It's just numbers on a page to them."

"Hang on a sec." I interrupted, finding myself being drawn into what was turning into a good old fashioned, stand-up row.

"Just who do you think the Diocese is?" I challenged the nameless besuited man in the hope of drawing his venom away from the beleaguered Area Dean who was in danger of becoming the epitome of everything that was wrong with the Church of England in the other man's eyes.

"You know who I mean. All those who work at Church House... those advisors and officers, the Bishop and all his cronies – sorry – staff."

"Well I'm no expert," I continued, stating the obvious and starting to regret my intervention, unsure as to which side of the argument I would come down on. "But, the Diocese is effectively three secretaries typing in an office, trying to do the best they can. It's just too easy to blame those whom we don't really know and whom we regard as faceless bureaucrats. It's always the fault of 'them upstairs', those we consider powerful, but we are the ones who have all the real power. We can change things. We can oversee decline or we can plan for growth. If there is any crisis in the Church it is a crisis that we have allowed to happen by letting others do our thinking and make all the decisions. It's not resources we lack, it's imagination!"

I was getting quite wound up now, but I still didn't know where my arguments were leading. My rising self-assurance was in danger of being undermined when the focus of debate suddenly started to centre upon my own contribution.

"Well what do you suggest then? If you were Pope what would YOU do?" Suddenly the nameless man in a suit was sensing a new clergy victim he could pick on as the earthly manifestation of all that he perceived was wrong with the Church. Now I had to think on my feet.

"Me?" Suddenly having drawn the sting of the argument away from the Area Dean I started to feel increasingly vulnerable. I hadn't thought through my argument in advance and if I was honest, I too shared many of the man in the suit's frustrations. It was time to use irreverence to lighten the atmosphere and give me space to collect my thoughts.

"Well, the first thing I would do is forget all that medieval nonsense about celibacy and let's modernise and get on down and get groovy with all the hot prots..."

An eerie silence descended as I realised levity was not called for at such a moment, my audience didn't share my sense of irony.

"You know what I'm getting at. I didn't literally mean 'Pope'." Suddenly the man in the suit realised he hadn't cornered the market in speaking rubbish and was starting to get a bit frustrated with what he saw as a professional who should know better, not taking his opinions seriously.

"If I was in charge? Pope. Bishop. God. General Secretary, whatever title you want." I countered, filling in once again whilst trying to organise my mind into rational thinking at the end of what had been a very long day and a very boring meeting. "I would start giving out cookery lessons!"

"Cookery lessons? What DO you mean dear boy?" interjected the Area Dean in a manner that said, 'I am still here' and 'remember I've been in parish ministry for a lot longer than you, so this better be good'.

"Well......" I said, hoping that my illustration would bear the weight of intense scrutiny. "We have been defining the issues we face as a resources problem, rather than a conceptual one. What we have essentially been arguing about this evening is the scarcity of resources. Clergy numbers are declining, congregations are shrinking and we all still trying to do what we have always done plus lots of extra things with fewer resources. Agreed?"

"Keep going. I still don't see what this has to do with cookery?" The man in the suit replied. His curiosity nonetheless aroused.

"To use a metaphor. We have been talking about the size of cakes. We all bring ingredients to the table, notably money as well as our voluntary help, experience, gifts and good will, but essentially financial resources. This money is then sent off in the form of our quota payments to Church House. In other words, the Bishop and those who advise him."

"Where they waste the money on committees, Synods and advisors," interrupted the man in the suit, sensing an opportunity to reinforce his previous point.

"Whatever. Well these ingredients are then mixed up and baked into a cake which then has to be sliced up and shared around. What we are all arguing about is the size of the slice. Some people are saying we deserve our slice because we are a larger and more successful church. Others say that we deserve a bigger slice because we are a poor and struggling with all sorts of social problems. Others say they are a special case because they have multiple numbers of congregations and buildings to manage. Others claim special treatment because they represent a particular style or tradition. So on and so forth. But no-one ever questions why we are all baking cakes in this way? Why don't we bake our own cakes instead?"

"Ah yes, but WE are the Church of England." the Area Dean countered, assuming an air of authority. "We are not congregationalists. We are the national church, with responsibility towards the whole nation and not just to our congregations. If we all did our own thing and only looked to our own congregations, then large parts of the country would be essentially de-churched. Churches would not be able to pay for their own priests and so would close and the church would have to withdraw." The Area Dean came to a triumphant conclusion, restored in the knowledge that he had made what he regarded as a stout defence for the comprehensiveness of the Church he had served for so many years.

"That's precisely my point." I announced triumphantly sensing my inner spirit coming alive as my passion started to awaken after many years of defeated slumber. "We would claim we no longer think this way, but essentially we still operate the same model of church that has been around since the middle ages." I decided to take the argument to the Area Dean, more confident playing the role of poacher rather than game keeper.

"We see Church as the building, plus the priest plus the appropriate financial support. When these are withdrawn, the church is absent, the gospel is silenced and God leaves the building." I suddenly found myself re-energised at half past ten in the evening in a soggy car park following a miserable meeting. "So why not use those ingredients to make something other than cakes? Why do we need clergy anyhow? Why does every function of leadership have to rest within the ministry of one person? Why do we expend all this energy in propping up a structure whose time has come? Why not think outside of the ecclesiastical box? Why not trust God to build His Church and then we'll worry about the structures later?"

I awaited the applause. The calls of 'hear, hear' or 'Amen, brother, preach it'. But none came.

"Yes, but... to use your analogy, not everyone can bake their own cakes." The nameless business man replied thoughtfully, now sounding more like the face of conservativism and restraint, rather than the hot-headed activist he had initially resembled.

"Yes they can." I maintained.

"No they can't! It's okay for you. But many of us haven't got churches with huge amounts of gifted people who want to do things. We have a few capable individuals who do just about everything. Without such people our church wouldn't function. But they are few in number and they all have jobs and families, they have lives to lead and less and less time to offer. Whilst those who have time on their hands are either too old, too frail, too young, too confused, or just plain worn out from having done everything for years. It's as though the willing aren't able and the able aren't willing."

"Snap. Same with us." the Area Dean interrupted. Then followed a brief pause in which he composed himself, whilst the rest of us waited in expectation, assuming that he was about to offer some hugely significant and penetrating theological insight, but it never came. It had been a long day for him as well.

"We're still missing the point." I felt the heavy hand of responsibility upon my shoulder. After all, I had initiated this three way debate; it now seemed to be falling to me to bring it to some sort of conclusion. The car park was suddenly plunged into total darkness by the activities of a diligent caretaker closing up the church hall building in a rather loud and deliberate manner which said, 'You might like standing in the rain talking theology, but I'm bloody cold and want to go home to my nice warm bed and nice warm wife.'

"We don't have to do it the way we have always done it. There's more than one way to stuff a mushroom. And there's more than one way to do Church. We are all talking about how to do what we have always done, but now with less money, fewer resources and less available time. What we should be talking about are the fundamental questions."

"And just what ARE the fundamental questions?" The Area Dean at last recovering his poise and experience sufficiently to ask a relevant and penetrating leading question.

"Well I don't really know..." I admitted in a moment of brutal, yet depressing honesty, fearing that I had painted myself into a theological corner without really thinking about an escape route. Then a much needed adrenalin rush kicked in to rescue me from looking a total fool and gave birth to the kernel of an idea which energised my creative thinking sufficiently to allow me to continue.

"... But I guess the fundamental questions have to be found in the area of, what is the good news revealed in Jesus Christ for us in the twenty first century? How should that good news be lived out and presented? What forms of community do we need to develop in order to present that good news and to sustain people in their understanding and experience and what kind of leadership is required in order to deliver all of the above."

"Are those your cars over there?" The grumpy church caretaker interrupted our lofty theological discussion with the cold hand of practical realism. "Because if they are, you'll be walking home in the rain, because I am about to lock this car park and any cars left in here will have to be recovered in the morning."

Marjorie, the man in the suit, the Area Dean and myself all quickly got the message and dispersed to our various means of transport like guilty school children caught out by the teacher.

"Do you need a lift?" I enquired of my un-named, suited companion.

"Wouldn't mind. But I also need to get something to eat on the way home. I came here straight from work."

"Fancy a doner kebab?" I asked hopefully.

"Now you're speaking my language," came the reply.

Chapter Two

Life after Julie and Elvis getting into 'hot' water

"*RADIO TWO...*"

A familiar tune broke the silence and darkness of the following morning. The clock radio began its comforting routine of banal banter and cheery observations.

I awoke slowly and with a mixture of regret and confusion. Regret not only for having been quite so outspoken the night before but also for my decision to have extra chilli sauce on my doner kebab. Why did I never learn such simple lessons in life? Late night food is an evil temptress. Often promising what you think you need, but leaving you feeling sore and sorry the day after and wondering just what attracted you to the idea in the first place?

Confusion also numbed my mind following a vivid dream that lingered in my memory with a powerful sense of menace and bewilderment. I rarely remembered my dreams but this one rested powerfully in my waking thoughts as I recalled seeing myself live out scenes from *The Matrix* in which the Area Dean had inexplicably shape shifted into the dominating figure of

Morpheus and was now offering me in the role of Neo, a tantalising choice of two different cakes, one red and one blue. I kept insisting that that there should be another choice and that there were other options to explore with the ingredients he had been given me, but Morpheus was insistent and kept forcing me to eat slices of brightly coloured cake.

Meanwhile in the background of my dream Ainsley Harriot was lurking for some unexplained reason with a 'goody bag' of different ingredients that he kept suggesting Neo could combine together in twenty minutes to produce an exciting range of cakes and pastries. I was also aware of the presence in the room of the business man I had argued with and with whom I later shared a doner kebab with, now playing out one of the minor characters, complete with designer sunglasses and long black trench coat. For some bizarre reason Marjorie had taken on the entrancing persona of Trinity, complete with slicked back hair and black leathers. I was just trying to understand and come to terms with the idea of a stalwart member of the Mothers Union in tight leathers Kung Fu kicking Agent Smith's baddies, when the character of Trinity suddenly became a pretty brunette in her thirties and a warm glow of familiarity and home-coming came over me along with the growing recognition that this was indeed a dream. Reality was a lot harsher and less welcome than my dream world. Once again I was on my own.

Life on my own had been something of a struggle. I remembered a Delia Smith cookery book my Mum had bought me during my student days entitled, *One is Fun*. Never had such a title seemed so inappropriate. Contrived by those who never had to come to terms with the raw edge of living on their own following a time when they had been part of a loving couple.

Bereavement had become my middle name. I had studied the subject as part of my theological training. I had also gained some formative experience – a school friend killed in a car accident returning from a sixth form party had a profound and disturbing influence on my adolescent years. Later came Mum's sudden heart attack and death followed by Dad's illness and his withdrawal into a private world brought on by Alzheimer's. This is a sort of living loss in which the mind slowly dies while the body lives on making increasingly onerous and unfair demands on all of those around them as if to say, 'Yes, when I was younger I didn't cause anyone any trouble, but now its pay back time and I am going make sure that you know that I'm around.'

I had certainly dealt with grief on many levels. Professionally, as a parish priest I had conducted numerous funerals. I had developed skills of listening and empathy, whilst offering emotional and spiritual accompaniment to those travelling the road of bereavement. I had buried still born babies; seen teenagers killed in drug overdoses and comforted the confused families of suicide victims. I had listened to stories about 'a wonderful Gran' and heard the often repeated story of how she was, 'always there for the whole family' and how 'she never did anyone a bad turn.' Sometimes I had even been overwhelmed by other people's experiences. I had struggled to deliver a eulogy to the young family of a soldier brought back from Afghanistan. I had grown close to members of my own congregation, only to see them slip into illness, decline and eventual death. I had been shocked by sudden deaths. Worn down by lingering deaths. Overcome by unnecessary deaths, even relieved by premature deaths which brought blessing and avoided further suffering. Often I had been inspired by instances of selflessness, faith and hope demonstrated at the end of someone's life. I had even laughed at numerous funerals when good endings and happy memories were recalled and had also encountered on a number of occasions that strange and illusive phenomenon of a 'good death'.

Yes I knew a lot about bereavement. In fact in a society in which death is frequently marginalised or at least effectively hidden from most people's view and sheltered from their everyday experience, parish clergy represented something akin to experts in bereavement counselling and aftercare. I knew all about the bereavement process. How there were no short cuts. No routes to avoiding the pain and impact of loss. How each person entered the bereavement journey at a different stage, yet each experience had to be entered into in some way in order to come to terms with the reality of the loss. I knew how important it was to enter fully into that process and failure to do so could cause later psychological and emotional problems. I knew that there was no shame in tears – they were sacramental – an outward sign of the inward reality of someone's love for another. Death after all was a totally natural and normal human experience. I also knew that ritual was important in processing that experience and part of letting go, in order to arrive at what our American cousins are fond of calling 'closure', although we never really recover from bereavement, but rather learn how to live with loss and to carry its memory and burden.

Yes, I knew all about bereavement, or so I thought. But then one day I discovered that I didn't know anything at all, indeed I was a rank amateur because nothing I had learnt or experienced had equipped me to deal with my own loss, when Julie had been taken from me four years previously after our happy, yet childless marriage of twelve years. Nothing had prepared me for that journey. It was a roller coaster marked by teasing promises and false dawns in which breast cancer treatments and subsequent remissions had provided a very cruel and strangely modern curse, namely that of 'hope' for Julie and myself. Some people recover whilst others don't, however, if only we had known the destination at the beginning of our journey; if only someone had told us that Julie would have two more years to live and then would die, it might have been easier for us to cope with. Together we might have been able to make plans, do something mad and impulsive – go on a world cruise, get a tattoo on a drunken night out in Thailand, run a half marathon, go to all our favourite restaurants or start a Mexican wave during a General Synod debate. But no-one ever spells it out to you like that. No-one quite knows where you are heading when you set out on a course of treatment for breast cancer. So instead doctors discuss your options, present treatment scenarios, offer therapies, coping strategies and pain relief, but no-one ever tells you that none of these options can insulate you from the long and cold reach of cancer. As a result we heroically hung onto hope, but the prospect of hope brought pain as well as healing.

Julie had remained positive right up to the end. Probably because she didn't want to crush me, realising that I wasn't coping with her illness and the possibility of her premature death. Julie had always recognized my vulnerability which I had laboured so hard to hide. Perhaps it was this characteristic she most loved about me, along with my self-deprecating personality. This vulnerability had become even more protected once I was ordained. Ordination had always been held out as a special calling for me, once embraced, I assumed such a call brought with it the responsibility of being a role model to others. Julie often reminded me I was called to wear a clerical rather than a Superman shirt. The need to be myself, rather than trying to be perfect or superhuman. To learn how to be content within my own skin. But I had found it hard to admit my doubts and fears to others. I often felt obliged to toe the party line of trusting God to heal and then to trust in His strength if He didn't. Indeed I had used such words to provide comfort for others, but couldn't find comfort in them myself. To admit this would not only make me look insincere but might also undermine the confidence and healing which others had derived from my pastoral ministry. Therefore my instincts drove me to hide my vulnerability and uncertainty so as to avoid letting other people down when they discovered the private reality behind my public persona.

Secretly I was pissed off with God for what happened to Julie. Not just because she died, but because she suffered and in the midst of so much suffering she was further tormented by many false hopes in her treatment. Julie recognised this emotion and tried to tell me that it was ok to be angry, after all, wasn't that part of bereavement and hadn't I always explained to other people how they shouldn't feel guilty about directing their anger towards God.

I tried to move on in my bereavement. To not remain permanently angry with God, the doctors or anyone else. As the years passed, my anger did indeed recede into the background but only to be replaced by that most destructive of all human emotions, namely disappointment. The feeling that things could have, and indeed should have, turned out better. The bitter taste in the mouth that occurs when you feel you have been cheated and made to settle for less than you hoped for. I felt that God still owed me something. I had carried Julie's death and had made a number of sacrifices in order to commit myself wholeheartedly to my calling. I had paid and paid BIG. I had surrendered my hopes and dreams of an idyllic stable family life for a commitment to a shifting community. I had exchanged company and friendship for solitude and detachment. I had swapped warmth and affection with Julie for the coldness and remoteness of vicarage life on my own. I had forsaken intimacy with Julie for intimacy with God and quite frankly the equation didn't match up, I was in deficit on my intimacy account and as a result God still owed me big time.

I had worked through many of these feelings and emotions. I had taken time out. I had received the love and support of many good friends. I had been treated sympathetically. People had given me space when I needed it and provided company when I needed companionship. Friends had sensitively marked anniversaries of Julie's death by acts of thoughtfulness and generosity. They even risked speaking about her with me, even when the tears welled up or I became strangely withdrawn and quiet. I had received counselling and support, both formal and informal, professional and with my peers. I had indeed been blessed with glimpses of 'closure.' At times I was even capable of speaking about Julie and the effect of her death upon my life and ministry, although I would often avoid dwelling in that place for too long when preaching, for fear that I would become self obsessed.

Despite all this, I have a message for the blessed Delia. 'One is not fun'. I knew the solitude of outer loneliness in my personal life and inner loneliness in my spiritual life. I guess that something had died in me also. Something had departed and not returned despite the passage of time. I was scarred and injured by the whole process in a way that I still didn't understand despite all my vicarious experiences. There was a huge chasm in my life and nothing that had entered subsequently was capable of filling this gap. I just knew I was diminished. I was incomplete. 'It is not good for man to be alone,' [3] was a scripture I would often repeat to myself.

I smoothed the bed sheets out where I had slept, trying not to allow my gaze to dwell on the space which someone else once occupied. I found comfort with the thought that there were many people much worse off. I found comfort in the familiar

3   Genesis 2.18

tones of Terry Wogan flowing from the clock radio beside my bed and discovered the phrase 'mustn't grumble' floating across the airwaves and briefly occupying almost profound philosophical significance.

The day now lay ahead of me and there were important things to attend to. Downstairs I could just hear the muffled tones of the phone ringing in the study. I briefly contemplated whether it might be urgent or important business, but decided against a mad rush downstairs to intercept the call before the answer phone cut in. A short period later I heard the familiar tones of Douglas, one of the local undertakers, or 'Deadly Doug' as I liked to describe him, although never direct to his face. The message droned on for some time. Somehow Douglas never seemed able to adjust to the electronic age and the use of answer machines, mobile phones and email. He still tended to shout his message down the phone as if it might be possible to penetrate the confines of the machine and stir the recipient of the message into actually speaking with him face to face.

I couldn't quite make out all the details from upstairs, but felt sure that it would probably wait and later on form part of my agenda for the day.

Breakfast was successfully negotiated without any further interruptions. As I tidied up, I organised used crockery into my newly acquired dishwasher, which I had purchased at the suggestion of Barbara, one of my church wardens who following Julie's death had taken me on as some sort of project. She would often insist on doing little household tasks for me she felt sure that a widower would not be able to master by himself. She was the one who insisted I needed a dishwasher, even though I didn't do a great deal of entertaining and didn't generate much in the way of neglected washing up. Nevertheless it seemed easier to give in to Barbara's insistence and buy a dishwasher, even though I felt sure that this would dramatically increase my carbon footprint and what was more I secretly quite enjoyed the experience of washing up. I would sometimes have my best thoughts over a sink full of dirty pots. I also enjoyed the experience of listening to the radio which I never seemed to have time just to listen to elsewhere, but when the washing up needed doing, I would always tune in. I often enjoyed the topics of debate that comprised talk radio and felt a strange liberation, tinged with some guilt, as many minutes were passed away over the pointless trivia of why Gerrard and Lampard can't form an effective midfield partnership for England and why young people today ought to be given more discipline and time in military service in order to cut down on the number of ASBOs being issued to the 'hoodie' generation.

I cleared the table and briefly wondered why I always ended up with marmalade between my fingers when I had toast for breakfast. The answer phone was checked and yes it was just another funeral. The third that week. I would attend to the details later.

The vicarage stretched out before me offering many rooms to intrigue the curious visitor. However, to me they represented more of a burden than a blessing.

"How wonderful to live in an old place like this," many a visitor would suggest. But they never have to heat the cold and draughty, high ceilinged rooms. Nor do they have to decorate and furnish them. I would have preferred a modern house that made fewer demands and offered the possibility of a conservatory or better still a garden shed to escape into and call my own, rather than a formal study. The curse of acquiring middle class values, along with working class income tugged on the ambiguity of my circumstances adding to my sense of alienation. Often my heart would ache for the modern comforts of fitted kitchens, decking and laminated floors, rather than the moulded plaster, parquet flooring, velvet curtains and sash windows of a typical vicarage. However, without such familiar icons of British suburban living, I had learnt to carry on the pretence portrayed to the local community that I actually belonged in such a cavernous structure and had the income and the knowledge to know just how to sustain a lifestyle appropriate to its grandeur and somewhat faded glory. How I had grown weary by the often repeated local stories of summer fetes and Sunday school parties held in the vicarage and its grounds by previous incumbents. 'It must have been easier for clergy in those days. It must have been different in some way.' I'm sure, but certainly, I never really felt at home in my grade two listed Victorian six bedroom detached town house, and I harboured a secret ambition that one day someone would release me from it and turn it into a nursing home – a destiny shared by other similar properties in the local area.

The vicarage stood some distance from the nearby main road and busy bustling streets of outer Sheffield, screened from the swish of trams and the rumble of regular buses by a large garden and a tree lined perimeter. Even then, the outside world would still make an occasional unwelcome intrusion into vicarage life signalled by the arrival of cans of *Carling* and *Stella* bottles along with the remains of chips and curry sauce and even the odd chicken biryani hurled into the bushes or else left in the middle of the drive. I recalled my initial lasting impressions gained in my first week in the vicarage, when the only person Julie and I met was the local police constable who popped around looking for a discarded knife apparently left in the vicinity after a disturbance outside the nearby balti house the day before. He never found the weapon, but the suggestion that such an event was not uncommon in the area laid down an uncertain marker for us both. The sense of coldness and veiled hostility was not helped by the first encounter I had with my next door neighbour in which I was greeted by the friendly honesty and warmth for which Yorkshire folk are known. "Aye lad I see you've finally moved in. Good. You'll be wanting to get that bloody hedge of yours cut back now then."

Today such memories were a distant reminder that I didn't really belong where I live. I like Sheffield. I love its straightforwardness: the sense in which it didn't pretend to be something that it wasn't. The fact that the local people all held great pride in their city as well as a sense of resentment for the industrial rape that had been forced upon it during the decline of heavy manufacturing and coal mining. I even enjoy the fact that Sheffield was the only city I knew of on the edge of a National Park with the hills and lakes of the Peak District beckoning on days off and forming a pretty garland around the neck of a once grimy industrial neighbour.

Mid morning I walked the familiar ten minute journey across town to church. Sheffield was enjoying considerable redevelopment of its city centre and new offices and retail developments were bringing a real buzz of economic optimism to the city, however, some of this energy and investment was still to trickle down to the parish. I passed by the Pound Shops, betting shops and sports bars that formed the shifting face of a local economy in transition and arrived at the dry stone wall of St Ebbs parish church. I entered the church grounds, mercifully spared the demands of an active graveyard, over which so many of my fellow clergy found themselves spending increasing amounts of time in maintenance and management.

Once inside the grey stone building, I shut the door, somewhat tentatively, feeling that I really should be making a statement to the local community, that myself and Jonathan, my curate, were there to pray and that others could join with us. I would have preferred a glass door and an open plan building which would then make the statement, 'We are here and we are not ashamed to do what we do,' to all who passed by. However, the Church's planning authorities had other views and as yet the debate about the building alterations remained unresolved. Some mornings I would leave the door open in order to show people that there really was someone there, praying for them. Over the years I had come to suspect that no-one really cared whether I was there praying for them or not, so long as I was available when they needed me. So when the wind blew the door shut or when an icy blast coming down from the moors penetrated deep into the building sapping the spiritual warmth and energy of the devout, I reluctantly retreated behind the certainty and anonymity of St Ebbs substantial wooden entrance door.

Today I was by myself and I completed an uncomfortable twenty minutes in prayer and bible study which I somehow managed to convince myself was more like half an hour because I knew that I really should be praying more than I actually did. As I emerged from the church building I was met by Arthur, the church caretaker sweeping up broken glass from one corner of the churchyard.

"How do Kev?" Arthur greeted me.

"Morning Arthur." I replied. I liked Arthur. Arthur was uncomplicated and undemanding. A former steelworker who had been made redundant and having failed to secure any permanent work had decided to retire early. He stood over six feet tall and broad chested with enormous rough hands scarred by many years of manual work. I found him the caretaking job partly as a form of therapy to keep him busy and give him something to get up for each day, and partly because there really was a great need for such a role. Church buildings need someone to keep a casual eye on them. To potter about and to notice all the little jobs that need doing. I had managed to convince my parish church council that such a role was needed and that Arthur would be ideal for the post. Arthur was also a real God-send, because he didn't share the same demographic as the rest of the congregation. He was more working class. Blue collar instead of white collar and consequently, not afraid to get his hands dirty and embrace all those little cleaning and repair jobs that many others were unwilling or unable to take on. Arthur was good news. I also appreciated the fact that Arthur was one of the few members of the congregation in whose company I could escape. I would often pop around to his small terraced house, or 'Camelot', his Arthurian Kingdom as I liked to refer to it in order to hide away, watch football or rugby on Sky TV and have a few beers without feeling the need to justify or explain myself to anyone else afterwards.

"Are you OK to do another funeral for me on Friday?" Arthur would also double up as verger for funerals and weddings. A welcome sideline for Arthur and a source of much needed cash in his pocket.

"Ah right. Thou'll do no doubt. Anyone we know?"

"Not really. Just the usual."

"No problem... Have you spoken with Jonathan yet?"

"What about?"

"Oh you haven't heard then?"

"Heard what?" I enquired becoming curious.

"About that there music for funeral he did t'other day."

"What about it? As I recall it was a couple of hymns and a CD."

"Well I'll say nowt more about it. Just talk to Jonathan. I think he's still a bit upset over what happened."

Arthur and I parted. I retreated back to the vicarage. Even though it was Jonathan's day off, I knew I had to get in touch and see what had happened. Funerals can be so much hassle, especially when they go wrong. Often people make the same joke about how it must be wonderful only having to work on Sundays, but they often don't realise all the hard work that goes into preparing and leading funerals throughout the week. Especially post Diana. Ever since the death of Princess Diana when the world witnessed her traumatic funeral, many clergy had perceived a significant change in people's expectations of funerals evidenced by more and more creative demands made upon funeral directors and clergy. Whereas once people had been willing to more or less hand over the arrangements to the professionals to do what they felt best, now the families were more actively involved. Tributes from family members, poems, songs, flowers, orders of service, taped music tastefully chosen to reflect the mood and character of the deceased were now all common place where once they had been rare. People were even known to take photos or arrange recordings of the services. Sometimes, I half expected to see Sir Elton John at St Ebbs providing an appropriate musical tribute. Such developments were generally welcomed as a 'good thing' and helpful in allowing families to participate more fully in the letting go process following the death of a loved one. However, it did create a lot more work for clergy and a lot more potential for something to go disastrously wrong.

> *"Hi Jonathan. It's Kev. I know it's your day off, but Arthur has just spoken to me and I understand there was a problem over the funeral you did yesterday. Give me a ring if you want to talk about it. If not, then we'll chat on Monday. Bye..."*

I hoped that Jonathan would receive his recorded message so that I could get to the bottom of the problem. I hated mysteries. My mind runs amok and imagines something a lot worse happening than is often the case.

Sure enough, ten minutes later the phone rang in the study. It was Jonathan.

"Hi Kev. Have you got a minute? I've not slept all that well since the funeral yesterday and it would be good to chat."

"What happened then?"

"Well everything went OK except for this CD they wanted played at the end... some sort of Elvis track."

Jonathan wasn't particularly musical. His background was in finance and insurance. He had come from one of those smart and self confident churches in London which seemed to produce smart and self confident candidates for ordination. We got on well. But in many ways we came from very different worlds. Whilst I was from the industrial West Midlands, my Father an engineer, the son of an engineer, the son of an engineer; Jonathan was from Crawley, the son of a management consultant and with impeccable middle class credentials. Public school, London University, a job in the city and then called to ordination. Sheffield had therefore proved something of a cultural baptism of fire for him, but he was capable and bright and very, very earnest.

"So what was the problem?"

"Well I spoke with the undertaker."

"Not Deadly Doug?"

"No, it was the Co-op. And anyhow they seemed fairly cool about the request. I think that they had a new chap in the office. But I left it with them. As you do. No sign of any problems. Assumed everything was OK."

"But it wasn't OK," suddenly realising that I had a good idea what problems Jonathan had encountered.

"No, it wasn't. It was a strange funeral anyhow. All sorts of unusual requests and weird sights."

"What do you mean?"

"Well it was a sort of country and western funeral. The woman who had died had been really into her line dancing and everything associated with popular American culture."

"Hence the Elvis request."

"Exactly. There were all sorts of strange things going on around me. A real interesting mix of people. Apparently not only did they all go line dancing, they were also members of a

Wild West recreation society and so a number of the mourners came dressed for the part as it were."

"What do you mean?"

"You know. Cowboy hats. Boot lace ties. Rhinestones over everything. Cowboy boots and those suede jackets with all the tassels around them. A few of them had Confederate flags sewn onto the back of their jackets. One guy even described himself as 'Dancing Bob', apparently when he's not line dancing and sharp shooting he presents himself as the local Monster Raving Loony candidate in some of the local elections... Really nice bloke though... does loads of good work for local charities, so I'm told..."

"What does any of this have to do with Elvis playing at the end of the funeral?"

"Not a lot. The funeral in church went OK more or less, no major faux pas, although they all stood up at the commendation and saluted the Confederate flag that had been draped over the coffin. But apart from that rather strange sight everyone seemed happy."

"So what went wrong then?"

"Well it all came unravelled at the crematorium after I gave the final blessing and they wanted to listen to this Elvis track called 'Burning love.'"

"BURNING LOVE! They played *Burning Love* at the end of the crem service?"

"Yes, I thought that it was a bit strange. But I just assumed that it was an expression of their love for the lady who had died, and that it was some sort of special family request."

"Have you ever listened to the words of *Burning Love*?"

"No, not then... but I have now... not very appropriate I thought. Something about, 'I feel my temperature rising. Higher higher. It's burning through to my soul'."

"Didn't you realise what was happening?"

"No, I just thought that it was just an unfortunate phrase or two, but then I started hearing other lyrics like, 'You gonna set me on fire. My brain is flaming. I don't know which way to go,' and 'the flames are reaching my body. Please wont you help me I feel like I'm slipping away... it's hard to breath... my chest is a-heaving... Lord almighty, I'm burning a hole where I lay.'"[4].

"So what was the undertaker doing?"

"Not a lot. He was just hiding his face and trying not to wet himself. Laughing most of the time."

"Who was in charge?"

"Richard."

"He's normally able to see the funny side in most things, but what about the mourners? Were they very upset?"

"They didn't appear so at the time. After a few verses of Elvis, one of the relatives came down the aisle of the chapel to tell the crem staff that they wanted track thirteen instead of eleven or something like that. By this time some people were sniggering whilst others were crying. I couldn't work out if they were tears of laughter or just tears."

"How about you? What were you doing?"

"Well I just didn't really know where to look or what to do. By the time I realised that something was wrong, the damage had been done. So I just got up and apologised and made some lame excuse, saying something like, I'm sure that the deceased would have seen the funny side and the tears and laughter are all part of our shared human experience."

"So did you get any bad feedback?"

"Well not from the immediate family. But there was a nephew there who was fuming and said something about coming round and breaking my legs. The others seemed to take it in better cheer."

"Look Jonathan. It wasn't your fault. Did you explain?"

"Oh yeh. Sure did. But you know how it is. I just feel so wretched and foolish."

"Look Jonathan. No-one has cornered the market in looking foolish as much as me over the years. I once got tongue tied at a committal and referred to bringing 'the whole Church living and

4   Lyrics to 'Burning Love' written by Dennis Linde
(March 1972)

departed in the Lord Jesus to a joyful erection' instead of a 'joyful resurrection'. Not quite the Christian hope I had in mind, but at least it put a smile on the widow's face."

"Gosh Kev. How dreadful, but what am I going to do?"

"Well don't worry. I'll give the Co-op a ring and try to smooth things over with them. I'm sure that it will blow over and be forgotten about in a few days time."

"Oh I hope so Kev. I've been so worried ever since. It's just that you only get one chance with a funeral don't you. It's not as if you can call everyone back together and go through it all again, this time with no cock ups."

"I'm sure we'll all see the funny side of it one day. But in the meantime, don't worry. Enjoy your day off. Go and play with your kids. Have fun and put it all down to experience."

I put down the phone secretly and rather selfishly relieved that this incident had happened to Jonathan and not to myself. It had been a very theatrical day. Starting with *The Matrix* and ending with Elvis. Little did I realise that this artistic theme would continue in the days ahead.

Chapter Three

Ian's crazy offer

Mourners outraged as Elvis gets all shook up

Shocked mourners failed to see the funny side of a misunderstanding over funeral music at a Sheffield Crematorium last week. Grieving relatives were said to be distraught following a mistake over the choice of music at the end of the service. The funeral of 80 year old former 'buffer girl' Eileen Stapleton descended into farce when instead of the carefully chosen Elvis standard of 'You were always on my mind' a very different upbeat song was played over the Crematorium's public address system.

The Elvis ballard was much loved by Mrs Stapleton to expressher love for her family for whom she had been a devoted 'Gran' and always there for them in times of need. Imagine their shock and horror therefore when instead of their timeless favourite tune, the words and music of *Burning Love* rang out as the coffin disappeared behind the crematorium curtains. Some mourners might have seen the funny side as the tune would have reminded them of happier times enjoyed by Eileen line dancing with her friends; however, some of the family were visibly shocked and upset. As Wayne Stapleton a family member recalled, "We didn't find it amusing at all. Even though the undertaker and priest tried to put a positive spin on it. To me it just showed a lack of respect and it ruined what should have been a moving moment for us to say goodbye to Nan."

Staff at the Crematorium were not available for comment, but a Council spokesman did say that it was part of their mission to deliver a sensitive and ap-propriate act of reflection for all their clients in a way that reflected their wishes and expectations. An internal review had been launched and in the meantime they would want to extend their deepest sympathies to Mrs Stapleton's family and assure them of the seriousness with which the Council would investigate its procedures in the future.

"Well Jon, I think that you got out of that one pretty lightly," I conceded whilst folding up my copy of the local newspaper and returning it to the kitchen table around which Jonathan and I were gathered.

"I just hope that this is the last of it. I couldn't bear anymore hassle with that family. They're asking for their money back now you know. What should I do about that?" Jonathan added tentatively.

"Well that's a tricky one. Strictly speaking it wasn't your fault. The Co-op should have told you what Elvis track they were intending to play at the end of the service. They should have realised when they spoke with the Crem, that the words weren't appropriate... so you weren't really to blame. Just remember to check out the lyrics if you have any doubts whatsoever in the future."

"Yah, right of course. Learnt my lesson on this one Kev. But what about the family getting some sort of refund?"

"Well the undertaker will have expenses to be paid no doubt, irrespective of what took place, so why shouldn't the Church? However, having said that, people think that they are hiring the clergy and paying them to deliver a product or in this case a service. They see themselves as the customer and if they aren't happy with the service provided, pardon the pun, then they see that they have every right to complain or in this case, ask for their money back."

"Okay. So what do I do?"

"Give the Co-op a ring and try to work something out. Go back to the family and talk about a good will gesture in view of the upset caused. Whatever we do, it will bound to be wrong. You're always in a lose, lose situation here. The family are upset anyhow, and often that upset is displaced onto something that isn't quite right about the funeral service..."

"... or the funeral music in this case." Jonathan interrupted.

"Quite. If people are looking for someone to kick, then it is usually one of the professionals involved. In this instance the clergy often fit the bill. I mean, after all they never see us until one of those times in life when their world falls apart and we turn up on the scene trying to help them make sense of it all. If we are perceived to having failed in that regard, we are culpable. It's hard to blame God directly, so why not do the next best thing. Blame His human representatives here on earth – 'The Men in Black'."

"Or grey as in our case... or even pink, bearing in mind the increasing numbers of women being ordained to the priesthood." Jonathan added with all his earnestness bursting out with irritating predictability.

"Yes, ladies in lilac as well. But it wouldn't make such a good film title though."

"I'm sorry, you've lost me now."

"Men in Black? Heroes secretly saving the world from undercover alien invaders? See any parallels there?

Jonathan remained rather puzzled. "Um... not really... kinda... not sure."

"It doesn't matter. Just an obsession of mine."

I resigned myself to the fact that Jonathan was a more concrete thinker than me. More given to managing the details of everyday living and less given to dreaming and imagining. My tendency to look at the world with a sideways glance had been shaped at a very early age. Often I was told off at school for not controlling my wild imagination and creative behaviour. I would regularly be ticked off for gazing out of the window in chemistry lessons or for talking too much in mathematics. I would always try and make connections between subjects, especially using humour and plays on words. My imagination would often spring to life in the world of television and cinema. Even my history projects would be laced with film, and then more latterly, musical references.

I must have been a disappointment to my Father. He is so practical and mathematical, whereas I have always struggled with numeracy as well as the discipline of formal education. I owe much of my academic career to the warm and wise intervention of an experienced English teacher, who took it upon himself to discover the things that really interested and motivated me. I will always be grateful for that. If it hadn't been for this timely mentoring I'm sure that I would have failed at school completely, but thanks to his support and understanding I was able to change my options at school to embrace those subjects which reflected my more imaginative personality. It was the same school teacher who encouraged me to take up the guitar. That led to my involvement with a school band, to my decision to go to art school and that ultimately set me on the path of Christian faith and eventual full time ministry in the Church of England. All because I used to gaze out of the window, make jokes and doodle.

The following day I found myself taking another funeral. This one was with the Co-op and this gave me the opportunity to have a quiet word with Richard, one of the undertakers who had been involved with Jonathan's funeral fiasco. Richard and I got on well. He fancied himself as something of a stand up comedian and saw it as his mission in life to put the 'fun' into 'funerals'. Just because he did a serious job didn't mean that he couldn't have a laugh with the pall bearers and clergy on the way to and from a funeral. Richard even used to moonlight as an Elvis impersonator on the local night club circuit, although not many people knew that. A fact that had only come to light following a former 'Teddy Boy' funeral, several years before. So it was not surprising that Richard took the initiative in approaching me to check that Jonathan was okay.

"How's tha lad bearing up Kev?"

"Oh, all right. His career should recover. He's the sensitive type though. I think that he's been losing a bit sleep over it all."

"Well tell he'll do and not to worry. Worse things happen at sea." Richard reassured me. "I had one a bit like that about a year ago," he continued. "Tha family just produced this CD at crem door with note saying track three. I didn't have time to check it all out. Anyhow it were track three but they'd put wrong CD in t'case. Instead of *Unchained Melody* we got *Smoke gets in your eyes.* Didn't go down well I tell you."

"Were the family really annoyed?"

"Aye… they were fuming!"

I paused realising that Richard had probably set me up for his punch line whilst the broad smile on his face revealed that this wasn't the first time he had relayed this particular story. Anyhow he re-assured me that this latest grieving family had now calmed down somewhat and were starting to see the funny side of the incident, especially when he had offered them a discount on the funeral fees.

Later on that evening I sat down to a microwave ready meal for one which I consumed whilst avidly watching an episode of *Masterchef* on BBC2. The irony of the situation was not lost on me. It was a Tuesday evening and that meant band practice. This was an important time in my week. I jealously protected this evening slot from church planning meetings, worship preparation and pastoral visits. This was time for me to indulge one of my great passions in life – popular music.

I entered my study. There before me sat an array of disparate items, emblematic of my obsessions. A large wooden desk sat in the middle of a tall bay window around which were draped heavy velvet curtains to keep out the draughts. The magnolia coloured walls were covered by various watercolour paintings of trees, seascapes and mountains. My own more recent efforts. Among them sat some dark and strangely sinister oils of scenes from the *Alien* series of films. These had formed an art school project many years ago, but I still enjoyed their visual impact and would occasionally lose myself in the visual imagery. This study space was carefully guarded from many of my parishioners. Some of them had seen these pictures along with some pop art based upon the comparative imagery of the various rock music album covers employed by *Meatloaf, Tangerine Dream* and *Yes*. Admittedly a somewhat strange eclectic mixture, but one that fascinated me yet worried the morally scrupulous and artistically conservative members of my congregation. Some of them were sufficiently worried by what they saw of my artwork and heard about my musical interests that they had started to pray for me to be delivered from their perceived dark and satanic influences.

Fortunately others were more understanding; however, I still regularly had to defend my choice of old vinyl records when visitors commented upon my choice of *Black Sabbath, ACDC, Iron Maiden, Motorhead* and *Led Zep*. Theories concerning hidden messages contained within such sinister records which if played backwards would reveal the name of the anti-Christ or spell out some satanic curse, were occasionally relayed to me by concerned visitors. I ranked such urban legends alongside the stories that Paul McCartney was really dead because he was photographed not wearing any shoes on the front cover of the Abbey Road album. As Paul McCartney remained resolutely one of the most alive former *Beatle,* it was difficult to take such concerns seriously, but still for some people my art and music remained impenetrable and provided a possible stumbling block for their sincerely held faith and moral perspectives, or a reason to question the judgement of their vicar. Overall it was just a lot less hassle to keep church meetings in particular and earnest visitors away from the study rather than have to justify my interests or explain my fascinations.

The rest of the study was a mixture of library and music room. A large racked bookshelf covered one wall and various books and journals jostled against each other competing for space and attention. Many of my books had been purchased during training at theological college when assignments beckoned and I still believed that New Testament Greek and the doctrinal reflections of selected dead Germans would play a part in my future ministry. Since then, many of the books had gathered dust. An impressive series of bible commentaries had been carefully organised according to canonical order, but only occasionally would they be called upon for sermon preparations. More recently, the world of information technology and the internet had taken over as reference sources so that my library of theological reference books has not been added to for some time. Indeed, I must confess to not having read a serious theological book since Julie's death, although CS Lewis's *A Grief Observed* sat on my desk, providing a constant source of comfort and inspiration.

The rest of the study was taken up by an old computer, a laptop, printer and all-in-one scanner which now formed the tools of my trade, along with a large photocopier left in the vicarage by the previous vicar and although still in working order I nevertheless found it rather heavy and complicated to use. Indeed, I had intended to take it to the Council dump or else to find a local skip to dispose of it before members of the church found out and gave me a lecture about how it was perfectly adequate for the old vicar. Nevertheless, the old photocopier now operated as a very effective display table for some experimental sculptures retained from art school. The strangely shaped pieces of old driftwood and copper piping would often provide a talking point for trusted visitors, even though I couldn't remember what they represented but enjoyed keeping hold of them because they reminded me of simpler and more innocent times.

Next to the old photocopier sat my collection of guitars. When I applied for the job of vicar at St Ebbs, the selection panel noticed that I was a musician and perhaps this swayed my application in their eyes. The church was looking for someone who could develop their music in a more modern and creative direction and immediately made the connection between guitarist and contemporary worship leader. Although I've done a great deal to develop the musical life of St Ebbs, establishing a number of worship groups who now took responsibility for the leading of different worship services, I remain a reluctant musical worship leader. At a time when just about every young Christian man able to hold a guitar wants to step onto a stage, stand under a spot light, close their eyes and lead worship, I recoiled at such a role. I naturally gravitated towards the back of the stage, rather than the front. I was happy to be involved, but preferred a supporting role. This reluctance had required some clever manoeuvring of musicians within various worship groups as well as many hours spent with potential leaders, developing their skills and giving them confidence in the art of leadership. However, recently the fruits of my labours had started to pay off, with two distinctive worship groups emerging with increased confidence to lead worship without the need for me to transpose, initiate, organise or direct. Not only had this given me immense personal satisfaction but it had also allowed me to indulge my musical passions outside of the context of Christian worship. In fact, if I'm honest I preferred so called 'secular' gigs and mainstream music to the niche market of Christian 'worship music'.

I appreciate the intentions of worship music, but I find much of it vacuous and shallow, often involving meaningless love language and the mindless repetition of archaic Biblical imagery. Although well intentioned it seems to reflect the triumph of form over content, devoid of concrete language or poetic sophistication or meaningful teaching come to that. I liked the experience of being part of the performance culture surrounding worship music and occasionally found myself uplifted and inspired by the better and more thoughtful examples of the art, but generally much of it felt like a trip out to see *Mama Mia* or *We Will Rock You* in the West End – a series of enjoyable anthemic sing-alongs, with little narrative component, designed to provide temporary euphoria rather than lasting enlightenment. Something more enjoyable than meaningful.

My lack of enthusiasm for much contemporary worship music was a pity because music generally plays such a huge part in my life. My guitar collection is a source of great pride and delight. One American built 'Guild' acoustic guitar and one Japanese Yamaha six string acoustic occupied pride of place in my study, alongside a cheap Les Paul copy electric which I picked up at a car boot sale in Rotherham. However, these six string guitars were not played as often as my collection of bass instruments. An acoustic Eko bass sat beside an electric guitar as a reminder of the first bass guitar that I seriously took up. This now rather battered example had provided many happy hours of amusement when learning the bass and had been given to me by my former guitar tutor. It provided the perfect platform to learn the musical disciplines and structures of bass technique without the need for amplification and without the potential to upset the sensitivities of the neighbours. Next to the acoustic bass sat an Epiphone Thunderbird electric bass leaning on a guitar stand. This was my workhorse bass on which I would practice regularly and learn new routines and riffs. This was the bass I often used in church or when called upon to join worship bands at other churches or at various Christian worship events. However, it was not my favourite bass. That sat in an undistinguished black guitar case on the floor. My most recent acquisition was a classic Rickenbacker Electric Bass bought on eBay two years previously with some insurance money left over following Julie's death. I'm sure that Julie would have approved of my choice and would have consented to the excessive amount of money required to secure this wonderful example of craftsmanship. It was an iconic musical flagship. This was the bass I used when performing with the *Manic Tuesdays;* the local rock band I had played with for several years.

I picked up the Epiphone preferred for rehearsals, located an appropriate hard case and practice amplifier and set off for Ian's house.

Ian is the same age as me yet taller, leaner, more striking, more outgoing, more self confident and in possession of significantly more hair. He has strong piercing blue eyes and a shock of thick dark hair which he wore tied back in something trying not to resemble a pony tail. He would often dress younger than his years and liked to be seen as something of a rebel and creative force. He lived in a terraced house in an inner city part of Sheffield which provided an ideal venue for the band to practise as it had a specially converted basement into which we could squeeze equipment along with keyboards and even a drum kit when a drummer was available. I rang the doorbell and shortly afterwards Ian appeared with his back half turned away from greeting me, in one of those distracted postures which said, 'I might be a bloke, but I can multitask as well'. He was absorbed by a conversation on his mobile and waved me indoors, gesturing towards the basement door as if to say, 'come in and get started, I will be with you in a minute.'

I lowered myself down the basement stairs and was greeted by Bryan the keyboard player who was setting up a series of small black boxes and assorted electronic equipment as well as practising his scales. I returned the greeting with a nod in his direction. Bryan was something of a gadget man and technology lover. His work involved computers or servers or something of that ilk, and he worked for a bank, but I had never really penetrated his information technology world, other than when I wanted help in setting up the wireless internet at the vicarage, at which point Bryan had been a great help in dealing with all the complexities and problems encountered. I enjoy what technology can offer, both in my work life and my musical interests, but I really don't understand a great deal about it. A bass guitar is a fairly simple piece of equipment with few technological needs or complexities. That's probably what I liked about playing bass. Certainly I feel secure within this role in the group, Bryan could handle all the PA, digital sequencing, balancing, effects and mixing issues, so long as I could just turn up, plug in and play. I enjoyed being part of the *Manic Tuesdays,* the band that Ian had formed five years ago whose name was both a nod towards his favourite band, the *Happy Mondays* as well as a description of what band practice was often like when all the band members came together on a Tuesday evening for a practice and jam session in Ian's basement.

Bryan provided all the technical wizardry for the group and was an excellent, classically trained musician. In many ways Bryan should have commanded greater authority within the group. He had superior musical abilities over all of us. He was bright and creative and very well informed concerning how to put together arrangements and adept at getting the group to play according to our strengths. However, he was also shy, awkward and unassuming, not given to the limelight and often found it hard to engage with an audience. As a result it was very much Ian's group. Ian had formed the band, decided upon the name, written most of the songs and performed as the band's front man, guitarist and vocalist. Of all the members of the group, Ian was the most comfortable in the spotlight. He came alive when performing and seemed to enjoy the attention and the spotlight which usually falls upon a band's front man. He could be very outgoing, outspoken and even cocky at times as a result of a strong sense of self belief and trust in his own judgement. Ian was a good social mixer, naturally gregarious and something of a 'ladies man'. The band also met at Ian's house, so I guess that made it game, set and match to Ian; if ever there were any musical issues or differences of opinion, he always held the casting vote.

Ian harboured what Bryan and I regarded as foolish and unrealistic ambitions for the band. We had set out as a pub band playing some of Ian's own material, but recently as Ian's ambitions had grown, and we had taken on more gigs, often playing at weekends for weddings and birthday parties where we would perform cover versions of popular songs and classic 'get everyone onto the dance floor' favourites. I quite enjoyed such engagements although I occasionally grew weary of playing *Come on Eileen*, *Daydream Believer* and *Hi Ho Silver Lining*. At times, I have been unable to play some gigs due to church commitments; this seemed to rankle Ian who couldn't really understand why so much church work took place outside of a Sunday.

Ian's ambitions for the band had recently stretched to hiring a local recording studio and putting a few tracks down. Unfortunately, this could only be undertaken on a Saturday night because Ian had a mate who worked at the studio and allowed him to use the facilities throughout the night when no-one else needed it. This had led to an all-night recording session in which the three regular band members were augmented by the services of a drummer, instead of Bryan's usual drum machine backing track. Ian thought that this recording could be the start of something big for the band, but the rest of us felt obliged to point out that not many bands were headed up by a forty five year old web designer, had a father of four on the keyboards, a widowed vicar on bass and a drummer who was a school friend of one of the keyboards player's children.

Fortunately our friendship is robust enough to survive such brutal honesty. I had come to know Ian through Julie's work. At the time Ian was living with Sharon, a friend and work colleague of Julie's from the hospital where they both worked as physiotherapists. Ian and Sharon had become an item, whilst Ian was on secondment to the hospital from his employer and their relationship grew stronger and more serious even after Ian left the hospital to start his own web design business. Ian and Sharon eventually ended up moving in together and shared the small terraced house that later became the venue for the band's practice sessions. Ian and Sharon remained good friends after Julie's death and provided an interesting secular counterpoint to the support and care I received from many of my Christian friends. They recognised the physical and sexual side of my bereavement and even clumsily tried to set me up with a few casual dates in the months following Julie's death. Although such attempts were appreciated, the idea of dating just felt so adolescent to me and I struggled to find the enthusiasm for the various unattached friends they repeatedly lined me up for. However, this didn't affect our friendship and Ian and Sharon remained trusted companions in whose company I could relax, talk about music, go to the cinema and share a few beers. On a couple of occasions, I managed to have one or two more beers than normal and found myself sleeping over at Ian's house on a Saturday night before emerging early the next morning to conduct an 8 o'clock Prayer Book Communion service, ever so slightly hung over. Fortunately I can rely upon the grace of God to always forgive such an indiscretion and certainly Ian and Sharon would never mention it.

My friendship with Ian even survived the eventual break up of his relationship with Sharon. I had been aware of tensions in their relationship for some time. Ian had a child from a previous marriage with whom he had little contact, but Sharon was desperate for children and Ian didn't really want the commitment. I never found out exactly why Sharon left, Ian had just rung up one evening in tears saying "She's left. The bitch has left me." I went around and tried to comfort him, but never really found out the exact reasons for the split. I suspected that Ian might have also been 'playing away' and that when Sharon found out, it provided the final straw in their separation. Ian wouldn't tell me the full story, he kept saying that it was complicated and that he wasn't a good person, unlike me. However, Ian did ask me to pray for him on that particular tear-soaked occasion. This was something I was happy to do, although prayer and God seldom received a mention again in our friendship, but it had seemed right and appropriate for me to pray with Ian at that point in his life and Ian appeared grateful often referring to me as 'his friend in high places'.

"Now do you want the bad news, the good news or the really good news?" Ian emerged into the basement with a broad grin on his round and unshaven face, looking like a cat who had just found the cream.

"Better have the good news first then," replied Bryan looking up from a mixer desk.

"Well the good news is that Siobhan is willing to join the band."

"Who's Siobhan?" I enquired, suddenly feeling as though everyone else was in on some great secret of which I was unaware.

"You know. That girl I was talking to at the gig in the *Irish Club* the other week. The one who used to play with *Marillion*. The sax player?"

"Oh I see the opposite sax is muscling in on our band now." Bryan chipped in with a typical ironic pun. He had such a dead pan tone and such a distant disposition, that it was easy to think that he wasn't listening at all and then he would often jump in with a witty remark or observation that would reveal that no details had escaped his sharp mind.

"And just why would we need a sax player?" Bryan continued.

"That's where the really good news comes in..." Ian paused for dramatic effect. "We are going on tour!"

"ON TOUR?" I squeaked in a voice rather more high pitched than I had intended. "When... and where... and come to that... why?" I enquired, deliberately lowering my voice to spare my embarrassment.

"This is the really cool bit." Ian was now winding up into something of a frenzied state. "I've landed us a tour as the support band for *Zoo Two*!"

"*Zoo Two*? Who the hell are they?" said Bryan in a rare outburst of frustration brought about because he didn't like the way this conversation was developing and felt increasingly steamrollered by Ian.

"They are only one of the top *U2* tribute bands. That's who. They are the ones that 'The Edge' heard playing and said that he thought he was having an out of body experience in which he was watching himself on stage."

"Presumably dying on stage," added Bryan. "I'm not sure that this is going to work for me. But you might as well give us the full SP. Just what is the bad news that you were talking about?" he continued.

"Ah yes, I was going to tell you. The tour starts at the end of next month and goes on for six weeks across much of the country. I am aware that that might create a few problems for you Bryan."

"Not just Bryan," I interrupted, reminding Ian that I was still in the room and Ian hadn't given any thought to my availability either?

"Yeh, yeh I know it's going to be tricky for both of you. But what a great opportunity this is."

"Look Ian. I know that you have all these great plans for the band, but Kev and I just like it the way it is," said Bryan, suddenly speaking for both of us. "Just a few mates, having a lark, playing a couple of gigs, a bit of beer money here and there. Just for fun. We really don't buy into all this 'let's have a career' bullshit. I certainly can't get that sort of time off work and in case you've forgotten, my eldest has got his A levels this summer and I need to be around for him and for all the kids. It just isn't that easy for me. You tend to forget that."

"But...?"

"No buts Ian. You don't think these things through. This could be the worst idea someone had since Mrs Lincoln asked her husband if he fancied going out to see an opera tonight...? Just get real."

"Come on fellas. You've got to see the opportunity here. This could be BIG!"

"Big? We will be the warm-up for the warm-up band." Bryan's comments introduced the icy blast of realism once again.

"Anyhow," insisted Ian, refusing to bow to Bryan's cynicism. "Bookings like this don't come along very often. We've got to seize the day with this one... haven't we?"

Later on that evening in Ian's kitchen I expressed my reservations to Ian as well. "Let me think about this gig Ian. It's all come rather out of the blue as far as I am concerned." Bryan had gone home fairly promptly after practice had finished and there had been an awkwardness and cool atmosphere around the rest of the evening. Ian, however, was apparently unaffected and undaunted.

"Come on Kev the Rev. It will be a laugh," urged Ian, using the nickname he had coined for me.

"Let me get back to you. Even clergy can't just take off and hit the road like that. We have a responsibility to our churches, colleagues and communities... and to our calling."

"Kevin... I think that the God you try to serve would understand, if you took some 'me time' occasionally. Why are you so hair-shirt about things? You are due some R and R, especially after what you've been through."

A silent moment descended. Part of me did just want to take off with Ian and be irresponsible – to indulge my passion for music – to be spontaneous. I had never really done anything that was particularly reckless or daring before. Even before college I had never gone along the backpacking route or gap year response that many of my contemporaries had favoured. Instead, I'd worked in the Tamworth branch of *WH Smith* for a year and had saved up my money instead. I have always managed to do the sensible thing and something deep within I just wanted to tear the place up and stop being a role model of sobriety and reasonableness. I felt that Ian might have some other agenda operating, but secretly I envied the freedom he had to follow his dreams. I thought back to the late night car park conversation a few days earlier in which I had told the angry business man that we shouldn't blame the church as an institution for all our problems – we have freedom to change things if only we used our imagination. If that was true, then shouldn't I be willing to follow a dream as well – to 'seize the day' as Ian had suggested?

A tinge of fear entered my mind. I was starting to frighten myself with the thought that I might be about to break the habits of a life time and start to act irresponsibly. But wasn't I just running away from my problems, my loneliness, my frustrations with the Church, my unease with my role as a vicar? Was I looking for escape, a way out of the questions and complexities of my life, or a way through them?

"I'm not sure Ian. Let me go and see one or two people and pray about it first. You must understand, I have to do that?"

"OK, but don't take too long. The tour starts in just over four weeks and to be honest, I've already said yes to the promoter. So if you don't want to be part of it, then I need to know."

It all felt a little unreal and threatening. I had sympathy with Bryan and in some ways I would have welcomed the excuse of having a family to consider. Having no-one to think aloud with or to bounce ideas or choices off is a great problem once you find yourself suddenly living on your own again. However, there were people I could talk with. Jonathan for starters, and my church wardens. I would definitely have to have a word with the Bishop. I was also due to see my spiritual director next week, maybe I could run it pass her and see what she thought. I would also have to make arrangements with the nursing home, just to let them know that I wouldn't be visiting Dad for a few weeks.

As I mentally made a checklist of all those people I needed to talk to and test this idea with, I felt a sense of relief. Surely such a process would either wonderfully confirm this idea or else expose it all as a vain folly and the symptom of some sort of mid-life crisis. For once I felt reassured and fortunate. I wasn't as isolated as I sometimes assumed. I was indeed part of a community of people who cared about me and to whom I was accountable in some way. I would lay a fleece in prayer, seek advice and see what developed over the following few weeks.

Chapter Four

A day out in Derbyshire

Gravel crunched under the wheels of my six year old blue Rover 45 diesel as I guided it up the immaculate drive of a large Regency town house on the outskirts of Buxton, Derbyshire. I loved this journey across the Peak District to Buxton, especially at this time of year. It was one of those winter days when everything appeared fresh and crisply turned out. The low winter sun shone out of a cloudless blue sky across a cold and frosty landscape. Sheep were grazing on the wintry hillsides of Buxton feeding on bales of hay that the hill farmers had lovingly put out for them. The journey down had been a pleasant distraction from a particularly hectic and complicated last few days in the parish. But now I was off to see Bridget Hamilton, my spiritual director.

"You need to find someone to whom you can be accountable. Someone who will support you, but outside of the parish and your immediate friends." The Bishop had insisted at the time. "Have you ever had a spiritual director?" I fielded such a question in the same manner as being asked, 'Have you ever been to a *Harvester* before?'

"No, not really, in fact, not at all." I admitted. Feeling a little bit guilty as well as ignorant of how a spiritual director was going to fill the void left by Julie's death.

It was after that meeting I was given Bridget's phone number and further encouraged by my church wardens to meet up with her. At first, I was a bit reluctant. Just who was this woman and how could she help? I also felt more than a little vulnerable, like being invited to undress in front of a stranger. How would I feel discussing my internal world and emotional and spiritual state with a complete stranger?

My fears were unfounded. The first time I met Bridget, I sensed huge warmth and an emotionally reassuring presence. In her company, I felt increasingly at ease and a rest. It felt a little like coming home after time spent away at college when I was a student. Bridget made a good impression on our first meeting. Following the initial assessment time in which I had explained to her all that had taken place during Julie's illness and death and how this had made me feel, she just sat back in her chair and pronounced.

"To me, it sounds as though you need to get drunk, get angry and get laid! But not necessarily in that order."

After that I realised I was in the hands of someone who combined great sensitivity with brutal honesty. I subsequently learnt that she didn't always literally mean everything she said, however I still respected her integrity and straightforwardness. Such comments were more comforting and permission giving than shocking. Sometimes Bridget provided a substitute mother figure, although I had never been that close to my own mother and certainly would never have discussed my problems with her in such a frank manner.

Bridget was in her late 50s, short and stocky with close cropped perfectly coiffured grey hair that never looked unkempt, even in the most blustery Derbyshire weather. She wore half rimmed glasses that she would often use as a prop to either stare over in mock disapproval or else remove in order to heighten her sense of earnestness and intensity. She was a bright as a button and as sharp and quick witted as anyone I had ever met. She also oozed warmth and wisdom born out of profound experience and quiet reflection with the God she loved, worshipped and trusted.

Bridget had spent a number of years on the mission field, working in Thailand and Burma as a school teacher. She had been engaged to a young Burmese doctor, but shortly before the wedding he had left her and returned to his family. She later found out that he had made one of the local nurses pregnant and was running away from the situation, unable to deal with the shame and unwilling to ask for Bridget's forgiveness. A period of many years of singleness followed in which Bridget applied herself to sterling work in the area of health education and literacy, even writing books and articles that had received international critical recognition. During that time she served in her local church, taught in the Sunday school and helped with various community projects.

She had never married and in many ways, the Church or the mission field had become her bridegroom. She made many friends and committed her life to the education and social development of the various rural communities in which she served. Then one day, whilst having a short break at a mission house in Bangkok, she met Roger, an international banker and credit controller who was visiting Bangkok on business and whom she bumped into when she saw an Englishman struggling with the local language whilst negotiating with a taxi driver the going rate from the airport. She had immediately offered her language skills and negotiated a reasonable charge for the taxi. That led to an offer of lunch and romance later blossomed.

Two years later, she and Roger were married, they came to settle into a large rambling Regency town house in Buxton, from where Roger commuted to Manchester each day, often making regular trips to the airport to fly overseas for business meetings and conferences. Bridget and Roger enjoyed what appeared to be an idyllic life in Buxton. Roger continuing with his work in credit control in Manchester and abroad, whilst Bridget who had now returned from the mission field felt that she still had something to offer the church and so trained as a counsellor and spiritual director, offering her services particularly to those engaged in full time Christian ministry. Bridget was good news and good to be with as far as I was concerned.

We met at the door. Kissed on the cheek and was shown into her study where a large raging fire and cafetiere of fresh coffee greeted me. Her home felt like an oasis in a spiritual desert. A deep calm pool of reflection and re-assessment in which I could bathe and emerge feeling refreshed, affirmed and re-focussed. There were indeed, some consolations and perks to Christian full time ministry!

"So how is it going Kevin?" asked Bridget as she stooped to pour a particular large cup of fair-traded, ground coffee into a blue Denby pottery mug. "Would you like some cake?"

Bridget immediately produced a large carrot cake she had made that morning and placed it on the table before us. This was a much nicer image of cake being offered than I had recently encountered in my dream world. In fact, Bridget would often encourage me to recall my dreams and then discuss them in a non-Freudian, but analytical manner.

"I shouldn't really. But I will. Thanks Bridget," I replied placing a large slice of carrot cake on a matching tea plate which I balanced on the arm of a large, loose covered armchair into which I had sunk. I rested in the moment, enjoying the warmth of the log fire as I looked out across Bridget's front lawn to the snow covered hills in the distance.

"It's been a funny sort of period recently." I explained. As ever, I was a master of the understatement. I then proceeded to recall all the events of the last few weeks beginning with the late night argument in the sodden car park, and running through the Elvis funeral story to the offer Ian had made to go on the road with the band.

"So what's the problem?" Bridget moved annoyingly straight to the point.

"The problem is I don't know whether I should go on this tour or not. It's a big commitment and it might be tricky getting the time off."

"Aren't you due some sabbatical leave?"

"I guess so, but you're meant to do some scheme of study on a sabbatical. Produce some written work to show for your labours and to present to the Director of Ministry upon your return. Not sure if going on tour with a *U2* tribute band would count towards that."

"And I'm not sure that producing a scheme of study sounds very 'sabbath-like' to me," observed Bridget. "But that isn't your problem is it? There's something else."

"You can always suss me out Bridget. It really is irritating at times. It would be good if you could just play on the line a bit more before you land me on the river bank and remove the hook from my mouth. I guess the problem is that I feel as though I am running away."

"Running away? What from?"

"From my problems. From my grief. From the pressures of parish life. From living alone in a huge Victorian vicarage which is used as target practice by the local *Stella* bottle hurling community."

"Ah..." Bridget took a deep breath and gave me one of her, 'haven't we been here before' looks. "What is the difference between running from and working through?"

"I don't know. I guess that one is a retreat from having to deal with issues and the other is a willingness to work them through as part of a process."

"A good text book answer."

"So what does the text book say I should do?"

"What do you want to do Kevin? What would you say if I was to appear before you now in a fluffy tutu and wand and say, *'I am your Fairy Godmother and I grant you three wishes'*."

"I would say, 'where did you get that fluffy tutu from and have you kept the receipt?'"

"Come on. Take the question seriously."

"Well you know what my first wish would be, don't you?"

"Yes, but these are wishes, not miracles. Julie is not coming back. What would 'Kevin' like to receive as a gift right here and right now?"

"Space I guess."

"And will this tour with your band give you space?"

"Yes I guess so."

"So what's the problem?"

"The problem is unfinished business. There's so much to do at church at the moment. So many people who depend upon me in one way or the other. So many plates to spin. So many expectations to meet."

"You remember what we said about 'expectations' before?"

"Yeh, the only expectation I should have, is to be faithful."

"That's right. All you are expected to do is to be Kevin, a follower of Jesus. Everything else is just the working out of that."

"So how does playing support to a *U2* tribute band fit into that?"

Bridget sighed and then looked down at her notes and back up to me.

"Tell me about the other evening in the car park," said Bridget, suddenly changing tack in a way that surprised me.

"The other evening? What's that got to do with it?"

"That's what I want to find out," replied Bridget in a voice that suggested she already knew.

"You know it was just one of those moments. A fairly ordinary day, but the discussion just felt sort of... sort of poignant, I suppose. As if time, froze at that point, and suddenly I glimpsed another reality present itself. Like the scene from *The Matrix*"

"*The Matrix*?"

"Yes, just an obsession of mine. Like the scene when Neo has this nagging doubt that reality doesn't quite make sense and that maybe there's an alternative explanation or perspective available that will provide some sort of metanarrative..."

"Metanarrative?"

"Yes, you know an over-arching theory that explains everything."

"I know what a metanarrative is. I live under one. It is called the grace of God, but I still don't know what made that evening so special for you?"

"I guess, that standing in that car park, arguing with those people made me realise. I don't really belong here. I don't really buy into all the arguments that other people feel so precious about. It just feels like we are trying to prop up a failing organisation all the time and I just want to say, 'No more. Stop let me out!'"

"Failing? What do you mean by that?"

"You know. All the indices are moving in the same direction. Declining numbers, ageing congregations, loss of young people in particular, fewer clergy trying to do more and more with less and less."

"Meaning?"

"Meaning that there are now eight and half thousand Anglican clergy in England, whereas there were thirty thousand after the Second World War. Many clergy now have a number of different churches or parishes to look after. We are struggling to pay for the clergy we have, whilst there are now twice as many retired clergy than active ones. The Church is the largest voluntary organisation in the world, yet the numbers of volunteers are falling as employment increases. We are the custodians to nearly half the nation's grade one listed buildings and expected to be on more than nodding terms with the charities act, the children's act, health and safety legislation and double entry bookkeeping. We're meant to be experts with young people, old people, newly weds and never weds. To act as counsellors, teachers, entertainers, liturgical experts, surveyors, builders, architects, accountants and committee secretaries. But more than anything, we are expected to manage. I didn't sign up to become a manager, but that's what I've become."

"And what are you managing?"

"Decline, I suppose?"

"Oh I see. And how does that make you feel?"

"Knackered for most of the time. You know the other day I was taking a funeral in church and towards the end of the service... I just gazed across to the coffin... just sort of gazed at it... and found myself thinking, 'Wouldn't it be great to have a nice lie down?' What an appalling thought."

"Kevin, what attracted you to the Church in the first place?"

"I'm sorry?"

"I mean, what made you want to become a vicar, a minister in the Church?"

"Well, I guess it was all the obvious things like the money, the power and the black sexy uniform."

"Come on Kevin. What did you think it would be like? What did you buy into?"

"I guess that in my more idealistic moments, I bought into the whole idea of a calling."

"Meaning?"

"Meaning that I felt called to proclaim a message and seek to live by it, to inhabit a counter culture, a Kingdom built on alternative values that would be transforming personally as well as challenging socially and politically. You know a place where the hungry are fed, the mighty humbled, the marginalised empowered and there's dancing all night to the sounds of the seventies."

"And is that what you saw happening?"

"Occasionally. Occasionally something truly wonderful would occur that would give me a glimpse into such an alternative reality. But even when it didn't, I still hoped that such transformation and renewal was just around the corner."

"So what gave you this hope?"

"Faith you might call it, but not blind faith. I saw tremendous signs of hope when I first sought ordination and started my training. There was a new evangelical Archbishop committed and personally gifted in leading mission. There were record numbers of evangelical ordinands being trained and appointed. A Decade of Evangelism was underway. We had seen how the renewing power of the Holy Spirit could transform our experience of worship and bring about greater intimacy with God through the ministry of John Wimber and those who had followed. There were signs of hope and optimism everywhere. I guess that I just felt that we were on the cusp of something significant in the life of this nation."

"A big agenda. Expectations that high would always be difficult to live up to. We all have hopes and dreams Kevin. We have to learn how to accommodate them to the reality of our lives."

"But I didn't sign up in order to fail. I really felt that the church could grow. I wanted to facilitate change, not manage decline."

"And were those expectations reasonable or realistic? Remember our ministry is about people, not processes or outcomes."

"I know, but I wanted to make a difference and be part of something good, something that grew and brought blessing to other people, not something that struggled to maintain itself."

"So what happened?"

"I don't know. I just feel like I was sold a pup. I bought into a kingdom and what I got instead was the Church. I wanted to help people learn more about Jesus and to learn how to deal with their problems through faith and prayer, but I ended up running an organisation. I set out to be a holy man and ended up a manager."

"So how does that make you feel?"

"Disappointed mostly. Disappointed with myself, with the Church and with God, but also trapped."

"Trapped? In what way?"

"You know how it is? You try and change things. You start to think that you might be able to make a difference. You try to implement all these bright ideas you've had over the years. You try events and programmes and initiatives... you work your socks off, but nothing changes, the ground just doesn't shift beneath your feet. I feel like Joshua circling the town of Jericho seven times, raising the shout and blowing the trumpets, but after all that effort, the walls still don't fall down." [6]

"What exactly do you feel trapped by?" said Bridget, leaning over to pour another cup of coffee and offer me some more cake, which I declined.

6   Joshua 5.13-6.19

"Sort of trapped by the system. Like I've stopped believing in it"

"The system?"

"Yes the Church. The way we do things. The delivery system for the gospel."

"It's very easy to have a go at the Church. It's a very large and very soft target."

"I know. I'm part of it. But it just wears you down with its fake promises."

"What you do you mean by fake promises?"

"Well with my evangelical hat on I would say that there is always the hope of change held out. We evangelicals look at the world and want to change it. So we are always marketing some latest programme or big idea that will transform the church and ultimately change the world. Through our programmes and campaigns we try to manage or market our way out of decline..."

"So what problems does that cause?"

"It just exhausts me and makes me feel as though I've failed when things don't go according to plan. Whereas with my charismatic hat on, we rely upon often repeated 'just-around-the-corner-isms'. Always living in hope that the revival cavalry will come charging over the hill at the last moment to save the day. If I had a pound for every time I heard that revival is just around the corner, or that God is doing a new sovereign work among this generation, then I would have... um... £27 by now."

"And how does _that_ make you feel?"

"Increasingly cynical... and I don't like that feeling. Cynicism is not the friend of faith."

"So what's the alternative then? Shall we all go over to Rome?" asked Bridget with a knowing smile.

"No, I wouldn't feel at home there either. The old categories just don't seem relevant any more. I guess that I'm looking for a third way – another path.

"So what will this path look like?"

"I just don't know, but I know I'll recognise it when I see it."

"That's not a bad path to explore. The path that recognises that there are no easy answers… just questions."

"I used to be uncertain, but now I'm not quite so sure." I added whilst sharing a smile and a coffee with Bridget.

"In fact I used to have such great certainty, but now when I open my mouth, I often don't know what side of the debate I am going to come down upon and then often I find myself offering some sort of alternative perspective. It's not as though I have thought it all through or have all the answers or even know what I am talking about. It's just that I sense that something has departed from me and now I'm about another agenda. Sort of, on a journey but I don't know the destination yet I feel drawn to explore the path. Maybe in the hope that there is more to life in the Church of England than just Deanery Synods and arguments about quota payments and clergy redeployments."

A pregnant pause followed.

"Kevin you're a bit of artist aren't you?" said Bridget in a knowing manner.

"Let me draw you a picture and let us see if this speaks to your situation or not."

Bridget then got up, straightened her tweed skirt and cardigan and walked across to her desk from where she returned a few moments later with an A4 writing pad and a felt tip pen.

"I like felt tips. They remind me of school." Bridget explained.

She then proceeded to draw a large mountain on which she placed a small stick man. *'Not a bad attempt'* I thought. *'May be she is more of an artist than me.'*

"From what you are telling me. And from what you are showing me in other ways, I would surmise that this figure is you standing on top of a mountain and looking around for direction." Then suddenly drawing another similar mountain opposite, Bridget continued.

"You sense that there is another land not far away, to which you really belong. Like the Babylonian exiles who couldn't remember what it was like when they lived in Israel, but sensed that they didn't belong where they were and needed to return home."

"That's right. That's exactly right. How did you know?"

"Because I have stood on a similar mountain and gazed across the valley to a far off peak that I desperately wished to explore. It's called longing and it is very natural and very human. We all do it. Sometimes, people who live without God have all these doubts that disturb their agnosticism and secular outlook. They don't know how to deal with them. They often won't admit them, but they just feel a longing for 'the other', for spirituality, for the unexplained, for holiness, for truth or virtue or wisdom. For something beyond themselves and beyond the goals that they have been striving for. The Bible is full of this stuff. Read Proverbs and Ecclesiastes.[7] So they glimpse another land, but this is the mistake that everyone makes. They automatically disregard the space in between. They assume that you can just step across to the other mountain. That there is some sort of quick fix or a bridge out there to take them on a short cut to the object of their spiritual yearning. They try to jump across without taking account of the grace of God. The grace of God is the space in between," explained Bridget labelling the gap between her two mountain peaks.

"What do you mean by 'the grace of God'?" I replied whilst making inverted comma marks in the air and knowing that grace was such a big idea, that it could often become empty of meaning.

"Well it can mean something different for each person. But in this case, I feel that it is the space that God allows us to occupy."

"Space?"

"Yes, the freedom he gives for us to make mistakes, to explore life, to learn, to struggle, to get things wrong occasionally. It marks the dimensions of his capacity to forgive, the extent of his patience with us, the boundaries of the freedom he affords us, the limits of the good he has in store as part of His purpose for our lives."

---

7   Proverbs chaps 4 - 8 - 9. Ecclesiastes 3. 10-12

"So why can't I just swap one mountain for another?"

"You can, but you can't jump across. You have to leave the mountain you stand on, climb down from it and enter the valley in between before you can climb up to the other mountain peak."

"And what lies in the valley?" I probed fearing an uncomfortable answer.

"Well it's different for every person. But often there is some sort of wilderness experience. Some kind of experience of lost-ness or leaving or giving up or moving away. Often it is more like a forest than a desert. A place where there are many distractions and obstacles to push through on route to the mountain peak you have glimpsed. You can't see it from the valley bottom or the forest floor; you just have to trust that it is still there and if you continue on your journey, that you will find it. You have to explore the space marked out by the grace of God."

"It all sounds a bit mysterious and mystical to me Bridget. Like an episode of *Kung Fu.* I half expect to see David Carradine with a shaven head trying to walk on rice paper and snatch a pebble out of an old monk's hand. What does it have to do with my car park conversation and Ian's crazy rock and roll odyssey?"

"Ah that's the question Kevin," said Bridget sitting back in her chair and folding her arms as if her work were completed. "And I think you already know the answer to that question. The question is, can you trust yourself or God to embrace it?"

A great sense of relief suddenly overwhelmed me. As if some of the clouds surrounding my life and ministry were finally starting to part and allow light to penetrate. I instinctively warmed to the picture that Bridget had drawn and to the explanation she had given. The idea of home coming and longing for another country struck a significant chord. I remembered a TV mini series based on the Stephen King novel *The Stand* and how the motherly figure of Abigail Freemantle seemed to draw travellers to her simple cottage whilst dispensing divine visions about a new, post apocalytic beginning for all those who had been hurt or displaced.[8] Maybe it was Bridget's maternal influence, but intuitively I felt like being beckoned home by the idea of exploring something illusive yet attractive and comforting.

As I drove home from Bridget's house sustained by a combination of caffeine from her coffee, calories from her carrot cake and her gentle wise counsel, I wrestled with my future options and how to respond. I still had other people to meet with and business to discuss. This was still not a done deal.

8   'The Stand' was published by Stephen King in
     1978 and made into a TV mini series in 1994

     In the story the human race is wiped out by a
     government invented super flu. The remaining
     survivors take sides in the forces of good and evil.
     A mysterious old woman, Mother Abigail
     Freemantle is a servant of God and the
     personification of good. She lives in a farmhouse,
     and initially appears to some of the survivors in
     dreams, drawing them to her home in order to
     become followers in the battle against evil.

Chapter Five

'Love all' with Justin and Pippa

The following day I came down to breakfast to be greeted by a pile of post strewn on the carpet of the vicarage entrance hall.

Most of it appeared to be circulars and unsolicited post. As I picked up the various envelopes and guided them towards the paper recycling bin I couldn't help but wonder why it was that junk mail never gets lost in the post?

Among the offers of credit cards, pizza delivery menus, step-in bath promotions, clerical garments catalogues and offers from local landscape gardening companies to quote for essential tree maintenance, one white A4 envelope stood out. It was hand written and bore an Edinburgh post mark.

I returned to the breakfast table in order to open this more promising looking item of post. It turned out to be a letter from Daniel Grey, an old school friend, I hadn't heard from for years. Daniel and I had been close friends at school, but when I left for art school we drifted apart. Daniel had gone on to university to study Drama, and since then we had pretty much lost touch although interestingly I had met his sister recently in *B&Q* whilst browsing the solid wood flooring section. It had been one of those strange occurrences when I had become aware of someone staring at me in a public place, followed by that uncomfortable greeting that clergy often have to deal with.

"Hi, its Kevin isn't it?"

"That's right. I know who I am, but you've got me at a disadvantage."

I had done one of those double takes when I would stare hard at someone and try to look interested in the hope that during the thought process I would remember just who they were and where I knew them from.

"Don't you remember it's Catherine? Catherine Bridgen, although I used to be Catherine Grey when we knew each other."

Certainly she was vaguely familiar, but was she someone I had married, whose offspring I had baptised or whose relative I had buried? Was she a former member of my church? Was she a member of the local school governors or the Community Association or a member of the Women's Guild or one of Julie's former work colleagues? Then suddenly I remembered. Catherine Grey, the older sister of Daniel from Tamworth High School in the 1980s.

Re-acquainted Catherine and I chatted at length, exchanged life stories along with more recent news and reflected upon how the world was really a small place in that old school friends could bump into each other over the solid wood floor section of *B&Q* without even the need for the 'Friends Re-United' website. Catherine had spoken briefly about Daniel and promised to remember me to him next time he got in touch. It was good to meet up with Catherine again and talk about old times, but I hadn't thought any more about our chance meeting since. I guessed that event and this letter must be connected in some way.

Daniel explained that his sister had spoken with him recently and how he had 'Googled' me in order to find out where I was living. Sure enough, a church website had thrown up my name and contact details. It's so hard to hide away these days unless you are a Serbian war criminal. Daniel had clearly taken his chance to get in touch. He gave a brief potted history of what he had done with his life since leaving university. His career path seemed to have involved a few small acting parts in *The Bill* and *Brookside* and long periods of unemployment punctuated by working in a bookshop in Edinburgh. Finally, he had decided to further his career in the realm of experimental theatre in Montreal and New York after he made an ignominious appearance as a corpse in an episode of *Cracker*. Upon returning from New York he had increasingly turned to writing, directing and performing as a solo artist, although he still did some television work, including a couple of appearances in *Midsomer Murders* as well as a season of pantomime in Watford. He was now performing in a one man touring play of his own composition based on the life and imprisonment of Dietrich Bonhoeffer.[9] He was due to come to the studio theatre at *The Crucible* in Sheffield very soon and asked whether it would be possible to meet up, or failing that could I at least circulate a few flyers for his one-man play around the churches in Sheffield?

Glossy leaflets bearing the face of Daniel dressed in 1940s period costume and seated in a prison cell fell out of the envelope with a little persuasion. It was strange to see someone with whom I had shared so many childhood memories now appearing on the stage. I examined the dates of the Daniel's tour, but discovered he was performing in Sheffield when I was due to be on the road myself. Was this some sort of sign that I shouldn't go on tour after all, rather I should meet up with an old

---

9   Dietrich Bonhoeffer (1906 – 1945) was a German
        Lutheran theologian who participated in the
        German resistance movement against Nazism. He
        was arrested and eventually hanged just before the
        end of the World War II. In his *Letters and Papers*
        from Prison Bonhoeffer's argued that the
        dependence on organized religion had undermined
        genuine faith. He called for a new religion-less
        Christianity free from individualism and
        metaphysical supernaturalism. The abstract God
        of philosophical and theological speculation is
        useless to the average man on the street, who
        needs to hear the gospel.

school friend and try to re-acquaint myself with the person I once knew so well?

I noted Daniel's home phone number and email address and made a note to get in touch whatever I decided to do about the band's tour. It would be good to have a chat with Daniel again. It might even be interesting to pick his brains over the life and significance of Dietrich Bonhoeffer – a theologian I had always been intrigued by. I could certainly post a few flyers around the local churches. That was the least I could do.

I spent the rest of the day crouched over my laptop exploring the world of the internet. This was not the frivolous activity it might have appeared to a casual observer, but rather research and fine tuning for the big social event of my week - the church quiz night!

I had always enjoyed quiz evenings, especially when played with friends at a local pub, and preferably ones where the questions were heavily slanted towards popular music. However, upon arriving at St Ebbs I had endured some fairly high brow and competitive quiz nights and therefore had mixed feelings about the approaching event. The quiz night was to be held in the old church hall which was located about half a mile away from the church building in a less fashionable part of the parish. There had been plans to develop the church hall into more a dedicated community facility or even a café at one time.

Other people at St Ebbs longed to use the centre for worship and outreach into a part of the parish that was less well represented in the congregation due to its social deprivation and less attractive character. I had been caught in the middle of this debate and had spent many days and nights on different planning meetings, vision days and half nights of prayer all dedicated to discerning what God's will was for the church hall site. Now seven years after coming to St Ebbs, there remained no consensus concerning what God wanted for the future of the church hall. So badminton still took place on Monday and Thursday evenings, along with the activities of various uniformed, or 'uninformed' groups, as I often referred to them. A deliberate Freudian slip disclosing my tense and occasionally fractious relationship with these long term hall users. I had wanted to reach out to the uniformed groups but instead just found myself refereeing disputes about storage space and access to the premises and who was entitled to be a key holder and what was a reasonable rental charge for using the building. I felt like a whipping boy in the constant disputes between the uniformed groups and the congregation, one of whom saw themselves as the rightful guardians of the hall, subsidising its upkeep and management whilst safeguarding the original vision of those who built the hall in order to reach out to their local community whilst the other represented the interests of the local church.

I had tried to suggest that they could use the local football club bar as an alternative venue for the church quiz night – a sort of neutral ground that might provide an interesting way of making a connection with the football club and meeting with people who wouldn't normally associate with their local church other than through baptisms, weddings and funerals. Unfortunately this idea had been voted down by the church council on the grounds of cost. Also because it was seen as important that the church was willing to use its own facilities in order to lay down a marker for local community groups, like the scouts, who were prone to see themselves as having priority over the church on the grounds that they used the premises for so many of their activities during the week.

Church quiz nights had been fairly serious affairs before I arrived in the parish. With so many members of the congregation being school teachers or else involved at the university in some way, the questions were often highly cerebral and taken very competitively. The same teams tended to win each time and those teams would also provide the quiz master and questions when they were not competing themselves. Therefore I had decided that the best thing to do, rather than killing off such a long standing and preciously held church tradition, was to redeem the quiz night and take on the role of quiz master myself, thereby giving the event a more fun feel and contemporary edge. This had worked to some extent and now new and younger people would willingly come to church quiz nights, presumably attracted by my eclectic mix of TV trivia, pop music questions, silly spot prizes and movie clips. However, I soon realised the problems a successful project can bring. The amount of work that was subsequently required in planning and leading such evenings was immense, leading to hours spent trawling the world wide web for interesting trivia, exploring the local *Blockbusters* superstore for appropriate movie clips and raiding my collection of CDs and vinyl records for contemporary music. Even then, the competitive edge remained and I knew that if I didn't double check all my quiz answers that I would be gently, but thoroughly taken apart the following Sunday by disgruntled teams of ex-school teachers who had concrete evidence that the Captain Oates who famously said 'I am just going outside and may be some time' during Scott's ill fated Antarctic expedition, was really called 'Lawrence Oates' and not 'Titus Oates', which was just his popular nickname.

That night the church hall was alive and kicking with a very encouraging turnout for the quiz night. Many strangers turned up and quickly fell into groups of friends who formed teams. I assumed that they were in some way connected with the uniformed groups that used the church hall and felt such a strong sense of ownership over how the hall was used. Whoever they were, they seemed to have a good time although they didn't seem to mix with many of the church congregation who enthusiastically turned up and eventually formed teams, mostly based around existing circles of friends or their regular home bible study groups. I couldn't help but think that the quiz night had been set up in order to provide a social gathering in which new people could mix freely and feel included within an atmosphere of fun and frivolity. Instead it was becoming a forum in which competitiveness was expressed and social interaction was reduced to a minimum. The main competitive flashpoint of the evening centred around a challenge to the quizmaster by a group of university lecturers who disputed that the 'T' in Captain James T Kirk of the Starship Enterprise, stood for 'Tiberius' and not for 'Theodore.' I refused to give in and was treated to a cold icy stare throughout the rest of the evening, which gradually thawed in the light of my attempts to lighten the atmosphere by awarding a whole series of spot prizes for the most creative, stupid or amusing wrong answers. I wouldn't have minded, but this was a church quiz night and not *Mastermind* and we were competing for the modest prize of a tin of *Quality Street* and not for a gleaming trophy or a million pound jackpot.

Still apart from all that, the evening seemed to pass without further incident and many people expressed their appreciation and good will – even though the following day I did receive an email from one of the university lecturers, quoting some obscure Trekie's website which upheld their opinion about Captain James T Kirk.

As the day wore on I poured over my unopened emails and came across an email sent by Justin Mellor, one of my clergy colleagues and local church leader. Justin had emailed me the previous week to invite me to his home for one of the regular clergy social events, which he described as 'networking' occasions. Now I had to decide whether to go or not.

Justin was the rector of a large and wealthy church just up the hill from St Ebbs. He was well known and popular and his ministry was often held up as one the few local success stories in the Diocese since arriving at his parish some eleven years previously. During that time, the church had been scheduled for closure but Justin, ably supported by his wife Philippa, who for some reason now insisted on being called 'Pippa', had turned around a small, yet enthusiastic congregation. They had seen the church grow and develop dramatically, with various building projects being embarked upon over the years in order to accommodate the growing numbers of young people and upwardly mobile professionals who had started to worship there.

Having a popular and growing church on your doorstep can prove a mixed blessing for other local church leaders. There had been something of an exodus of church members haemorrhaging from St Ebbs over the years in order to chase the blessing under Justin's leadership. I could understand the attraction of a larger church where so many interesting developments were taking place, but often my morale was eroded by seeing so many enthusiastic and gifted members of my congregation drift away to such places because they perceived the pace of change as proceeding too slowly at St Ebbs. In exchange others did arrive at St Ebbs from Justin's church but often they came with severe emotional baggage or else suffering from spiritual burnout, hoping to find a less frenetic and more stable community where they could chill out for a while without having to constantly re-invent themselves under a continuous programme of change and development.

There had indeed been a number of interesting and exciting outreach and community programmes embarked upon at Justin's church. Alpha courses were blossoming with interested enquirers about the Christian faith. Music and teaching CDs had been produced and were now downloadable from an interactive and very funky looking website. A staff team had grown in order to embrace particular sector ministries serving the needs of children, young people, students, people in their thirties and forties and the elderly. There were even outreach projects for the victims of addiction and prostitution. Justin and Philippa certainly had been very effective and successful in their Christian ministry, so much so that they were often courted by the Christian press and had started to co-author a number of books on leadership and mission. Justin was gaining a reputation as a conference speaker and author. He had produced a number of 'How to...' booklets on Church growth and leadership, including such titles as, 'How to grow your leadership team', 'How to double your giving in two years', 'How to plan for growth whilst avoiding disagreements' and 'Ten ways to avoid a stress-filled life.'

Everyone liked Justin. The Bishop spoke well of him on many occasions and had even made him a Canon of the Cathedral in recognition of all his good work in the city. Young people would often remind me of what wonderful worship and youth work took place at Justin's church. Other young leaders would speak of Justin's charismatic personality and warmth, combined with such a humble spirit. There was nothing that this man couldn't do. He was born for this role in life. His father had been a parish vicar and university chaplain at an Oxford college. Justin had been educated at one of those public schools that constantly produce students who go on to be successful in their careers. They exude a calm confidence and swagger that suggests not only that they knew they were born to lead but also that they expected to succeed. Later on Justin had shone at Cambridge where he was the captain of the rugby team and

Christian Union president. After completing his degree, he took a year out to work in Peru building a school and helping out with a clean water project. It was there that he met Philippa, whom I had previously known from my teenage years at youth camps where Philippa was a young leader. In those days Philippa had been a striking red head, although for some reason, she had now become blonde without anyone else appearing to notice or being prepared to comment.

There appeared to be no end to Justin's talents and aptitude. A classical pianist whose range and repertoire covered the church organ, Vaughan Williams, classic jazz, rhythm and blues. He was also a technocrat who used to amuse himself by building computers for friends at college. He even made a small business for himself, building PCs for a while until it became unrealistic to compete with cheap high street alternatives. Was there anything this bloke could not excel at? I really wanted to hate him, or at least give his rather handsome and smug face a good slap. But I couldn't just bring myself to do it. Although I secretly wanted to see Justin trip up over something in life, make a hash of a task that came his way or let himself down in some way, he was such a nice bloke and he had been very kind and helpful towards me in the past. The bottom line was that Justin remained a thoroughly decent bloke, he had a gift of encouragement and by and large he was good to be around.

Perhaps I would go to his cheese and wine buffet after all.

Later on that evening I found myself in Justin's living room mingling with other clergy and local community leaders, some of whom I knew whilst others I only vaguely recognised. Justin's vicarage was more modern than my Victorian edifice. It had a light and airy feel, exuding confidence and optimism. Philippa was a brilliant designer and interior decorator and had tastefully furnished it throughout. I've always admired the middle classes for their ability to instinctively know what worked and what didn't work when it came to furnishing a house. Julie and I had acquired furniture over the years from various dead relatives, and when we had chosen new furniture we always seemed to go for the bargain end of the market, succumbing to the instant charms of flat pack versatility. Despite being an artist I've never really been able to quite get the hang of the presentation of art and always struggle to hang pictures and display collectables tastefully.

Philippa, however, always seemed to just know what looked good and what didn't. Where to put things. How to avoid clutter. How to blend different items together and create mood and atmosphere in each room of the house. She had style. She even gave talks and took workshops for vicars' wives groups on how to decorate your vicarage on a budget. Not only was Philippa great with interior design, but she was also developing a reputation as a counsellor, specialising in inner healing. She had recently brought out a book on the subject of healing, in which she drew analogies between the world of interior design and the interiors of our own minds and lives. She was even studying part-time for a MPhil in pastoral care and counselling and remained very much the intellectual power behind Justin as well as providing the personal rock, to the ebb and flow of his entrepreneurial energy.

Justin was in his mid forties. Tactile and blessed with good looks, confidence, and old money charm. He appeared at his vicarage door wearing a blue and white striped shirt open to the third button over which he had draped a red jumper and tied it around his neck in semi-casual style. The Hugh Grant look was completed by beige chinos and highly polished brown brogues. He was also physically imposing, standing over six foot four inches tall, a height that had not only been an advantage when playing rugby in his youth, but also provided a useful tool in Christian leadership when he wanted to get his point across or stamp his authority on a situation. I always felt that physical height and power over others were somehow linked, but in a way that I didn't quite understand. Indeed, some people would compensate for their lack of height by developing massive personal ambition. After all no-one over the height of five foot six ever tried to conquer the world – Alexander the Great, Napoleon, Hitler, Bernie Ecclestone. I rest my case. However, with Justin physical height was used more subtly. Often he would come up to people, put his arm around their shoulder and hold them in position whilst he initiated and managed the conversation. Many people found such body language affirming and reassuring, however, I always felt uneasy when on the receiving end, as if I could never say 'No' to anyone who treated me like that.

One of Justin's most noticeable faults was his irritating habit of looking over your shoulder when speaking with you, suggesting that he was only talking with you until someone else made him a better offer, in which case he would become '*too cool*' to remain in your company and would move on to someone else whilst assuring you that he would 'get back to you on that one', and to keep in touch because 'we really must do lunch together some time.' Or at least that was the impression he gave. This impression wasn't helped by his pathological attachment to his cell phone which was always going off during conversations and meetings, further suggesting that his presence in your company was only a temporary dispensation on route to something far more important. Justin was also known for his appalling time keeping and his propensity to arrive fashionably late for many a gathering, necessitating a grand entrance. This tendency had earned him the nickname 'Justin Time' among many of his fellow clergy. Would I receive Justin's undivided attention this evening?

Needless to say I was somewhat jealous of Justin. I guess I wanted to be like him, although I realised that I could never really compete with him, nor master his methods or charm. After all Justin came from Esher, a respectable commuter town and cultured neighbour to Hampton Court Palace. The sort of place where they eat their chips with a small wooden fork, where they knit their own furniture and even the Samaritans are ex-directory. Whereas I came from Tamworth, home of the Reliant Robin. The town that gave its name to a pig. A place outshone in terms of historical significance by its near neighbour of Lichfield, which at least can boast Chad as its own saint, and overshadowed strategically by the industrial legacy, municipal history and second city status of nearby Birmingham. Even my name didn't convey the same sense of cool confidence as Justin. No-one is called 'Kevin' these days. It is a by-word for 'un-cool'. The name is as 'last year' as prawn cocktails and black forest gateaux. I had conducted numerous baptisms of baby boys and although there had been numerous Jacks, Jacobs, Joshuas and

Justins, not one Kevin or Trevor had been seen in the register of baptisms since the 1970s.

More reasons to be envious of Justin and Philippa.

"Hi Kev. Fr...iend. How are you?" Justin suddenly appeared and put his arm around me in the usual manner of his greeting.

"Oh hi Justin. Thanks for the invite. How's things going?"

As soon as the words left my mouth, I knew it was a mistake to ask Justin how things were going. The answer would invariably make me feel inadequate. Justin always seemed to be engaged in enterprises, initiatives and missions that were far more interesting than the pre-occupations of my life. Often when I get together with Justin and the like-minded Christian leaders Justin likes to network with, we end up playing the game of 'my church is better than your church.' The rules of this game are quite simple. They involve talking about all your successes and plans and about how God is bringing blessing and working deeply in the life of your church or even your own personal life. This is in direct contrast to the game a number of my more traditional Anglican clergy like to play when they get together. This was conversely called, 'my church is worse than your church'. The rules are similar, but instead of your achievements, you boasted about how difficult the parish council was, how little help you received from your elderly or over-stretched congregation, how socially disadvantaged the parish was, how inadequate the church buildings were, how many funerals you had to do without the assistance of any curate and how many days off you had to work on recently.

Sure enough, Justin launched straight away into the familiar game. As always he played a blinder, recalling some mission he had just returned from in South America. He detailed how many thousands of people he had spoken in front of in Buenos Aires. I remembered where I was at roughly the same time. My parallel universe had involved covering a 6.30 pm evensong in a former mining village, accompanied by two elderly parishioners, a church warden and one of the terminally confused locals who had wandered in looking for refuge and for something to complain about. He proceeded to unwrap and suck *Fox's Glacier*

Mints rather loudly throughout the entire service. Once again, it was game, set and match to Justin.

"But anyhow, let's not discuss that now." said Justin, suddenly taking me to one side. "There's something I want to run past you."

This was a surprise. Justin wanted me to help him out in some way. This was definitely a new departure.

"Yah. You know the 'New Growth' conferences I'm involved with over the summer?"

"You mean the ones that take place in a cattle shed in Harrogate?"

"Well, actually it's the Royal Horticultural Showground, but yep, those are the ones. Well Pippa and I were wondering if you would like to come and do a seminar for us?"

"Gosh, yes... I've never given it much thought before. What did you have in mind?"

"It's just that we were really impressed by what you guys did during the floods last year. How you organised all that water distribution among the elderly and housebound when the mains supply got contaminated. How you took all those referrals and gave out all those buckets and made a fuss about the water tanks that got vandalised. We thought that a few of your folk could come over and speak about how the church can serve its community at times of crisis and what this could teach us about how to serve at other times."

"Well I'll certainly think about it Justin. Let me get back to you on that one." I just couldn't resist the temptation and nearly added, 'and we really must do lunch some time,' as a passing valediction.

The rest of the evening passed very pleasantly, although a young woman did manoeuvre me into a corner of the room and over a slice of quiche, interrogated me on the state of the worldwide Anglican Communion and where I stood on the Windsor Report and ordaining practising homosexuals. I wanted to pass a characteristically flippant remark along the lines of 'well I think that they should be allowed to practice a while before they get ordained and become professional homosexuals.' But I resisted. Instead, I tried to talk about the

Anglican Communion being a very broad church with lots of differing points of view and theologies, and then realised just how woolly I was sounding and tried to change the subject.

Later on that evening, Philippa came over and we chatted. We had known each other for some time, although not as close friends. Nevertheless I could still remember feeling quite physically attracted towards her during my teenage years when she appeared just that little bit older and therefore more mysterious and unavailable. However, this was a very different Philippa standing before me now. Gone was the red hair, jeans and college sweatshirt, replaced by this forty something blonde, immaculately turned out mother of three wearing a perfect Harvey Nichols' outfit trying to open up to me in a way that I'd never seen before.

One thing Justin had omitted to tell me earlier was about the problems they were having in their church staff team. One of Justin's colleagues had been rumoured to be having an affair with a young student in the congregation and Justin had confronted him about it. This had led to a very ugly argument between the two of them and a resulting break down in what had previously been a very warm and reciprocal working relationship. His colleague had even started to question Justin's motives along with his own marital faithfulness. In the meantime, the working relationship had continued to unravel and was starting to lead to a split in the church between those who believed Justin's version of events and those who supported his colleague. It had all come to a head last week, when the colleague concerned had taken an overdose as a result of all the stress he was under and was now in hospital in a serious condition.

Strange how Justin never mentioned any of this. But there again, it was not one of those topics that would be entered into as a conversation starter over a vegetable samosa.

"It's really knocked Justin's faith." Philippa explained. "He has always been so certain about everything he does, now he's questioning all the time. Not only the version of events he was told, but also his own pastoral techniques and leadership style."

"Gosh Philippa. I had no idea. Justin has always had such a good way with people."

"Yes, he has. But now some people are saying he is over-bearing and autocratic. That he sees things very two dimensionally. In terms of black and white."

"Well a lot of people like that approach. They appreciate the certainty that it can bring in a complex and often confusing world."

"I guess that we are just learning how to struggle and what being unable to cope feels like. I know that you have gone through the most appalling time of things, what with Julie's illness. But Justin and I have been so fortunate. We have never really – well, sort of – failed before."

All of a sudden I was faced with a stark choice. Do I just walk away or should I be prepared to chin a vicar's wife in her own living room?

"PHILIPPA! You can't talk about death and bereavement as if it were some Oxbridge entrance exam. It isn't a matter of pass or fail, win or lose, success or failure. It's just life… and in life, shit happens!"

"I know, I'm sorry, I guess it sounds a bit insensitive?"

"It does." I was genuinely angry.

"But to use your terms, less shit has happened to us than many other people and I'm not sure how we are going to get through this one. There's even talk about formal dismissal and then the threat of taking Justin to a tribunal if that happens."

"I know that it must be worrying. I don't really know what to say Philippa…"

"Well could you pray for us?"

"Yes, sure any time. You know I will."

"How about now Kevin? I just feel that this is something we both need."

This was not an activity that often happened at the end of a dinner party, even at the super-spiritual home of Justin and Philippa, but it just felt right for me to respond to Philippa's request. I often felt like a bit of a fraud on such occasions, especially in such company, after all, who was I to be ministering to the omnicompetent Christian celebrities of Justin and Philippa. They had written books about prayer and spoke at conferences on the subject. Whereas I was just the vicar from down the road who liked to paint, potter about and play his guitar.

Philippa beckoned Justin over and explained the situation to him suggesting that I was happy to pray for them both.

"Brilliant Kev. That would be super." declared Justin when he learnt that I was now within his loop. Then in the corner of their immaculate, Laura Ashley furnished living room, Justin and Philippa knelt down before me to receive prayer and asked me to lay my hands on them for the healing of their memories and for the restoration of their ministries.

"Pippa and I have always admired your gifts Kev," announced Justin whilst passing me my coat as I prepared to leave. This had certainly been an evening of surprises and an occasion when myths and reputations had been demolished.

"What do you mean Justin?"

"The way you just get on with things. Your sense of humour even in the midst of so much heartache. And all those guitars you have a home. It must be great to be part of a band. Whenever I do anything, it's always as a solo artist. Either musically or at church come to that. It must be good to be part of an ensemble where everyone just mucks in. What's happening with that rock group of yours at the moment?"

"Well it's funny you should ask…"

I then proceeded to explain briefly the events of the last few days and how I had been prayerfully considering Ian's offer.

"I think you should do it Kevin." Philippa added with great certainty. "What have you got to lose? At the end of your life, how many people look back and say 'I wish I had spent more time at the office'? Or the vicarage in our case. *Carpe deum* Kev. Seize the moment, you'll only regret it if you don't and you deserve some fun as well."

Meeting with Justin and Philippa felt like a real epiphany for me. Not only because of their encouragement to grab the opportunity of going on tour with the band, but also because of their honesty with me. I now started to see them and what their ministry represented in a new way. They too were fellow strugglers on the same journey as me. Their struggle was not with lack of resources or lack of affirmation, but with success itself. I no longer envied their popularity, giftedness or apparent success. Indeed, it seemed to represent a burden under which they were unable to express their vulnerabilities, doubts or failures. The need to have success stories in a struggling church produces the pressure to keep succeeding, to constantly re-invent yourself, to continually come up with new ideas, new programmes, new initiatives, new thinking and new blessings. They too were the victims of expectation. Their ministry, like mine, appeared as much driven by the need to prove themselves as being led by the activity of God.

With those thoughts echoing in my head I took my leave of Justin and Philippa. It had been a most illuminating evening and perhaps I had now received the confirmation I was seeking concerning Ian's offer. Just one more fleece to lay down. What would the Bishop say?

Chapter Six

Fluffy Fiona and
the Bishop's dog

The following day was spent on administration and preparing for Sunday worship.

It is an interesting feature of the life of Anglican clergy that they often have to defend what they do to the world outside. Often clergy appear as objects of curiosity to those who don't go to church or who don't know a great deal about how churches work. This curiosity frequently presents itself in the form of a leading question, namely, just what does a vicar do all day? Not even the popularity of the *Vicar of Dibley* or reality TV shows about parish clergy or monastic communities have dispelled the ignorance that surrounds this question. Often the question is asked obliquely in the form of comments about how 'it must be wonderful to only have to work on one day of the week?' To which I would regularly reply, 'yes it is, but the other six days are spent preparing for it.'

If you were to ask those people who don't come to church and who don't know a great deal about how churches work, the question, 'what does a vicar do all day?' They tend to imagine a vicar visiting the sick and elderly and doing pastoral work in the community. If the same question is addressed to regular church goers, they assume that the vicar spends most of the day in prayer and preparation of sermons, whereas the truth in fact, is far from both of these assumptions. Indeed, on average a minister works around 60 hours per week and of that time, more than 22 hours are spent in administration, whilst only 38 minutes are spent in prayer.[10]

This was certainly true in my case and today was no exception as I waded through a mountain of administration. This included preparing two references for church members who were trying to get their offspring into the local Roman Catholic secondary school, writing an article for the parish magazine, putting some final touches on an application for funding for a youth project that Jonathan and I had been working on for some time, preparing a report for the church council on the last Deanery Synod meeting, completing the coffee rota distribution list and drafting an order for some new candles and a replacement bulb for the video projector, although in the last instance, I still didn't know how the parish were going to pay for it, as such items are incredibly expensive. Not a bad day's work. Unfortunately, all this administration had still not left me with any time for sermon preparation or for being creative about putting together something for Sunday morning worship. As for prayer? 38 minutes seemed pretty excessive, apart from the twenty minutes a day, Jonathan and I would spend in church saying 'daily prayer' together, I must confess that I had little time or energy to devout to long periods of private prayer and as a result had developed the practice of 'speed praying'. This was very similar to 'speed dating' for those who were too busy to spend a great deal of time in getting to know people through the normal conventions of dating and developing relationships, but with some important differences. Rather than rotating different people every five minutes and then marking them out of ten, I would shoot off quick sixty second prayers on all the topics or

10   Alan Bartlett in *Humane Christianity* DLT 2004
       refers to an Evangelical Alliance survey of 1990
       which revealed that clergy spend an average 38
       minutes praying each day and 22 hours a week on
       matters of administration

people that were concerning me in the hope that God wouldn't be too disappointed about the lack of detail or time spent, but rather would be impressed by the sheer volume and scope of my concerns. A case of the triumph of quantity over quality. 'Let this be an eternal moment Lord,' I would pray as a preface to such rapid prayer requests, in the hope that God would not weigh the time given as an indication of my lack of seriousness or commitment to the task.

Sometimes it felt more like sending a heavenly email or text, rather than dwelling in the presence of Almighty God, so I decided to set aside a day for prayer and fasting in order to seek out what I should do about the tour with Ian and the band. I decided that a week on Monday I would set aside time for such prayer and then let Ian know my answer at music practice the following day. In the meantime, I would wait before getting in touch with Daniel and would try and get hold of the Bishop, in order to see what he thought about the opportunity as well as seeking his permission, if necessary.

A phone call to the Bishop's secretary however proved rather less than straightforward. It seemed that the Bishop's diary was booked solid for the next two weeks.

"I'm afraid the Bishop is at General Synod on that day and he has a speaking engagement then, and he is taking a confirmation service at the Cathedral on that day," said the rather brusque Bishop's secretary when I rang offering several dates in order to try and arrange an appointment. Many people were scared of the Bishop's secretary. She was affectionately known as 'Fluffy Fiona' to many of the clergy. Not because, she was soft and approachable, but rather because she resembled the triple-headed dog of the same name in *Harry Potter and the Philosopher's Stone* which acted as a ferocious gatekeeper to the forbidden corridor. Even the Bishop was a little scared of his secretary, but never owned up to knowing about her nickname.

This was getting me nowhere. Time to change tack.

"Is the Bishop there at the moment?"

"Yes, would you like me to see if he is available now?"

"That would be helpful" I said in growing exasperation.

After a few moments, a friendly, yet distant voice came onto the line.

"Hello Kevin. How are you?" A warm and gentle Scottish accent greeted me.

"Fine Bishop. I've just been talking to Fluff... I mean, Fiona, and trying to arrange for me to come around for a chat some time in the next few weeks, but it seems that you are all booked up."

"Aye... I am a wee bit busy these next two weeks, but I'm free this afternoon, did Fiona tell you that?"

"No."

"Oh why not come round then and we can have a cup of tea or a dram if you prefer something stronger?"

The Bishop had a habit of pulling surprises and his immediate availability coming after such an unpromising tangle with his secretary, along with the offer of a drink, was very typical. Sometimes the Bishop liked to shock his clergy by doing something unexpected and this was obviously one of those occasions. Two hours later I was ringing his front doorbell and being greeted by Fiona, thankfully only sporting one of her rumoured three heads and without the ferocious bite. She showed me into the Bishop's large study in which the Bishop sat with a small Yorkshire terrier at his feet.

The Bishop's study was adorned with a selection of water colours painted by the Bishop's wife along with photographs and sketches of various small dogs. I always assumed that these were predecessors of the Yorkshire terrier that had now taken up residence on the Bishop's lap or else favoured examples of much loved breeds. I know that his dogs meant a great deal to the Bishop and in the absence of children, probably formed something of a substitute family for him and his wife.

On the floor of the study sat a number of piles of books of all different shapes and sizes. These were probably books awaiting perusal by the Bishop who was an avid reader and academic or else having just been read, were awaiting cataloguing and filing away on the large wooden book shelves which covered two sides of the study walls.

In a bay window sat the Bishop's antique wooden desk on which was placed a very fine example of an Apple notebook and wireless printer. Another example of how the Bishop was full of surprises and the fact that he was obviously well up-to-date with the latest state of the art information technology therefore should have been expected. To the side of the desk was a large, marble fireplace over which hung various college photographs along with a Russian icon of the child and Madonna and a picture of the Bishop being greeted by Pope Jean Paul II. I guess that covered just about all the ecumenical corners.

The Bishop offered me a large arm chair in front of the fireplace directly opposite to where he sat. He rose to his feet, displacing the small lap dog.

"Would you care for a wee drink Kevin?"

"Just coffee please. That would be fine."

"How do you take it?"

"Milk, two sugars please."

At this point the Bishop disappeared only to re-emerge several minutes later with a large tray. It was strange that the Bishop, who had an over-officious secretary, still had to make his own tea and coffee.

"I've given Fiona, the afternoon off." he explained. "She's been doing some overtime for me recently, and besides, she makes awful coffee... and she won't use the fair-traded stuff as well. Says it's too expensive. I keep trying to explain to her that that's the whole point, but she just doesn't get it and insists on buying that cheap generic supermarket stuff all the time. I wouldn't mind... But I'm the Scottish one!"

Having been re-assured as to why the Bishop was waiting upon me, I felt slightly easier in accepting his hospitality. Soon we were both sipping fairly strong filter coffee and nibbling on home made shortcake biscuits courtesy of the Bishop's absent wife.

"She's off on one of her wee adventures again." Explained the Bishop, referring to his wife's absence. "Last year it was climbing Mount Kilimanjaro on behalf of Marie Curie; now it's jumping off some suspension bridge in New Zealand for the Children's Society. I don't know what will be next, but she's got this bug for thrill seeking recently and who am I to stand in her way?"

I must have looked incredulous.

"Nah... don't worry. She's tied onto the bridge with some elastic rope or something before she jumps off... So how is it going Kevin? Still battling with those scouts?"

"Oh that appears to have blown over for the moment. They'll come around eventually. They just want to flex their muscles a little. Try to gain some control over their circumstances."

"Aye, a bit like Bishops. Even though we are meant to be in charge, we are never in control."

"You don't do too badly. How about that recent liturgical issue. Didn't you finally get your changes to the prayer book through General Synod?"

"Oh yes, but that's not about gaining control. The Church of England might think that the word spoken is the word believed, and that all our theology is wrapped up in our various prayer books, but how often do people really read those prayer books? Or even use them? Do you use the latest version of 'Common Worship' at St Ebbs?"

"Um... uh... Gosh. That's a leading question. We use parts of it. But we tend to cut and paste bits into a video projector."

"There you go. You see my point. We are in charge, but not in control. We spend all this time and effort revising our centuries old liturgies and beautifying our prayer books and then computers come along and we end up with a pick and mix liturgical free for all. Most people get more Bible knowledge from the songs they sing than the prayer books they read anyhow. I call it the gospel according to St. Matthew of Redman."

"I see your point. Although I do quite like some of Matt Redman's songs. The words aren't bad either."

"Oh aye. Anyhow we haven't come here today to talk about liturgy versus modern worship songs. What can I do for you Kevin?"

"Well, ironically it's about music – sort of – that I wanted to talk with you. Do you know that I play in a band?"

"At church? I had heard, I..."

"No, I don't mean that. I play in a secular rock band. We meet together during the week for practice and then play gigs at the weekend."

"What kind of gigs?"

"Just entertainment really. Weddings. Birthday parties. The occasion pub gig. Nothing too serious."

"Oh good for you Kevin. I had no idea," admitted the Bishop whilst offering me another piece of homemade shortbread.

"Yes, just a bit of fun, up till now, although we did lay down a few tracks a short while ago. But Ian, he's the sort of lead musician and prime mover in the band, has this vain ambition about us doing our own stuff and getting some sort of career out of it. Recording our own material, setting up a website, making our music available to the masses – sort of building a following. You know, the way the *Arctic Monkeys* did it. I guess that the *Arctic Monkeys* don't mean much to you?"

"I might be a Bishop approaching retirement, but even I have heard of the *Arctic Monkeys*. They are a local band, but I don't quite see you in the same market as them. Also, don't forget you're a priest Kevin, not a rock musician."

"Precisely. That's what I keep saying to Ian, but now he's gone and got this offer to go on tour in a few weeks time. Supporting a tribute band."

"Which tribute band is that?"

"Oh, a *U2* tribute band. I think they're called *Zoo Two* or something like that."

"Oh aye… the one The Edge had an out-of-body experience over."

"Y-e-h…, those are the ones." The Bishop really was full of surprises.

"Well, it means being away from the parish for six weeks, maybe longer and touring up and down the country and that."

"And your problem is...?"

"My problem is that I want to go, but it feels like I'm jumping ship or running away from my responsibilities."

"Running away? Whatever from?"

"Parish life I suppose."

"And your problem is....?"

"Well six weeks is a long time and..."

"And...the parish will continue without you."

"Oh, I know that."

"And no-one will think you don't deserve it. How long have you been at St Ebbs now?"

"Over seven years."

"Oh... you'll be due a sabbatical then."

"Yes, but I don't want to have to do any serious study."

"Study?"

"Yes. Aren't you meant to go away and spend all such time doing something worthy and academic?"

"No, not necessarily."

"Well it is the sabbath part of a sabbatical that would appeal to me, rather than the study part."

"We could be a wee bit flexible over that. If you wanted to wait until you had some area of study in mind for a sabbatical, then we could defer that part and you could take the tour as the first instalment of the sabbatical. Call it fieldwork or research which could be written up or reflected upon at a later time."

"You mean that I could just take the time off"

"Oh aye. Why not? Look Kevin. Why do you always expect something horrible to be waiting around the wee corner in order to jump up and bite you? No one would begrudge you some time off, especially following the sadness that you've had to bear... Have you spoken with Jonathan yet?"

"No not yet. I wanted to speak with you first and to arrive at some sort of decision before I panicked him."

"Oh he'll no panic. He's a canny guy is Jonathan. I'm sure he'll cope. Have you spoken with anyone else at church?"

"Not really. Not at all. It's just that..."

"Just that what?"

"It's just that I'm not sure... don't know whether I will want... whether I can get back into, whether—whether I will want to come back if I go away for so long!"

There. I had finally said it. I had 'outed' myself. Owned up to how I really felt... and in front of the Bishop at that. What would he think?

"*Come back*, why for ever would you not wish to come back?"

"I don't know it's just this lingering fear I have."

"Fear? What are you afraid of. You don't strike me as the fearful sort. Are you telling me that your vocation is under threat?"

As the Bishop mentioned the words, I could feel myself welling up, becoming emotional and light headed. Oh no, I was going to start sobbing all over the Bishop's shag pile. How embarrassing having to admit to questioning my vocation. Bang goes any future career. If the Bishop thinks I'm damaged goods, then he would never offer me a decent parish if I wanted to continue in parish ministry in the future. Did I really want to burn all my bridges straight away? I had always felt a little uneasy with discussing personal issues with the Bishop or other senior staff come to that. I know that they were there to help and to support, but they were also my line managers, with the potential to determine a career and to flavour a reputation.

"Maybe I am? I'd never quite thought of it like that before."

"Oh dear... that's unfortunate... sorry Kevin I wasn't referring to your doubts." At that point, the Bishop got up, grabbed a box of Kleenex tissues from off a bookshelf and instead of offering them to me knelt down on the study floor and started to clear up some discharge that his Yorkshire terrier had just vomited up all over the carpet.

"Dogs have such a wonderful wee sense of timing don't you think?"

"I... I guess so," suddenly regaining my poise and realising that I wasn't the only object of the Bishop's attention.

"Aye and this one has a terrific sense of occasion. One time when the Archbishop came round to tea and we were breaking bread together in my chapel. This wee Yorky here wandered in and was sitting under the altar cloth. He then broke wind most violently half way through the eucharistic prayer, I'm afraid we both thought it was rather funny and became rather distracted... Sorry, you were saying?"

"Maybe my vocation is in doubt or maybe it isn't." I tried to return to my earlier conversation wrestling with my thoughts and feelings, whilst trying not to be distracted by the idea of the Archbishop and a farting dog. "It's just that I have always struggled with knowing just where I fit in. Where I belong."

"But you do fit in. You belong to Jesus and to His Church. You are loved by Him and everything else is just a working through of that amazing truth. You are also a fine priest and a good human being."

"Thank you. I appreciate that," I added suddenly feeling more secure and affirmed and growing in size as I sat opposite the Bishop.

"Are you struggling with your churchmanship?"

"Perhaps? The labels don't really seem relevant any more."

"Oh I always had you down as a committed evangelical."

"Well that is my background, but I no longer seem to possess the certainty that many of my evangelical brethren share. Nor their focus."

"Their focus?"

"Yes, their focus on scripture and scripture alone. I love the scriptures, I adore the Bible, but I love Jesus more. It seems that the written word often gets confused with the living Word."

"So evangelicals actually start worshipping the Bible?"

"It can feel like that, but I guess that we all worship our traditions at times and elevate them to divine status. We end up loving the gifts more than the giver."

"And the Anglo Catholics? Could you find a home among them?"

"If evangelicals can be criticised for worshipping the Bible, then Anglo Catholics can end up worshipping communion instead."

"A little harsh?"

"Yes, but I hear so many speaking about worship being eucharistically centred when I thought that we were meant to be Christ-centred in our worship."

"So, the Anglo Catholics worship the eucharistic. What about the charismatics?"

"They just worship worship."

"And us liberals? What do we worship?"

"Ah, what do you mean by worship? Let's all reflect upon that theologically for a time and get the House of Bishops to write a report."

"Aye, I hear what you are saying, fair comment, although I don't necessarily agree," replied the Bishop although smiling hugely to himself, "but let's get back to your particular ministry. I think that you have a lot to offer the Church and that won't change or be affected by you having a wee jolly with your rock band for a few weeks...When was the last time you took a decent amount of time off?"

"Last year, I suppose, during the summer holidays."

"And how long did you take?"

"Just a couple of weeks, unless you include the week I spent at that 'New Growth' Conference."

"New Growth? A week spent in a muddy field surrounded by a wee bunch of Christians who couldn't get tickets for Glastonbury. No Kevin, any such conference sounds like a busman's holiday to me. I call that work. It certainly felt like hard work whenever I had to speak at one of those events! How about your day off? Are you taking a day off every week?"

"Yes, most weeks. Occasionally they get interrupted by a special event or when a funeral occurs involving someone I already have a pastoral contact with. I kinda feel obliged to accept those funerals."

"Obligation? Obligation, that's a hard one. I wonder how much of what we all do, is actually led by love or rather driven by guilt? You must take your days off. Don't let anything get in the way of that!"

"The problem is that it's just a day. I never fully unwind in a day. It usually takes most of a day just to go shopping or to cut the lawn or catch up on my sleep. The next thing I know and the day is over and I'm back to work still not having unwound."

"Hmm. Yes, that is a hard one for sure."

"By the way, why do we only take one day off a week? Most people have two days, they call it a weekend, why should we be any different?"

"Because we are different. We are set apart to live a life, not to do a job."

"And that life doesn't allow us to take time to re-charge or relax?"

"I suppose it's all to do with the Sabbath principle again. Marking a creative pause in the week from our labours. It goes back to the wee Jewish custom and practice."

"I see. But if I understand you correctly, you say we work six days a week because that is what the Sabbath established as a pattern of life. Correct?"

"That's broadly true. Although there is a wee bit more to it than that."

"And the Sabbath pattern was based on God resting from the creation of life, the universe and everything in six days and resting on the seventh?"

"That's the common understanding, although some of us understand the story more symbolically."

"So when did we become God?"

"I'm sorry?"

"Well, we're not God are we? He might only need a day to rest, but he's God and we aren't. Quite frankly if even God needs a day's rest, how much more do most of us need to re-charge and reflect after being creative?"

"I see your point. But that's the way it has always been for clergy and it's not going to change overnight I'm afraid."

"Even when it's pointless and not grounded in sensible theology?"

"Especially when it's pointless and not grounded in sensible theology. This is the Church of England after all."

With that we both laughed and then continued chatting but in a more personal and free ranging manner. We started to share about how we had both wanted children but it had never happened and how life never worked out exactly as planned, but that didn't mean that God wasn't involved in the big picture as well as in the details.

There were times in my life when I hated being a priest and despaired of the Church of England. But there were also times when I felt as though I was part of something really rather wonderful and glorious. That the Church was a bit like a batty old aunt who was something of an embarrassment to be around for most of the time and then when it really mattered, she would do something magnificent to make you proud and all would be forgiven and forgotten. This was one of those moments. Suddenly, I could see that there was a point in having Bishops, they were there to actually help rather than get in the way.

"So, do you want me to speak to your church wardens about this?"

"No, I'll tell them. I'm sure they'll be OK." I re-assured the Bishop, realising at that point that I had effectively already made up my mind to say 'yes' to Ian and to the tour. I wouldn't need a day of prayer and fasting after all.

The next week just shot by. There were many details to attend to following my meeting with the Bishop. I spoke with Barbara and Phil, the church wardens and they appeared to be very supportive and understanding. I also spoke with Jonathan who looked a little pale initially when told, but then began to warm to the task once we discussed the details and started to make plans for the transition and hand over. As the following days passed by it became increasingly apparent that Jonathan was starting to relish the opportunity to spread his wings a little and even to use my absence as an opportunity to introduce a few of his own ideas that he had been considering. It was as though a cork had been released from the bottle with Jonathan. I was a little concerned by this growing positivity, fearing that it revealed I had been holding him back in some way, but we were able to talk together very openly and it emerged that Jonathan just needed some affirmation and the freedom to express himself, which he couldn't always find whilst working alongside someone who was trying to formally train him and shape his ministry. Perhaps my sojourn would therefore prove beneficial and character building for Jonathan. A win-win situation all round.

The following week I went to band practice with a warm fuzzy glow of assurance and conviction surrounding me. When I arrived at Ian's house the door wasn't opened by Ian, but rather I was greeted by what appeared to be one of the 'Corr' sisters – a stunningly attractive slim, dark haired Irish lady in her early thirties who Ian immediately introduced to me as Siobhan. I hadn't remembered her from the *Irish Club*. I know that I would have remembered someone who looked like her. Perhaps she really was an overlooked 'Corr' sister – kept in some kind of solitary confinement in case her public appearance made the others look dowdy in comparison? It was then, that the penny started to drop, this was one of Ian's potential conquests. There was another agenda operating here. As if to confirm my suspicions, as Siobhan made her way down to Ian's basement to get her saxophone reeds warmed up, Ian grabbed me by the arm to hold me back and then caught me with a wink and a knowing look.

"Eye candy Kev. Never under-estimate the effect of eye candy."

I was shocked that Ian could be thinking this way, but as we entered Ian's basement practice room the bigger picture began to emerge. Bryan was absent and Ian explained that he wouldn't be coming back due to irreconcilable musical differences between the two of them. I would miss Bryan. He could appear miserable at times, but he always understood my sense of humour and self parody. We had developed a strong musical connection as well and although I never really shared all of Bryan's technical insights and concerns, I always felt that I had an ally in Bryan and felt secure when he was around. Ian, on the other hand, was always full of mystery – smoke and mirrors. Just when you thought that you knew him and had him all worked out or had won his trust, then something like this agenda with Siobhan would happen, proving just how impenetrable his personality was to me.

"Still the good news is that Siobhan is also able to double up on keyboards," announced Ian. "And Bryan has agreed to run through all our set pieces with her in order to get her up to speed as it were. So everything should be OK. How about you Kev? Are you able to get the time off? Are you in or out?"

"As far as the band is concerned, I am in, but I can't help but feeling a little sorry for Bryan. Will he be coming back when we return from the tour?"

"Oh yeh. I'm sure he will. We'll sort something out by then." Ian lied.

The rest of the practice proceeded without further hitches. In fact, it started to sound rather good. Siobhan was offering a lot more than just eye candy. She could really play and her soaring sax solos offered a richness and subtlety that had eluded the *Manic Tuesdays* previously. I comforted myself with the thought that whatever had happened with Bryan, this was going to be a very interesting musical journey for the band. Perhaps that would authenticate my decision to join in with the tour after all?

The practical and musical arrangements for the tour were falling into place neatly, however, I remained spiritually drained and somewhat troubled. Even though the Bishop had been so helpful and so supportive, I was unable to shake off a sense of unease. I felt vulnerable, exposed, as though I had indeed 'outed' myself, and disclosed some awful embarrassing home truth that I had been previously unaware of or else unable to own up to. Just saying the words about not wanting to return to parish life had been an admission about how I had really felt for some time. I recognised that some part of my life had departed at that point. As though preparing to leave and go on tour represented a leaving of a deeper kind. The Bishop had suggested that such feelings were still the outworking of my grief over Julie and perhaps they were? But the experiences of the next few days would make me realise that despite all the positives that came out of my meeting with the Bishop, there still remained unresolved issues that needed to be worked through.

Chapter Seven

Chewing the cud
with Matt and Co.

An email stood out among the collection of correspondence, newsletters, committee minutes, jokes, petitions and spam emails advocating natural *Viagra* that filled my in-box.

From: "Matt Samuels" <matt.sams@hotmail.co.uk;> sams@globalsolns.co.uk	
To: KevtheRev@fish.co.uk Sent: Thursday, February 20, 2006. 2:18 PM	
Subject: Let's get together	
Hi Kev	

Do you remember me? We talked in the car park after Deanery synod the other week and then enjoyed a great late nite doner. Well I was wondering if you fancied a pint? I would also like you

> to meet a few of my friends. If you are up for this, then we meet every Friday evening in the Fleece and Firkin on Bridge Street. 8 till late.
>
> Be good to meet up again and to chew the cud.
>
> Matt

I had been thinking about the angry young businessman I encountered all those weeks ago. Our conversation still haunted me. I felt a strange sense of responsibility towards him. I also felt that there was some unfinished business between us in that I had spoken up for a kind of third way forward for the Church, without really knowing what I meant by this or understanding exactly where my theological journey was leading. Why did I hold out the hope that there was such a third path to explore having never properly travelled that path myself? Was such speculative thinking just a little bit reckless in the company of an impressionable person? What did I know after all? I'd never been much of an innovator at St Ebbs. Nor had I earned a reputation as an expert on the future of the Church of England. I just instinctively felt that there must be a better way forward. Another way of 'doing church' that didn't involve working harder at what the Church already did or re-labelling existing projects as new innovations. Like the second peak that Bridget had described, I just passionately believed that there was new territory to be explored, so a pint with Matt might just be fun and offer the opportunity to explore that territory further. I wasn't sure about the friends that Matt wanted me to meet. Who were they and what was their agenda? But an offer of a pint is an offer of a pint. I had learnt that such offers were few and far between in parish ministry and even if it might come with some strings attached, opportunities for male bonding should always be embraced.

I quickly pinged back a response to say 'yes' before I was able to change my mind.

The following Friday evening I took the tram to Bridge Street and located the Fleece and Firkin which I hadn't previously visited since it had been taken over by a new brewery and received one of those stylized make-overs, the results of which end up as themed pubs. I therefore entered somewhat hesitantly but was pleased not to be greeted by old bicycles and washboards hanging from the ceiling and food menus offering a terrine of goats' cheese, apples and celery and a salad of toasted walnuts, raisins and balsamic vinegar. Whatever happened to good old pub grub?

A figure stood up and waved at me from within a small group of people crouched in the corner of the room and I forced my way towards the waving figure pushing past a group of scantily clad young women who were wearing bunny ears and talking rather loudly whilst endeavoring to hold each other up. Presumably they were en route to a night club or the venue of a hen party, or both.

Matt greeted me like a long lost friend, rather than a new acquaintance.

"Hi Kevin. Glad you could make it. What can I get you?"

He was dressed in a business suit and tie which was part loosened in a manner that suggested he had been working hard all day and now was trying to relax a little. He then manoeuvered between us in order to take up residence at a part of the bar not occupied by bunny eared young women. Trying to hold each other up. Shortly afterwards we returned to our table and to the assembled group of friends with two pints of creamy Yorkshire ale.

"Have a seat Kev. Do you know anyone here?"

"Only the one I think."

The individual I was referring to was Melanie, a woman in her late thirties that I knew from church. Melanie had been someone Julie had befriended shortly after her arrival in the parish. She lived just around the corner and had knocked on the vicarage door the day after we moved in with a bottle of wine and a box of *Thornton's* chocolates. We had been touched by such a welcoming gesture but hadn't really got to know Melanie that well in our first few years in the parish. However, a friendship eventually grew between Julie and Melanie, especially following the marriage problems that Melanie was having. She had endured a fairly unhappy marriage for some time. Her husband proved to be a very demanding character and had subjected her to a tirade of verbal and emotional abuse for a number of years. We had wondered what ever had endeared her to such a manipulative and unpredictable character in the first place. He had even appeared at the vicarage late one night in a drunken state accusing Julie of turning Melanie away from him and poisoning her mind.

Melanie could look a little strange or even severe. She had dyed bright red shoulder length straight hair, blue or black lipstick and often cultivated something akin to a Goth image. She would wear strange combinations of clothes, such as skirts with socks and trainers along with torn blouses and stripy jumpers, mercifully not all at the same time. She also had acquired two distinctive tattoos. One on her shoulder in the shape of the Celtic cross and another at the very small of her back which could only be seen when she would lean over or crouch down. She was a former English and Drama student and a very accomplished actress and poet. At one time she had tried to start a drama and creativity group at church, but it didn't really get off the ground. I suspect that some people found her a bit off putting and intimidating, although I had often found her to be a lot less severe that her physical appearance might have suggested. She once performed some dramatic monologues and improvisations during Holy Week on the theme of Jesus' passion. I was happy to allow her the freedom to experiment and push the creative boundaries, but some found her approach rather shocking, especially as it involved stage blood and the use of a couple of swear words. Blood and abusive language should never be allowed to spoil a good crucifixion.

Melanie had ultimately gone through a very difficult divorce in which there had been all sorts of issues about access to her children. However, despite all her problems she had remained a great support to Julie and myself during her illness and would often come around to the vicarage bringing amusing and unexpected gifts or else a casserole because she falsely assumed that I was unable to cook. The gesture was always appreciated though and Melanie had often shed considerable and much needed light into some fairly dark and desperate times for Julie and me.

Her relationship was Julie had grown very close and intense during Julie's illness. Occasionally I felt that she had become too emotionally involved, even to the extent of excluding me from some of Julie's most vulnerable and darkest moments. There was one time in particular, when I had come home only to find Melanie sat up alongside Julie in bed, with the pair of them eating chocolate and watching back-to-back episodes of *Friends* from a DVD box set that Melanie had bought for her. I don't know why, but something just snapped inside me and I found myself telling Melanie rather forcefully to leave immediately and that I could cope with looking after Julie perfectly well on my own. Although I later apologised for my outburst, there remained coolness and distance between us after that and the atmosphere cooled further following Julie's death which Melanie found incredibly overwhelming emotionally.

Since that time, our relationship remained rather distant. I guess that I had come to resent anyone else sharing my grief for Julie to quite the same degree. I just couldn't understand what she was feeling and why she felt so strongly. It was as if she was trying to steal my grief away from me or muscle in on it in some way and I came to resent her for it as that was all I had left of Julie – my love for her and my sense of loss.

I tried to explore these feelings during one of my regular visits to Bridget but I didn't feel that I got very far. Bridget suggested that they might have developed a powerful exclusive emotional link that provided Julie with something I could never provide for her, but I was uneasy with exploring such an idea. Whatever lay behind it all, I felt an ambivalence and awkwardness towards Melanie for a while, although my coldness started to thaw in time as I grew to recognise all that she had done for Julie and how she had been a special friend to her during her time of need. For that in particular I would always remain personally grateful although I had often struggled to adequately express my appreciation and thanks to her in the past. As the months went by I saw less and less of her at church. Once I became sufficiently concerned to go and visit her and ask if there was anything concerning her that was keeping her away from regular worship, but she just came over all coy and elusive, and seemed unwilling to explain herself. Subsequently I hadn't seen her for about a year, although mutual friends said that they thought she was now attending another church, whilst others said that she had stopped going to church altogether. Whatever the reason, it felt good to see her again.

Melanie sat next to a rather large lady I didn't recognise who was momentarily absorbed by a text message she was trying to compose. Next to her sat a rather scruffy looking man with a beard and beer belly. He wore a black leather jacket, black leather trousers, black boots and an orange helmet, covered in stickers. Just a shot in the dark, but something about him told me that he was a biker.

"I gather that you already know Melanie."

"Yes, hello Mel. How are you?"

"Fine, fine. Good to see you again." Replied Melanie although she remained uncharacteristically withdrawn and unsure of herself.

"This is Andrea, a friend of Melanie and all-around good egg. And this is Bill the Biker. Don't worry he doesn't bite. We were expecting Richard, but he's not sure if he can make it tonight. Everyone...! This is Kevin, the vicar I was telling you about. The one who likes to make cakes."

"We could call him, 'Kev the Rev'," said Andrea suddenly looking up from her mobile as if enlivened by a new sense purpose.

'Oh no' I thought. *'I've joined one of those groups in which everyone has a nickname or title. They've already got 'Bill the Biker'. I thought that only Ian called me Kev the Rev. Ground please swallow me up.'*

However, fortunately that was the first and last occasion that nicknames were apportioned that evening. After such an unpromising start, warm and wise conversation eventually started to flow along with the beer.

"Kevin took me to task the other day after I got rather hot under the collar following the last Deanery Synod." Matt explained to the small group around the table. "Then he started to blow my mind away with all this stuff about baking cakes and using our imagination. It was a real Jose Mourinho moment".[11]

I didn't quite understand the footballing reference, but gathered that this was meant as some sort of compliment and conferred approval upon my unexpected use of an analogy.

"So what do cakes have to do with the Church of England Kev?" asked Bill from behind his rather untidy beard as he took a sip of non-alcoholic lager.

"Are you a fan of Eddy Izzard?"

"Uh no. Not really."

"That's a shame. I was going to mention his observations about the Church of England. He does this routine about how the Catholics during the Inquisition offered people the choice of renouncing heresy or death, whereas for the Church of England it was probably a choice between death or cake? In which case most people would reply, 'Yes please, I'd rather have some cake if that is all right with you'."[12]

A cold icy blast came over me as silence greeted my procrastination and once again I became aware that people were staring at me as though I had suddenly started to speak in fluent Chinese.

"Don't worry if you're not familiar with his material. The whole cake thing was just an analogy. A way of explaining how we all avoid taking responsibility for living out the gospel because we like to get other people to do all our baking instead

---

11   Jose Mourinho – manager of Chelsea Football
      Club 2004-07, known for his exraordinary
      statement to the press and media: such as
      comparing being a football manager to making
      omeletes from eggs.

12   The comedian Eddie Izzard speaks a lot about
      faith and religion. One of his best known routines
      parodies the fact that the Church of England
      doesn't do religious fundamentalism: "Church of
      England fundamentalism is impossible because
      you can't have: *You must have tea and cake with
      the vicar... or you die!* Cake or death!"

of using what we have to bake our own cakes." I explained quickly, hoping to redeem myself in their eyes and recover my illustration.

More silence.

A picture of tumbleweed blowing along a deserted wild western street immediately came to mind. Suddenly my newly acquired expertise on the subject of the Church seemed to be ebbing away. My reputation now in tatters, I felt the need to beat a hasty retreat.

I decided to break the icy silence. "Now I come to think about it. It's a rubbish illustration. Forget all about it."

"No. I see where you're coming from." Andrea rescued me, whilst remaining thoughtful and unconvinced in appearance. "But we've all become somewhat bogged down in the details of pastoral re-organisation recently. We've gone through a real battle at church since our vicar left and now they want to push us together with St. Agnes. And we all know what that will lead to." The three of them exchanged knowing looks, whilst Melanie examined her shoes, looking furtive.

"But why let other people 'do Church' for you? Presumably you all worship together?" I enquired.

"Well I don't really worship that much these days." Melanie explained. "Since I left St Ebbs and since last time we met. I haven't really gone anywhere. Just sort of, drifted I suppose."

"I'm sorry to hear that Mel. I just assumed that Matt knew you from his church."

"Oh no, we just kind of met up recently. I only started coming along to the pub because of Andrea. She brought me along."

"So what if you don't mind me asking drew you away from Church in the first place?"

"Well there were some personal issues... which I won't go into at the moment, but I just felt that Church wasn't scratching where I was itching. It didn't resonate with my life as much as it used to. I still believe and pray and that. In fact I don't actually consider myself to have left the Church, more that the Church has left me. It just wasn't able to follow me where I was going..."

"The problem with Church is that it is trying to answer questions that nobody is asking any longer," interrupted Andrea. "All this talk about sin and sacrifice, heaven and hell, good and evil belongs in the middle ages if you ask me. I'll give you an example: 'washed in the blood of the Lamb' – what's that supposed to mean?"

"I guess it comes from the biblical images of the sacrificial love of God displayed in Christ who gave up his life for us," I suggested. "Lambs were often used in the ancient Jewish sacrificial system as sacrificial offerings whose blood was seen as atoning for the sins of the people."

"Precisely – it's meaningless," replied Andrea immediately dismissing what I thought was a very well constructed and measured answer.

"It might be Biblical language and Biblical images, but what is the point in retaining Biblical language if the language no longer speaks to our culture." Andrea continued. "We no longer live in a world of animal sacrifices. Most people no longer believe in sin, unless in some sort of sniggering, childish, naughty kind of way. They might live under it, see its consequences, but they reject it as a meaningful description of the human condition. So why do we continue to use it?"

"In fairness Andrea," said Melanie, suddenly butting in. "Kevin was very good in teaching about sin at St Ebbs. Many of us never really knew what sin was until he arrived {PAUSE} – sorry, that came out all wrong."

At that point the whole group fell about laughing at Melanie, whose facial colour gradually began resembling that of her hair. It was then decided that it was time for more drinks, so not wishing to appear mean spirited, I decided to get the next round in.

When I returned the mood of the group was growing warmer and less adversarial. Melanie's faux pas had lightened the atmosphere somewhat and allowed us all to laugh at ourselves, rather than to mock the Church from afar or mount our various soapboxes.

"What irks me," began Matt. "Is the way that people operate a hierarchy of sins. It's like there are some sins that are worse than others."

"You mean mortal sins?" asked Bill the Biker.

"No not really. We are all Prots. We don't officially operate under such labels, but we do in practice. It's like anything to do with sex is immediately seen as worse than any other type of sin."

"Well sexual sins usually involve other people... and broken relationships can cause great hurt," explained Bill.

"Yes, but if someone has an affair, or if a same sex couple arrives at church and wants to get involved in ministry... it's like everyone panics. But if someone is gossiping around church or being critical, then everyone makes excuses for them. 'Oh it's just their way 'or 'Old Mrs so and so always likes to speak her mind, think nothing of it.' But that's ridiculous because all those kinds of sins are condemned just as harshly as sexual sins in the Bible. And what's more..." Matt was starting to get energized by the debate but this time rather than the rant I had witnessed in the car park all those weeks before, he spoke with warmth and passion. "When we talk about addictive behaviour, drugs, alcohol, gambling and so on, it's like they are such terrible things to get involved with... and of course they are. But what about being addicted to work and power and ambition? It's like it's OK to be a workaholic and neglect your family and stress out those around you, but have a few drinks or buy a lottery ticket and then you are condemned to burn in hell!"

"Does that mean that it's your round Matt?" asked Bill moving his empty half pint glass towards Matt across the table.

"I guess that part of the problem is that we have adopted an intrinsically Greek, rather than Christian way of looking at life." I decided to get all theological. "The Greeks basically saw the body as inferior to the spirit or the soul and so of less concern to God. When the Church started to develop its ethical thinking, it took on this mindset so that anything to do with the body was regarded as impure, unholy or unspiritual – *de facto* the abuse of sex was seen as more sinful than other abuses. This was basically moving away from what Jesus said on the Sermon on the Mount, when he made the connection between intention and outcome – thought and deed."

"Here endeth the sermon for today," added Andrea with a bemused look.

"Well you did invite a vicar along. What did you expect?"

"It's good to have you with us Kev. It's just we are all feeling a bit hacked off with trying to be part of this thing called 'The Church' and we don't know what to do about it," Matt explained. "In my work life if something isn't working, then we have the power to change it – in theory anyhow. But at church if something doesn't work, we're expected to make do... to accept the received wisdom... to live within the limits and learn to love the odd ways and traditions, but traditions should be living and active. A tradition is only something we have done two weeks running. Like us coming to this pub. Just because we have always met on a Friday night in the past doesn't mean that we can only ever meet on a Friday night in the future."

"Ok. So let me play devil's advocate here. Why do we have to go to church in the first place?" I was starting to get provocative again.

"Most Christians would say that it is important that we meet together for the purpose of worship and fellowship and for mutual encouragement," answered Bill.

"That's right, but there are a number of different ways for that to happen. I wasn't trying to get at why we need to meet together as much as to why we have to GO and meet together. Why is Church seen as an event? As something that always takes place at a particular location on a particular time and day of the week and in a particular manner or pattern? The early Church met in houses and in trade guilds as far as we know. It hasn't always been like this."

"So are you saying that we should all meet together in someone's house, because I've tried one of those house churches and they have just the same problems as everyone else" added Melanie.

"Just what are you getting at Kev?" asked Matt.

"I'm getting at our mindset. We all keeping falling back onto the same default mechanism. We still want to make cakes from our ingredients. We keep seeing the Church in terms of an event and location, not as a people or a community. We say come along to church. See if you like it. Try to fit in and find your place within this organisation. Then when things don't work out, we want to fix the organisation."

"But every community needs some form of organisation."

"That's right Matt. But not every organisation is organised in the same way. Many people participate in a community without joining an organisation."

"You've lost me now Kev," admitted Matt.

"Me too," chorused the others.

"Well for instance. The parish system. Much loved by the Church of England. Why do we still operate that way? It's based upon a medieval pattern of settlement in which people were born in one place, grew up there, got educated, started work, got married, had a family and died. All their significant relationships were expressed within a fairly limited spatial location. Nowadays, we are born in one part of the country or even abroad, grow up somewhere else, get educated in a different place, work miles from where we live, shop somewhere different, mix socially in another part of town and probably travel to a church miles away because we like the way they worship and the coffee they serve. It's crazy to talk about serving your local community because you can be on better terms with someone in Australia via email or Facebook than you are with the person who happens to live next door to you. We express community relationally, through networks. So why not do Church in the same way?"

"So how do we do that then?" asked Matt.

"To be honest... I don't know. I'm just as clueless as the next person. But I'm prepared to keep asking the question."

"So you haven't got any answers either?" added Andrea, ruefully, looking rather disappointed.

"Not really. You shouldn't expect your clergy to have it all worked out you know. We are just as much victims of the system as everyone else."

"Can I make a suggestion?" Bill the Biker stirred from behind a packet of cheesy quavers, some of which had collected in his untidy beard.

"I might have got the wrong end of the stick here but hearing you talking like that has made me think about my own situation. You won't know this Kev, but the others know that I'm off work. I haven't done a days work for the last?... Oh it must be six years now. I'm not lazy or anything, it's just that I had an accident at work in one of the steel mills and ever since then I haven't been able to walk very well and if it wasn't for the trike I'd never be able to get anywhere."

"Trike?" I enquired. "What's a trike?"

"Sort of three wheel cross between a motorbike and a car."

"Like that monster machine that Billy Connolly rides all around the world?"

"Kind of. But it's more like an A-frame with a Mini Metro engine bolted onto a Goldwing front fork. But it gets me around. I can't cope with getting in and out of a normal car and a conventional bike is a little too finely balanced for my condition. Anyhow, what I was about to say..."

"Sorry." I apologised for interrupting.

"The one thing I am able to do is to pray. And ever since my injury people have started to tell me about their pain and problems more and more. So I would always ask if it is all right if I prayed for them. And so I started to keep one of these."

At this point Bill produced a small, red hardback book from inside his biker's jacket. "It's just a record of those people that I am praying for. Well this has gone on now for some years now..."

"A bit like your story Bill," interrupted Matt. "Do come to the point."

"I'm sorry, but Kevin won't know all this. Well all these people just kept coming into my life and after a while I guess folk just learnt that I was basically harmless but that I'm always prepared to pray for people. So I started to hand out these cards."

Bill placed a small business card on the table, with a cartoon of a hairy biker on a trike, plus the invitation, 'Can I pray for you?' along with his contact details.

"I'm not very high tech. Not like these folk here," Bill pointed to his friends around the table, "So I haven't got a computer or internet, but I do have an answer phone and people can leave requests and if they want me to ring them back, I will... So I guess the question I am trying to ask is this: do this group of people who send me their prayer requests make a sort of network?"

"Yes absolutely Bill," I replied confidently.

"Then I guess that you could say that I am part of a sort of church with these folk, although we never actually get together on a Sunday."

"Definitely Bill, and what's more – from what you've just described to me – I would say that you are the pastor of this church of yours in that you are exercising a valuable pastoral and teaching ministry to those people you are in contact with."

"Bishop Bill!" Andrea added to hoots of laughter, at which point Bill started to put on his motorbike helmet in the manner of a Bishop ceremonially putting on his mitre, whilst kissing his scarf and draping it around his shoulders in the manner of a priestly stole. Much amusement and general leg pulling followed.

"If Bill is our Bishop, then this must be our church," added Matt, "because we meet here every week, drink alcohol and consume cheesy potato based snacks."

"I see where you are going with this Matt." I replied trying to drive the image of Bill as a biking bishop out of my mind. "But Church is still more than a few like minded believers meeting together in a particular place. It must be a conscious gathering, aware not only of itself, but also of its mission and place within the bigger picture. It must see itself as part of a larger body, responding in worship to God and sharing a sense of belonging in some way."

Just then the familiar sound of a bell ringing out cut across their conversation announcing last orders.

"Our church bell?" suggested Andrea.

"Yes but this one is telling us to go home rather than calling us together," added Melanie.

As our gathering gradually broke up and each person started to make preparations to return home, I decided to take Melanie to one side.

"Mel, it's been really good to see you again tonight. And to see that you have found some great new friends. How are you keeping? You seem a little quiet if you don't mind me saying. Is everything OK at home?"

"No things aren't great at home, but they are better than they have been."

"And the kids? Are they OK? Who's baby sitting tonight?"

"Oh they've gone over to be with their Gran tonight. They like that."

"But what about YOU? How are you coping?"

"I'm all right really. Just in a bit of turmoil at the moment."

"I'm sorry to hear that."

"Are you free to get together some time?"

"Yes, but it's a matter of when," I explained, and then gave her a potted history of the last few weeks and how I would shortly be taking some time off to go on tour with the band.

"Oh I see your problem. Perhaps we could get together when you return. There is something that I want to share with you, but it's not for here and now. It'll wait."

"Ok, call me when I return. I will hold you to that Mel. Remember, I know where you live!"

Then we parted. As we did so a significant look was exchanged between us, although I didn't really recognise its meaning. Melanie was trying to look away, her eyes started to go red as tears began to well up. Unfortunately I didn't notice. I was distracted by the intensity and informality of the evening. My mind awash with new information, new friends and new possibilities.

"Right Kev the Rev, how about another visit to the late night kebab shop?" enquired Matt as he slapped me on the back sufficiently hard to register the fact that he had probably had just a few too many ales and was about to start to get all tactile and lucid like many blokes do once they have had one too many.

I didn't fancy bonding with Matt and discovering that I was now his '*bestest mate in the whole wide world*', over a dona and extra chili sauce. So I decided to decline his offer and set out into the clear and frosty Sheffield night air in search of the tram stop and the comfort of my grade 2 listed vicarage.

Matt set off in the opposite direction in search of the evil temptress of late night fast food.

Chapter Eight

"We just feel that we are not being fed at St Ebbs"

The next week was spent making preparations for going on tour with the band.

News of my impending absence received a somewhat mixed reception on Sunday morning when I told the congregations at St Ebbs, particularly when I explained that I would be taking some time out of the parish in order to honour a commitment arising from my extra parochial interests. I felt unable to spell out publicly that I was going away for six weeks in order to play bass guitar in a rock group supporting a *U2* tribute band. I just sounded rather trivial and selfish. I would have preferred to have revealed that I was going away to complete some rather important theological study, or about to undertake an extended silent retreat in order to commit myself to quiet contemplation or even to go to Africa to work among refuges or Aids victims. Anything but the truth would have been preferable. However, I did disclose more details at the church door after morning worship when the more curious enquired further about what I would be doing during my time away from the parish. Some were shocked, others a bit puzzled, whilst still others were quite dismissive, assuming that I was having some sort of mid-life crisis. One or two even appeared jealous, making comments such as 'it must be good to do a job that lets you take paid time off to go and play your guitar around the country' and 'I can imagine what my boss would say if I asked for time off for musical therapy.' In many ways, they did have a point. Although comparing the demands of parochial ministry with the demands of secular employment was a bit like comparing apples with pears; it was nevertheless worth conceding that whatever the drawbacks were to full time Christian ministry, there were also benefits and freedoms.

As ever Marjorie was wonderful and supportive when she found out what I would be doing, even though she didn't really understand much about rock music and had certainly never heard of *U2* or the idea of tribute bands.

"I think that this is a terrific idea Kevin. It will be so beneficial for you to have a break; and playing your music will be such a blessing I'm sure."

'Someone really should canonise this woman before she is taken up to heaven in a chariot of fire before my very eyes'.

"Do let us know how you get on. Perhaps we could come and see you play some time?"

"Yes. That might be an idea," I replied, whilst secretly praying one of my please get me out of goal prayers.

> *"Lord I know that you love Marjorie massively, but much as I appreciate her offer, please don't let her or any other members of St Ebbs Mother's Union come to see me play live.*
>
> *They wouldn't like it and I would feel really awkward and it would be so hard to explain to everyone back at church when I return and so hard to explain to other band members if they catch sight of them expecting a happy clappy sing song.*
>
> *I don't mean to be unkind…you know how it is… although I guess this didn't happen to*

Jesus all that often, but I guess he had a mother and he knew what it was like when people from a particular generation and background with all sorts of expectations turn up at an awkward time and an awkward place.

Can you just fix it so that it doesn't happen please Lord? I don't want to tell you your job, but I think it would be best for all concerned.

In your name – I hope – Amen."

Not one of my most fluent, liturgical or theologically balanced prayers, but an honest one.

Generally, however, I was affirmed and supported in my decision to go on tour. A decision that was confirmed in another way by a meeting I had during my last week in the parish.

Alison and David had rung me asking if they could come around and see me before I went away. Alison and David were a young couple who had joined St Ebbs from another church some three years previously and had always appeared enthusiastic and full of good ideas. Alison was a full time mum to their three young children whilst David worked as a local GP. Alison had been a real blessing at St Ebbs. She was bright and articulate and a very good organiser. She also had a real heart for mission and for work in the local community. She had been the driving force behind setting up a holiday club for children to attend during the summer months and without her leadership and organisational flair the event would not have taken place at all, let alone become the success and encouragement it had been to the whole parish.

The door bell rang and Alison and David entered, appearing friendly but looking serious.

I showed them into the living room, avoiding the study, the contents of which I was sure they would not understand or else have some issues over.

"Do you want a drink?"

"Thanks. David will have a coffee, but just hot water for me." Alison replied. I still hadn't grown accustomed to Alison's practice of answering on behalf of her husband. He was a doctor for goodness sake. People trusted their lives into this man's hands. Why can't he answer for himself when asked if he wanted something to drink?

A little while later after drinks had been distributed and pleasant small talk exchanged by way of preliminaries, the real business of the evening began.

"We wanted to have this little chat with you before you go away." Alison explained. "We thought it only fair to tell you personally that we will be leaving St Ebbs in order to go to the New Life Christian Centre."

"Gosh Alison. I hadn't seen that coming. I'm shocked. What has brought about your decision?"

Sometimes I just couldn't help myself. I had been in this situation before and always found it difficult to deal with. Such decisions troubled me deeply and I often took them as a sign of my own personal failure to engage people with vision and passion for their parish church. As a result I was usually left feeling personally inadequate and discouraged. I had spoken at length with Bridget about similar occasions. Bridget's advice had been to keep such meetings brief and business like because once people have announced that they are going to leave then there is realistically very little that can be done to change their minds. Such instances are quite common, and therefore shouldn't be dwelt upon excessively. Although finding out the reasons might satisfy my curiosity, it would also invariably play upon my self doubts and feelings of inadequacy. On such occasions it would be better to shake hands and just say 'thank you for letting me know and I wish you every blessing in the future. Goodbye and God bless.' However, I was still hadn't learnt this lesson and couldn't resist the temptation to probe further as to the reason behind Alison and David's decision.

I had always endeavoured to be friendly towards all members of the congregation. Indeed, I would often explore and probe the boundaries that surrounded the demarcation between effective warm pastoral relationships and that of open and genuine friendships. Alison and David's visit revealed the conditionality of their friendship. They expected something tangible in return for their friendship over and above that of my personal appreciation, love and support. The conditionality of such friendships demonstrated how difficult it can be to cultivate honest, open and reciprocal friendships with members of your own congregation. How many friends will announce that they are leaving in order to become someone else's friend because they don't approve of your work methods or business strategy? As a result, Alison and David had now moved from one set into the other, from friends and colleagues to becoming 'hoppers and shoppers'. A group of people who had caused me so much heartache in the past.

Work colleagues or business partners occasionally fall out when they can no longer work together, but Church offers very fuzzy boundaries between business and friendship, between work and leisure. As a result I always felt disappointed when those I had previously regarded as friends suddenly announced they were taking themselves elsewhere. It sometimes felt as though it wasn't sufficient just to offer people my support and friendship; they sometimes required entertainment and stimulation as well.

"Well to answer your question…"

Suddenly my attention returned to the unfolding conversation and the reason for Alison and David wanting to leave.

"… We just feel that we are not being fed at St Ebbs any more."

I had faced similar situations before. Growing expectations, the allure of increased choice and decline of personal loyalty meant that 'hoppers and shoppers' often withdraw their support from churches which they perceived aren't going fast enough down some prescribed route towards renewal or growth. Inertia or lack of progress towards such outcomes can lead to frustration with those who want to worship in a more traditional fashion, labelling them, as 'unspiritual' or 'not listening to God' or worst still were 'trying to squash the work of the Holy Spirit'. In the past such tensions had precipitated the arrival of a delegation of concerned parishioners. A conversation would ensue as to how a particular issue should be handled or how a new work might be initiated. Such conversations were often couched in spiritual language and good intentions, but would often carry a subliminal threat that if a particular course of action was not followed or a particular outcome arrived at, then the 'concerned delegation' would have to pray about where God was leading them and whether they could continue to worship at a church that didn't exactly correspond to everything they wanted.

I found this strange mixture of accountability and sociability difficult to manage. Were we all in this situation together or was I in some way meant to provide those things that 'hoppers and shoppers' were looking for from Church? Was Church a family and community or a social institution which was meant to make people happy and fulfilled? Dealing with such issues had broken my heart on a number of occasions, especially when I heard that people had simply moved to another church, only to repeat their same unsettled pattern of behaviour. I nevertheless felt I had failed them and failed God in some way. Like the owner of a small, local convenience store feels, when they are known and loved by their local community for generations and cherished for their standard of customer care and service, only to find themselves competing with a large superstore who moves into town offering instant bargains, bright lights, convenient parking and 24 hour opening.

"Not fed? In what way?" I replied, trying not to sound hurt or indignant.

"It's not us so much, as our children. We feel that it is so important that they receive a proper Christian education and upbringing. But often they don't get the right nurture and ministry that they need at St Ebbs."

"I'm still not sure that I follow."

"When David and I were younger, we used to be part of a large youth group at our local church. In fact that's how we met. Didn't we David?"

"That's right." The doctor was briefly cajoled into a response.

"And during those years there was always something interesting going on at church. We had socials together, weekends away, half nights of prayer spent sleeping out in the church hall. We used to go and see Christian rock bands and concerts and the like. It was great. But at St Ebbs it just isn't like that. If we don't organise activities for the children and young people it's like nothing ever happens. There's little going on that would be of interest to them."

"And often there are only a few of them there each week," added David. "Their fellowship groups are so small. How are they going meet other Christians and find Christian partners when they get older if there are so few of them? It's always going to be a struggle." Alison continued.

"I see what you are saying. But we have seen great growth in our children's work, especially since you and David arrived. Look at how successful the holiday club was. I'm sure that over the years the ministry among our children and young people will continue to grow and develop and your children will be part of that and benefit accordingly." I tried to rally their spirits and help them to gain another perspective.

"I hear what you are saying," continued Alison. "But we just can't be sure and it is far too important for us to take the risk with our children. We just want them to have what we had and we feel that the best place for their spiritual development would be at the New Life Christian Centre."

"What about Christ Church with Justin and Pippa?"

"We have looked into that, but some of their school friends already attend a midweek club at New Life and so it would be a natural progression for them to follow on there as well."

"I see."

"We don't want you to take this personally Kevin." [Too late! I already had] "We think you're a really super chap and all that."

"But…" I interjected, anticipating the train of their thought.

"But, we feel that we can only grow spiritually if we move on to another church. I'm sure that you will understand."

"I'm sorry that you feel this way Alison... and David. I am grateful for all that you have done at St Ebbs. I was looking for your support for various projects and ideas for the future, but I guess that there is nothing I can say to change your minds?"

"I'm afraid not."

At this point. I really wanted to say something unchristian like, 'Oh sod off then, see if I care.' But instead some clerical reflex mechanism kicked in causing me to be kind and sympathetic instead. So I offered to pray with them and then afterwards escorted them to the door, feeling rather deflated by the whole experience.

Not only would Alison and David leave a leadership vacuum in the current over-stretched children's leadership team at St Ebbs, but as committed Christians who took their financial stewardship very seriously, they would be greatly missed in other ways. I tried not to find out how much each member of the congregation gave by way of regular giving to the Church. Knowing too much about such issues could inevitably skew personal relationships causing clergy to ingratiate themselves with certain people whom they knew were making a significant financial contribution towards the ministry of the church. However, knowing the whole hearted manner in which Alison and David approached everything in life and the kind of income that local GPs attract, meant that I suspected that the church finances would record a substantial down turn as a result of their departure.

I went to bed feeling really depressed and disillusioned. Perhaps I would explore an alternative career as a musician after all? Or else get a job that didn't raise any personal issues about self worth and achievement. Perhaps I could get a job delivering pizza on one of those little mopeds or else stack shelves at *Tesco*? Anything but this.

That night I fell into a troubled sleep. I dreamt that I was working in a supermarket on the bacon and cooked meats counter. Lots of couples kept walking past but no-one ever stopped to buy anything. Then at last I saw someone I recognised. It was Alison and David, complete with their tribe of three hungry, malnourished children.

"Oh hello Kevin," said Alison. "We were looking around, but we didn't want any of your bacon. We just don't feel that bacon is feeding us as a family any more…"

At that point a motorised pizza delivery man arrived in the supermarket and when he took off his helmet it revealed Jamie Oliver who started to entice Alison and David's children with offers of exotic 'pukka' foods… explaining that in the Church of England there was only the choice of cake or death. Then after a while he began to play a drum kit, which had inexplicably appeared, explaining that he was also the new drummer that Ian had arranged for the band whilst they were on tour…

I awoke feeling disturbed and confused by the collision of so many stories but relieved that it had all been a dream.

Much of the rest of the day was spent with Jonathan running through rotas and various lists of who was doing what and at which service whilst I was away. Jonathan looked a bit overawed by the prospect, displaying the fragility of his growing confidence, but I assured him that he would be able to cope and let him have my mobile phone number, which I usually strenuously guarded so as to avoid being bothered by voicemail messages in addition to email and the answer phone. However, I trusted Jonathan to only contact me if there was some kind of emergency or a situation that he couldn't deal with on his own. In which case, he could get in touch and I could be available to return to the parish if needed.

Later on I just had enough time to make a couple of house calls to families of those I had taken funerals for. The first visit was a bit awkward, as the widow didn't really seem to understand why I had called around and assumed that I wanted a donation of some kind. I stood resolutely on the doorstep trying to re-assure her that I had only called around to see how she was coping after the funeral. She eventually seemed to understand, although she still didn't take the hint and invite me in. After a few awkward minutes, I made some excuse and took my leave.

The second visit was more appreciated. The family of an elderly relative, who had died in a nursing home, seemed genuinely pleased to see me and invited me in. They even offered me alcohol. Usually a good sign of warmth and openness. I don't normally accept such an offer, but a kind of 'Oh what the heck' attitude overwhelmed me and shortly afterwards I found myself sitting in their living room with a glass of malt whiskey putting the world to right. This was one of those 'Arthur type occasions' that I enjoyed just slotting into someone else's family and world. The family talked about their feelings surrounding the funeral and how difficult it had been visiting their relative in the nursing home. I explained that my Father was also in residential care and shared how I felt about visiting him. This seemed to spark some kindred spirit in the family and pleasant warm conversation started to flow, eventually moving onto the subject of the band and going on tour. It transpired that the teenage son of one of the family members had actually heard of *Zoo Two* and had seen them in concert before. This put my credibility through the roof and before the visit was ended, the family started to make all sorts of positive noises about wanting to start coming to church and how I should come around and see them when I returned in order to share my experiences of going on tour.

The pastoral visit had reminded me that it would be appropriate to go and visit Dad before I set off on tour. It would be possible to take time out from the tour to visit Dad, but somehow I felt that I owed him an explanation before I set off, and although it was unlikely that he would understand what was taking place, nevertheless, I still wanted to touch base with him before embarking upon my travels.

The following day I drove into Whiteview Nursing Home – a large Victorian sandstone building which stood a little distance back from one of the main arterial routes that led out of Lichfield. At one time, the building had been used as a private school and then as an up-market restaurant, but the restaurant had struggled to find the right sort of clientele in Lichfield and had closed after only a year, after which it was soon bought up by a chain of social care providers who converted it into residential accommodation.

Dad had been one of their first residents. Without a brother or sister to share the burden of care with once Mum had died, a great deal of responsibility had fallen on me. Dad had lived by himself at home for a number of years after Mum's death and had seemed to be doing very well at first. He had learnt to cook and had even joined the local bowling club as a kind of social support group. However, it soon became apparent that although he remained in good physical health, his mental faculties were deserting him. I would often be rung by Dad's friends and neighbours to let me know that he had been seen wandering about in his dressing gown and slippers or else sitting at the bus stop all day singing to himself. His friends at the bowls club had been brilliant with him and very understanding, but his behaviour had become more erratic and harder to manage. One day he just picked up one of his bowls and sort of froze on the spot as if he had forgotten what to do next despite all manner of advice and encouragement. Friends at the bowls club rang us and Julie and I came to collect him and take him home. He never returned bowling after that and although we tried caring for him at the vicarage for a while, it soon became apparent that his condition would require more long term and specialist care, especially when Julie became ill and my focus inevitably had to shift to her immediate needs. Julie had been brilliant with Dad but when her own illness started to consume all her energies and fighting spirit, it was as though a watershed had been crossed and I knew that I had to take decisive action.

The decision to sell Dad's house and admit him to a nursing home had been very difficult. During easier times Dad had often joked that I must promise to shoot him rather than admit him to a nursing home. This thought had played on my mind for some time, although I knew that the Father, who had joked with me, had now long departed, to be replaced by a more dependent person whose future I now had the power of attorney over. I owed Dad so much. Although not a believer, it was Dad who had conveyed a sense of political discipleship to me and who had encouraged me when he was considering my vocation to Christian ministry.

He had previously been a staunch trade unionist and shop steward who saw the world as wholly susceptible to improvement and redemption. He often spoke about the need to leave the world a better place than you found it, and that whatever I decided to do in life, to make sure that I invested goodness and a sense of the self worth in the people around me.

Although this sounds a bit trite, it nevertheless stuck. Dad was an engineer by trade and committed to providing solutions to practical problems. He saw the world in a similar way. Each person had innate value to society and was capable of self improvement and change.

It was Dad who had given me a love for music. Although he personally couldn't play a musical instrument and struggled to sing in tune, he still had a brilliant musical mind and appreciation of different musical genres. This enthusiasm was conveyed to me during my youth and even though Dad struggled to understand the point in the more self-indulgent guitar solos that I loved to emulate, he nevertheless endeavoured to talk about music with me and to understand my tastes and preferences.

I tapped a security code into the electronic entrance of Whiteview Nursing Home. The heavy Victorian wooden door yielded as my nostrils were confronted with the smell of urine and bleach. A cheerful, rather large lady was mopping down in the entrance hall whilst listening to her ipod.

"Hello Father," she greeted me.

Even though I seldom wore my dog collar when visiting Whiteview, many of the staff seemed to know who I was somehow and had even retained the habit of addressing me as they would a Roman Catholic priest. In the early days of his visiting, I used to try and correct people, insisting that they just call me 'Kevin' instead, but more recently I had decided that it was easier just to let this greeting rest.

"Jim's in the TV lounge. Your Dad's in a good mood today," she reassured me as I made my way into a large room off the entrance hall where a number of residents sat in an arch around a large flat screened television. No-one appeared to be watching television at all, but I knew that it would precipitate a small riot if I took the initiative to turn the set off.

In the corner of the room sat a steel bird cage in which a blue budgerigar sat talking to itself. Next to the bird cage was a well dressed lady stroking the hand of a frail elderly resident, slumped in a chair with her chin in her chest looking at the floor. Next to them were some empty orange vinyl cushioned chairs propped up on wooden blocks so that they leaned slightly forward in order to assist residents in getting out of their chair. Behind the chairs was a tall, grey haired man wearing a grey pullover, blue shirt and dark tie over a pair of blue track suit bottoms and slippers. He was absorbed staring out of the window and rocking backwards and forwards on the balls of his feet.

"Hello Dad."

The figure twitched as if to register some form of recognition.

"How are you keeping today? Shall we sit down?"

I guided Dad into one of the empty vinyl cushioned chairs.

Taking hold of one of his hands I squeezed tightly, as if to say, 'Here I am Dad'.

"Have you brought them?"

"Have I brought what Dad?"

"Have you brought me my tools? Have you brought me my tools? You know that I need them, but they won't let me have them in here you know. They won't let me have them."

"I know Dad. But its best that I don't bring them isn't it?"

This was painful. I had grown accustomed to the bizarre topics of conversation that shaped our meetings, but it still broke my heart.

"I've got to find my spanners to put the new sink into the kitchen. I promised your Mum. Mum will be expecting a new kitchen. A new kitchen."

"Mum's not here Dad. The kitchen is OK now. You fixed it. Remember?"

"Fixed it. Fixed it. Yes, must fix it. Jim'll fix it."

When I was growing up I loved the fact that Dad was always so practical. He instinctively knew how to sort out a whole series of manual problems. Not only could he help me with my maths homework, but he could also turn his hand to re-wiring the pick ups on my guitar when they became dislodged during a particularly frenetic guitar solo or changing the oil filter on my first car or fixing the central heating boiler in my student flat. He had applied his practical skills to many household tasks and DIY projects over the years. However, following retirement and then shortly afterwards, the sudden death of Audrey, my mother, Dad had become increasingly withdrawn.

At first Julie had thought that it was a depressive state brought on by grief and indeed, the doctor had shared a similar diagnosis, prescribing him anti-depressants. However, it soon became apparent that there were serious lapses in memory and losses of concentration. This was followed by a series of financial problems arising from Dad's inability to cope with money. He would repeatedly pay the same utility bill or else would take money out of the cash machine and then forget where he had hidden it. After we sold Dad's house, we discovered piles of cash stashed away in various envelopes in the airing cupboard and in the bathroom cabinet. These financial problems had alerted us to the seriousness of Dad's condition and the speed of his decline. The diagnosis of Alzheimer's was given soon after. This was followed by the general loss of the ability to take care of himself and the onset of his eccentric and erratic behaviour.

"Where's Julie? Where's Julie? Why isn't Julie here?"

"Julie's not coming Dad. She can't come." I had repeatedly told Dad about Julie's illness and death, but reality struggled to register with him, even though on a good day, he seemed to remember and to understand.

"I know Julie's not coming. Julies gone to be with Jesus hasn't she. Gone to be with Jesus."

"That's right Dad. She's gone to be with Jesus."

"Dad there's something I've got to tell you."

"Got to tell me. Got to tell me."

"Yes, I'm going away for a few weeks. I won't be seeing you for a little while... I WON'T BE SEEING YOU FOR A LITTLE WHILE." I found myself shouting at Dad. I knew that I didn't need to do this. There was nothing wrong with his hearing. It was a kind of instinctive response that I kept falling back upon whenever I felt exasperated and unsure how to communicate.

"I'm going on tour with my band Dad," I continued in a quieter voice. "You know, the band I play in with Ian... the rock band."

"Ah yes. Ah yes."

"Do you remember?"

"Yes, yes, I remember. There's a nice young man who came to visit me, he plays in a band as well... a bit like you."

"Yes, that's me Dad. That's Kevin. The one who leads the church. The one who plays guitar. Who used to be married to Julie."

"That's right. That's right."

"We've got an offer to provide the support act for another rock band. So we've got to go away and play a series of concerts around the country."

"Ah yes. Ah yes. What about Julie and church?"

"I'm taking some time out of church Dad, and I'm sure that Julie won't mind."

"To play in your band? The rock band? Yes... good. Will you bring me my tools when you get back?"

Every now and then, glimmers of recognition and coherence would lighten up our conversation, but generally we kept returning to the same topics and I found myself repeating the same information.

After a while, a young male nurse came round with a cup of tea and a plate of custard creams. It seemed to jog us out of the conversational loop into which we had descended, and shortly after sipping my tea, and helping Dad to drink his, I made an excuse and discharged myself from Dad's presence, sensing that a job was done, but feeling little satisfaction or peace over the situation.

I knew that the staff did a brilliant job in looking after him. But I still felt a twinge of guilt in leaving him behind at Whiteview. Just as I was about to leave, I heard the sound of someone playing a piano down the corridor. I remembered that there was a music therapist who visited the home and organised sing-along sessions and workshops with musical instruments. Hopefully Dad would want to get involved... and maybe if he enjoyed himself, he would remember and understand that his son liked to play music as well.

Later that day I found myself practising my bass guitar hard in Ian's basement. My fingers were starting to ache and become sore. I hoped to avoid blisters if I was to go on tour. It would be fun but also a gruelling schedule of events. The bass guitar's strings could feel like lengths of electrician's cable at times and I hoped that my fingers would be able to cope with all the extra work required.

It wasn't a Tuesday, but rather an extra practice day that Ian had suggested as preparation for our imminent musical touring debut.

Tonight we were joined not only by the delectable Siobhan, but also by Tim, the nineteen year old friend of Bryan's eldest child who occasionally helped out with the band when they needed a live drummer. Tim was enjoying a gap year before he went off to university and so he would be available to play for the entire tour, hence his attendance at practice that night. Tim was also hoping to earn a little much needed money from the tour. A topic that I had not thought to pursue with Ian.

"By the way Ian. Tim was asking about how much we are being paid for these gigs and I wasn't able to tell him."

"Ah right. Well I have to tell you that it won't be a great deal. In fact we will get about as much as we do for a wedding gig once you have taken out all our expenses."

"Expenses?"

"Yeh. We've got to hire some more decent mikes, although we can use the PA and lighting rig from *Zoo Two*. Then we've got to find some transport and source all our own digs and that."

"Oh great. We are meant to pay our own hotel bills and transport."

"There is a small allowance, but it won't go very far. I was hoping that we might be able to subsidise ourselves through the sale of our CD at the gigs and that?"

"What CD is that?" enquired Siobhan.

"It's the CD we recorded earlier this year, with Bryan. We've got a few boxes left over to sell at each gig."

"Gre..at.." said Siobhan in an ironic fashion.

"Look luv. I know that you've only just got involved with the band, but we've been together for some time, and if this tour works out, then who knows what will follow and how the band will develop. But at the moment, we just have to use what we have and hope for the best."

"Sounds like the story of my life!" said Siobhan with a long and knowing Irish sigh and a twinkle in her eye.

Chapter Nine

"It was going so well until the first song"

It was a cold and foggy morning in Sheffield as I opened the door to Ian and Siobhan.

"Are you ready to rock?" asked Ian, who for some reason, despite it being ten o'clock in the morning on a cold, foggy March day in Sheffield, was wearing sunglasses and a beanie hat. A sort of perverse fusion of Bono and The Edge.

"Uh... Yes, I guess so. What's with the shades then Ian?"

"Just trying to get into part. You know, if Bono can, then..."

"Yeh, but—Oh never mind."

"Are you all packed then? Did you remember the smoke machine?"

"Yes, I did manage to get hold of the smoke machine, but I warn you it's a still a bit temperamental. Bryan gave it the once over, but we'll have to keep an eye on it... Hi Siobhan"

Siobhan slinked into the vicarage entrance hall like a little girl let loose in a sweet shop. She was also wearing sunglasses, above a black, shiny bomber jacket over faded jeans, ripped at the knees and tucked into snake skin boots.

On the back of the jacket were embroided the words: 'On the road with... *Marillion*'. Somehow, I felt on edge and nervous around her. She was like an electrical storm, full of energising power, yet carrying the threat of menace and collateral damage. It was taking some getting used to having a girl in the band and I guess you could say that Ian's 'eye candy' strategy was starting to work on me.

"So... this is what a vicarage looks like on the inside" said Siobhan. "Kinda cute isn't it."

Her reaction to the inside of my vicarage puzzled me. What did she expect to see, St. Paul's Cathedral? A huge piped organ thundering away in the corner? Rows of hooded monks processing around ancient cloisters? Aled Jones singing in a vaulted gallery?

"It's just a house... only it's a bit too big for me these days."

"Oh yeh. Ian told me you lost your wife some years ago. I'm sorry to hear about that. It can't be easy?"

"No... it has its moments." I could never get used to how people described my circumstances. Talk of 'losing your wife' always sounded rather careless, as if I had misplaced her in the same way that you put down a diary on a cluttered desk and then can't locate it.

"Where's Tim then?"

"Oh, we're picking him up on the way." Ian announced. "Siobhan and I weren't quite sure where he lives, I gather that you know though."

"I've got a pretty good idea."

"After that we shouldn't have any more navigation problems, we've just picked up a 'sat nav' to get us to all the gigs." Ian awaited my reaction, expecting me to be impressed at the addition of the latest computerised gadgetry. It never came.

I was musing over the developing internal relationships within the band. I was gaining the distinct impression that Ian and Siobhan were forming some kind of alliance or partnership. Indeed, they might already be an item. This heightened my already elevated feeling of apprehension. What was the atmosphere going to be like in the band if Ian and Siobhan became an item?

"Hey Kev. Come and have a look at the tour bus."

Ian was determined to make a favourable impression and ushered me outside where a shiny new blue Volkswagen Transporter Shuttle van was sitting on the drive.

"Gosh. Where did you get this from Ian?"

"Oh it's hired. It cost a bit more than I envisaged. But just look at all the comfort we get inside." Ian slid back the side door and invited me to drool over the upholstery.

"Great. Its official then. We're now the 'A-Team'." At this point I descended into juvenile mode starting to hum the tune to the popular 1980s TV series in the hope that others would join in. They didn't. "I'll tell you what, I'll be B.A. Baracus and you can be Howling Mad Murdoch. If we ever get into any tight scrapes at least we will be able to build a tank from our guitars and PA equipment and come out fighting."

"I'm sorry?" said Ian.

Ian and Siobhan were still looking incredulously at me without a flicker of recognition. Clearly they didn't share my formative memories.

"Never mind. Have you thought this one through Ian? We're not going to fit all the gear into there, plus the four of us."

"Yes, we will. We're not taking too much with us. We don't need all our usual PA and lighting rigs. Just our own equipment and luggage."

"But even so..."

"Oh take a chill pill Kev. We've even got a roof box if we need the extra space."

"Seems as though you've thought of everything."

"Oh he has, he has," assured Siobhan.

After packing up my luggage and gear, we were soon on our way. We arrived at Tim's house to be greeted by his parents. Tim was a wiry nineteen year old, six foot tall with short spiky light brown hair and acne. He had a cheeky face and a personality to match. He was wearing typical adolescent uniform of a grey hoodie, jeans, somewhat at half mast and smart Nike trainers. It must have looked like we were taking on an apprentice or receiving the lad on work experience, but Tim could really play and he had become a valued member of the *Manic Tuesdays* ensemble. After helping him to load his drum kit and luggage, I noticed how there seemed to be a painful drawn out parting between Tim and his parents.

"Do make sure that Tim uses his inhaler, won't you?" asked Tim's mum.

I hadn't realised that Tim was asthmatic.

"… and keep an eye on him for us. It's his first time away from home."

I started to feel somewhat paternal and responsible towards Tim. I hadn't thought much about Tim's situation. He was just this quiet lad who used to drum for us occasionally when he was available on a Saturday night. I hadn't considered that this might be a significant rite of passage in his life. I knew that he was taking a gap year, but hadn't realised that this was probably Tim's first time away from home during that year.

"Don't worry. We'll bring him back safe and sound. Mrs Lawrence." Ian reassured Tim's mum. "After all what harm can come to him? We've got a vicar on our tour bus!"

And with that parting comment, we swept Tim off in the tour van to join two menopausal men living out their childhood fantasies along with a mysterious Irish sex kitten, the potential object of Ian's affections, en route to play a number of unfamiliar venues supporting a group of rockers that we had never met before. What harm could possibly come to him?

"So tell us what it was like playing with *Marillion*?" Tim started to interrogate Siobhan as Ian drove the tour van up the A1 en route to our first gig at the Gala Theatre, Durham.

"Well I only did a couple of shows with them. I was a replacement for one of their regular band members who was taken ill."

'I detect a theme emerging here,' I thought.

"… But it was great. Quite hard work though. All that touring around and having to learn my parts pretty quickly."

"Must have been amazing!" said Tim, slightly star struck and dewy eyed over the idea.

"This is going to be even more amazing," claimed Ian.

"Let's just remember that we are the warm up act to a tribute band. In another words, we are a warm up act to another warm up act." In the absence of Bryan, it felt that it was now my duty to inject a little realism into the world of the '*Manic Tuesdays*'. "It's not as though we are on tour with the *Rolling Stones* or anything."

"Chill out Kev. It's going to be fun. Let's just see what happens and all try to enjoy the experience," added Ian.

"I was going to ask Siobhan if she remembered, 'chalk hearts melting on a playground wall' and did she also remember 'dawn escapes from moon washed college halls'. Do you remember the cherry blossom in the market square?"

"I did I remember that 'I thought it was confetti in our hair' " Siobhan replied, suddenly bursting into song, to show that she really did know the lyrics to *Marillion's* best known hit single.

"Kay...leigh is it too late to say I'm sorry? And Kayleigh could we get it together... again?" The three over thirties suddenly joined together as one, belting out the words of 'Kayleigh' in a raw and rather untuneful manner, much to the consternation and embarrassment of Tim, who started to become aware of the age gap that separated himself from the other band members. Perhaps it might be fun after all?

Later on that afternoon we arrived at the *Gala Theatre*, Durham - a large modern theatre and cinema complex on the banks of the River Wear. Once inside we found our way to the 500 seater auditorium where *Zoo Two* were setting up and preparing for their sound check. This suddenly felt like foreign territory, both exciting and challenging. A proper theatre – a grown up venue with potentially a large audience, even though, they had only come to try and get close to a version of Bono, Edge, Adam and Larry that were usually out of reach in the large stadia and mega venues that the real U2 were playing. However, this was impressive, and a huge step up from the pubs, clubs, hotels and community halls that the *Manic Tuesdays* usually played.

"Bloody hell. Is this for us?" enquired Tim as he entered the auditorium.

"GREAT isn't it" extolled Ian. "I told you that this could be BIG"

"Yeh... very impressive," I added, trying to master the understatement.

"You must be Ian?" asked a short, stocky man who suddenly stood up from his position occupying one of the front row seats. "I'm Chaz. I'm the manager of *Zoo Two*... Good journey?"

"Yeh, not bad. We just got a little lost in the town centre when we stopped off to check into our accommodation."

"Sat nav?"

"Yes. How did you know?"

"'nough said. The curse of the Devil," Chaz mumbled.

I looked at Ian and we exchanged knowing looks. "Some of us prefer the tried and tested methods" I added, unable to resist the opportunity to reinforce my suspicions about Ian's latest gadget.

"Where are you all staying?" Chaz enquired.

"I've got an address of a B and B nearby," added Ian, grateful to change the subject.

"Forget about that. I'll try to get you booked in to where we are all hanging out from now on. It will make life much simpler. Have you met the band?"

At this point Chaz led us up onto the stage where a group of rather scruffy men wearing black tour tee shirts were huddled over various pieces of electronic equipment and musical instruments. A bald man with a cigarette in his mouth was strumming an electric guitar with one hand whilst listening to one side of a pair of headphones with the other.

"Chris. I'd like you to meet the support band. Chris, this is Ian of the *Manic Tuesdays*, I'm sorry I don't know the rest of your names?"

The group quickly introduced themselves along with an explanation as to what role we all played in the band.

Chris greeted us all in a gravelly voice through cigarette smoke.

"You'll need to get rid of that Chris," explained Chaz, referring to his cigarette. "No smoking in all these venues."

"Yeh sure, sure."

"Chris is the brains behind the outfit. Although you could be forgiven for not realising that" explained Chaz, who then went on to give a potted history of how he and Chris had worked together on a number of projects and bands over the years and how it was Chris who had the idea of putting *Zoo Two* together after seeing the popularity of other tribute bands.

"It's the only way that fans can get close to their heroes these days," explained Chaz, who obviously felt the need to justify why he had ventured into the tribute band market.

"I guess that you'll be wanting a sound check?" asked Chris suddenly finding the power of speech, once his cigarette had been extinguished.

"Yeh, when you're ready. I understand that we can use your PA and lighting blokes," said Ian.

"Yeh, that's cool" grunted Chris.

The rest of the day was spent setting up equipment, familiarizing ourselves with the backstage facilities and undergoing a rigorous sound check. I felt rather over-awed by the occasion and the prospect of hanging around with *Zoo Two* over the next six weeks. The other group members probably shared my nervousness because the sound check took an eternity to get right and even then our fairly well rehearsed back catalogue of songs seemed to sound rather strained and feeble in the cavernous 500 seater auditorium.

"It'll be all right on the night." Ian re-assured everyone. "Let's just do what we do best. Play a standard set, get the feel for how it is going and then try to improvise and develop some more."

It seemed like sensible advice from Ian, but I was really nervous. It all seemed like a big step up from our usual pubs and parties programme.

Before the concert we mingled backstage with members of *Zoo Two*. It was an interesting game to see them off stage and out of character and to try to guess which member of *U2* they were representing. This game was made all the harder by the fact that there were five members of *Zoo Two*, an additional member being required to provide the right sort of stage sound, we were assured. We were not disappointed when we met Steve, aka Bono. A former butcher from Bolton who was a dead ringer for Bono once in costume. I was disappointed that he didn't have an Irish accent and access to Barak Obama's mobile, but otherwise, he was really convincing, especially given his ability to remain in character off stage, an artistic commitment that required him to wear his sunglasses even in the darkest recesses backstage and constantly meant that he was falling over power cables and staging.

That evening the excitement and tension began to grow as the auditorium filled up and excited expectation entered the room.

"Have you thought about your stage outfit?" Ian probed.

"No. Not really. I just thought I'd wear what I always wear." I replied.

"Oh I see," said Ian dispassionately, with a look of disappointment.

"I thought that it would be good to make a special effort as we are in front of all these people."

"Yeh, but I'm just the bass player. I usually hide away at the back somewhere... I like hiding away at the back." I explained, but I soon realized that Ian's line of questioning was really by way of explanation for the fact that he was going to be wearing a purple silk shirt tonight, along with the sunglasses he had worn earlier.

"Whatever... just a thought." Ian added.

As the band's front man and vocalist, I expected Ian to make more of an effort than me and Tim, however, I hadn't anticipated what Siobhan would be wearing.

Siobhan entered our changing room wearing a tight fitting red satin three quarter length dress, plunging neckline and high heels. It was difficult to take your eyes off her and Ian exchanged a knowing look with me whilst the words 'eye candy' once again passed between us unspoken.

'Well at least that will take the audience's attention away from me' I thought.

Twenty minutes later the house lights dimmed and the *Manic Tuesdays* stepped onto the stage. Ian made the fatal mistake of coming out and shouting, "Hello Durham" to a disappointed audience who were obviously expecting to see the headline act and hadn't realized that there was a support act on first. It all went downhill from there. A few disappointed jeers and whistles rang out around the auditorium.

The band immediately launched into one of Ian's own composition numbers followed by two other numbers that the audience didn't recognize and hadn't paid good money to hear performed. Mistake number two and three. Cold indifference started to turn to thinly veiled irritation among the audience. Sensing that we were struggling. Ian prompted me to switch the smoke machine on for the next song. However, rather than presenting the band in a more atmospheric and mysterious light, we just disappeared altogether behind a curtain of fog whilst Siobhan's hair started to un-straighten and form a number of ringlets much to her irritation. After the fog finally dispersed Ian made another fatal error, namely trying to engage the audience with amusing banter by introducing the other band members. The 'lovely Siobhan' in the red dress was introduced as a former member of *Marillion* and attracted a number of wolf whistles and jeers. 'Kev the Rev' was introduced on the bass guitar, along with the explanation that his Bishop didn't know he was moonlighting. The ice age descended further. Once 'Tim who is taking a gap year' was introduced, you could start to hear audible sniggers and hoots of derision. At that point, mercifully Ian took the hint and thought better of adding further biographical information. "And I'm Ian Ross..." he said and then immediately launched into a cover version of *Before I fall to pieces* by *Razorlight*. The irony of choosing this track was probably lost on Ian in the heat of the moment, but at least it had the effect of calming down any potential rebellion and winning part of the audience over to the band's cause by exposing them to a more familiar tune.

During the number I became aware that Tim was struggling to keep time and looked round to find that he was drumming one handed whilst fumbling with his inhaler in the other hand. He must have been having some kind of mild attack brought on by the panic and pressure of the moment. Distracted by Tim's predicament, I kept losing my way in my bass line, as I failed to connect with Tim to form a strong rhythmic foundation for the song. The lyrics of the songs were starting to become increasingly descriptive as we were in real danger of falling to pieces musically. Just then I became aware of objects being thrown onto the stage. A half eaten *Big Mac* appeared at my feet for reasons I never did quite work out, whilst a curtain of lager spray from a precisely thrown beer can swept across Ian and I with Siobhan dodging what looked like a cloth thrown directly at her. She bravely played on before turning round to wiggle her bum before the audience and pick up what we thought was a cloth or a tee-shirt but proved to be a pair of discarded boxer shorts. Siobhan stoically held up the item of clothing, wiped her brow and cleavage with it and then threw them back into the audience much to their amusement and appreciation. As the number finished she grabbed Ian's microphone and said, "Thank you for your kind gift. The owner can see me afterwards if his Maam doesn't mind him being out too late!" Hoots of derision and cheers followed in equal proportions.

Clearly the joke had been lost on Siobhan. She hadn't realised that the audience literally thought that we were pants. Nevertheless, we ploughed on, forcing another couple of original songs upon an unsympathetic and increasingly hostile audience. Siobhan had clearly decided that the best form of defence was attack and chose to demonstrate her considerable prowess on the saxophone during these songs whilst Ian improvised vocally. Gradually the audience started to turn slightly more positive, perhaps impressed by our sheer balls and persistence. Finally, Ian fell back on our 'bankers' which were designed to get any audience on our side, launching into a cover version of 'I predict a riot' by the *Kaiser Chiefs*. Once again, the irony of such a choice was lost on us all in the adrenalin required for the stage performance. The audience reluctantly started to enjoy themselves, swept along by the driving guitar riffs and pounding rhythm which gave them permission to act as an unruly mob and jump up and down with gay abandon. Finally we finished our set. Ian shouted "Thank you and good night" and we all made a hasty exit before the lyrics of our final song became a self-fulfilling prophecy.

"I thought that went well," I announced to the recovering band members, falling into unappreciated irony.

"It was going so well until the first song." Ian remarked mournfully.

"Come on guys, first night, climbing a steep learning curve. It could have been a lot worse," remarked Siobhan. Clearly she had experienced such a reaction before.

"Could it?" said Ian, his head in his hands. This had not turned out as he had expected.

"Yes, we could have been playing for a hens night in Cowes on the Isle of Wight, and you could have greeted the audience in a similar way," I pointed out.

"Thanks for softening them up for us," said Chris, aka 'The Edge' as he and his band pushed past us backstage.

"Yeh, thanks fellahs," said Bono, now totally in character and speaking with a strong Irish accent.

"Break a leg," said Siobhan as if she actually meant it.

Tim was just staring at the ground in some sort of state of shock. He had the appearance of a rabbit caught in the headlights and all of sudden I once again felt strangely paternal towards him.

"Don't worry Tim. This is just our first gig. We've got a long way to go, but no-one is going to fire us. Let's just learn one or two lessons here. I thought that you were great. I could never have done any of that at your age."

Tim looked up at me as if to say 'thanks, but that doesn't help.'

The rest of the evening was spent in our dressing room, eating jelly beans that had been thoughtfully placed in large bowls for us by *Zoo Two*'s roadies and drinking bottled water.

"They're taking the piss," remarked Ian.

"What do you mean?"

"Jelly beans. Hard on the outside and soft in the middle. Someone is trying to tell us that we aren't up to it."

"Ian. You're becoming paranoid. I'm going to get changed," announced Siobhan, and with that left the room.

Tim was absorbed in a computer game in the corner of the room. A thoughtful inclusion in the itinerary of essential items needed for a teenager when going on tour with a support band of middle aged musicians.

"I just wanted them to love us," explained Ian.

"Come on Ian. This is our first night and don't forget that the audience haven't come to see us. They just want to indulge in the fantasy of pretending that *U2* are playing in their town... It's a bit like Church..." I couldn't stop myself from becoming all serious and theological. "You never really know why people have turned up and what their motives are. Sometimes, like at weddings, they don't even want to be in church at all. They just can't wait until you get off the stage of their big day and they can get on with the real business of having a good time and getting drunk at the reception afterwards."

"Bit cynical Kev?"

"Just realistic Ian. I've taken a lot of weddings and seen the look in people's eyes. You think that tonight was a hard gig to carry off?"

"I never thought of church as being a bit like a gig before."

"Yeh... there are some similarities."

"So how do you get through one of your 'weddings from hell' then? What do you do to retain your integrity and sanity?"

"Well it's a bit different. 'Cause God is involved and He can bring something good out of even the most unpromising situations."

"Wasn't God in the building tonight?"

"Yes definitely, but when I'm in church I'm more focussed upon pointing people towards Him."

"And how do you do that?"

"I guess I just try to show His love, be true to myself and put on the best show I can. Then the rest is up to Him."

"So it's all just a show to you then?"

"Hum... good point. Sometimes the way we do Church does feel like we are putting on a performance for people every week, but that's another story. Like I said, there are some similarities, but also some differences. I guess that I was getting a bit carried away by the theatrical metaphors.

"I don't see God as a fan of rock music anyhow. Do you?"

"Yeh... why not? Think of the universe as one huge rock concert, playing a brilliant tune all the time and what God wants is for us to recognise the tune and just join in with what He is doing."

"So God is some sort of divine rock musician then. Well I wish He'd been playing in our band tonight or controlling the audience's reaction."

"I think that we sometimes have all the wrong ideas about God. Like the fact that He is always on the outside of our lives. On the edge of the universe, controlling things, making good things happen and then when they don't we dismiss the idea that He is involved at all."

"This is getting heavy Kev."

"Just bear me out. Instead of thinking of God as some sort of divine puppeteer, think of him as part of the band. The Bible talks about how Jesus came and dwelt among people. The idea behind that was that he has pitched his tent among his people.[13] That's a bit like saying that God is part of the band."

"So if He is so much involved in our lives, then why can't I see Him, feel Him, hear from Him? Why does He keep letting me make a fool of myself in public?"

"Dunno. Can't give you a quick easy answer to those questions Ian, but I'm sure that God is closer than we think. It's like He is playing a song around us all the time. A song that is written on our hearts. Some people instinctively hear the tune, others don't. Some just get it and hear what's going on and join in with the tune."

"So why do so many Christians appear to live just like everyone else? Sharing the same values and ideas. In fact, there

13   John 1.14

are some people who call themselves Christians who seem to be even less Christian than me. If you see what I mean."

"Yeh, I know what you mean. I guess that some people recognise the song, but they still can't join in with the tune. It's a bit like us, when we are rusty and not in the zone together. We all know what the tune is and what the song is all about, it's just that we don't click, or harmonise or listen properly to each other."

"You mean they just play crap, like us tonight?"

"No. We weren't that bad. It's just that we didn't connect with our audience and perhaps we have to get used to that. Perhaps we never will, as long as we are piggy backing onto someone else's show."

"So how do we know when we are in tune with God then?"

"I think that it is when we start to resonate with His purposes and character. It is hard to think about God in an abstract sort of way, but we can get our minds around love and mercy and justice and compassion and generosity. So when those values and beliefs start to shape the people that we are, then we know we are resonating with God's tune."

"And what if you are the drummer?" A detached voice came from the back of the dressing room. I had forgotten that Tim was still there, absorbed, so we thought, in his computer console.

"I think that God's tune has also got a rhythm to it as well as melody. Think of it as a rhythm track if you like Tim."

Just then Siobhan re-emerged in dressed down appearance.

"So what's the crack? What's happening fellas?"

"Kevin was just explaining why we were pants tonight. Apparently it all God's fault." Ian explained.

There were times when Ian and I could have the most profound and meaningful discussions that would make me feel as though we were just crossing some kind of rubicon in terms of openness to spirituality in our relationship, only for Ian to snap himself out of his serious and thoughtful mood with a quick one liner.

In the background, we could hear *Zoo Two* getting stuck into a series of well known hits and Bono starting to interact with the audience.

"You hear that?" said Siobhan. "It's the gift of the Irish. We know how to have a good time."

"I think that you will find that the person in question is from Bolton. But I hear what you are saying." I reminded Siobhan.

"So let's either hit the town or hit the sack."

"Sounds good to me," replied Ian. "Let's hit the town."

"I'm afraid it's going to be the sack for me," I explained suddenly feeling rather old and as though I'd left such activities far behind in my youth. I also still felt that one of us should try to be a responsible adult, if only to provide a role model for Tim and to avoid leading him astray as his parents probably feared.

"Ok. You can go back to the B & B to say your prayers, but we're going to drown our sorrows in style. How about you Tim? Fancy a bit of fun?" Siobhan enquired.

"Yeh, why not," said Tim starting to pack away his computer and peripherals into his backpack. "Let's lock and load."

So much for me as a strong guiding influence.

Chapter Ten

I still haven't found what I'm looking for

When Love came to Durham Town

The Gala Theatre saw an apparent invasion of Irish megastars last night, when *Zoo Two* the premier U2 tribute band came to town, bringing their anthems of love and social justice. Bono, the Edge, Adam and Larry all appeared on stage to enthrall the near capacity audience with a medley of timeless classics such as *When love came to town*, *Pride*, *The Fly*, *Sunday Bloody Sunday*, *Bad*, and *I still haven't found what I'm looking for*.

Unfortunately for all *U2* fans in Durham City, the alter egos of the Bono and the Edge were played by Steve Darling, a meat processing supervisor from Bolton and Chris Cowley an electrician from Eccles. Suspension of belief was called for in order to imagine the real Giants of Rock and Stadium performers coming to play in the *Gala Theatre*, however, for one night only it was just possible to get caught up in the whole tribute band alternative reality in which Bono could be found vocally sparring with the appreciative audience and illuminating the Edge for his mesmeric guitar solo in *Bullet in a blue sky*.

Many similar old favourites were belted out by the popular five piece tribute band, who were once described by the real "Edge" as being so convincing that watching them play felt a little like an 'out of body experience' for him.

The Durham audience were treated to most of their well known hits although many of the songs from their recent *Vertigo* tour were omitted in favour of a classic '80s and '90s back catalogue.

The evening was briefly in danger of being overshadowed by a comical interlude from the *Manic Tuesdays* the warm-up act, who contrived to play a number of original numbers whilst their guitarist paraded around like Neil Diamond on *Red Bull* and their saxophonist tried to distract the audience with her appearance as Miss Scarlet yet only succeeded in provoking the audience to rain a variety of projectiles upon the hapless band. After a while the mist descended on their performance, literally, after an over zealous smoke machine totally obscured their closing number. This had the effect of transforming Miss Scarlet from an Andrea Corr look alike into a bedraggled Nigella Lawson. So there will be no more longing for the *Fog on the Tyne* from her, or was that the fog on the Wear instead?

[Durham Gazette *Out and About*]

The following morning I woke early. I hadn't enjoyed a good night's sleep in the small bed and breakfast in Durham town centre that Ian had booked us into. Having retired early to my attic room, I had been disturbed by images of the evening's performance. I tried to dismiss most of the unpleasant memories and was just nodding off when I was cruelly woken at 1.30am by Ian, Siobhan and Tim. They could be heard giggling outside of my room, whilst singing the words and presumably doing the actions to the *Music Man* song. Clearly the result of the effects of alcohol on three vulnerable carbon based life forms.

"I am the Music Man I come from down your way. And I can play. I play piano. Pi-a, pi-a, pi-an-o Pi-an-o, Pi-an-o Pi-a, pi-a, pi-an-o Pi-a, Pi-an-o. Come on Kev, join in" they shouted and banging on my door.

"Pi-a, pi-a, pi-an-o Pi-an-o, Pi-an-o Pi-a, pi-a, pi-an-o Pi-a, Pi-an-o." the chorus continued.

At which point I thought I might as well greet them as try to ignore them. So I opened the door to find the three of them sat on the landing carpet cross legged in boat race configuration, miming the actions to the song.

"Hi Kev... we've had a brilliant night," explained Siobhan. "This young lad has been teaching us some wonderful new songs, Ian and I think we can include them into a new routine, what do you think?"

"I think that I should have come along with you. To keep an eye on you all."

"BORING!" Ian and Siobhan chorused together.

"Come on Mister Bass man. Play your bass for us. What does a bass sound like? Baa, Baa, Ba, Ba, Baa, Ba, Ba, Baa." For someone so gentle on the eye Siobhan could sound rather harsh upon the ear at times.

"I don't feel very well," announced Tim.

"That's OK, because you don't look very well," added Ian, helping Tim to his feet. "Let's get you to bed... you naughty boy... and then let's get YOU to bed you even naughtier girl," said Ian helping Siobhan to her feet as well in a manner than appeared more than helpful.

After that I didn't want to know what followed. My promise to look after Tim seemed to have lasted only 24 hours before he had been led astray in old Durham town and I would rather not think about how Ian and Siobhan would finish their evening. I settled back into an uncomfortable and disturbed sleep. What was I doing here? Why was a forty something, widowed clergyman touring around the country with such a bunch of misfits and 'wannabees'? How was I going to keep up the pace of my nearly acquired rock and roll lifestyle? Can you acquire a rock and roll lifestyle?

The morning provided time for reflection and clearer thinking. I went down to breakfast but strangely the others didn't join me. Having decided to leave them to lie in a little longer before waking them, I was somewhat surprised to find that Siobhan and Ian hadn't spent the night together, but upon seeing the state of Ian, I decided that it would be better for all concerned if I volunteered to drive the van that morning and to take responsibility for getting the group to their next venue on time.

As the milky daylight gave way to a wintery half light we made our way across the Pennines to Cumbria. I loved this part of the world. Julie and I had enjoyed many happy times in the Lake District on various walking holidays. It also reminded me of the hills surrounding Sheffield and similar happy times spent enjoying the Peak District. Unfortunately there would be no time to explore the hills and lakes of the surrounding countryside this time. We would be performing in the *Brewery Arts Centre* in Kendal. A poignant name for a venue given the previous night's activities for three of the band's members. The *Arts Centre* was a smaller venue, about half the size of the previous theatre and represented a good opportunity to try and develop our act in a more intimate setting.

The journey across had been a rather quieter and more reflective affair than the previous day, but at least it presented a chance for Ian and I to talk through some changes to our running order and choice of songs.

"Why not slip in a quieter acoustic song into the middle of the set somewhere?" suggested Ian trying to shake off a splitting headache.

"Such as?"

"Well we could do... um... 'More than words' – the old 'Extreme' hit. We haven't done that for ages. And we could start with 'I predict a riot', rather than end with it."

"What about the guitar arrangements."

"You could play rhythm Kev. Just like in the old days. You could use my other acoustic."

"OK. But I'll need some practice."

Having agreed these changes we both felt more settled. I am more at home in the world of music, than in socializing and organizing. It would also make for a nice change to play an acoustic, although I would need some practice in order to improve my hammering on and off technique for 'More than words'. However, it would give my fingers a rest from the rigorous pressure required to pluck and slap the bass strings as six strings always felt easier and gentler to turn to afterwards.

Having arrived at our hotel in Kendal, a venue that Chaz had hastily arranged in order to allow us to share accommodation with *Zoo Two*, there was just enough time for me and Ian to find a room in which we could run through the new number for that night's set. An hour later and we were all sorted and both felt a lot more relaxed and confident than we had on the previous night. When we emerged from our rehearsal we bumped into Chris, aka, 'The Edge' from *Zoo Two*, who was clutching a packet of red stripe and looking sheepishly around the hotel for a door by which he could exit for a breath of un-fresh air.

"You can't have a decent smoke anywhere these days." Chris announced. "It's enough to turn a man to drink I tell you. How are you getting on Ian? You and... um... Keith?"

"It's Kevin actually. All right I think. We've made a few changes to our set from last night. So we'll see how it goes tonight."

"Oh right I see. I understand that you had one of those 'Spinal Tap' moments with the smoke machine last night."

"The smoke machine wasn't the only thing we made a cock up over last night. Never mind. We're just glad to be here. I'm sure it'll go better tonight," explained Ian.

Just then Siobhan arrived followed by Tim complete with earphones and iPod.

Siobhan was wearing a scowl of disapproval.

"Come on then. Let's get to the venue and get the sound check done." She announced in a matronly style.

"Who's rattled your cage then?" Ian got straight to the point with Siobhan in the tour bus on route to the *Brewery Arts Centre.*

"What do you mean?" she replied, pretending that everything was all right when it was self evident that everything was not all right with her.

"Your mood and tone. What's the problem? Have I upset you?"

"Look Ian. I appreciate that this band is your baby and that I have only just come along in the last few weeks and that you and Kev have known each other for a long time and that. But it might still have been good to have been included in your decisions about the running order tonight. You know, I might have had something to contribute?"

Perhaps Ian and Siobhan really were an item. This sounded like one of those frank discussions that only couples have together.

"Look Siobhan. I really appreciate all that you contribute to the band. But it's just that this song is an old standby for Kev and me. We've played it loads of times, although not recently. In view of the steep learning curve that you spoke about us all having to climb, we are just going to have to try out some different materials. And this song is best done unplugged... with just two guitars and vocals. It's nothing personal. Just practical."

With that Siobhan retreated into her shell.

Later that evening we left the stage following our half hour set a lot more satisfied with our performance and the whole experience of playing live in front of so many people. The smaller, more intimate *Art Centre* venue had suited us and the acoustic ballad in the middle of the set had gone down well with the audience and allowed us to connect in a way that had not been possible previously. We all emerged from the stage with a warm and satisfying glow of a job well done.

"Good set fellas. You really rocked tonight," said Chris as he and the band passed by en route to starting their set.

The sense of euphoria lasted sufficiently long enough for Ian to venture into the entrance of the *Arts Centre* and set up a stall selling back copies of the band's CD. I declined the offer to join him, and instead decided to listen to *Zoo Two* go through their routine from the wings of the theatre.

It was great to see other musicians hard at work and to know something about the process of making the magic happen on stage. They really could play and were fairly convincing alternatives to the Irish super group. Steve, aka Bono appeared to be born for the role and had an amazing ability to connect emotionally with the audience, frequently reaching out to them as he belted out the familiar lyrics as well as reaching out to them spiritually as he threw his head back and banged out the anthemic words of *U2*'s back catalogue of hits. The sense of connection was heightened by the shared narrative held in common between band and audience; Steve's vocals being sung back to him or else mouthed along to in what frequently resembled a giant karaoke exchange between band and audience.

As I looked on, the words of one song had particular resonance for me.

I have spoke with the eternal angels
I have held the hand of a devil
It was warm in the night
I was cold as a stone

But I still haven't found
What I'm looking for
But I still haven't found
What I'm looking for

I believe in the Kingdom Come

When all the colours will bleed into one
Bleed into one
Well, yes I'm still running

You broke the bonds
And you loosened the chains
Carried the cross
Of all my shame
All my shame
You know I believe it

But I still haven't found
What I'm looking for
But I still haven't found
What I'm looking for

The words seemed to resonate with my spiritual location. They seemed to tell the story of my life far better than many sermons or conventional devotional literature. The sense of longing that I had discussed with Bridget returned to me once more in the words of that song. I still believed, but hadn't really found what I was looking for. I also thought about how I had 'outed' myself in front of the Bishop, admitting to my doubts and fears whilst questioning my vocation. Perhaps I should be grateful that I wasn't supporting an *R.E.M* tribute band who would be singing about *Losing my religion*.

As I examined my sense of longing, I felt reassured that it wasn't so much a conventional crisis of faith, but rather a crisis of confidence and belonging. I still believed in God. I still believed the gospel of Jesus. I even believed that God had a plan and purpose for my life, a song that He was singing over me and inviting me to join in with. What I was struggling with was more my confidence in the system of which I was a part. I was still committed to travelling in a particular direction, the way of faith in Jesus and the values of His upside Kingdom. I had just lost confidence in the means of transport I had inherited to get me to my destination.

As the words of another Irish pop anthem were blasted out by *Zoo Two*, the lyrics *Sunday Bloody Sunday* seemed to reflect my disillusionment. "But I won't heed the battle call. It puts my back up, puts my back up against the wall." I started to realize how I had come to resent Church – it had become my office, my coal face or factory floor, rather than my home and first love. We had drifted apart like lovers who become over-familiar with each other and forget what had drawn them together in the first place. I wasn't sure whether I was drifting away from Church or the Church had moved away from me. All I knew was that I still believed in the ideal, but for me is just wasn't working out in practice.

I thought about our travels around the country and my introduction to Ian's 'sat nav' gadget. Having to rely on such technology seemed to represent my dislocation and lostness. I know that I should trust such devices to safely lead us to our future location, but using it seemed to offer as many problems as solutions. I preferred to scrutinize a map which could display our journey in some kind of context. Road maps reveal not just the best routes to follow now, but also they retain a connection with the old settlement patterns and roads based on the experiences of travellers throughout the centuries. The problem was that I felt as though I was heading on a personal journey where there were no road maps available to help me navigate my way and no way of connecting my journey with past experience. A shifting cultural landscape accompanied by a loss of confidence in conventional church seemed to depend upon untried new methods and processes I didn't understand. I felt completely out of my comfort zone, yet strangely energized.

The words of the song once again formed in my mind and encapsulated my philosophical position:

'You know I believe it,

But I still haven't found what I'm looking for.'

That night I made an important decision. Not a theological one, but a practical one. I decided to engage more wholeheartedly with those around me. To abandon myself to the consequences of the journey and the experience that I had entered into. I didn't want to give the impression of being a 'kill joy' who disapproved of the other band members' behaviour. So I would commit myself to the whole process of being on tour, doing strange things in strange places and see where it led me.

As a result when I was invited for a post-gig drink in the Hotel bar I accepted without hesitation. This time the band was joined by members of *Zoo Two*, who rejoiced in the anonymity they could be afforded in a public space once their wigs and stage clothes were removed.

As the evening wore on, voices started to become raised and less coherent – obvious signs of the effect of alcohol on tired musicians. I found myself positioned in a corner seat in the bar, squashed between Siobhan and Tim. Ian was distracted by his new found friends in *Zoo Two* and was happily swapping stories and information in the hope that he could garner some inside track into how to succeed in the music business.

In the meantime I found myself in the slightly awkward position of having to entertain and respond to Siobhan, whilst also being aware of my somewhat paternal responsibilities towards Tim. During the evening Siobhan was becoming increasingly relaxed and familiar with me. She was obviously flirting with me and playing with my emotional reactions as she became more and more tactile. This made me want to turn my focus even more towards Tim and direct my conversation and attention to his concerns and interests. It was increasingly apparent, what a blank canvas Tim was. I had forgotten what little life experience I had at a similar age and the naivety and straightforwardness that youth produces in people. Tim seemed to see the whole world in very simple terms and respond to that world with very simple solutions.

"So, if you can't get enough young people into your church, then why not take the church to where the young people are?" Tim asked.

"It's not always that easy," I explained.

"Why not? You could get some skate ramps and play stations and mixing desks, then you'd get loads of skaters and greebos coming along."

"Well, many churches already provide such things. And many Christians are working with young people in such ways. But it still doesn't solve all the problems. It might provide entertainment, but it doesn't necessarily build community."

"But don't communities form around entertainment?" Tim asked. "It must be worth trying. There's more than one way to be a gang. It isn't just about sitting in circle, strumming a guitar and drinking coffee."

At this point, I became aware that Siobhan was starting to drape herself more and more over me whilst she continued a conversation with a member of *Zoo Two*. I tried to catch Ian's attention, as if to say, *'Look what's happening. What should I do with her?'* Unfortunately, Ian was by now engrossed in conversation with Chris about how to set up an interactive website from where you can download audio files of the band's songs and didn't appear to notice Siobhan's flirtatious behaviour.

My attentions were being pulled in opposite directions. Torn between wanting to continue my conversation with Tim, whilst becoming aware of the need to deal with the physical presence of Siobhan. I had already been struggling with my hormones in relation to Siobhan. Standing behind her in the band whilst she wore that tight red satin dress was starting to become a distraction. The 'eye candy' that Ian had in mind for the band, was intended to provide a focus for the audience, but it was also having the same effect on me. How would I be able to concentrate on my bass playing if every night I was confronted by the rear view of Siobhan in 'that dress'? It reminded me of an incident that had occurred many years ago, when I was a young and inexperienced curate still learning to lead worship. A young, attractive female student had joined the music group a number of weeks previously and on one occasion when I was leading a Communion service my gaze became fixed on her rear view in a particularly tight pair of jeans. I then found myself struggling to announce the post communion prayer as the music group lined up in front of me. 'The closing prayer can be found on the rear of the communion card—no I mean the backside of the communion—no, the back of the communion card.' At which point the congregation started to giggle and look knowingly at me in that manner that is reserved for all curates who make bumbling errors when learning how to lead a very solemn moment in a service. It was one of those Freudian slips of the tongue that I just about got away with, but the cause of my distraction remained for many other weeks and I had to find a way of setting aside my natural reactions as a man, with my duties as a priest. I also remembered times when a Bride would appear in a rather low cut wedding dress and the visual problems this would cause when I would invite the wedding couple to kneel in front of me for a blessing. It wasn't quite in the same league as *The Thorn Birds*, but at least it helped me to understand the temptations that human sexuality throws up to all those who seek to minister in the church as well as teaching me how to avert my gaze in certain circumstances.

Suddenly Tim stood up and declared that he wanted an early night, especially after the experiences of previous night. This was fortunate as it provided me with an opportunity to move away from the amorous advances of Siobhan and to catch Ian's eye across the bar. Eventually the cosy gathering started to break up as various group members and roadies began to drift away to different parts of the hotel complex.

I found my way back to my room having deposited Siobhan with Ian in the hope that he would instinctively know how to deal with her.

I decided to try and relax properly before bed time. I put on the TV in my room and started to run a shower in the en-suite bathroom. I was still a little bit in awe of the experience of being on the road and also with staying in a hotel. Hotels were not places that I had a great deal of experience with. Often Julie and I would go away together in cheap self-catering accommodation or else would camp or stay with friends. Only rarely did we ever book ourselves into a hotel as a special treat. On such occasions we both found ourselves captivated in a child-like trance by all the offers of complimentary towels, sachets of tea and coffee, minibars, hairdryers and trouser presses as well as seduced by the availability of free shower gel and shower caps in the bathrooms. It still remained one of the great mysteries of life as to why the toilet paper was always folded into a neat point by the maid at such hotels, as if most guests were so stupid that they didn't realise which end they were supposed to use. Still under the spell of hotel complimentary gifts, I decided to avail myself of the en-suite facilities of the hotel room and make the most of the hospitality offered.

At that point there was a gentle knock on my door and when I opened it Siobhan was standing there in front of me.

"Oh hi there Kev. I heard you moving around and I was wondering whether you had any spare tea bags, they seem to have left me short in my room?"

"Sure, help yourself."

Siobhan slinked her way into the room and collected a few sachets before turning to leave.

At this point I retreated into an increasingly steam filled bathroom to lower the temperature of the shower. I heard the door of the room close shortly afterwards. I started to take a shower, frantically trying to get a decent lather out of the complimentary shower gel, having rejected the offer of the shower cap, although secretly wanting to try it out just for a laugh. It was at that point that I gradually became aware of movement in the adjacent room and then the presence of another person on the other side of the shower curtain. Briefly the shower scene in *Psycho* entered my mind as my heart started pounding vigorously whilst I imagined a crazed knife wielding assassin about to jump out on me. In desperation I reached for something to defend myself, but all I could locate was a *Body Shop* banana and guava shampoo and conditioner set. Perhaps I could squirt this in the face of any unwelcome intruder? Suddenly the shower curtain was abruptly pulled back to reveal Siobhan naked as the day she was born, who then immediately stepped into the shower to join me.

"I hate to see a good shower wasted on just one person," she announced as her arms reached out to embrace and enfold my startled body.

Suddenly huge quantities of adrenaline and testosterone surged through my bloodstream and I found myself responding accordingly, swept up in the spontaneity of the moment and unable to resist the offer of intimacy. We continued to embrace and caress, discovering each other's bodies and then began kissing under the pressure of the cascading water. This was madness but I felt alive in a new way as Siobhan started to make me feel like a man and I responded in kind. My passion continued to rise, internally and externally, emotionally and physically.

An overwhelming desire to go along with the moment overtook me as years of sexual restraint and longing came to the surface. Nothing like this had ever happened to me before. I had all sorts of moral questions about the situation, but I just couldn't help myself from being swept up in the glorious insanity and unpredictability of the situation. *'Why not go for it? Why not go all the way?'* I kept thinking. Perhaps this was all part of my new personal journey? A greater sexual freedom, marking a break from my past? The re-awaking of my sexual drive as a means of re-discovering my spiritual energies? My whole life had been lived within limits defined by my upbringing and belief system. Now that those beliefs and values were being challenged it was as if my passions and instincts were exploding and heading off in new directions under the spell of this gorgeous, yet predatory woman. This was a perfect opportunity. An opportunity to move on from Julie and from my former life and lifestyle, and all the responsibilities they brought. It felt good to be close and vulnerable with a woman again, although strange to be so intimate with someone I hardly knew. Great torrents of raw passion started to flow through my body, stimulated by the cascading waters. It felt like the perfect opportunity had presented itself. What was I waiting for? Why hold back? It was the equivalent of an open goal at Wembley on Cup Final day with only minutes left on the clock. All that was needed was for me to symbolically put the ball into the back of an empty net and seal the deal.

Somewhere along the corridor an unknown hotel guest decided to flush a toilet and the resulting effect on the hotel's ancient plumbing sent a sudden burst of cold water through the shower head in the bathroom, disturbing our sensual moment and bringing me back to earth with a bump.

"Hang on... NO!!" I found myself saying. "I'm sorry Siobhan, but No. This is not the way I wanted it."

"Come on Kev. You can't say that you don't want this."

"I do, I do. I think that you are gorgeous. But I just don't want it like this. This isn't right. This isn't how it should be. I thought that you and Ian were an item anyhow. You're just using me to get at him aren't you?"

"No, it's not like that" said Siobhan as she tried to grab me and pull me back into her embrace.

"Well what is it like Siobhan?"

"It's just sex Kevin. No big deal. Just sex. Just adults having fun."

"I'm sorry, but you've got me all wrong Siobhan." I tried to reach out for a towel whilst turning off the shower spray.

"I thought I had you about right a moment ago" Siobhan replied, enjoying the double meaning. Then realising that I was serious, she continued, "God! You holy Joes can be so sanctimonious at times. You do my head in," she complained as she stepped out of the shower while grabbing my towel.

"What do you mean?"

"You think being good is all about saying 'No' to everything. That God doesn't want you to have a good time...

I can show you a good time." Siobhan reached around me with her towel, pulling me towards her once again and wrapping us both up in a towelling embrace.

"I'm sure that you can Siobhan. And I really want to have a good time. And part of me desperately wants... you... right here... right now." I said holding Siobhan tightly.

"So what more can I do? What's holding you back?"

"It's just that this isn't how I wanted it." I took hold of the towel and firmly pulled it away from both of us, making a hasty naked exit into the other room, before I could change my mind.

Once in the bedroom I sat down on the bed and suddenly found myself crying uncontrollably. Huge, gut wrenching cries started to pour out of me from a place so deep within, that I hadn't thought myself capable of crying like that before. It was as if an obstruction had been removed or a dam had been breached, releasing so much emotional energy and turmoil that I was no longer in control. Deep whooping rhythmic squawks eventually turned into more polite and controlled yelps as years of pain and frustrating were expressed in a most inelegant and primal manner before fading into muted sobs and whimpers.

As I sat there, I became aware of the embrace of Siobhan. But this was no longer the embrace of a lover or of someone who just wanted the satisfaction of a sexual conquest. This was an arm of comfort and understanding, reminiscent of maternal affection. I continued sobbing all over Siobhan, my tears mixing with her damp skin and the aroma of the complimentary shower gel. Eventually my self control and emotional equilibrium returned and we both fell backwards onto the bed, still naked and damp from the shower, but in another emotional location.

We must have lain there for several minutes. Both without saying a word. Staring at the ceiling. Neither knowing nor understanding the emotional structure of our situation, nor daring to bring the situation to a premature conclusion. Strangely I found the moment both wonderfully releasing and profoundly healing. A spiritual epiphany, like being back in the garden, when Adam and Eve were naked, yet felt no shame.[14] Eventually Siobhan broke the silence.

"You were right. I guess I was just trying to get back at Ian." She explained as she leaned forward to pick up items of her clothing that were scattered over the floor. "It wasn't really about you. It was about what you represent."

"Same for me. I guess."

"I've always been able to get what I want with fellas you know. I am aware of how I appear to them. And over the years you could say that I have used my womanly wiles to not just have a good time, but also to get my own way. When I saw how Ian excluded me from the band's decisions, I thought. Sod you. I'll show you. I'll show you who has the real power around here..." She paused for further reflection. "Shit, did I say that or just think it. I never talk like this. I'm never this open. Not even back home, when I go to confession."

"Perhaps it's because I'm a priest."

"Perhaps it is. Perhaps that's what I wanted as well. After all, I've never had a priest before... especially in a shower."

"There's a huge difference between a confessional and a shower cubicle."

"Yeh..."

A huge sigh passed between us.

"What do you really want Siobhan? Because I don't really think that you truly want me."

"Don't put yourself down Kev. You are kinda cute... and there's more to you than most fellas I meet... a kinda mystery and depth to you as well as a sadness. That's quite appealing. I guess I also feel kinda sorry for you, like you have this inner emptiness I want to reach into and say, 'Come on Kev, loosen up a bit and have a good time.'"

14   Genesis 2.25

"Is that what you really want then? Is sex just a route to a good time?"

"What's wrong with sex? Sex never hurt anyone. It's just physical. Something we do with our bodies. It's how adults play. It's no big deal."

"I guess that it's a big deal to me. It's spiritual as well as physical and I thought that after Julie died, that the next person I would share that with would be someone just as special as Julie was."

"Oh get real Kevin. No one thinks like that any more. This is the twenty-first century not the nineteenth."

"Well that's the way that I think."

"Is that why those blind dates that Ian arranged never worked out?"

"Oh he told you about that did he?"

"He kinda filled me in on one or two details about you."

"Yeh... probably... I dunno... I guess that I'm just not ready. It's as if there's no-one who's able to replace Julie. She was the love of my life. Even though I know that I need to move on, I just can't help but measure everyone up against her. As the years go by and the more I miss her, the more I remember her wrongly, not as she really was, faults and all, but as the ideal that she represented. The notion of the perfect life partner, the perfect friend, the perfect lover. No-one can replace that ideal, because it is a perfect ideal and perfection can only be properly replaced by similar perfection... and that is unfair and unrealistic to expect of anyone else. So I carry on, living by myself and getting more and more lonely. I guess."

"Is that what the tears were all about?"

"Possibly. I just don't know, I'm going through a lot of emotional and spiritual turmoil at the moment."

Siobhan and I then continued to talk as we got dressed and returned to being friends and colleagues, not lovers.

We carried on talking into the early hours. Siobhan explaining about her childhood in Ireland, her abusive father and how he used to be violent towards her and her brothers and sisters. How he used his power over them in a way that made them all feel worthless. As a result when she had grown up she had resolved to use the power she had at her disposal to gain control over other people, particularly men. In fact, she seemed to have problems with men and father figures generally. She spoke about the fear she had of an over-bearing God derived from her Catholic upbringing and how she had identified the character of her heavenly Father with that of her earthly father, ultimately rejecting both of them. For her, God was a cruel and vengeful teacher, who would always be disapproving of her conduct whilst using His power over her to teach her tough lessons.

As I listened to Siobhan's life story, a very different person emerged to the person Ian had introduced to into our band. This person was a lot more likeable and vulnerable. Multi-layered and three dimensional, rather than the caricature of 'eye candy' that Ian had introduced into the band, whilst still remaining mysterious and slightly unsettling. I was told about an abortion she had endured shortly after moving to Music College in Dublin and how she had kept that from her strongly religious family and friends. I also learnt a little more about her musical career and how not everything was quite as it had initially appeared, including her involvement with *Marillion*. Apparently she had been part of their tour party, but not as a backing musician, but rather as a roadie and former partner of one of the band members. She had ended up playing with the band, but only during rehearsals or improvised jamming sessions. She never performed with them on stage, but had told Ian the story because she wanted to impress him. Her real musical career had been a lot less rock and roll, and a lot more conventional, involving giving saxophone lessons to school children, performing in a jazz and blues band and the occasional amateur orchestra along with a considerable time spent playing in a backing band on a number of cruise ships.

"Gosh Siobhan. Tonight has been crazy and rather unreal, even by present standards. I've certainly discovered a lot about you and you've discovered a lot about me…" I started to blush.

"Especially in the shower." Siobhan added with a return of that Irish twinkle in her eyes I had seen earlier.

"Yes, well that's the problem. Where do we go from here? Usually people either become lovers or else they part and never see each other again. What about us? We can't ignore each other. We've still got the rest of the tour to complete."

"I don't know," admitted Siobhan. "This has never quite happened to me like this either. I guess that we can continue as friends can't we? If anything else happens, then it happens. But I don't see why we can't just stay as we were before tonight's events."

"That would suit me. But can you try and back off a little."

"What do you mean?"

"Well can you stop some of this slinking around and coming on to everyone act?"

"Fuck off. That's just the way that I am. It's just the crack that I put out there. You'll have to get used to it."

"And the red satin dress?"

"That cost me a bloody fortune. And I like it. It gives me a chance to show off… and I like showing off."

It was at that point that I realized that despite all Siobhan's candour and the softer side to her personality that had been on display that night, there was still a huge void of understanding and personality between us. She was certainly very different to Julie and any attraction would always be purely physical, so it was up to me to deal with that, learn to live with it and to move on.

Chapter Eleven

A drink with
Kronenberg

The following day I was aware of a certain awkwardness between Siobhan and myself. We both avoided making eye contact with each other during breakfast and confined our conversation to the essentials required by politeness and the conventions of sharing a dining table. Our awkwardness in each other's company was the only tangible sign of the intimacy the night before. Those events felt strange and unreal as if they had happened to someone else whilst I looked on as a casual observer. Had I really been so un-clothed physically and emotionally with this woman? I knew that all those extraordinary events had taken place but it still felt like another world a million miles away from the frantic travel details and musical demands of touring with the band, and the casual friendships that usually orbit around such occasions.

Mercifully breakfast had been a brief and business like affair in which all the band members hurriedly grabbed various items of food and knocked back tea and coffee before collecting cases, musical instruments and equipment. There was not even time to worry about marmalade between the fingers as there was an urgent need to hit the road early if we were to make our next venue on time.

When Ian first described the idea of the tour I hadn't paid a great deal of attention to where we would be heading each day. The truth had only slowly started to dawn on me and on other members of the band that our itinerary required us to crisscross the country in an apparently random and haphazard fashion, clocking huge distances between gigs. The practical and physical demands of travelling such distances hadn't really been considered. The large number of gigs in the programme also meant that there would be very little in the way of down time between different events for the band in which to gather our thoughts and catch our collective breath. The venue today was in Cardiff. A distance of some 260 miles from Kendal and this therefore required a very prompt start if we were going to arrive with sufficient time to practice and set up before the gig. There was also something about the name of the venue that concerned me.

"Ian? This gig we are playing in Cardiff?"

"Yeh, I know that it is a lot of travelling, but we will just have to start getting used to it."

"No, it wasn't just the travel I was thinking about. Have you seen the name of the venue we are playing?"

"Yeh, ur no, sort of…" replied Ian, trying to cover up the fact that he didn't have a clue what the name of the venue was.

"Sin City Nightclub! Any alarm bells ring for you?"

"Not really… it's just a name… do you have problems with it?"

"Well possibly… possibly not. Does the name suggest anything to you?"

"No. It's just a name. Like The *Marquee* or *Convent Garden* or the *O₂ Arena*. You shouldn't take it all so literally. The *Marquee* isn't really a marquee and *Convent Garden* isn't really a convent. *Hammersmith Palace* isn't a real palace and the O₂ Arena isn't really filled with pure oxygen or mobile phones. They're just names!"

"Yes, but don't you think that it might at least suggest something about the sort of audience we can expect. Don't you at least think that we should be prepared in some way?"

"Look Kev," responded Ian, now becoming a little exasperated. "I'm sure it's just a name. But I'll have a word with Chaz and see if he knows any background to the venue. Will that satisfy you?"

"Yeh, yeh. Don't worry. Just asking. Just curious."

I had a bad feeling about this venue. I suspected that I was being unreasonable by reacting to the name, but it felt like we were entering enemy territory in some sort of way, or at least an unfamiliar culture. What would people back at St Ebbs think if they knew that I was appearing for one night only at a place called *Sin City*? That might be a hard one to square with my church council and with the Bishop, albeit a broadminded one. Still, I re-assured myself, it was just a name. It didn't necessarily mean that it was any more sinful than any other place, did it? Then I remembered that even if it was, then so what? Jesus had been criticized for keeping strange company and for associating with those considered to be 'sinners' during his lifetime.[15] If Jesus was prepared to associate with dodgy characters, then why shouldn't I be prepared to at least give the venue the benefit of my probably groundless scepticism?

Later than morning, as we travelled down the motorway, Ian leaned back in his seat and spoke over his shoulder to reassure me.

"Don't worry Kev. You're not being asked to play in a den of iniquity. I've spoken with Chaz and he says that it's just a name for a sort of small and intimate nightclub, frequented by mostly students and young people, so at least Tim should feel at home."

"Oh I see. Will they be a bit too young for us? Might they expect something a bit more edgy or hip and happening?"

"Look Kev. As you keep reminding me. It's not us they're coming to see anyhow. It's the alter-egos of Bono, Edge, Adam and Larry. So if that's what they've come to see, then they won't mind seeing blokes of our age on stage as well. After all, the real

15   Matthew 9.10-13; Matthew 11.18-19; Mark 2.15-17;
      Luke 5.29-32; Luke 15.1-2

U2 are actually older than we are… and a lot less good looking. Right Siobhan?"

"Um, what… what was that?" replied Siobhan, waking from a light snooze she had fallen into sitting next to Ian.

"I said that we are a lot younger and better looking than the real *U2*. Right?"

"Sure we are… but a lot less Irish as well," said Siobhan whilst stretching and yawning.

After being re-assured by Ian, I started to relax and to enjoy the journey a little more. We stopped at a service station just south of Worcester after which Ian and I swapped over as drivers. Siobhan decided to join Ian in the back seats of the bus to continue her sleep, which indicated that she still wasn't entirely at ease in my close company, so Tim and I found ourselves driving and navigating instead. Tim appeared more at home with the 'sat nav' than myself and Ian. He even managed to programme in an alternative route which avoided the need to pay the toll fee for entering Wales by way of the Severn Bridge.

"Have you ever seen the Severn Bore?" asked Tim as we drove around the outskirts of Gloucester.

"No, I haven't. Isn't that some kind of wild pig that roams about these parts?"

"No, you fool. It's a huge tidal surge. A kinda wave that comes up the River Severn at particular times of the year."

"Oh yeh." I replied, trying to recover my poise and nonchalantly suggest that I knew that all the time. "I think I've seen the pictures."

"Must be amazing sight? All that water just surging through the countryside. I understand that they can predict to the exact minute when it will come along.

"Apparently people swim out in wet suits, ready to surf it." Ian explained.

"Wow. Cool. That would be amazing. I'd love to do that. Wouldn't you?"

"I'm not much of a surfer Tim." I said stating the obvious and adding another sport to the sum of my ignorance. "Just the odd bit of body boarding whilst on holiday."

"I love surfing. Spent most of last summer down at Newquay. Hitting the waves. Really cool place."

"Unfortunately, I don't think that we are playing Newquay, or else you could give me a few lessons."

"Must be cool though. Just going with the flow for so long. Catching the wave and just hanging on in there. I'd love to give it a go."

"I never knew that you were such a keen surfer." Ian added.

"Oh yeh. I'd love to be able to just surf all the time, but I suppose I've got to go out and get an education and get a job some time."

"Can't keep surfing the waves for ever I suppose." I said, trying to introduce a note of pseudo parental realism.

"No. I guess not... It'd be good if you could though."

Thanks to Tim's creative use of the sat nav, we managed to arrive in good time in Cardiff. Having checked in to a Travelodge in the middle of town we then proceeded to find the venue which was near to the university. Once inside we were confronted by a very dark and compact interior which would offer the gig a certain intimacy and character. It also meant that if things were to go wrong there would be no space to hide.

"Lovely to see you lads. Lovely. Welcome. Welcome to Carr...diff."

A small squat man appeared from behind a very large and expansive bar wearing a pair of round metal framed glasses on his balding round head. He had a black tee shirt and black drainpipe jeans with a metal belt which appeared to be comprised of a number of imitation bullets. He resembled a cross between Captain Mainwaring from *Dad's Army* and a welsh Ozzy Osborne.

"Thank you. It's cool to be here." Ian announced.

"And we're not all lads," added Siobhan, "there's some of the fairer sex as well."

"Lovely... I must say though, I can't quite work out which one is Bono and who's The Edge man?"

"That's because we're not *Zoo Two*, we're their support act" Ian explained.

"Oh, I see. I see. Well I expect I'll meet the others shortly. Have you ever been to Carr...diff before?"

Once again, it felt like one of those 'Have you ever been to a Harvester before' moments.

"I have" I replied, "But I'm not sure about the others."

"Oh, you'll have a grand time here I'm sure. They're a lovely crowd. They can get a bit boisterous at times, mind. But they've got heart of gold you know. Even the young ones who come in."

"Yeh we were wondering what sort of crowd you get in?" asked Siobhan.

"A good mixture usually. A lot of students and young people, but we get some locals as well. Tonight's sold out, so there should be a good crowd here. Although we do get some heavy metal fans and some Goths coming in. I'm not sure whether they'll be here tonight. But they're really harmless. Lovely people even though they can look a little strange at first."

I felt as though some of my earlier fears were being confirmed. I imagined a rough set of hairy bikers and Hells Angels throwing beer bottles and hurling abuse. A bit like the scene in *The Blues Brothers* film when the band find themselves in a rough country and western bar that didn't appreciate their choice of music and the whole gig takes place behind a wire cage against which beer bottles are constantly thrown.

"I'm sure it will be fine." Ian's confident reassurance snapped me out of my morbid mental recreation of the *Blues Brother*s in a Cardiff nightclub.

"I think I'll wear something a little less showbiz tonight," muttered Siobhan.

'Great', I thought. *'She won't stop wearing that red dress because of what it stirs up in me, but she will if she thinks that she might get beer spilt over it.'* I started to feel a degree of hurt and jealousy, and then realised just how stupid I was and how little I understood about the female mind. *'Remember Tim's outlook on life.'* I told myself. Tim's previous words took on added poignancy. *'Just go with the flow'*.

At this point Chaz, Chris, Steve and the rest of the *Zoo Two* crew arrived and the nightclub manager's attention was shifted towards them and their technical requirements. Similar introductions followed and very shortly equipment started to arrive before being puzzled over and eventually forced into the limited space on the tiny performance area.

Later on that evening the club filled up with a noisy and lively clientele. The small stage and the compact nature of the venue meant that there were great difficulties with squeezing both bands equipment onto stage whilst it quickly became apparent that if you didn't immediately connect with the audience, then it would be difficult to deflect any negative reaction thereafter. As a result we all felt the need to meet together in one of the smaller venue bars before the concert for a quick briefing and group discussion as to how we were going to handle the occasion. It was decided to cut out a few songs and to rock it up a little, leaving out the ballad that had gone down so well previously, but which had rankled Siobhan to such an extend.

"Ok. It's time for some blue sky thinking. Has anyone got any creative ideas that could rock it up a bit for us?" asked Ian.

"Let's get the old smoke machine out again?" suggested Tim.

"Let's not get the old smoke machine out again, thank you very much," added Siobhan abruptly. "In fact, I was thinking that a bit of good old rock and roll excess might be in order. How about an extended DRUM SOLO?" said Siobhan glaring in the direction of Tim.

"Ah, there might be a few problems with that. I could give it a go, but I'd need access to my inhaler if it had to go on for too long" explained Tim, not realizing that Siobhan was trying to get back at him.

"Great! How rock and roll is that? An asthmatic drummer. Keith Moon must be spinning in his grave," Ian replied rather forlornly.

"Keith who?" asked Tim.

Ian and I exchanged glances resigned to give up on a whole generation.

"Ok hear me through. Why not fall back on one of our old favourites?" suggested Ian, rediscovering his 'can do' attitude. "Let's do 'A design for life'. After all, we're in Wales. The heartland of the *Manic Street Preachers*. It's a real rock number.

You, me and Tim have played it before. Our band is even partly named in honour of the *Manics*. It'll go down a storm."

"Hang on a sec Ian." Once again it fell to me to inject a note of caution and to take Ian gently by the hand for a walk down reality street. "First of all, we haven't played that song for about a year. Secondly, we don't have any rehearsal time left. Thirdly, Siobhan doesn't know it and it would be unfair on her to have to wing it. And fourthly, can you remember the words for it?"

"Yeh, I'm a bit rusty, but I'm sure I could brush up on them."

"Fair enough, let's do 'A design for life' in front of a mob of drunken, bottle-throwing rockers and sing to them about 'I wish I had a bottle. Right here in my dirty face to wear the scars. To show from where I came.' Ecetera, ecetera. 'We dont talk about love we only want to get drunk…' Need I say any more?"

"Yeh, but no-one really listens to lyrics… except you. What do you suggest instead?"

"I suggest we keep our nerve, stick to what we do best…Oh and pray quite hard."

"OK. I'll keep my nerve, Siobhan can stick to what she does best and you can pray hard."

"What about me?" asked Tim.

"Just keep us in time," added Ian. "God knows, we always need that."

Two hours later, the band were relaxing over a drink having come off stage and having completed a more rocky version of their usual set.

"I think we got away with it then fellas." Siobhan's assessment seemed to sum up the mood of the group.

"Yeh, I wasn't sure there for a moment. The audience was really in my face tonight," said Ian.

"Sorry!" I shouted over the noise of *Zoo Two* launching into *Where the streets have no name*.

" I SAID: THE AUDIENCE WERE REALLY IN MY FACE" shouted Ian across the crowded bar.

"I didn't think the audience were a disgrace. They were quite kind to us."

Ian looked bemused. We then attempted to continue our conversation, reflecting upon what had worked and what had struggled to provoke a positive reaction from the audience, but it was obvious that *Zoo Two* were in good form and going down well and the noise levels meant that any conversations would have to wait until after they had played their set.

Towards the end of *Zoo Two*'s set a particularly large and scary looking bloke approached the bar. He was probably in his twenties, although he looked older. He was powerfully built and completely bald apart from a small goatee beard and a thin platted pig tail which extended half way down his back. He also had the most number of body piercings in one individual that I had ever seen. He had piercings through his lip, eyebrow, nose and ears as well as a large number of silver rings on both of his heavily tattooed hands. He was wearing a black leather waistcoat over an *Iron Maiden* tee shirt and black jeans. He was with a tall Goth looking girl of about the same age who was dressed in a black ripped tee shirt and dark three quarters length skirt and doc martin boots. She was wearing a great variety of silver jewellery, including a large pendant around her neck. She had purple hair and black lipstick and considerable amounts of pale face make up. They were joined by a really skinny looking young man, with long, thick black hair that cascaded over a long black, crushed velvet jacket that resembled something that Adam Ant might have worn in the height of fashion excesses in the 1980s. He had long and spindly legs whose appearance was exaggerated by black, tight fitting drainpipe jeans and full length doc martin boots. He looked like a cross between Dr Who, Edward Tudor-Pole of Tenpole Tudor and Richard O'Brien from the *Crystal Maze*.

"Brilliant... fucking brilliant tonight." He announced in a loud voice audible enough to cut through the closing finale of *Zoo Two*'s set. Then noticing the rest of us within earshot he added the rider. "Not you mate. You were crap. But that *U2* lot were fucking brilliant."

It was not a terribly auspicious start to any meaningful conversation.

"Please excuse my mate," explained the body pierced man, holding up his hand in an act of consolation towards Ian before slapping him on the back. "He can't help it. He's such a rude bastard at times. He doesn't mean it."

"Yes I fucking do!" added Mr Tenpole Tudor.

"Let me get you all a drink." The body pierced man then proceeded to grab the attention of the bar man by his sheer physical presence and familiarity and arrange for a round of drinks to be made available for the much maligned support band.

Shortly afterwards various drinks arrived including an assortment of soft drinks and tonic waters.

"I thought that you did OK. I liked the *Kaiser Chief's* song," added the Goth lady.

At this point, the body pierced man, who clearly held some kind of authority or primacy among the three eccentrically dressed friends, took it upon himself to introduce themselves to the assembled members of the *Manic Tuesdays* who were by now able to converse more easily following the end *Zoo Two*'s final encore.

"This is Deb, my partner," referring to the Goth lady. "This is Razor," which was a wholly inappropriate name as he clearly hadn't been acquainted with such a device for some time. "Or you can call him Raze, just as long you don't call him Carl, he hates that... and I'm Kronenberg!"

I looked across to Ian incredulously, to check that I had heard correctly. "Yeh, I know it's a weird name. I changed it by deed poll. I thought that it would be really cool to be named after a lager at the time, but since I've been on the wagon, I grew to like the name for other reasons and it kinda stuck with all my mates. Kronenberg Casstle. Sounds impressive hey? Like Mordor or Helm's Deep."

"He really is called Kronenberg," explained Deb. "We feel that it like sounded like really primeval. Like a Celtic warrior. Sort of goes with our life journey. Even though we're vegetarians and pacifists these days."

"I see..." I said, falling back into my nodding, active listening mode that I usually reserved for parish ministry when someone had just told me something outrageous or appalling, and rather than appearing shocked, I would give the impression that I had heard it all before. Only after so many years I had finally arrived at the stage where I had indeed heard it all before and consequently didn't have to pretend quite so hard.

Meanwhile, Tim turned away and whispered under his breath. "Pity she wasn't called 'Stella', then we'd have the complete set!"

"It can't be easy having to warm up the crowd for this lot," Kronenberg added, nodding in the direction of the heaving throng.

"We're getting used to it." I added.

"Yeh, you've got a lot of balls if you ask me," added Razor before going on to ask me that question that so many people asked shortly after meeting me in some neutral venue or context. That question that I had grown to fear over the years. The question I wished I had a stock false answer to, because my habit of answering it truthfully usually led to me having to defend myself in some way. "So what do they call you and what do you do when you're not playing in a band?"

"I'm Kevin. Kevin Birley and..." Briefly I considered an alternative career for myself; wouldn't it be much easier to tell people that I was a sales executive, or TV producer or hairdresser or abattoir inspector or anything other than A VICAR! "... and I'm a parish priest in the Church of England."

"A what?" Razor replied, cupping his hand to his ear as if he hadn't quite heard correctly.

"I'm a vicar in the Church of England." As if this was something that someone would make up in order to impress a stranger when there were a lot more sexy and interesting false occupations available to try and impress them with.

"Fuck me!" said Razor. "Whoops, sorry vicar."

"Yes, he really is a vicar," Ian added reassuringly. "He's even got all the gear and that."

"Are you all amateurs then?" asked Kronenberg, as if such a question was necessary having heard us play.

"Yeh, I'm a website designer and businessman, Tim's a student at the moment, enjoying some time off before college and Siobhan is... Siobhan is a mystery..."

"Actually I'm a music teacher and occasional session musician," Siobhan added in a moment of self-effacing candour.

"So are you all into God and that?" asked Deb.

"No. Just Kev... 'Kev the Rev' we call him." Ian explained.

"That's cool. We're all pagans," Kronenberg explained.

His reply perfectly illustrated the reason why I was often so reluctant to explain to strangers who I was and what I did for a living. It always seemed to lead onto a religious debate in the most inappropriate places and at the most awkward of times.

"So what do pagans do?" asked Tim, once again showing that he was really listening, even when it appeared otherwise.

"Well apart from drinking and listening to rock music and coming to places like this, we follow the ancient religions and traditions that shaped our islands and try to show our care for each other and respect for mother earth."

"So, a bit like Kev then. But with slightly more weird clothes?" added Tim with all the youthful naivety that came from someone who having made such a comment, would never assume that anyone could take offence at it.

"You could say that," replied Deb looking down at her ripped tee shirt and across to where Razor stood. "Some people do find us a bit strange. But what brings you out to such a place as this Kev? Shouldn't you be like home in church, praying and that?"

"Probably, I..."

"He's not like that." Siobhan suddenly interjected. "I mean, he doesn't kinda force his religion upon you and bash you with the Bible and that." Suddenly I appeared to have found an advocate in Siobhan.

"Thank you for that endorsement Siobhan. Even if it was a back-handed compliment. In truth I'm having some time out of the parish. But I've been playing in this band for a number of years, haven't I, Ian?" I looked across to Ian for emotional support.

"Cool," chorused Kronenberg and Deb.

"That's right and he still hasn't converted me," added Ian, rather unhelpfully.

"So what made you choose the pagan path then?" Siobhan asked the three strangely dressed friends.

"I've like been involved in paganism and witchcraft for a while" explained Deb. "I like sort of dabbled in Wicca and that, but never really settled at anything."

"Perhaps it was just a spell you were going through?" suggested Tim, demonstrating not only his ignorance of witchcraft but also the naivety of his generation who had no idea how close he was coming to provoking a stranger into a violent reaction through such an inappropriate attempt at a joke.

"Just ignore him," Ian suggested, "He's on a gap year."

"Yeh, but what gap is he filling," asked Kronenberg, "the one between his ears?"

"It's so not about potions and pointy hats you know. There's a strong, noble tradition of paganism and witchcraft in this country that like pre-dated the Church and Christianity." Deb explained. "What we are doing is just like exploring those ancient roots and like connecting with those traditions and spiritualities. Anyhow, I was about to tell you how I sort of dabbled for a while and then met Kronenberg and we like so got it together and became like real soul companions and fellow travellers. Later on we met Razor here, during another gig about six months ago."

"Are you all into the same stuff then?" asked Ian.

"No. Pagans follow many paths. I prefer the traditions and customs of the ancient Celts, druids and mystics. Deb has a slightly different spirit companion and Razor different again. We are all following our own guides and paths. Do you know much about the Celtic tradition?"

"Don't they have the same football anthem as the Liverpool kop?" added Ian, just to show that Tim didn't have a monopoly on stupid comments.

"I know a little," I interjected, trying to show that at least one of us was prepared to engage them in some kind of serious dialogue. "I'm from Tamworth and nearby in Lichfield they have a tradition about Chad and Cedd the ancient Celtic Christian missionaries."

"Yeh, but they were the ones who tried to remove the pagan gods and traditions from Europe," explained an increasingly impassioned Deb. "Even worse, they supplanted their Irish Christian traditions over the ancient Celtic customs and beliefs and religious sites. You know that many of the places of Christian worship and veneration were originally pagan sites."

"Yeh, I do. I know that it is a lot easier to Christianise a tradition, than it is to remove it or deny it. And often the Church tried to hold together those ancient traditions whilst giving them a Christian reference or interpretation."

"You stole our clothes."

"Don't worry. No danger of that happening nowadays" added Tim, unable to resist another opportunity to send up his Goth companions.

"Pratt." muttered Razor, shaking his head.

"Perhaps, the Church did. It happened elsewhere, but sometimes there was antipathy as well. Patrick and others used to see pagans as the enemy. He lit bonfires to drive away their evil spells. Columba had a number of run-ins with local Druids and ended up in a Mount Carmel-like competition over who could heal diseases."

"Yeh, that's right" said Kronenberg. "You either tried to stamp out our ancient ways or assimilate them."

"Yeh but it wasn't always as confrontational as that? Didn't the Celtic Christians in this part of the world plant little prayer cells all around the country? Weren't they called 'llans' or something, which later came to mean 'church'. Isn't that why so many Welsh place names begin with 'llan?'"

"Dunno mate. But what I do know is that one way or another, our traditions got lost. And when they re-appeared in history, then the Church used to come down hard on them and burn witches and destroy pagan shrines. That's how we lost so much that was so precious. We are just trying to re-capture what the Church has Christianised out of our culture," explained an increasingly agitated Kronenberg.

Suddenly, I felt guilty. As though I needed to vicariously apologise for the history of Christianity in our land, even the good bits. I decided to change tack.

"Look I'm not here to defend or apologise for two thousand years of church history. What happened in the past is in the past and no-one can change it, we can only choose to interpret it from our differing perspectives, but what fascinates me..." I added starting to mount one of my hobby horses on which I would ride the debate "... is how the Church is struggling today in a secular or pluralist or some would even say, pagan culture to try and re-capture the culture in order to Christianise it all over again."

"But you can't Christianise a culture." Deb added. "Culture is like complex; it doesn't belong to anyone. It is shaped by many sets of beliefs and values and defined by many languages. There is no such thing as a Christian culture in the same way as there is no such thing as a pagan culture. It's just culture. Although it's complex, it's essentially neutral. Like you can put into it or take out of it whatever influences and values you want and then like use your belief systems to decide whether those values are any good or not?"

"So you wouldn't describe our culture as Christian or secular then?"

"No, it's just what you make it. We've all got choices. We might choose to celebrate Halloween and you might want to think about All Souls or All Saints. One way or another, we're both remembering the spirits of the dead." Clearly Deb knew her way around Christian tradition and doctrine. "Yeh but somebody's got to be right haven't they?" asked Tim. "I mean you can't have Christians and pagans both being right. You can only put one snooker ball on a spot can't you? You can't put two in the same place. One has to be in the right place whilst the other is just a bit off the mark, if you see what I mean. Someone has to yield. Don't they?"

Blank looks were exchanged among the group, as if both sides were unwilling to take the debate any further for fear of provoking offence.

"Well I wish you all the best with the rest of your tour," Kronenberg said, whilst gripping my hand in a firm but friendly, two handed handshake. "If ever you come back down this way, look us up. I've got a web page." At which point Kronenberg pulled a business card out of his top pocket and thrust it into my hand, closing my fist around it so that I couldn't refuse. "It's more of a blog space I guess and a portal for those who are following different spiritual paths. We'd love to hear from a rock and roll vicar. We get all sorts of hits... some even from people trying to find cheap alcohol for obvious reasons." With that passing valediction Kronenberg slapped Tim on the back. "Look after this young lad, if I wasn't so committed to non violent protest I'd have chinned him tonight."

Deb then produced a crumpled piece of paper from inside a small bag hung over her shoulder. "This is a kinda prayer I use each day. We don't really pray like you do, but perhaps you'll like it and it's something that we can both pray, or hope for each other. Keep it, I've got another copy."

With that our gathering broke up and the four of us set off to pick up our kit and make our way back to the Travelodge. Once safely back, I examined Deb's prayer in more detail. It read:

A Prayer To Make Me Strong in Spirit

Make me strong in spirit,
Courageous in action,
Gentle of heart,

Let me act in wisdom,
Conquer my fear and doubt,
Discover my own hidden gifts,
Meet others with compassion,
Be a source of healing energies,
And face each day with hope and joy.

My trip into the *Sin City Nightclub* had not proved to be a fall into the den of iniquity that I had feared and had probably provided a more inspirational spiritual encounter than many a late night church meeting.

Chapter Twelve

Exploring
the Tardis

Information technology can be wonderful. Informing the mind, expanding the imagination, enabling trade in goods and services, lubricating industry and commerce, connecting people across huge distances and creating a sense of inclusion and community. Also it can be a pain in the backside.

Half an hour into a number of increasingly bad tempered cyclical attempts to gain access to my electronic mailbox by means of 'Outlook Express' had led to me calling down heavenly fire and retribution upon Bill Gates and the entire information technology industry.

> *'I hate you Bill Gates. You've ruined my life. Why don't you understand that your technology has advanced beyond most people's ability to operate it? Why can't it just do what it's supposed to do? You techno twat!'*

My inability to gain access to the Travelodge 'wifi' network via my laptop was causing my descent into a Basil Fawlty like rant directed at the software.

*'What do you mean 'Error 686. You have
performed an illegal operation'? What in
God's name am I meant to have done? Have
I set up a secret people trafficking network
in order to bring Ukrainian sex workers
into the country? Have I carpet bombed
Dresden or something? All I'm trying to do
is to look at my email. It's not an
unreasonable request. That's what you were
created to do in life Mr Microsoft Outlook
Express. It's not as if I asked you to find the
square root of minus one, or the solution to
cold fusion or to bring about world peace. I
just want you to work properly!!*

Finally I succeeded in gaining control over my emotions long
enough to take the cause of action that any self respecting
technophobe would do in such circumstances; namely, I asked a
nearby teenager to sort it out for me. A knock on Tim's door and
the bribe of chocolate from a motel vending machine managed
to coax him into action and sure enough three minutes twenty
seconds later the wireless connectivity problem was solved.

"How did you do that?" I asked Tim incredulously.

"Dunno, just did."

"But how do you know? Have you done some sort of IT
course at school, or read up on the subject or something?"

"Naa... just trial and error, instinct and loads of messing
around."

Thirty two new emails were awaiting my attention. One of
them was from Justin. Hopefully not a re-match of 'my church is
better than your church':

| From: "Justin Mellor" <Justin@christchurchrocks.com> |
| To: KevtheRev@fish.co.uk |
| Subject: New Growth this summer. |

Hi Kev

Just trying to touch base about the New Growth this summer. Seems as though events are moving apace. God is really blessing abundantly at the moment. Team across from Buenos Aires staying here at the mo... Pastor Don Domingues. Have brought a wonderful really anointed ministry to us. Healings, amazing prophecies, signs and wonders. We are seeing a real sovereign move of the Holy Spirit in this generation. You must come across to one of his leadership nights when you return. In meantime, we need to re-jig the New Growth programme this summer to make room for Pastor Don and his team. He is back in the UK again for only a few days in the summer, so need to use that time well – might not be poss to have your slot about engagement with local community and water distribution as well. So if you and your folks are cool about it, then can we put it on ice and try to share your insights locally instead. Perhaps at a Diocesan or Deanery Synod?

In meantime, thanks for your prayers the other night. Real blessing for me & Pippa. God has really moved in that area recently. All sorts of answers to prayer. Must fill you in some time. Why don't we do lunch when you get back? Give my secretary a ring to arrange a date.

Trust that God is anointing your music and opening doors for you as well. I'm sure that God has wonderful things in store for you in the future Kev.

I'm really praying hard for you.

Every blessing

Justin

Another blinder from Justin. I guess there goes my chance of ever becoming a conference speaker.

Among the various items of church business, correspondence and minutes from committee meetings I was still copied in on, despite most people being aware that I was out of the parish and therefore should be considered unavailable to deal personally with any such business matters, were two more personal emails which stood out demanding my immediate attention.

The first was from Daniel Grey an old school friend and struggling actor who was touring the country with his one man show concerning the last days of the German theologian and anti-Nazi conspirator, Dietrich Bonhoeffer. I had already emailed Daniel expressing a desire to meet up, but explaining that I would be away on tour myself when Daniel was appearing in Sheffield. Daniel appeared to be genuinely pleased to have heard from me and couldn't believe that I was likewise on a nationwide tour, albeit in the music business. Apparently he had accessed the website of *Zoo Two* in order to obtain details of the tour dates and venues and made several suggestions as to how we might be able to meet up on our respective travels. The best option appeared to be an opportunity to meet up in Edinburgh where Daniel lived and where the band would be playing in a week's time. I quickly pinged back a reply suggesting that we could go for a drink in Edinburgh city centre the day before their gig at the Liquid Room and asked for Daniel to suggest a good venue.

The second email that took my attention was from Matt:

From: "Matt Samuels" matt <sams@hotmail.co.uk>

To: Kevbirley@fish.co.uk

Subject: Biker!

Hi Kev

hope that this fnds you OK. Rather late, a little tired, but had an amazing few days.

There have been interesting developments with Bill (the Biker!) since we last met. I know that you are on tour at the moment, but is it possible to get together some time for a coffee. I am attending a sales conference in Worcester tomorrow. Any chance we can meet up afterwards, I understand that you are down in that part of the world – or is your rock and roll lifestyle taking up too much time?

Matt

I was intrigued to know what amazing news Matt had for me, especially as it concerned Bill the Biker. Had he finally taken a shave or was it perhaps something more significant? I was also intrigued that someone else seemed to know my whereabouts in the country, probably by virtue of the same *Zoo Two* website and tour programme. Putting these concerns aside, I decided to get back to Matt and arrange a meeting for the following day. There would be ample opportunity as the band were enjoying a few days off from gigs and there were limited opportunities available for interesting ways to pass your time in a Travelodge. I suggested that we could meet up in Tewksbury on Tuesday afternoon before the band played their gig at the *Roses Theatre* that evening and then go in search of a decent cappuccino.

I composed my reply but before I had the time to hit the 'send' button, an email dropped into my in-box from Daniel, who must have been live on-line. He was available in Edinburgh at the same time and suggested I stay with him in his flat. We could then have some more time to catch up on news and talk about old times together. I felt a little concerned that I would be spending so much time with someone I hadn't seen since I was sixteen years old and wondered if it might be pushing the boundaries of our friendship a little far to immediately feel at ease in each others company after so long. Nevertheless, Tim's image of riding the wave popped into my mind once again casting aside any reticence or ambivalence I had over staying with Daniel, and I felt sure that our friendship would be strong enough to find itself again after so many years. Besides it would make a pleasant change to be staying in someone's home rather than in a hotel and it might well still be helpful to keep some distance between myself and Siobhan. I drafted a quick reply and arranged a rendezvous.

The rest of the day was spent trying to kill time in Cardiff. I hadn't seen Ian and Siobhan since breakfast, but later on they knocked on my door to let me know that they were going down to the Cardiff Bay to join a Dr Who walking tour and see where *Torchwood* was filmed and did I want to come. I thanked them for their offer, but declined. As a Dr Who fan, I would actually have loved to gone along, but I feared feeling a bit of a gooseberry with Ian and Siobhan and thought it better all round if Siobhan and I backed off from each others' company whilst not performing. I also hoped that allowing Ian and Siobhan to spend time together might allow romance to blossom between them if it hadn't done so already, with luck that might help to resolve the awkwardness that still existed between Siobhan and myself. Having declined the offer of company I explained that I might wander down to the waterfront on my own later. By way of an excuse I suggested it might be good if I could keep an eye on Tim as he was still a bit out of his depth in terms of the age profile of the band and might be feeling a little lost at times. It was important for him to have responsible adults around him as a role model who could honour the promise given to his parents, to look after him.

Sure enough about half an hour later Tim knocked on my door having finished the supply of chocolates that I had bribed him with in order to help me get on-line.

"What's happening then Kev?"

"Not a lot. I guess you could call it relaxing and catching up with ourselves after all the busyness of the last few days."

"Where's Ian and Siobhan?"

"They've gone for a walk. They're taking in a tourist tour of Cardiff Bay. Something about a Dr Who guided walk."

"DR WHO! Wow. Why's that here then?"

"It was filmed around here. Do you like Dr Who?"

"Yeh, of course, one of the few reasons to watch telly on Saturday night. I didn't know that they filmed it here."

"Oh yes, and *Torchwood*."

"Cool, that's really cool... do you want to go as well?"

"Well...I don't really want to gate crash on Ian and Siobhan... and I am a little old for Dr Who conventions. On second thoughts I am probably a little too young for Dr Who conventions, so hey...why not? Let's explore."

Forty five minutes and a bus ride later Tim and I were wandering around Cardiff's redeveloped waterfront taking in the sights. Marvelling at the slate clad *Millennium Centre* and puzzling over the Welsh Assembly building, which resembled a bus shelter.

"I don't know where the tour starts from or what time it begins," I explained to Tim.

"Don't worry I'll find out," said Tim, taking out his mobile phone from deep inside his hoodie. "I'll go on-line and Google it."

"You can get on-line with that phone?"

"Yeh, of course. These phones have been around for ages. Haven't you got one?"

"No… mine just makes phone calls I think. I can't even text."

"Bloody hell, granddad. Where have you been? You're nearly fifty aren't you, not nearly eighty?"

"Yeh, but I just don't really 'get it' with technology as you know. I missed out on it at school and then I found myself working in a fairly low-tech world."

"But you've got computers and things haven't you?"

"Yeh. We do most of our church business via email. We have websites even blogs, although I never use one myself. It's just mobiles, I don't get this dependency thing. People always plugged into them. Won't go anywhere without them. 'I text therefore I am' philosophy. It just attaches strings and invites other people to pull them. It's a lot less stressful if you know that no-one can contact you via your mobile… mind you I am fortunate, I can avoid such things to an extent, I guess other occupations don't have the same freedom as clergy."

"Yeh, right. But I still think you're a dinosaur."

At that point we stopped abruptly in our tracks transfixed by the sight of a Cyberman walking past *Starbucks*. Alongside him was a man in a long brown coat, black felt soft rimmed hat and multi-coloured scarf attempting to give out jelly babies to unsuspecting and moderately terrified toddlers accompanied by their young mums. On his back was a poster with the words "Dr Who tours – every hour. Outside Welsh Assembly. £5.50"

"I think we're going in the right direction Tim," I stated the obvious. At which point Tim put away his phone as we both started to follow the Cyberman and Dr Who in his Tom Baker persona. By now the Doctor and the Cyberman had started to attract a certain amount of attention. Various young people in the vicinity started to hurl abuse and some even managed to muster up sufficient imagination to start singing the Dr Who theme tune: 'Duddle da - Duddle da - Duddle da – Duddle –da - Duddle da – da ---- da da da, dada da, da – da, dada da, da – da dada da da da, da, da, da.'

Unfortunately other passers by reacted less favourably. Young children in prams started screaming or hiding their faces beneath woolly hats and coat hoods. One terrified child was so distraught that the Cyberman tried to console her with offers of the Doctor's jelly babies. The sight of a Cyberman crouching besides a buggy and offering a child sweets might be a common sight in Cardiff Bay, but it certainly presented a surreal image as we made our way towards the Welsh Assembly building.

Sure enough outside the Assembly building was a full size fold away model of a Tardis advertising Dr Who tours – every hour on the hour. A small group of people had assembled outside the Tardis whilst prying hands were observed probing its surface looking for a useable entrance. This was obviously a deliberate omission, as many others who no doubt shared my child-like curiosity just ached to open the door of that famous 1960s police box and take a look inside. Such a curious nature would no doubt be shared with other interested tourists congregating around the Tardis resulting in endless attempts to gain access only to be disappointed that it really wasn't that big on the inside. I reflected upon what a powerful symbol the Tardis was. How its appearance on the streets of urban Cardiff could in itself draw a crowd of curious people, attracted by the mystery surrounding an iconic object which represented in many people's minds the possibility of exploring the endless reaches of time and the boundless limits of the universe. The Tardis acted as some kind of touchstone for people's imagination and their childlike desire to explore the mysteries of life, offering both disturbing and yet glorious possibilities of new worlds beyond the limits of our daily routines and physical world. No Christian symbol could evoke quite the same reaction, even though like the Tardis, the cross was much bigger on the inside once its meaning and significance was explored.

I spotted Ian and Siobhan approaching holding hands and clearly in a happy, relaxed mood.

"Hi Kev... Tim. Are you up for the Dr Who tour after all?" Siobhan enquired.

"Yeh, should be cool. We've already seen the Doctor and a Cyberman frightening the local under fives," announced Tim.

"Well, have fun. We did." said Ian turning away and heading in the direction of the *Millennium Centre*. "We're going to explore the wonders of Welsh culture." He explained, whilst wheeling Siobhan around to join him in his cultural quest.

Siobhan caught my eye with a slightly uncertain look which said, 'I might have accepted an offer, but I still haven't exchanged contracts.' Then she and Ian disappeared in the direction of the *Millennium Centre*. Perhaps she wasn't quite as committed to her partnership with Ian as she appeared, or else she had a burning desire to visit the Welsh Assembly instead in order to explore the concept of regional devolved government. Whatever the reason, Ian and Siobhan soon departed and we were left to make arrangements to pay for our walking tour and to join the happy throng of devoted Dr Who worshippers on their pilgrimage around the sites of Cardiff associated with the various TV series.

An hour later we were back outside the Welsh Assembly building having both enjoyed a walking tour of the Cardiff docks and surrounding streets which were associated with Dr Who or with its spin off programme *Torchwood*. During the tour we had been entertained by what were clearly seriously sad and deluded part-time actors who remained in character within the make-believe world of Dr Who, occasionally contriving scary moments when Cybermen or Captain Jack look-alikes would jump out from dark alleys or else appear around corners of the street. The whole experience proved thoroughly entertaining and surreal and afterwards we retired to *Costa Coffee* in the *Red Dragon Centre* to succumb to the tempting charms of strong coffee, warm paninis and Danish pastries.

Later on that evening, back at the Travelodge Ian knocked on the door and entered looking excited and purposeful.

"Great you're here. I've been trying to get hold of you Kev. Is your phone off?"

"Ian, how long have you known me? My mobile is always off!"

"Never mind. I wanted to see if you are up for a jam session with the *Zoo Two* boys tonight?"

"Ah... not sure, I'm a bit tired..."

"Come on Kev. It will be great. Chris has been in touch and they've got access to some rehearsal space in a nearby hall and offered to have a joint jam session. It should be a laugh..."

"I don't know Ian..."

"We'll have the opportunity to use their top equipment. We can practice some new materials together..."

"Umm... still not sure..."

"We can play some of their back catalogue..."

I remained unconvinced.

"We can also go out for a drink together afterwards."

I was still hesitant.

"Followed by some late night fast food!"

"I'll get my bass."

Later that evening the four of us drove the bus to an old chapel building in inner city Cardiff which had been converted into a night club and music venue. After unloading our equipment, we joined Chris, Chaz, Steve and the rest of the *Zoo Two* crew who were already inside and were working up a good head of steam with *U2*'s back catalogue. The tiny performance area usually wouldn't have been large enough to contain our collective equipment and extra bodies, but the absence of any audience allowed us to spill out onto the dance floor and spread ourselves around the venue. After a few technical problems and some musical awkwardness surrounding the choice of songs the collective bands were finally ready to start and launched into a version of *U2*'s *One* with Ian sharing the vocals with Steve. I was encouraged to follow the bass player of *Zoo Two* whilst Siobhan improvised some passionate sax solos around the musical riffs and constant vocal sparrings.

After about ten minutes of improvisation the song finally arrived at some sort of conclusion and everyone appeared pleased with the results.

"That was amazing," announced Chris, "You guys can really play. We should try to do something together as part of our set... and I love that sax... we miss that brass sound."

"It's all part of her obvious sax appeal," added Tim from the back of the stage.

"Could you possibly play *Angel of Harlem*?" continued Chris, "It would be great to be able to add that to our set."

The rest of the evening was spent practicing *Angel of Harlem* with Siobhan taking responsibility for the brass section backing, whilst Ian joined Chris on guitar and I started to explore the freedom I had from not being the only bass player. This released me to experiment with my own ideas and improvise without the responsibility of leading the whole band off in a different musical direction. We spent what felt like about an hour practicing the anthemic *Bad* with me being encouraged to provide rhythm guitar whilst Tim and *Zoo Two*'s drummer worked themselves up into a rhythmic frenzy with the two drum sets pounding out their percussion backing. Finally, *Zoo Two* joined in with one of Ian's own compositions which he took great delight in teaching them and explaining its subtle nuances and structural musical flow.

"It's good to do some original material," announced Chris as the session came to a weary, yet satisfying end. "We used to do all our own material, but no-one was really interested until I put a tea cosy on my head and Steve joined the band. As soon as we became someone else, everyone suddenly started to love us."

"Yeh, I know what you mean," said Ian. "I get really pissed off, with the lack of opportunities for new and original bands. But I guess that we've just missed the boat now and so we have to do all these weddings and birthday parties and that. It's fun, but you can have too much of the popular hands in the air, everyone on the dance floor moments. I long to be appreciated for what we do and for who we are, not for what we remind people of, or what we can successfully re-create."

"I know what you mean. But what can you do? At least, this tribute band crap pays well. And it gets you out of the house and living the rock and roll lifestyle all around the country. I'd rather have that, than remain unsuccessful yet authentic."

"Why can't you be both? After all the real *U2* are... aren't they?"

"Depends on who you ask, but yeh it would be great to be both successful, original and true to ourselves, but in the meantime, I'll settle for what pays the bills."

"Speaking of which, there was mention of a drink afterwards. Are you and the lads still up for that?"

"Too right. Just give us some time to clear up here first."

Two hours later the entire group had settled down to a large round of drinks at a down town Cardiff non-themed public house. Ian was holding court entertaining the *Zoo Two* lads with tales of Welsh Goths and body pierced pagan warlords named after lagers despite being teetotal, vegetarian pacifists. This whole story caused some amusement especially after it became somewhat exaggerated in the telling. Eventually the topic of conversation turned towards the tame vicar that played bass in the group and how strange it was to have such a person as part of their rock and roll outfit. I was aware that I was once again becoming the object of people's curiosity and fascination. Why couldn't I just be a coat hanger salesman from Wigan or systems analyst from Reading? I felt a bit like the Tardis I had been drawn towards earlier in the day. An iconic symbol that many people found mysterious and intriguing. I wanted to scream, to shout, swear or do something to break the mould of expectation or failing that, just to hide and fade into the background.

As the drinks kept flowing and the decibels kept rising, I was aware of my own increasing struggle to speak coherently and quietly. I was becoming increasingly raw and edgy in my conversation, probably as a result of my weariness with handling the expectation to be polite, measured and reasonable at all times in order to maintain my persona of a respectable clergyman. I was also becoming a little hoarse and high pitched from having to raise my voice above the background noise in order to speak with different members of what had become a large group of drinkers.

Gradually as my level of intoxication grew I briefly recalled Bridget's flippant comments about needing to get drunk, get angry and get laid. I had narrowly avoided one of those experiences, but felt myself being inextricably drawn towards another. Fortunately we had all walked to the pub from the Travelodge so I didn't have to worry about who would be driving the A-Team battle bus home that night. Normally I was fairly in control of myself when having a pint. I recognised my comfortable limit of two or three pints and often enjoyed working up to such a point, but beyond that ceiling lay virtually uncharted territory and my previous forays into such a place had caused discomfort and regret. I enjoyed the experience of having a drink, I even quite enjoyed having a little more to drink, but I didn't enjoy the experience of having too much to drink. I remembered previous experiences of the room spinning and feeling like I was in a boat being tossed about by the waves. Then the following morning feeling so ill and hung over that I really wanted to die. I had resolved after such experiences never to visit that place again. However, as more and more people seemed keen to buy me drinks, I lost the capacity to say 'No' as well as my ability to count the numbers of drinks I had actually consumed. I was re-visiting that place of alcohol-induced excess and I didn't know where it would lead.

As the evening wore on my self-control progressively loosened to the point at which I found myself becoming best buddies with the drummer from *Zoo Two* whose name I couldn't even remember, but to whom I was now swearing undying loyalty and friendship because he kept buying me drinks and saying nice things about my bass playing. I was also aware that once again Siobhan was getting very tactile and what's more I couldn't stop myself from reciprocating the gestures by placing my hand on her leg and referring to her as my 'bostin Irish buddy'.

"I might be your 'bostin buddy', but don't you think that a vicar in the Church of England should be watching how much he's drinking in public?"

"Naa. It's all right. Didn't you hear about that bishop who got smashed the other Christmas and started thinking he was Santa Claus and kept throwing gifts out of his taxi window? Well worse things that can happen after a few drinky winkies... Anyhow Jesus got criticised for hanging around too many parties and associating with some dodgy characters. He even kept a wedding party going when the bar ran dry."

"I see. So that's how you see us is it. A group of dodgy characters?"

"No. No. Not at all. I think you're all wonderful, fabulous, beautiful people, I really do... although you can be a very naughty girl at times." Once again I found myself patting Siobhan on the leg and trying to give her a knowing look which due to my heightened state of alcohol induced relaxation came across as more of a lurid squint instead.

"So no room for people like me in your version of heaven then."

"No. No. It's not MY heaven is it? It's just the place where we get to hang out with God and I don't see why you wouldn't want to hang out there as well... If it was up to me you could all come... yes, why not, everybody's invited. God throwing a great big party and you can all come along." {*Why had I chosen such a tired and emotional state to tell my non-believing friends all about heaven?*}

"OK, but why would we want to go somewhere populated by a bunch of boring Christians?" asked Ian.

"It won't be boring!"

"How do you know?"

"I don't, but Jesus said it was like a party or a big feast that God throws and invites everyone to come along."

"A bit like KFC?" Tim interjected.

"What?"

"Party bucket? Big feast? Never mind. Carry on."

"Um... uh... sort of, but not really. More like a great big gig."

"Ah that explains it," added Ian, "it'll be like a *Pink Floyd* re-union concert."

"You've lost me. Just what planet are you all on because it doesn't share the same orbit as mine?"

"You know, *Dark side of the Moon... the Great Gig in the Sky*"

"Ah yeh, sort of, but the light show will be even better. The Bible talks about noise, music, praise, worship and appreciation all being expressed."

"You mean it will be like Church?" suggested Siobhan.

"Yes, kinda... but no, not really."

"Because church going on for all eternity sounds more like hell than heaven to me!"

"Yes it does a bit to me as well," I admitted in a moment of candour. At times of great stress or heightened relaxation, I would often fall back on my default mechanism of saying what I really felt. At such times, my true feelings would just pop out like a shirt tail that refused to be tucked into a trouser waistband.

"Like one of his sermons, going on forever." Ian explained to my assembled audience much to their amusement.

"You've never heard me preach."

"Not in church, but elsewhere else we all have."

"REALLY. Am I getting to be an old fart?"

"No, not really. In fact, you've become a lot more interesting recently, but sometimes you can get a bit intense..."

"Intense? What d'you mean?" I snarled... intensely.

"You know. Like you've gotta to solve all the world's problems as well as your own. Just loosen up a bit. Have some fun. You don't have to provide all the answers to all life's questions. Just relax and take a chill pill... in fact, have another drink, it won't kill you and it might be interesting to see what happens the more drinks you consume."

"You're trying to get me sloshed aren't you?"

"No, that's your job and so far you're making a better fist of it than me."

"Well, I'm sorry, but I just can't face another... but I want you all to know that you're really, really special to me. And if there is such a place as heaven then I'd love to spend it in your company, just as long as you didn't expect me to take lead vocals and we didn't have to play *Hi-Ho Silver Lining* anymore."

With that I inelegantly struggled to my feet and attempted to offer the assembled gathering a blessing and benediction.

Unfortunately my words became somewhat slurred and mostly unrecognisable whilst my blessing resembled more of a wave and a waft of the hands as if to announce my departure rather than any formal liturgical gesture. My journey to the exit was punctuated by a necessary visit to the Gents which coincided with me feeling increasingly unwell and disorientated. So rather than providing the opportunity to re-gain my self control I found myself returning to a room now spinning in a disconcerting manner. I knew it was time to leave before making an even bigger fool of myself.

I recall being taken home by Tim who suddenly occupied the place of sobriety and responsibility which had previously been my territory. Tim was wonderfully patient and tolerant, even when I threw up in the street outside the bar. Tim guided me to the Travelodge and forced me to drink over a pint of water in order to avoid dehydration. In a surreal moment I remember Tim helping me into bed fully clothed, wishing me good night before turning off the light. '*Shouldn't that have been my role?*' I thought before passing out into what transpired to be a deep and not very pleasant night's sleep.

Chapter Thirteen

Doing a Dr Ruth
with Dr Ruth

MSN Chat Log

$$Lorro0$$[/c] says:
   hi matt

You have just sent a nudge.

[2l2||éé+MATT+éé||2l2][/c=31] says:
   hi tim

$$Lorro0$$[/c] says:
   wuu2

[2l2||éé+MATT+éé||2l2][/c=31] says:
   nufin hapnin. Borin… wat wiv U

$$Lorro0$$[/c] says:
   cool, sub 0. band kickin ass. Keep
   meeting weirdos. Goths. Welsh
   witches. Drunk vicars.

[2l2||éé+MATT+éé||2l2][/c=31] says:
   gota get dwn wiv the details.

$$Lorro0$$[/c] says:

oh okay.

Ian cool but bit up himself. Finks hees bruce spring. Good axe man...got hots for sheborn (sex goddess big time). Kev is a grandad. Serious but kind...sad inside. Keeps talkin bout X church, god etc. he is a rev. knows loads of stuff...mostly old music + film. Went tardis hunting n Cardiff today. Kev the Rev got pissed last night. Lol. Well wicked. Should have seen sheborn... keeps coming on 2 everyone n trousers! well wicked. None of them get it. All livin in an arc for oldies. Fink they so cool. Livin n past. Band just 4 fun but ian hed n clouds.

[2l2||éé+MATT+éé||2l2][/c=31] says:
RU straight up about pissed Rev?

$$Lorro0$$[/c] says:

straight up. Thought was meant 2B looking after me... sort of responsible figure...but really lost it last night. Kinda lonely, but means well. Keeps me entertained. No techno though, complete airhead. at least he gives me choc.

[2l2||éé+MATT+éé||2l2][/c=31] says:
wat wiv goths & witches?

$$Lorro0$$[/c] says:
n bar last nite

[2l2lléé+MATT+ééll2l2][/c=31] says:
> spill t beans

$$Lorro0$$[/c] says:
> look like orks... warhammer + skinny
> crystal maze man. Really primal. All
> veggies & tree huggers. Peace & tee
> total crp. Wouldn't liten up. Thought
> they were gunna chin me. But cool.
> Named after lagers. Tossers.

[2l2lléé+MATT+ééll2l2][/c=31] says:
> how about tardis – meet the Dr??

$$Lorro0$$[/c] says:
> n only exhit – cool though. Cybermen
> scaring kiddies, Cap Jack look alikes.
> Streets like full of darleks... i fink
> not!!! Cool idea though.

[2l2lléé+MATT+ééll2l2][/c=31] says:
> ahh ok fair enuf. how RU 4
> drummin?

$$Lorro0$$[/c] says:
> ok

[2l2lléé+MATT+ééll2l2][/c=31] says:
> so wuu. gizza the form

$$Lorro0$$[/c] says:
> cool. OK so far. no long solos. need
> my spray w me. hope i OK in next gigs.
> who is keith moon by way?

[2l2lléé+MATT+ééll2l2][/c=31] says:
> dunno. weird!! sumat about bloke
> who dropped his trousers on stage?

$$Lorro0$$[/c] says:
> ahh ok. fair nuff

[2l2ǁéé+MATT+ééǁ2l2][/c=31] says:
    fair nuff

$$Lorro0$$[/c] says:
    gota go now. have convo wiv ya soon.

[2l2ǁéé+MATT+ééǁ2l2][/c=31] says:
    cya timbo

$$Lorro0$$[/c] says:
    c

I awoke feeling like I had just gone ten rounds with Mike Tyson. My head throbbed, my throat was dry and sore and my limbs felt heavy and reluctant to move. I dragged myself into the bathroom where I prepared to throw up in order to relieve my symptoms. After briefly toying with the idea of putting my fingers down my throat to induce vomiting, I decided against such self inflicted torture and instead chose to drink as much water as possible in order to re-hydrate after the excesses of the night before. I briefly considered whether this had been the worst good time I had experienced? Why had I put myself through such an ordeal when the outcome was always so unpleasant and enduring?

A quick check on the time revealed that breakfast was still available in the pub adjacent to the Travelodge, provided I could get ready in time and face the prospect of food in my hung over condition. After a shower and shave I started to feel more human again. Although the idea of breakfast remained unappealing , it would provide a good opportunity to make up with those I had previously considered to be my friends whom I had inconvenienced with my general loutish behaviour the night before.

Upon arrival at the breakfast table I was surprised to find that the others had all made it to breakfast despite the excesses of the night before. Eating alone would have been less complicated, but I also felt contrite and wanted to draw a line under the whole episode in order to move on. Having to face people therefore had both advantages and disadvantages.

"Ah the creature from the black lagoon emerges." Ian's greeting was not entirely inappropriate.

"How are you feeling Kev? You look crap," enquired Siobhan.

"I'm OK," I lied and then sat down trying to avoid the gaze of Tim who had so successfully reversed roles with me the night before and to whom I now owed a really big favour. Such a debt would take a lot more than just vending machine chocolate to repay.

Trying to steady myself, I drew together all my faculties, took a deep breath and stood up to address the breakfast table in the manner I usually reserved for an expectant 8.00 am congregation.

"Before anyone says anything. I would just like to apologise profoundly for my behaviour last night…"

"Oh sit down and shut up Kev!" Ian barked.

"But?"

"Just do as you are told," added Ian, impatiently.

And with those words my drunken behaviour during the night out was never mentioned again.

After a somewhat muted and restrained breakfast gathering, the band succeeded in packing up all their equipment in the A-Team battle bus, whilst Ian took the wheel en route to the *Roses Theatre*, Tewksbury. The restrained atmosphere continued inside the bus during the journey with no-one willing to take the initiative in conversation. It was apparent, despite my indiscretions, that I wasn't the only one of our group feeling a little delicate the morning after. However, I decided to break the silence by offering some interesting social history by way of a running commentary upon our future destination.

"Has anyone visited Tewksbury before?"

No they hadn't and they weren't particularly interested, seemed to be the consensus view evident from the lack of response that my question provoked.

"I used to have a great Aunt who lived here, and we occasionally visited her when I was a child." I added trying to personalize my travelogue.

Still no response.

"Of course Tewksbury was entirely cut off by the floods in the summer of 2007. It sits on the congruence of two major rivers and is somewhat susceptible to flooding; however, the experiences of that year were exceptional. Did you know that someone actually drowned in the High Street during the storms."

Still no response.

"And the *Roses Theatre* in Tewksbury is the place where the great Eric Morecambe died."

"Well let's hope that we don't die there as well." Ian replied.

"No, I mean, actually died... in that he completed his performance and then collapsed backstage."

"Who's Eric Morecambe?" asked Tim.

It was such comments that reminded me of the generational and cultural gap between Tim and me. Is there any hope for him?

Arriving in Tewksbury, the band settled into their small high street hotel near to the theatre and awaited the arrival of *Zoo Two* and the opportunity to set up their equipment. Meanwhile I managed to penetrate the mysteries of my mobile phone's sub-menus and ring Matt to check on our arrangements. Sure enough Matt was only five minutes away and so shortly afterwards we met up outside the theatre before setting off to locate a supply of caffeine delivered through the medium of a frothy fair-traded coffee.

Settling back into the fake leather upholstered armchairs in a suitably convenient half timbered high street café Matt remarked upon how entire provincial towns were being taken over by coffee shops and estate agents, who between them now dominated economic activity in many provincial high streets.

"I'm not one to suggest a conspiracy theory. But isn't it interesting that estate agents like to greet prospective clients with the smell of fresh coffee when showing them around a property. A cosy little arrangement if ever I saw one. Need I say more?" added Matt, tapping the side of his nose in a knowing fashion and then sniggering as finally he could keep up the pretence no longer.

"Anyhow Kev. How are you keeping? Still burning up the place in true rock and roll style?"

"Oh you've heard have you?" I briefly wondered if my behaviour from the previous night had suddenly become public knowledge.

"So where have you parked the tour bus? In the hotel swimming pool."

"It's not quite like that. It's been a lot of hard work. A lot of travelling. Late nights. A steep musical learning curve to climb and loads of interesting people along the way... Oh and the occasional Welsh witch and Cyberman to deal with!"

"What?"

"Don't worry. I'll give you the full story one day."

"Sounds fun. All I get is a day sales conference about globalised credit control systems. Still at least we get some free stationary."

"Really? That's what I always wanted at church conferences, but it never happened. Did they give out any of those mint imperials as well?"

"Better than that. We had pens, mouse mats and complimentary bottles of water."

"*Evian*?"

"How did you guess?"

There was an obvious growing warmth and respect shared between myself and Matt, evidenced in our irreverent chat and common skewed perspective on life. After such initial sparing and preliminaries, our conversation eventually turned to more serious matters, although it is always difficult to be entirely serious with frothy milk being deposited up your nose every time you take a sip of cappuccino from a cup the size of a small soup bowl.

"So what's been happening with Bill the Biker since we last met?"

"Well, you remember his amazing ministry of prayer among all the people he meets on his travels."

"Yeh, I also remember the low tech networking techniques - calling cards and an answer phone."

"That's right. Well apparently the other day he was having a hospital appointment. A sort of six monthly regular check up and MOT on his spinal problems. He's a bit of a walking miracle that bloke. He didn't give you all the details, but he really shouldn't be able to walk at all, let alone ride that monster trike of his. Anyhow all the problems and treatments he's had over the years mean that he's now on pretty good terms with some of his carers and health professionals. So he goes in to see his regular consultant and after giving him the once over their conversation turns to more personal matters. This consultant, name of Ruth, starts to open up to Bill about how things aren't quite all that rosy at home at the moment. So they chat about the pressures that she and her husband are under and how she suspects that he is having an affair with someone from his work, but keeps denying it. You know the sort of thing?"

"I've come across the situation before. But not in a medical consultation." I re-assured Matt. "Is that what they mean by NHS direct?"

"Yeh it does sound a bit strange, but you know what Bill's like. Things just happen around him. Anyhow, he offers to pray for them and hands out one of his cards, then just as he's doing his sales pitch on her, he suddenly stops and says, 'I have this strange feeling that there's some urgency over this matter and that you should have it out with your husband as soon as possible.'"

"That's brave."

"Yeh. Some might even say foolish. But he doesn't stop there, he just carries right through with it, saying that if she can get home tonight promptly then there might still be time to save the marriage, but if not then it could be too late. Powerful stuff hey?"

"So what happened next?"

"That's where the amazing bit happens. Bill doesn't usually go out on a limb like that. He just doesn't say those sorts of things normally. He's not really the intuitive type – not that touchy feely with people. So I think even he was a bit shocked at what he found himself sensing and saying. So he thinks that this must be special and he sort of braces himself for a phone call that night or soon after. But nothing happens. No call. Not a word. He even calls the hospital after a few days later to see if he can get a message through to Ruth that way. But they just keep saying that she's not available and won't say if she's at work or not. So he just dismisses the whole episode as some sort of freak occurrence or a sign that he's been inhaling too much engine oil or something."

"Like you do."

"Absolutely. Then about a week later he gets this message on his answer phone from the Doc saying that she really wants to talk with someone and she's feeling really scared but doesn't know what to do. Bill doesn't know exactly how to respond, so he gives me a ring and we try to think about how to handle the situation. We feel that he should go ahead and see her, but Bill didn't feel comfortable going on his own. So I suggest he takes a woman colleague with him. You know the whole man to woman counseling thing can be quite tricky. Initially we thought about getting our own vicar involved, as clergy are meant to be sexless or neutral or something?"

"I beg your pardon?"

"You know. Sort of professional. Safe pair of hands and all that."

"I can assure you that we aren't sexless and we have all the same temptations and need all the same safeguards as anybody else."

"Fair enough. Well I had a word with our vicar, but he wasn't much cop. He made a few suggestions, but didn't seem that keen to get involved and appeared a bit too busy really. I even wondered about getting in touch with you at that stage."

"Gosh, you must have been desperate."

"No, I just thought that you might be able to advise us as to what to do next. But Bill said that we should let you enjoy your magical mystery tour of the UK. Anyhow, eventually we thought of Andrea, Melanie's friend. Do you remember her?"

"Oh yes."

"Fortunately she was available and so Bill and Andrea arranged to see Ruth at Andrea's place and Mel and I met elsewhere and just sort of prayed for them whilst they were meeting. Just kinda asking for a bit of inspiration and protection for everyone involved. Anyhow it transpires that God has been doing some amazing things with Ruth. Apparently she actually took Bill's advice and cancelled a late meeting that day in order to get home much earlier than usual. I think that she half suspected she would find her husband in bed with another woman or something. But rather than getting a nasty shock she had a pleasant surprise. Her hubby was just sitting on the bed, deep in thought and alongside him were his packed bags because he was about to leave at that precise moment. Apparently, he had been having an affair and it had been going on for some time, they had even started to make quite well advanced plans for a new life together. Opening bank accounts to put money in for rented property and all that. Apparently the other woman had kids as well. She was actually making plans to take them with her. It was all planned and decided. Really far down the road you could say. But her husband was just having a quiet moment to reflect on what he was doing. He wasn't particularly religious or anything, but apparently he had just prayed for the first time in years for some kind of sign to confirm that he should leave. At that precise moment his wife comes home early, which never usually happens and starts telling him that a strange hairy biker patient of hers had a premonition that she had to go home straight away in order to save her marriage. How about that?"

"You're right. That's pretty amazing. So what happened next?"

"Well they are pretty shook up by these events as you can imagine. But they end up talking and talking for hours together in a way that they'd never talked before. In fact they go on for so long that this other woman actually rings the husband up whilst they are still sat on the bed talking and he ends up telling her that he's not leaving his wife after all and that he had received a sign that he should try and patch up his marriage.

Anyhow days go by and that's when they end up getting together with Bill and Andrea to tell them the whole story. But instead of a good heart-to-heart counseling type of session, they just came around to Andrea's house and sort of crumbled emotionally before them. They just both end up on the floor sobbing and holding each other up, apologizing and asking for forgiveness. Bill doesn't know what to do. So he just prays over them and this seems to bring them a sense of peace or calm and Andrea then reads some scripture and then they ask Bill if he can give them some sort of absolution. Apparently, Ruth had a catholic background and knew all about that sort of thing. So it had a special meaning for her. So Bill ends up telling them that God forgives them and wants to give them a new start."

"We said Bill would be a bishop one day didn't we. Well he's already become a priest by the sound of it, by the time I get back to Sheffield I expect to see him wearing a purple coloured crash helmet."

"I know incredible isn't it? But that's not all. A few days later and Ruth and her husband come and join us for one of our Friday night get togethers. We all get on famously and they start to ask all sorts of questions about God and Jesus and the Bible, the virgin birth and all sorts of things that we couldn't tell them the answers to, but we just sort of agreed to meet together again around at Andrea's to look at the Bible and pray some more for them. And guess what, they turned up to that as well. It's like you had a prophetic word for us Kev. When you said that we were a bit like a church. Well I can now see that we are becoming a bit like a church. It's exciting, but real scary. We're just ordinary people. We don't know what to do and we don't have all the answers to all the questions. So to put in bluntly, what do you suggest we do next?"

"Well it's interesting that you are starting to use the 'C' word?"

"C word?"

"Yeh, 'Church'. What's happening does sound a bit like church to me."

"Yes, its church Kev, but not as we know it," announced Matt in a mock *Star Trek* tone. "Certainly not as I recognise it. So how do you know when something becomes church?"

"That's a crucial question but there are a lot of different answers. Some people say it has to do with the preaching of the gospel, others the offering of baptism and communion, whilst others think it has more to do with leadership, authority and structure."

"So what do YOU think? How would you recognise church when you see it?"

"I think that I would look for some kind of intentionality."

"What does that mean?"

"Umm... let me think. Do you enjoy art Matt?"

"Some art... it all depends. I like pictures more than sculpture or that weird stuff that gets nominated for the Turner prize."

"That weird stuff you refer to is probably some kind of installation art. Installation art often divides opinion. To some people it is pushing the boundaries of what is art and begging important societal questions. To others it's just an un-made bed, a cow cut in half and pickled in formaldehyde or a bowl of rotting fruit."

"To me, it's just a bowl of rotting fruit."

"Yes, but what you must take account of is the artist's intention. What they are trying to communicate; in that case that nothing lasts. They are inviting the observer into the world they have created and challenging their perceptions or understandings."

"So how does that make an un-made bed into art?"

"Well, the un-made bed is more than an un-made bed because of the artist's decision to install it in a gallery as a representation of something about her life. The artist's intention makes it into art—well, according to some people."

"So do you like all that weird art stuff then Kev?"

"Some of it. What I admire is the ambition in the whole exercise. Pushing the boundaries of what is considered to legitimate. No other discipline does that. Constantly broadening definitions and trying to be more inclusive and expansive. Bringing into the fold new concepts and ideas. Challenging existing understandings and categories. I admire the adventure that such an enterprise involves."

"So, it's all about the intention ultimately. What the artist is trying to say and trying to reach out in order to achieve."

"Yes, broadly. I guess so."

"OK then. So running with one of your weird analogies once again. Are you saying that when we act like a church that we become a church. Such as when we get together in the pub?"

"Perhaps. It has more to do with what such gatherings effect among you. Does the experience of coming together create a community of believers who live out the values of Jesus and His Kingdom? If so, then your little group is starting to operate intentionally as a kind of church."

"But we don't know what we are doing. We are just stumbling upon needy people and experiencing the work of the Holy Spirit among us. We're not trying to start an organisation or movement, we're just people thrown together by circumstances and shared faith. We don't have a grand plan, huge resources or even any agreed roles."

"Sounds like the early Church to me. First of all, if you feel vulnerable, unsure of yourself and de-skilled, then don't worry because you're in good company. Join the club."

"You mean the early disciples were like that as well?"

"Yeh, of course, but I was also thinking more close to home, because I often think that way myself. None of us have all the answers. We're all amateurs in that respect. No-one knows exactly what to do all the time; we're called to live by faith and trust, not by sight and merit. The best advice I can give you all is to carry on carrying on. Just do what God tells you to do. It sounds as though that has worked out fine so far, so keep trusting that He will show you what to do and will give you the strength to do it."

"Simple as that?"

"Simple, and as complicated as that! Then when you find out exactly what to do, come back and tell me about it, so that I can learn from you as well."

It had been an incredible experience to learn what was happening with Matt and his friends. Matt seemed genuinely transformed by the whole experience – as if coming alive spiritually and learning to hope once again. It was also good that he had been so keen to get in touch and to make himself and his group of friends accountable to me in some way. I felt affirmed and encouraged by the display of faith and trust that Matt had obviously invested in me, especially given the events of the last few weeks which had made me feel so unspiritual and a bit of a failure as a priest and as a follower of Jesus. If only Matt knew the situations I had found myself embroiled in during my time on the road – the shower incident – *Sin City Night Club* – the drunken night out. As a result I felt unqualified and unworthy of offering any model of holy living to anyone. But it was good that there was apparently still a place for me within God's great economy. I might be a lousy Christian and a rubbish vicar, but that didn't mean that God couldn't use me to help others and to provide support when it was needed.

Matt and I agreed to keep in touch and to get together as soon as I was back in Sheffield. Before we parted, Matt went to leave but stopped in his tracks and turned on his heels Lieutenant Columbo style, although without the scruffy raincoat.

"By the way Kev. Just one more thing. I think that Melanie would like a word with you when you return."

"What makes you say that Matt?"

"I don't know. Just a feeling I get. I sense that she's got something to get off her chest, like she's carrying a weight around and you might be able to help her to deal with it in some way."

"Ok Matt. I hear what you're saying. I don't understand what it could be. I've tried to talk with Melanie on several occasions over the last few years and we just don't seem to get anywhere. Sort of skirt around the subject as if she is hiding something or afraid to bring it out into the open in some way."

"Look Kev. I'm no psychologist. Just a hunch. Get in touch. That's all."

Matt then departed in order to tackle the automotive challenges of the over-congested motorway system on his journey back to Sheffield.

Upon returning to the hotel I discovered that the rest of the band had already decanted themselves along with all their gear to the *Roses Theatre*. I located my Rickenbacker, along with a rucksack full of various leads, tuners, junction boxes, pedals and spare strings and set out on foot to walk the short distance to the theatre in order to practice and complete a sound check before the evening gig.

The gig went really well that evening. The jam session with *Zoo Two* had obviously proved beneficial to both bands in allowing us to develop more confidence within our own spectrum of abilities and experience. Everyone seemed more relaxed on stage and less concerned with proving themselves and getting all the details of the performance correct. Ian was a lot more confident with his vocals and upfront role following his brief foray into the world of Bono when he and Steve had duet-ed together. Siobhan continued to be a revelation musically. Not only was she continuing to look amazing on stage, but her sax improvising and even her keyboard work were becoming a lot stronger and more intuitive. She was starting to have a real impact on the way that the group lined up. No longer hanging around at the back of the stage with me and Tim, but rather increasingly confident in occupying the public gaze at the front of the stage with Ian. Perhaps it was the effect of 'that dress' – but she was clearly becoming more self confident and I was aware that she was fulfilling Ian's expectations in providing an alternative visual focus for the band as well as attracting quite a lot of adoring attention and wolf whistles are a result. Tim was also proving to be a revelation. He was rock solid in his performance, but also increasingly willing to improvise, experiment and challenge himself musically. Despite what he had said about needing his inhaler for any demanding drum solos, he was certainly putting in a physical performance and tanning the drum skins pretty hard at times, even venturing into the occasional solo and over theatrical closing, cymbal thrashing climax. Not only were the band avoiding what Ian knowingly referred to as any further 'Spinal Tap' incidents, we were also attracting some positive feedback, not just from members of *Zoo Two*, but also from an appreciative audience. We even heard a lone 'encore' shouted following the completion of our set, which we all took as a huge vote of confidence given that the audience had assembled in order to see *Zoo Two* play rather than us.

After a moderately early night which followed a lot more sober evening's entertainment, the band members awoke refreshed and sustained, basking in our growing self confidence that we had earned the right to perform alongside such a professional outfit as *Zoo Two*. We made good our arrangements with the hotel and set off early in the A-Team bus to travel the considerable distance required to makeour next gig in Norwich.

Chapter Fourteen

Speaking off the record

"Can't we just use a road atlas like everyone else?"

"Atlases are for wimps and mini metro drivers. Everyone uses 'sat nav' these days. You've gotta move with the times Kev." Ian insisted.

"Yeh, but what's the point in moving with the times, if the technology doesn't work?"

"It does work!"

"No, it doesn't."

"You've just got to know how to use it. It's no use just shouting out at it when it doesn't do want you want it to do, it's just a dumb machine. It only does what you tell it to do."

"Well why does it keep telling us to take detours when we don't need to?"

"Someone must have fiddled with it. Programmed it to take us everywhere via B roads or to go the pretty way or something, I don't know. I can't be expected to programme the thing perfectly whilst I'm driving."

"Well, I'll drive then. You're meant to work with computers anyway. It should be right up your street... Unlike this particular sat nav which is right up every street other than the one we are meant to go along."

"Tim. Can you fix this sat nav? Just get it to do the basics right. We just want to get to Norwich city centre by the shortest possible route."

"Yeh, I'll take a look at it." Tim emerged from his iPod and palm top computer to take a quick look at the small silver 'sat nav' box attached to the inside of the VW Transporter windscreen. We were a few miles outside Evesham in search of the quickest route to our next gig at the Waterfront in Norwich. I sat perplexed alongside Ian having already spent half an hour trying to re-programme the sat nav which kept trying to direct the A-Team bus to Norwich via Peterborough. In desperation I decided to tackle the instruction manual for this latest electronic gadget Ian had placed so much faith in to get us to our gigs on time. However, I quickly became exasperated and confused; my head set spinning by the technical language and baffling illustrations.

"I just wish it wouldn't keep nagging me in such a condescending, maternal tone," I complained.

"It's just a machine Kev. It only does what you tell it to do." Ian insisted, as we started to sound not unlike a squabbling married couple.

"But..."

"There you are. All done," announced Tim.

"What do mean, all done?" I asked incredulously.

"All sorted. Shortest route between Tewksbury and Norwich. I've even changed the voice to a male one, if that will help."

"Well you both haven't got much experience in taking advice from a woman," added Siobhan from her position wedged against the inside of the van, pretending to be asleep.

"Yeh. You can have a selection of different voices if you want," explained Tim.

"Any Irish ones?" asked Siobhan.

"Probably not, but you can have Norwegian, Croatian or Swiss if you like?"

"I bet the Swiss one doesn't nag you," I suggested, "it just sits on the fence remaining neutral."

"Yeh and I bet the German one keeps directing you across the Rhine lands to occupy Poland," added Ian, sensing it was now time to indulge in some blatant national stereotyping.

"And the Italian one reverses you into the nearest restaurant and keeps you there for a three hour lunch break."

"And I bet the Swedish voice explains the route by saying locate road junction A to the interconnecting slot next to flange F with the aid of the roundabout tool labeled D, remembering to turn in a clockwise direction…"

"Meanwhile, the French voice…"

"Ok fellas. Enough is enough. I want some shut-eye, without all the 'crack', going down," insisted Siobhan.

Four hours later, having spent a pleasant lunch in a wayside pub just east of Huntingdon, we were inching our way through the congested city centre streets of Norwich circling the venue looking out for a suitable place to unload and drop off.

"This could be quite an experience," claimed Ian, "a lot of famous bands have played here and the venue can take up to seven hundred people. Potentially our biggest gig yet."

"Yes, but have they got a car park?" I enquired, trying to deflate Ian's pomposity.

"Oh take a chill pill Kev. I'll get it sorted out soon."

At that point Ian turned a corner and manoeuvred the van into a small car park adjacent to the venue.

"See. What did I tell you?"

"I love it when a plan comes off." I quipped, falling into A-Team speak, but Ian wasn't listening.

Grateful for the opportunity to stretch our legs we staggered out of the bus, blinking in the diffused sunlight in a manner lacking any of the military precision demonstrated by Colonel John "Hannibal" Smith, Lieutenant Templeton "Faceman" Peck, Sergeant "B.A Bachas" and Captain "Howling Mad" Murdoch in the popular 1980s TV series. We made our way into a large redbrick building, previously a brewery and bottling house now the local student's union and a well recognised live music venue. Once inside we were met by Chaz who was looking rather excited, yet nervous and anxious to please.

"Hi fellas. What took you so long? We've been here for ages."

"Blame it on the sat nav," Ian explained.

"Oh right I see. Whatever did we do before we had such gadgets?"

"We used our sense of direction or a map," I added, seeing another opportunity to make my point about reliance upon technology.

"Anyway, whatever... there's someone I want you all to meet. We're starting to attract some media interest. There's a TV crew here who are researching something about the popularity of tribute bands and there's also a music journalist from *The Guardian* who's running some sort of article."

Chaz led the four of us through the entrance of the club and upstairs into a small bar which was being used as an improvised hospitality area and had a coffee machine set up, along with numerous bottles of water and plates of sandwiches and Danish pastries laid out on paper plates covered with cling film. Not very rock and roll, but a welcome sight having just arrived in a new town and venue. In one corner of the room sat Chris and Steve from *Zoo Two* who were earnestly engaged in talking to a young lady with a clipboard alongside a young man fiddling with a microphone that resembled a large grey and fluffy rodent on a stick. Lying on the ground next to him was a large video camera along with various leads and black boxes.

"I think that Steve is quite over-awed by it all. They apparently want to do a feature on him especially," explained Chaz, "you know the human story, contrasting home and work life against his own stage persona. 'Butcher from Bolton becomes Bono' sort of thing."

"Well it certainly has a ring to it," said Ian.

"Yeh, well hopefully it will give us some free promotion, because they want to do some filming tonight, both on stage and off stage. Sort of day in the life I suppose."

"So who is it for?" asked Ian.

"Not sure. I think that they are one of those independent film outfits who do stuff for all sorts of channels."

"Just as long as it doesn't go out on a comedy channel," added Siobhan.

"No, I think that they are pretty mainstream. Probably Channel Four or BBC3 or one of those freeview channels."

"So, how does this all involve us Chaz?" asked Ian.

"I'm not sure about the TV, but the journo is interested in your band, especially you Kevin!"

"Me?"

"Yes, having a bass playing vicar seems to have captured the journo's imagination."

"So how do they know about me?"

"Well, she's a friend of Chris's and he contacted her first, to see if she could get any publicity for the band. Just kinda put out a few feelers. Anyhow she ends up passing the idea on to her friends in TV and then Chris suggests that they all come along to a gig. They're all based in Manchester, but we're not going up that way and today was the only day they were free to get to a gig. Chris thought they might show up, but he didn't know for certain until this morning when they gave him a call. Hence we got here pretty promptly because they don't have much time available for filming. They were all waiting for us when we arrived."

"But you still haven't explained, why the journalist is so interested in me?"

"Oh yeh. I was coming to that. Well Chris asked me to do some sort of press release about how the tour's been going. Where we have played, what reaction we got. All that sort of thing. So I mentioned that we have a full support band in tow and that one of them used to play with *Marillion* and another member was a vicar taking time out from his church. The next thing I know, this journo not only wants to do a feature on our band, but is also interested in running a separate article on people taking gap years or time out from demanding jobs or respectable professions in order to do alternative lifestyle things. And guess what, Kev? You fitted the bill! Come and meet her."

Chaz took me across to meet a slim, blond haired girl who was sat in the corner of the bar tapping away on her mobile phone with a very dexterous thumb. She was wearing a white tailored blouse and thin black tie and black leather waistcoat over blue jeans. Her hair was scraped back into a short pony tail and she had bright red lipstick and dangly ear rings. She looked up and beckoned Chaz and myself over, whilst Ian, Tim and Siobhan sidled towards where the TV crew was camped hoping to attract their attention or failing that to at least be able to avail themselves of the hospitality thoughtfully provided by the venue.

"Are you Kevin? Sorry about that," referring to her activity on the phone, "just trying to get in touch with my boss and arrange some copy... You don't look much like a priest to me."

"I don't normally dress up for the role while I'm playing in the band."

"Sure, I understand." The journalist looked right into me as if she knew more than she was letting on.

"Have you got a few moments. I'd like to get some background on what's going on here. First of all this is me..." She passed across a business card which introduced her as "Danny Short. Journalist. Guardian Newspapers Group."

"Hi Danny, I'm Kev. What's Danny short for?"

"That's a very direct question. I don't have to justify..."

"No, I mean, what would Danny stand for?"

"Uhh... I would stand for a number of things, such as..."

"No, I mean what's Danny an abbreviation of?"

"Oh, I see, nothing really. It's just Danny. I'm not normally asked such a question. I never mention Danielle, she was someone I left behind a long time ago."

"OK, just Danny it is then." This relationship had not started well.

"Look, I'm working a little out of the box here. I've been sent to get some copy on *Zoo Two*, you know the whole tribute band phenomenon – a kinda feature for a glossy article, when my IDIOT photographer arrives to take a few snaps." She raised her voice and looked around the room when referring to the photographer as if to show everyone just how ticked off she was by his non arrival. "But I understand from Chaz that you've taken some time out of church life to pursue a musical career?"

"Well it's not really a career. Just a bit of fun and a change of scene for me. Ian wants to take the whole band thing a lot further, but I just feel…"

"Yeh, sure, whatever. Look I appreciate you seeing me like this, but this other article is a bit of freelance work and my boss is always a bit sniffy about how much of that I do on company time and expenses as it were. So I'd be really grateful if you could give me some background as to why you up and left your church in order to play in all these live music venues… it's a bit inappropriate for a clergyman isn't it?"

"No, not really. I actually like getting out and about. You meet a lot of interesting people in parish life, but going on the road and coming to places like this is a whole new experience…"

"Hang on, hang on… I should get some of this down. Wait a sec."

Danny then proceeded to search in a small shoulder bag for a mini disc player and note book. The tools of her trade.

"Right can we first of all put down some formal stuff on tape? Please just tell us your name and spell it out for me."

I then proceeded to give my name, age and background details of where I lived in Sheffield, although not every detail as I didn't want to attract too much personal interest and place my whole life in the public domain.

"So Kevin, you live in a large vicarage in Sheffield. You've got a church of about two hundred people. You share the work with a curate and two readers… what do the readers do?"

"They help to lead and speak at different services."

"I see… So what about your family Kevin? What do they think about all this?"

"It's Kev, just call me Kev… Actually I haven't got a family. My wife died four years ago and I don't have any children. The only person I've left behind is my Dad and he's in residential care these days."

"Oh I see. I'm sorry to hear about your wife… Ummm…*was hoping to do something about family reactions…*" Danny whispered as if thinking out loud. "Never mind. What did your church think about you giving up being a vicar and coming on tour with a rock band?"

Danny's rather insensitive dismissal of my bereavement started to irk me and get under my skin. It felt as if I should apologise to her for not providing the sort of story she was looking for. Nevertheless, I had learnt from being a parish priest not to wear my personal feelings too near the surface and try to disregard other people's insensitivity towards my circumstances. So I decided to ignore her reaction and carry on providing all the biographical details she was seeking to garner in order to build up a picture of why I was on tour with the *Manic Tuesdays*. I was sufficiently experienced to know that when dealing with journalists they are often looking for a particular angle on a story and that I should therefore be fairly careful in providing any information that was 'off the cuff' or too spontaneous. I decided to treat this conversation as a formal interview rather than a chat with a friend. I didn't have to feel any warmth towards my interviewer in order to honour my part of the arrangement and I was anxious to avoid treating her as a friend or confidante, because journalists can be quite skilled in using such apparent friendships as a way to obtain fairly personal or frank comments that can be later seen as injudicious or even incriminating.

"So have you got all the information you need?" I asked wearily.

"Yeh, I think so. You're not the first person I've interviewed for this feature. I met with a top city lawyer the other week that was going to Africa to work in an Aids orphanage for a year."

"Good for him."

"Her actually. Never mind. Thanks Kev, that's really helpful. Hopefully, Joss will be getting here a little later and he'll want to take some photos of you if that is OK. Performing with the band and that."

"I'm sure that'll be OK. Especially as far as Ian's concerned."

"I wonder if I could ask you something more personal?" said Danny, deliberately switching off her mini disc recorder and putting away her notebook in an exaggerated manner, designed to show me that anything that followed would be strictly for private consumption.

"Does that mean 'off the record'?"

"Sure. Most of my readers wouldn't be interested anyway, it's just for me and my own interest."

"OK. Fire away."

"Well I guess it's the 'why now?' question. You've been playing in a band for some time. You're on your own. Your only commitment is to your church and to God I suppose, so why haven't you done this before? You obviously enjoy playing. I just don't get what's keeping you in the church? Why not just leave and jack it all in for something else?"

"It's like I said earlier. I'm just having a bit of fun with it all. It's not a serious career path I'm following. I'm too old and too set in my ways for that."

"Yeh, fair enough. But why don't you just get another job, you don't strike me as someone who is all that happy and fulfilled in what they are doing."

"I see, you're playing a game with me. Pretending to be disinterested and distant, when all the time you are really perceptive and weighing it all up."

"Well you have to use all your faculties as a journalist. That's why we women are so good at it. We use our intuition as much as our reasoning. But I've met other people taking time out from their professions, and your profession should be different shouldn't it. Aren't you meant to be 'called' or something? Isn't it a commitment you make to a lifestyle – a sort of lifetime commitment you can't just take time out from?"

"I'm not sure whether I am taking time out from it?"

"What do you mean?"

"I think that I'm exploring a new way of relating to people outside of the formal conventions of Church and outside of the formal role of a vicar. I'm finding a new freedom outside of parish life to discover new ways of being Church." I then proceeded to give a few outline details of the conversation I had with Matt the other day and what had been taking place in Sheffield during my absence.

"Wow... that would be good to include. Can I use that?"

"No. You said that this would be 'off the record'."

Danny sat back in her chair, looking slightly aggrieved, as if she had been caught out breaking the speed limit. Then looking deliberately past me she announced. "What if I said 'Flame Proof' to you?"

"Meaning?"

"Meaning, the experimental Christian community that operated in Manchester over twelve years ago."

"I know a little about it, but not a lot."

"They used to meet in places like this," said Danny looking around the room, "and they tried to 'do' Church in another way, among the rave scene at the time, which was pretty strong in Manchester then."

"Still not sure I know where you are coming from."

"Well I used to be part of that scene. Used to be quite involved in that church, so when I hear about people trying to find new ways of being Church, my ears kinda prick up."

"Were you part of the church when it all went pear shaped?"

"Yeh, you could say that, I was there when it all went Pete Tong. I used to be a lay pastor and worship leader there, but after all the funds went mysteriously missing and after some of the goings on with Jake Parsons, our pastor, I got out pretty smart..." she paused. "And I haven't been near any church since."

"I'm sorry to hear that Danny. It must have been pretty tough for you. I know that some pretty serious things were said about those in leadership at the time."

"You don't know the half of it. No-one does. The whole story has never really been told. Well not by those who were actually involved... who really knew what was going on. It was trying to find out the truth that got me into journalism. I was pretty close to it all, but even now, I still don't have all the details. Some people are just too hurt to talk about it, or else they just live in denial... like they were never in the loop... or they never really bought into all the God stuff or something. It's just crap. Total crap."

"Wherever you get community forming, there will always be the potential for problems to occur. People get tempted by the allure of popularity. Relationships fall apart. They get seduced by the power and the control they can exercise over others." I tried to explain, for some reason feeling that I had to defend those involved, although I had no reason to.

"Too right. We were told not just what to say and what to think, but how to dress, how to dance, how to move, how to eat. We were all groomed to present an image more than a lifestyle. We were meant to be counter cultural, experimenting with new radical lifestyles not dominated by power or money or tradition or modernity. But we were seduced all right. We were sold a lie. It was all about trying to be cool rather than trying to be alternative. A monument to someone's vanity if you ask me. And your lot were complicit in the whole sorry story!"

"Uh... sorry?"

"Yeh, the good old fashioned Church of England leadership just cheered on from the sides. Allowed us to do whatever we liked, so long as it was popular. Provided we put bums on seats, or in our case sweaty bodies on the dance floor, they were happy. They were so keen to have a success story that they never really asked the important questions. They fast-tracked Jake through leadership training, just gave him everything he wanted. No questions asked. So when I hear about a vicar moving into the music industry and trying to set up new forms of Christian community, I think, God it's happening again. They never learn."

"It's not like that. And I'm definitely not another Jake Parsons. Look Danny, I'm really sorry for everything that must have happened to you. I'm sure you feel very bruised by the whole experience."

"Bruised? Yeh you could say that. But this was meant to be Church, it was meant to be a healing environment, not a place of hurt and exploitation."

"I know. You're right, but churches are comprised of people and people get stuff wrong, they are fallible, they get sucked into making wrong choices, like all human organisations do. The church is not a club for perfect people…"

"… But you Christians just don't get it do you? You act as if you have all the answers, you think that you are perfect and only you can save society. You think you can redeem the culture. That the Kingdom of God will come when you impose your political agenda. Look at George Bush and Tony Blair. The two most committed, born again Christians in the entire history of the 'special relationship'. And what do we get? The fucking Iraq war, that's what. Without the support of born again Christians there would be no George W and without him there'd be no war in Iraq or Afghanistan and no young muslim kids blowing themselves up on tube trains."

"I don't think you can blame the Iraq war on the Church of England or Christians in general. Many of us were opposed to the war. Some of us even marched."

"Yeh, but that's what faith and power does. Religion is the cause of so much suffering in the world and so many wars. Look at the Crusades, the Inquisition, Northern Ireland, the Gulf Wars, Iran and Iraq, the Balkans, Darfur, Nigeria, Indonesia, Al Qaeda. It's all about religion."

"You can't say that! It's too simple an analysis. Wars are more to do with power than religion, look at Hitler, Stalin, Pol Pot. They killed millions in the name of what? It's just seduction by power, that's all. Political idealism. Sometimes, people like to wage war under the banner of religion, but I don't see anything in my Bible telling me to go around killing people."

"What about the holocaust? All those Jews killed?"

"Yes, but you're not seriously trying to tell me that Hitler was motivated by Christian principles or that his anti semitism arose from him blaming the Jews for having killed Jesus. Jesus was a Jew after all and many Christians opposed Hitler." I was becoming quite animated and angry over what I saw as arguments based upon such a selective view of history."

"That's another thing. Why do you Christians make such a big deal of the cross and crucifixion? He died, so what? I never asked anyone to die for me. I don't need someone to die in order to get closer to God. All this death, judgement and punishment language – it's so violent and imperialistic, I just don't buy into. It's all mediaeval crap. What's wrong with the idea of an original blessing, rather than original sin. We don't need a human sacrifice to recapture our souls, do we?"

"Gosh. Where do I start in trying to answer all those questions... do you really want me to answer... are you looking for an open and honest exchange of ideas – or something else?"

"Something else if I'm honest," said Danny looking down at the floor, exhausted by her outburst. "There's nothing you or anyone else could say or do that would make me come back to any sort of church. Whether it was a church that met in a drafty old building or a modern themed pub. I just think we've all moved on from there. A worldview dominated by religion and ideas of heaven and hell, sin and a personal saviour has had its day – it's yesterday's news. The Bible is a very old book. No-one really believes that a book can show us all how to live today. Even when you wrap it up in dance music, its still the same old message. I can see that you're not the same as those vain egotists who did so much harm at 'Flame Proof', but you are still signed up to the whole God package and I guess you're still committed to propagating your idea of truth. You think that you're right and everyone else is wrong."

"But everyone has values and beliefs, not just Christians."

"What do you mean?"

"Well everyone believes in something. They have some moral code, some ethical framework or political creed that they live by."

"Yeh, but we don't all try to impose it upon other people."

"So are you telling me that you are completely neutral on every important issue in life and that your newspaper is totally value–free in its editorial policy and never attempts to influence people's ideas or values?"

"No we just try to tell it the way it is. We don't try to construct any particular platform for our view."

"You must stand for something. You can't be much of a journalist if you don't believe in anything."

"Yeh, I do stand for something. That's why I got so touchy when I introduced myself. I stand for free thinking individualism. I'm not swayed by any religious dogma. I'm open minded and I'd like to think I'm tolerant as well."

"Except when it comes to other people who don't share your 'free thinking' views" I replied ironically whilst making inverted comma signs in the air.

"But I don't try and force my personal values and beliefs on others."

"Of course not, but national newspapers exert a certain influence on the national psyche and our shared values either intentionally or unintentionally. They shape opinion as well as describe it and they all do that from a faith position, albeit a non religious one."

"Perhaps? Um... no... sort of... I don't know. I don't care. I just think that religion is part of the problem in our world today, not part of the solution."

"I wish I had your certainty and faith, because I think that it's both!"

"But you didn't live through what I lived through and hear the crap that I heard and even started to believe in for a while. I just can't get back into all that stuff again, which is why I can't understand why you can be part of this world and yet still part of the Church and trying to do God's work and all that."

"Look you're not the only person to have been hurt in life. We are all limping along in different ways, hurt by our loss or pain or confusion. It's just that I try to live in hope and to choose to live by faith in something bigger than myself. I prefer to follow Jesus than follow someone else."

"I have faith, just not in religion anymore. God would have to do something pretty amazing to convince me to believe again."

"Like dying and coming back to life again?"

"Yeh yeh, I knew you were going to say that. You Christians are so predictable. Look, all this stuff, I will keep off the record if you can just do me a favour."

"Well I'll try. It depends on what the favour is."

"Look, keep hold of my calling card and give me a call about your church in a pub thing in Sheffield."

"But I thought that you didn't buy into the idea of Church. That we are all planning the invasion of Iran or something."

"I don't buy into Church. I still need to be convinced that I need a church to help me to connect spiritually, but I do need to eat and this is what I do for a living. And I'm still planning to write up some of my experiences at 'Flame Proof' and need to do some more research about new forms of religious communities and I'd really appreciate some up to date fieldwork. So... is it a deal?"

"Yeh, I suppose so, but I'm really not sure if anything will come of what you call my 'church in a pub' thing. We don't really know if it is Church or whether it will become Church or not. It's just too soon to say."

"OK. Whatever happens, just cut me in on it, that's all I'm saying. I'll write you up in a good light, because I think that on balance you are probably one of the good guys, but now all I want is to see you lot on stage, because if you are shit tonight, then as far as I'm concerned any credibility you might have acquired in my eyes, goes right out of the window."

"Yeh, well you're welcome to see us perform, but remember, we are only the warm up act. Everyone is really here to see *Zoo Two*."

At this point a rather large man with a receding hairline and long black ponytail entered the room and greeted Danny.

"Yoh Danny. How you doing?"

"Oh, it's Joss, my idiot photographer." Danny whispered under her breath. "Hi mate, you need to get yourself set up before the TV crew exhaust everyone's good will and enthusiasm. The *Zoo Two* boys are over there. I'll give you a briefing in a minute."

With that Danny started to pack up all the tools of her journalistic trade. She punctuated her departure with an attempt to make polite conversation, something which had been missing in our rather intense conversation. She then joined Joss to get some material for the story about the rise of tribute bands. Ian, looking slightly concerned came across to rescue me.

"You look as if you've just been mugged."

"I think I have. This journalist was OK until she went off the record and then she gave me a right grilling over everything she hates about the Church, Christians in general and George W Bush in particular."

"Don't take it personally Kev. Everyone has their own axe to grind… even journalists."

That evening's gig opened to a fairly full auditorium. Some four hundred paying customers had responded to the publicity Chaz had skillfully networked through the music industry and local pop press. He felt a little discouraged that the gig hadn't sold out like others on the tour, especially given the fairly isolated location of Norwich, but the appearance of a TV crew and Danny more than compensated. Ian had been disappointed that the *Manic Tuesdays'* set had attracted so little interest from the TV crew, although the photographer had appeared quite keen to get some action shots of me playing bass. However, once *Zoo Two* came on stage the cameras began to roll. Chris and Steve relished the spot light and made a great show of their on stage routines. For *Bullet in a blue sky* Steve used a hand-held spotlight to illuminate the group on stage, especially during Chris's screeching guitar solo.

Putting aside the disappointment that we hadn't been the centre of attention for the music media, we packed away our equipment and decanted to our hotel to decide how we would spend the next two days. These were scheduled for resting up in Norwich before the long journey north to our next gig in Edinburgh.

Chapter Fifteen

In Edinburgh with Daniel and Clint

"Wow!

Ian have you seen where we are heading in Edinburgh?" asked Tim.

"Liquid something or other isn't it?"

"*The Liquid Room* in Edinburgh. Have you seen what bands have played here over the years?"

"No, should I? Is it another *Sin City* venue or another *Gala Theatre*?"

"Well according to this website the *Charlatans*, *Keane*, *Travis*, *The Zutons* and the *Fratellis* have played there as well as some cool tribute bands… Awesome!"

"Yes, but have they had the *Manic Tuesdays*?" asked Ian not expecting an answer.

"How did you find all that out Tim?" I asked.

"I just looked them up on the net with my blackberry."

"Ah. I should have known…" I suspected Tim's answer didn't have anything to do with the soft fruit that grew ferociously in my garden. I really wanted to ask him exactly what a 'blackberry' was, but decided against a further public display of my technological ignorance. "So if all those cool bands have played there recently, then boy are they going to be disappointed when we turn up."

"There you go again," added Siobhan, "putting yourself down again, or rather putting ourselves down. We've earned the right to appear on that stage. Well I have anyhow."

I had often struggled with my self-confidence. I found it difficult to remain positive during Julie's illness. The numerous false dawns and tantalising hope held out to us had nurtured a deep sense of foreboding within me. No matter what progress I saw, disappointment had a habit of tracking me down, smothering any optimism. My negativity had even extended into my spiritual life and had provided the subject of many lengthy discussions between myself and Bridget. Julie would often rebuke me for undervaluing my musical gifts and creative talents. It seemed that every significant woman in my life was giving me the same message to stop being so down on myself and try to develop a more positive mental attitude.

My faith should have provided me with greater positivity but I had struggled to find the correct balance between the realisation of my own spiritual fallenness and a 'can do' attitude towards life in general. There had been times when I had become highly motivated and even ambitious in terms of Christian ministry. But much of this enthusiasm had been sapped by Julie's illness and death and by the daily grind of parish life. Although I recognised this development, nevertheless I was powerless to prevent it.

An artist is afforded the satisfaction of stepping back from a completed work and then offering it to a critical public for their comments and response. But how does a priest receive affirmation and recognition?

I had seen a large number of positive outcomes in my parish ministry, people had come to faith, lives were put back together and people discovered a sense of identity and community, whilst others even experienced healing physically, emotionally and in terms of relationships. I got on with most people and at times even felt appreciated both personally and professionally. I had seen new projects and ministries developing, new people becoming more involved and discovering their own vocations and ministries. I had enjoyed good times aplenty, yet it was always the negatives that touched a raw nerve within me. The criticisms, the back biting, the misunderstandings, the feelings of disappointment, the projects that consumed so much hope and spiritual energy only to peter out in frustration and disappointment. These remained my enduring memories. Many people experience both positive and negative outcomes in their work life, but I found the positives to be subjective and hard to quantify. The negatives of falling congregation size, increased workload and declining church income felt more tangible and measurable and consequently felt more compelling.

I wasn't alone in my struggle to accept that the glass was half full rather than half empty. Marjorie and I once had an interesting conversation en route to another Deanery meeting in which she was able to vent her spleen about the world of education in which she had served for so many years. Marjorie lamented the times when teachers were more respected and appreciated by society at large, whereas nowadays they had become a convenient whipping boy for society's ills. In a world in which personal development is always cast in terms of social education, if something fails to improve, who is to blame? Usually the teachers or the parents. Such attitudes are not confined to the rants of *Daily Mail* readers, but also penetrate deeply into the ethos of an education system focussed upon attaining targets in the quest to bring about improvement. Reaching such targets is then acknowledged in terms of what could be further improved or made better, rather than in terms of celebrating the achievements already made. Even when examination passes increase, the response from wider society is usually that the exams are getting easier rather than the standard of education provided is improving.

Marjorie spoke painfully about the effect that such a performance driven culture had upon the morale of dedicated and experienced teaching staff. This was often fostered by the practice of offering 'conditional praise' whereby staff were appraised in terms of what could still be done further to improve their performance. Such appraisal techniques might well raise productivity and performance, but Marjorie knew of many hard working and gifted people who remained insecure and uncertain of themselves due to lack of unconditional, positive affirmation. Rather than being set targets for future improvement, there remained the important human need to be told, 'Well done good and trusty servant'[16] full stop, with no 'buts' or conditions.

The world of target-setting, performance indicators, outcomes and mileposts hadn't yet impacted upon the Church in the same way as it had elsewhere. In a profession whose workers don't receive a salary as a reward for their labours, but rather a stipend or living allowance to support them in their Christian ministry, there remain few ways of affirming and recognising achievements within the Church. Promotion, power, status, extra income and improved fringe benefits are officially off limits in Christian ministry, so positive strokes are offered in other less conventional ways. Sometimes, an honourary title or degree is conferred; sometimes clergy are made canons of cathedrals, or receive formal honours. One or two ascend the slippery pole to 'preferment' or promotion as it is known elsewhere, but generally speaking they're very few ways in which achievement can be recognised or marked in some way within Christian ministry. For many people in Christian ministry this lack of a career structure does not present any issues, especially if they have entered Christian ministry later on in life, following a successful career elsewhere. However, for others there remains the need to be affirmed and to have the value of their ministry recognised in some tangible way.

Most priests have a fairly high level of personal motivation or else they wouldn't have pursued the call into the priesthood originally, so drive and ambition cannot easily be wished away. For those with a more catholic spirituality, the calling is its own reward. Others might have their professionalism recognised by achieving expert status and going on to become conference speakers, retreat leaders, authors and columnists. But how does

16   'Make me strong in spirit' source: http://www.spiralgoddess.com/Homage.html Abby Willowroot @ 1998

a regular parish priest know if they are performing well or not and should it matter?

Whatever the pathology of my negativity, both professionally and musically, I remained unsure of myself and the tendency towards self-deprecation remained. As a result, it wasn't surprising that I found it difficult to accept that things were going well with the band. We had now established ourselves into a tight musical unit, with a variety of different skills and a wide ranging back catalogue of songs. We deserved to be occupying a stage on which other more notable musicians had already stood. Siobhan was correct. We had earned the right to be where we were and now it was time to enjoy the experience.

Entering the city of Edinburgh on a cold and slightly gloomy spring afternoon, could not detract from the evocative power and majesty of Scotland's capital city. I had previously visited the city as a student during the Festival and had enjoyed its bohemian feel during those heady weeks of artistic self-indulgence. Now I looked upon the city differently, but still with great affection. The wonderful imposing castle looking down over Princes Street. The wealth of historical buildings, monuments, churches, museums, art galleries and shops inviting further investigation. Princes Street itself had an iconic feel, the opening scene from *Trainspotting*, Euan McGregor chased through the city streets. Edinburgh was indeed a fine city and I decided that in the words of Tim, I would 'ride the wave' and enjoy whatever experiences the place had in store.

Having located a reasonably priced city centre hotel we made good our arrangements to unload and settle in. I still felt slightly nervous about meeting Daniel after all these years. I would rather have joined the others in the hotel to relax the night before the gig. However, it seemed important to Daniel that I should receive his hospitality and so while the others made plans for a night out enjoying the sights and sounds of Edinburgh city centre, I enquired at reception as to directions to the *Wetherspoons* bar where Daniel had suggested we meet.

I located the bar, and entered somewhat tentatively. I was assaulted by a wall of sound as raised voices competed for space above the background music of MTV pushed out courtesy of various mounted flat screen TVs. The ambience of a family eating emporium was gradually transforming into that of boisterous wine bar. Popular venue for the hard working young professional population of Edinburgh, anxious to let off steam at the end of a busy day. I quickly scanned the bar and the surrounding room for any faces that might be familiar. I was aware that my visual memories of Daniel were still primarily located in our adolescent years and despite the promotional literature that Daniel had sent, I still very much expected to be looking for a young, fresh faced, innocent man, rather than someone in their early forties marked by the experience of many years. I continued to scour the room looking for some vague signs of recognition or familiarity among the disheveled business suits, sport shirts and tee shirted males that thronged the establishment.

"I thought you might appear in full clerical gear." A voice from behind me announced. I turned to see a slim, dark-haired man with twinkling eyes, arms open wide in welcome.

"Kevin Birley I presume?"

"Daniel Grey?"

Daniel enveloped me in a firm hug, which took me somewhat by surprise. He was never like this at school!

"Although don't forget to most people I'm Daniel Graham these days. Apparently there is another Daniel Grey working in *Hollyoaks* so my acting pseudonym is Daniel Graham, even though it sounds a bit like a breakfast cereal. I still use my real name when I'm writing or directing or sending you strange emails. Anyway, gre...at to see you Kev. It's been too long."

"Gosh you've hardly changed at all," I observed more in politeness than in truth.

"Likewise."

"You are so kind not to notice my hairline heading north whilst my waistline heads south." Once again I fell back into my habit of self-deprecation.

Daniel was my age, but I remembered him as slightly taller. Some people develop physically earlier than others, so it is possible that Daniel had stopped growing since we had parted company at the age of sixteen whilst I continued to grow. It is also just possible that I had remembered incorrectly and the passage of time had dulled my perceptions and recollections. Whatever the reason, Daniel struck quite a pose. He was well built, but muscular, rather than over-weight, I suspected he had been working out, especially after the powerful embrace he had greeted me with. He had thick dark hair and deep-set eyes that seemed to penetrate into the gaze of those he met. He appeared well groomed, slightly tanned and gave the impression of someone who took a certain degree of care and attention over his physical appearance. Probably part of the lifestyle of an actor, albeit a struggling one. He wore a collar-less stripey shirt under a tight fitting velvet waistcoat, sports jacket and corduroy trousers.

"It's really great to see you again Kev. The years have flown by. I understand that you met Catherine the other week out doing some DIY shopping."

"Yes I must admit that she recognised me, rather than the other way around. I had no idea who she was at first…" I paused as new arrivals pushed passed us on their way to the bar. "I often have that experience when someone greets me like a long lost friend and I can't remember who they are, or where I know them from?"

"Must be an occupational hazard I guess?"

"Yeh, one of many."

"Who would have thought that all those years ago in 'Tamworth High', that we would meet up again, both touring the country as wandering minstrels."

"Yeh, I have to keep pinching myself every time we arrive at a new venue. I've played small local gigs for years, pubs or village halls but nothing on this scale before."

"So where do you want to go from here?"

"Well I'm not bothered, I just enjoy playing my bass, but Ian, it's sort of his band, and he had all these ambitions about…"

"No I mean. Here and now. Do you want to get a drink here or go somewhere quieter and get something to eat or go back to my flat?"

"Yes, one of those. How about some food. Where do you recommend?"

"Leave it to me. I'll find us a place."

With that Daniel headed in the direction of the door, forcing his way passed a group of singing rugby fans who were just arriving and obviously had something to celebrate. He beckoned me to follow, and I dutifully complied.

Back on the Edinburgh street, the decibel levels dropped and Daniel asked that tantalising question guaranteed to strike indecision into anyone who enjoys eating out.

"Indian or Italian? Chinese or Mexican? Thai or French?"

"You know what. I really don't mind. Surprise me."

With that Daniel looked pleased and slightly mischievous and headed off in the direction of the city centre with me in hot pursuit. "I know just the place," he replied reassuringly.

Ten minutes later we were seated at a table in a somewhat quirky Tex Mex restaurant where all the waitresses were wearing Stetson hats and short skirts.

"I love this place. It's so kitsch." Daniel explained.

"Did you get a liking for Mexican food whilst you were in the States?"

"Sort of. However, this stuff is nowhere near the kind of thing they serve up over there. I just think its fun," Daniel started to pore over a large laminated menu in the shape of Mexican hat.

"Let's just hope that it isn't anyone's birthday."

"Why's that then?"

"You don't really want to know. Suffice it to say that it involves staff standing on tables, singing and doing a dance – I warned you it was kitsch. So Kev. What's been happening in your life over the last twenty one years?"

"A big question."

"Well we have to start somewhere. Why not get the full biography? I've already given you mine in the email."

I proceeded to fill Daniel in on my curriculum vitae since I left school, but I sensed he didn't want to know all the details. So I started to talk about Julie.

"I understand from Catherine, that Julie died some years ago," said Daniel.

"Yes, that's right, although it doesn't seem all that long ago to me."

"It must have been very hard for you?"

"Yes, you could say that." I realised that I now inhabited a sensitive subject which probably shouldn't constitute the first topic of conversation with someone you haven't met for over twenty years. I didn't want to get too intense too soon with someone I was still reacquainting myself with, so I decided to turn the tables on Daniel.

"Are you married Daniel, Catherine didn't say?"

"No. Never married. Not the marrying kind, although I am in a relationship at the moment."

"What's her name?"

"Clinton."

"Clinton. That's an unusual name." I was fumbling for the right response and still failing to understand the structure of the unfolding conversation.

"Yes, Kev... Clinton is a bloke. I thought you knew I was gay. I've been out for so long I forget that some people still don't know."

"Oh right. I see. No I didn't know, Catherine never said."

"Yes, we've been together for about two years now. In fact I want you to meet him later. I'm sure you'll get on. He's been a real rock for me during some uncertain times in my life. He's religious too."

At this point I felt myself floundering. I was presented with a choice, whether to change the subject and just take Daniel's revelation in my stride as though it was no big deal, or else explore and examine some of the issues Daniels' lifestyle raised. Sensibly I decided on the former.

"So, tell me about your acting? Is Clinton an actor as well?"

Brilliant I thought to myself. I've managed to change the subject whilst recognizing it at the same time. A warm sense of self congratulatory smugness came over me just as the drinks arrived.

"Yes, we met when I was in New York... in Queens. But don't look at me like that. It wasn't like most people think it is. Anyway, he's been a great inspiration to me professionally as well as personally."

"I understand that being an actor isn't as glamorous as most people think."

"That's right. It's not. Most of the time you are out of work. The rest of the time is spent going to endless auditions for parts you're wholly unsuitable for and receiving constant rejection."

"Sounds not unlike being a parish priest."

"Oh come on Kev. It must be great; doing something that is so worthwhile and helping people out with all their problems?"

"It's not quite like that, although some of what you do can be very rewarding and satisfying."

"So what got you into religion in the first place? You weren't particularly religious at school as I remember."

"No, I wasn't. I guess that it all kicked off when I went to Art School or rather University, where I studied art."

"Art school isn't exactly awash with religious revivalism."

"No it wasn't then, and I guess it still isn't today, but we had to study the history of art and the ideas that determined various artistic movements, so I started to get exposed to renaissance art and some of the ideas that lay behind it. You tend to forget that the Church was the chief sponsor of the arts for many centuries before the days of the Arts Council or Charles Saatchi. I just started to do a lot of reading around a number of religious topics. I wanted to know what inspired people to produce their paintings and sculptures. You know, where their passion came from, the world views that sustained those passions and how their art could be used devotionally in a way that had power over people's minds and emotions. I started to get fascinated by the power of images and how they connected with the world of ideas. Then there was the whole debate over iconography and whether people are worshipping the image or the idea or power that lies behind that image. There was a lot to explore and think about."

"So is that what led you to God?"

"May be in part. But it's never that simple. All the interest in art and stuff I was exploring was just opening my mind to a whole new world, but ultimately it's as much about people as it is about ideas. It wasn't just an intellectual or academic quest; I also met people who inspired me as well."

"Other artists?"

"Some were, but not all. I started to see how Christian faith impacted on people's lives. The positive difference it made. How faith did more than just help people to cope with their problems, but rather gave them direction, passion, inspiration and—and most of all, hope. Ultimately, no-one is ever converted just by reading books and exploring ideas, although there are some exceptions, I think that CS Lewis came to faith that way."

"Who?"

"You know. CS Lewis, the contemporary of JR Tolkein. Author of all those stories about Narnia."

"Yes, just kidding I have heard of him. I did go to Drama college after all. By the way, have you noticed how all the popular best selling fantasy authors use their initials followed by their surname?"

"Not really."

"Yeh. Think about it. CS Lewis, JR Tolkein, JK Rowling."

"JR Hartley?"

"Who?"

"Never mind."

"Anyhow, you were saying..."

"What was I saying? Oh yes, I was saying that I found the idea of truth mediated through personality so compelling. God didn't send a book, or an idea or even a religion, he sent a man. A human being who encapsulated the nature of God. God took on human form. Even God needs people to fully communicate what He is all about. It is the same today. People are the best adverts for the gospel even with all the faults and contradictions. There's this bloke called Newbiggin who said that the only hermeneutic, sorry I mean the only way of understanding the gospel, is a church of men and woman who believe it and live by it.[17] In other words, the way to understand the gospel is to see it worked out in people's lives."

"So I gather that you met some good Christians then?"

"Yeh. One or two. People who believed it and lived by it. I won't go into all the details, but it was like finding what I had been looking for. The academic interest along with my philosophical or spiritual quest if you want to call it that sort of intersected with the people who lived out this passion and shared this hope. Both parts kind of came together all at the same time. It was like two blades of a pair of scissors. As far as I was concerned I needed both parts to cut the cloth in terms of authenticity. The intellectual system without any practical outworking is just wishful speculation. The practical working out without the intellectual rigor is self serving. Both parts are needed. Both came together, whilst I was at art school and over a period of about a year, I sort of came to faith and learned to trust God with my life direction."

"So that's when you became a vicar then?"

"No, not immediately. You don't just make such a giant leap overnight. I spent a year or so doing voluntary and part-time jobs before getting involved with the youth work at a local church. Eventually I ended up working with the young people at the church and the local school full time and getting paid as a sort of unqualified youth worker. It was from there I eventually explored the path that led towards ordination."

"Wow Kev. That's pretty amazing. I wish I had been there to see it. It might have inspired me and set me off on another path."

"Are you not a believer then Dan?"

"I am a believer. I just don't really know what I believe in. This latest play of mine has raised all sorts of questions for me. Bonhoeffer was an extraordinary man living in extraordinary times. I didn't know anything about him before, but Clinton sort

17   Matthew 25.23

of got me into him. It was he who had this idea of doing a one man play. He brought me this rough script and we kind of worked on it together. In fact you could actually say that Bonhoeffer brought us together, because we weren't really that close before then. But certainly I see that passion you spoke about in Bonhoeffer. Whatever you think about his politics or even his motivation and ethics. He was certainly someone who believed in the message and tried to live by it and in fact ended up dying for it. He said something about how it wasn't sufficient just to bind up the victims beneath the wheel, but that you needed to stop the wheel itself.[18] I guess that's why he took that approach of opposing Hitler and supporting the attempt to overthrow him. I find that very powerful, but unlike you and Clinton, I still don't really have that kind of certainty about what I believe, in fact I'm not even sure if I believe in certainty."

"There are just two certainties in life Dan. Death and taxation."

"Who said that?"

"I did, just then."

"You know what I mean. Who first said that? I've heard it before."

"I never reveal my sources."

Just then a sizzling platter of fajitas arrived requiring our immediate attention and curtailing the topic of conversation.

"Is there anything else you require Sir," said a pretty waitress in a short flared skirt and Mexican hat. "Any sauces perhaps?"

18   "How is it possible that the gospel should be credible, that people should come to believe that the power which has the last word in human affairs is represented by a man hanging on a cross? I am suggesting that the only answer, the only hermeneutic of the gospel, is a congregation of men and women who believe it and live by it." Lesslie Newbiggin *The Gospel in a Pluralist Society,* SPCK. London, 1989. p.227.

"Young lady." Daniel reached out to hold the waitress's arm in mock seriousness preventing her from going any further. "I'll have you know that this man NEVER reveals his sauces!"

At this point that we both broke into raucous laughter which was probably inappropriate and excessive by way of a response to such an awful play on words, however, the pun seemed to bring us back to childhood times once again when school boy pranks, silly names and plays on words were often employed to provide the commentary upon our changing lives. It was good to be with Daniel again. Even though so much had changed and we now lived very different lives, laughing together reminded us both of our shared childhood and all the important things that we held in common.

After the meal, which Daniel very kindly insisted on paying for, we caught a bus for a few stops to Daniel's terraced flat in a slightly down at heel, yet formerly very respectable part of Edinburgh.

"Edinburgh is becoming a really expensive place to live," Daniel explained, "despite what most people think. Actors don't earn a great deal, so it's a bit of a struggle to keep this place up. Hence why I needed a flat mate."

We then gained access at street level through a large green painted wooden door with a rather large and magnificent brass door knocker. Once inside the rather dark hallway opened up before us to reveal stone steps and wrought iron banisters. Once we negotiated two flights of bare stairs we reached Daniel's modest flat, which had a poster of his one man play stuck on the door.

"I need all the advertising I can muster," said Daniel tapping the poster and pushing back the door against a pile of takeaway food menus and glossy advertisements for patio steam cleaners and conservatories. "I don't know why they post these adverts through our doors. They can see that we have no need for a patio or a conservatory."

"I guess that they need all the advertising they can muster as well." I added.

Daniel's flat was an interesting array of the expected and the surreal. Tasteful practical furniture, festooned by a somewhat larger number of scatter cushions and candles than most men usually choose, accompanied by various theatrical posters and movie memorabilia, including a life size full costume and face mask of Darth Vader.

"Don't be put off. Come inside. There's a story about that which I'll tell you one day," said Daniel referring to the dark Jedi knight.

"I bet there is," I said knowingly.

"Come in. Make yourself comfortable. May the force be with you."

"And also with you." I found myself replying without thinking.

"Caffeine is called for, don't you think?" said Daniel who apparently hadn't heard my compulsive liturgical response. "Or are you a de-caff man?" asked Daniel as he disappeared into a kitchen off the main living room.

"However, it comes. I don't mind."

As I looked around I noticed a cello and music stand propped in the corner of the room beneath a few promotional posters and photographs of Daniel standing alongside John Nettles on the set of *Midsomer Murders*.

"I didn't know you were a musician as well."

"I'm not," replied Daniel from the kitchen, "I sort of dabble. I took it up whilst I was in New York, had a few lessons, but I find it quite hard to maintain the discipline of practising."

"You need to find an orchestra or a quartet or some sort of group you can join. Most people find it a struggle to play on their own, but it's much easier if you have a reason to practise and other people to play alongside."

"Are you trying to recruit me into your group?" asked Daniel popping his head through a serving hatch.

"No, it's just that musicians are meant to play together. It's much more fun… and it can also cover up your own mistakes."

"In that case I would need to be part of a very large and very good orchestra to cover all my mistakes" announced Daniel re-entering the room with a tray, cafetiere and a plate of large, interesting looking cookies. After sitting down, our conversation continued.

"Do you keep up with anyone else from school Kev?"

"No, not really. There was a school reunion a few years ago, but I couldn't get along to it as I was working. It was arranged by a couple of girls from our year, Jeanette Price and Tracey Wilkins, although they are now both married and called by other names."

"Oh yes, I remember them, I couldn't get there because I was in New York, but they kindly sent me some photos and a write up about it."

"Me too."

Daniel and I then proceeded to reminisce about our old school days, recalling eccentric teachers, funny incidents, appalling food and speculating over what had become of the school bullies and the class flirts. "I guess that they are still bullies and flirts, although bigger and older." Daniel suggested.

Just then there was a noise in the flat as the door opened wide and in walked Clinton carrying various bundles of books and papers.

"Hi there. You must be Kev-van. Pleased to meet you sir." He announced in a southern US drawl whilst offering a firm handshake. "Dan's told me a lot about you."

"That's always a worrying introduction, and its 'Kevin' or Kev."

"Help yourself to coffee and cookies Clint." Daniel beckoned Clinton into the room. "Sorry Kev, coffee and cookies is a kind of tradition I picked up from my time in the States," he explained.

"One of the better American imports I'm sure," I replied, without really thinking, before quickly looking across to Clinton to see if he was offended. However, he appeared not to have heard or registered my ill conceived remark.

"So you're some kind of pastor and a rock musician Kev. That's an interesting combination," observed Clinton as he sat down to make up a circle of friends.

"I suppose I am. The musician bit is just a passion and pastime. It's the pastor or priest bit that I do full time."

"Sure, sure you do. Must be great to combine both though. Where I'm from they tend to steer well clear of rock music. They've only just stopped banning people from listening to Elvis in some Baptist churches down south," Clinton commented with a wry smile suggesting that such a sweeping generalization was not entirely accurate.

"Is that where you are from Clinton?"

"Please call me Clint. Everyone else does."

'I'm sorry but I'm not going to call you Clint,' I thought, rather defensively. *'There is only one Clint and you aint the stranger with no name. Besides, it is just a bit too familiar and too soon to be drawn into such abbreviations straight away.'*

"Yes, I was Southern Baptist. Born and ill bred."

"You didn't appreciate your church upbringing then?" I said rather stating the obvious.

"You could say that. But in fairness, it wasn't all bad. It did give me a set of values and a direction, even a passion in my life. All of which I am subsequently grateful for. You never quite leave all that behind. No matter what happens later."

"Clint's Dad was a pastor of the church down there," Daniel helpfully explained in a manner which suggested that he was encouraging Clinton to be more forthcoming in explaining his background and upbringing.

"Yeh that's right. My little old Daddy was the pastor of the church. So I guess you could say that I was brought up to be a good Christian boy... Gee these cookies are good. *Duchy of Cornwall*?"

"No, *Sainsbury's,*" Daniel explained.

"Do I gather from your tone that you have struggled to continue with your Christian faith as an adult?"

"Gee... I thought us southerners were meant to be forward. You don't waste any time in getting to the point do you? Yep, it's been a bit of a struggle ever since. My faith has continued, but now it follows another less rigid path you could say. You may not know, because I guess it's very different over here, but in the

States and especially in the southern part of the US, we have a sort of Bible belt, a conservative Christian ghetto you might call it. Now that's just fine and dandy if that is all you know and if that is all you want, but if you find yourself questioning the rules that define that community or ghetto or else you find that you don't quite fit in with the expectations of that ghetto, then you got serious problems, sir and boy, did I have serious problems, especially when your Daddy is the pastor of the local church."

"Did you experience problems about your sexuality?"

"Well yep, you could say that. At first I was so deep in the closet that I was practically in Narnia. Although that wasn't the first problem I had. First of all, it was more political. I just started to question some of the policies that the church was backing and started to explore other political creeds and ideas. Unfortunately that wasn't entirely appreciated. All good Christians are expected to think and vote in a particular way in those communities. Then the gay thing cut in and boy... did the shit hit the fan over that. Sorry I didn't mean to cuss."

"It's OK. I understand what you mean."

"Well you can imagine if you're gay in some of the southern states of the America, you've got problems. I mean they believe in shooting faggots over there... that's what they call them. And if you are a radical Democrat as well, then you've got real big problems. They want to tar and feather you... and then shoot you afterwards. So it aint easy fella. It aint easy."

"Is that what brought you to move to New York?"

"Kinda, although it wasn't all ideological. I went off to Drama school in New York first, and in fairness my family supported me with that. Even paid my fees. I just think that they find it hard to accept me the way that I am. They never stopped loving me as their son. But anyway, they sent me off to Drama school and New York was a lot different place to back home and I just settled in there and felt accepted. Then I spent some time teaching Drama before I eventually met up with Dan here, when we were doing a drama in the community project working out of some tough schools in the Bronx and Queens and things kinda led on from there. Now he's taken up this Bonhoeffer project of mine, which is great because I've been trying to get someone to put it on for me for ages, but they weren't all that interested in New York. I guess they are still a bit parochial and European history doesn't make great box office there. People kept saying. 'Remember *Yentl*' as if it were some sort of warning as to what happens when Americans try to recreate European religious stories."

"Have you seen *Yentl*?"

"Yes, I have."

"No comment required then."

"Anyhow, Clint's been a real inspiration on this project," explained Daniel, "and now we have put this little tour together we have started to attract some favourable reviews, there's even some talk about taking it to the West End. Clint's just managed to secure a place in the Edinburgh Fringe for this coming summer, so things are looking really encouraging."

"I'll have to find a way of getting to see the production. It will probably have to be after we have finished this tour of ours," I assured Clint and Daniel.

"That would be great. And Clint and I want to come and see you perform tomorrow night. Don't we Clint?"

"Wouldn't miss it for the world."

"OK provided you promise to behave yourselves. I understand that these Scottish crowds can be a bit hard to please."

"Yeh should be fun. Don't worry, we'll behave ourselves. I saw the real *U2* in the States and they were amazing."

"You know that we're just the support band don't you. You're not expecting us to launch into *Sunday Bloody Sunday* or something are you?"

"No. Don't worry." Daniel explained. "I think we know what to expect. Not the real Bono, just like I'm not the real Bonhoeffer."

"And Bonhoeffer, what made you want to explore his life and beliefs?"

"He just sort of blew my mind" explained Clinton. "I suppose that I'm instinctively drawn towards people who go against the flow. Bonhoeffer didn't just stand up to Hitler and the Nazis; he also opposed the official religious hegemony of the state church. He helped to set up the Confessing Church and that, with all the criticism from within as well as opposition from outside. I guess I have a deep respect for that... He also had the good fortune to die just at the most creative part of his theological journey, when he was exploring so many new ideas. Consequently, everybody can now claim him as their own, because we will never know where his journey would have led him and so everyone who wants to explore radical approaches to faith and politics can extract bits from his final letters and sermons to suit their cause and no-one can find any later work of Bonhoeffer that will contradict the conclusions they draw. So Bonhoeffer is an ideal, postmodern prophet, he's an empty space you can put anything into. You can make him into a martyr for any cause you want – but there again, some people say that I'm just an old cynic."

"Well you might be an old cynic, but I'm a tired actor who needs my beauty sleep luvvy. So I'm going to bed now. Have you got everything you need Kev?"

"Yeh, no problem, I travel light. I only brought a toothbrush."

With that Daniel showed me into a box room where I would be spending the night.

"Clint and I will be next door if you need anything."

I found the very idea of two men sharing a bed in the room next door still quite unsettling. I was aware that such things took place, but only rarely did they become part of my life experience. I still hadn't made up my mind about the whole gay debate as it affected the Church. I was aware of the strong feelings that issues concerning sexuality created on both sides of the debate, so I had always tried to be measured and broad minded. I struggled personally to know how to respond when members of my own church tried to pin me down to make general statements about homosexuality, gay priests and civil partnerships. I found myself wanting to take the teaching of scripture and Christian tradition seriously, yet found that issues of morality never presented themselves neatly in black and white terms of right and wrong, truth and error, but rather came wrapped up in inconvenient parcels labelled 'people'. Therefore although I knew what the Bible said about such issues, I still felt uncertain how to respond pastorally to people who found themselves attracted to members of their own sex.

Despite the fact that I felt uncomfortable, I couldn't help but like Daniel, whilst Clinton seemed to be quite a character and obviously provided Daniel with inspiration in many ways. I didn't really want to pass a moral judgement upon their relationship, but yet I remained uneasy about their lifestyle and unsure how to react around two people who were obviously so committed and settled within that lifestyle. I felt like a pacifist invited to stay in a barracks. I might share a personal conviction that there is a better way to resolve conflict than through violence and war, yet the reality of the world around meant that wars still happen and soldiers are people who need love and understanding just like everyone else.

Ultimately I didn't want to spoil any new friendship that was being reconstructed between me and Daniel by engaging in a hot headed theological debate. I had had enough of such debates recently and like many Anglican priests I had no affinity for confrontation. Sometimes it was inevitable and occasionally I had been unable to avoid conflict in parish life finding that it offered the opportunity to clear the air, release tension and help to illuminate the absurdity of the issues that often divided people. Such as the rows with the Uniformed Groups that I had engaged with back in Sheffield. However, heated debate was never my preferred option. My Father had given me the childhood advice of avoiding debates on the subjects of politics and religion as they would often lead to arguments. However, as an adult, I was gripped by a passion for both politics and religion, which meant that it had proved difficult to abide by Dad's advice. Although I retained a profound dislike of arguments, I had often been drawn into a defence of the Christian faith which had degenerated into impassioned arguments with sceptics and unbelievers, such as with Danny in Norwich and although I felt more than able to hold my own in such debates, rarely did I notice any change among those with whom I locked intellectual horns. Such arguments often produced more heat than light and in my case I had never encountered anyone who was sufficiently convinced by my particular line of reasoning to change their own belief or indeed, behaviour.

Instinctively I wanted to be inclusive and embracing towards Daniel and Clinton. I just wanted to say 'yes' to them as people whilst retaining a discreet distance from the moral and theological debate surrounding their lifestyle. Friendships were thin on the ground for people in my position, I didn't want to jeopardise such a rare commodity by a show of public disproval. Once again I therefore decided to go with the flow or to surf the wave, however, I still secretly hoped that the subject of Daniel's sexuality would not arise again in conversation and that I wouldn't have cause to knock on their door for any reason during the night.

I fell into a deep and perplexing sleep.

Chapter Sixteen

Bono takes a dive

"Have you still not found what you're looking for?"

Danny Short writes....

Having personal doubts? Career going nowhere? Left behind whilst others climb the greasy pole of promotion? Entering a mid-life crisis or just considering a new career move?

It seems that we are never happy in our own skins these days. No sooner do we get educated, train and qualify for our chosen career, than we are off exploring new career horizons.

This is now a well worn path for many career minded people in the UK today. Last month we caught up with Alexandra Hopwood in Mozambique as she turned her back on a lucrative City Legal Practice in favour of working with Aids orphans and community development schemes. So a willingness to give up wealth, power and respectability is clearly a common feature of those exploring the path of 'Zen Employment' – exchanging material gain for personal fulfillment and worth.

However, what do you do, if you aren't wealthy and powerful and your social profile is no longer held in the same high esteem by your local community? What is the cost of giving up all you have for a foray into a new career? What if your situation is complicated by the fact that you are meant to be following a vocation, rather than a career in which a personal calling is the key criterion for entry?

This month we catch up with Kevin Birley, a recently widowed clergyman from urban Sheffield, who has turned his back on a thriving 'happy clappy' Church of England parish in order to pursue a career in the murky sub-culture of rock music and tribute bands. I recently caught up with Kevin, the bass player from the *Manic Tuesdays*, an appropriately entitled aspiring four piece rock band in Norwich where they were supporting the critically acclaimed, and much loved by 'The Edge', *Zoo Two* tribute band. Kevin managed to persuade his Bishop and his congregation to release him for a period of six weeks to go on the road supporting *Zoo Two* on their recent national tour. But isn't this a huge step away from the pastoral responsibilities of church life in Sheffield?

"Actually, I like getting out and about. You meet a lot of interesting people in parish life, but going on the road and coming to places like this is a whole new experience," confessed Kevin, a congenial balding, Brummie in his early forties.

In fact, for Kevin such a road trip is proving to be not only cathartic and therapeutic, but also educational and formative as it has allowed him freedom to explore his theological interests and passions, namely researching new ways of being Church. Since the birth and massive implosion of 'Flame Proof' – an alternative church for the rave generation in Manchester in the 1990s, there has been a powerful and potentially destructive connection between the Church of England and the contemporary music scene. Kevin could hardly be described as cutting edge though as his band, 'The Manics' dole up a safe menu of timeless cover versions and inoffensive original material. However, for him the time out of parish life has proved more personally fruitful, allowing him space to develop a new church community meeting in a pub in Sheffield.

Although Kevin didn't want to be drawn on what form this new church of his might be taking and whether he will become the new Jake Parsons complete with female acolytes and dance music, the striving towards innovation and significance is frequently a key driver for 'Zeners' as they often escape routine careers with little or no prospect of promotion or creative development in favour of paths that are more entrepreneurial and receptive to personal interests and life skills.

So what next for Kevin, as he closes off his tour around the small theatres, nightclubs and Art Centres of Britain?

Will we see him return to his parish or to pulling pints? Will he be able to fit back effortlessly into the dog collar after so much time within the music scene? Will he be able to exchange his bass guitar for a communion chalice and Bible? Worshippers of Sheffield look out. Next time you see a band tuning up in the corner or a group of drinkers meeting together regularly in your local, it might just be 'Kev the Rev' continuing his sojourn from the pressures of parish life.

[THE BIG ISSUE]

I awoke abruptly the following morning to a knock on my door followed by Daniel appearing in a silk kimono-style dressing gown.

"It's 8 o'clock. I didn't want to wake you earlier, but I guess you need to be up at some stage today."

"Thank you."

"Do you want a cooked breakfast?"

"Yeh that would be good."

"I'll make you a wee Scottish fry up. You've got to try this white pudding they have up here."

Somehow I hadn't expected Daniel to be a fan of fry ups. I had anticipated muesli and fresh fruit, or croissants and coffee placed next to copies of *The Independent* with Radio Four's *Today* programme playing in the background. Instead, I was greeted by a huge plate of artery clogging cholesterol. Bacon, sausage, eggs, mushrooms and indeed, fried white pudding, consumed with mugs of tea to the accompaniment of local commercial radio. More stereotypes shattered and pre-conceived ideas challenged.

"Is Clinton up and about? I enquired.

"Yes, but he left earlier. He's got a meeting with some promoters of the Festival today and he had to make an early start."

"Oh I see. He seems to be quite a mover and shaker. May be we could offer him a job as our band's manager?"

"He'd probably love to do that job. He's certainly a pretty driven individual and he has the happy knack of knowing how to make good ideas happen. It's quite a gift. He's been really helpful to my career. I would never have got anything like this one man play off the ground if it wasn't for Clinton. He seems to know all the right levers to pull."

"Obviously a useful guy to have around."

"Yes he is. So Kev if you don't mind me asking is there anyone significant in your life at the moment? It's been a few years since Julie died and you're still young. I can't imagine that you like being on your own."

"You certainly get right to the point sometimes Daniel."

"I think it's a Tamworth trait. West Midland bluntness and lack of pretensions I call it."

"Well, no there isn't anyone at the moment. I haven't really been in the market for another relationship you might say. Ian and his former partner, tried to set me up with various dates after Julie died, but I just wasn't ready and I was pretty poor company if truth be told. Since then, nothing really. Although…?"

"Yes… come on spit it out."

I paused briefly to consider whether to let Daniel in on the episode with Siobhan, and decided that it couldn't do any harm.

"Well, there's this girl in our band…"

"Ah hah…" Daniel's ears pricked up and he leaned across the breakfast table on his elbows transfixed by the prospect of some juicy tantalising gossip. I then proceeded to tell Daniel all about the incident in the shower and how shocked and surprised I was and then how I had fallen to pieces before her emotionally.

"What do you think caused you to react in that way?"

"I guess it's because I'm still hurting. Intimacy just felt like some sort of cheap thrill – an attempt to fill the gap that Julie left in my life."

"Kev you might be a priest and a good Christian, but you're also a bloke with feelings and needs. I know a little about that, although I have other feelings and needs, but we are all sexual beings and there's nothing wrong with acknowledging that."

"I'm sure you're right. I think that after that incident with Siobhan that I'm starting to understand my emotional life a little better. I think that I'm now more ready for a relationship than I have been for some time. I'm starting to move on."

"Maybe you and Siobhan?"

"I don't think so, she and Ian seem to have something going between them. I think she only came on to me as a way of getting at Ian."

"Oh, I see. But don't write yourself off Kev. You're quite a catch."

I decided to take this last comment purely as a compliment and nothing else. A slightly disconcerting side effect of discovering that one of your closest friends is gay is the troubling thought that they might actually have eyes for you or have had a crush on you at some stage in the past. There was no reason to make such an assumption, yet the idea stuck in the back of my mind in a place I hoped I would not have to revisit.

Later that morning I re-joined Ian, Siobhan and Tim at their hotel bar.

"Did you have a good night?"

The look that Ian gave me answered my question.

"Siobhan had a good night, but it was a bit quiet for the rest of us." Tim replied.

I went to ask Ian what Tim meant by his comment.

"Don't ask. I'll tell you later." Ian warned me off rather abruptly.

Siobhan was just looking embarrassed. Ian was sat vigorously stirring a cup of coffee. Their body language told me that something was up; I decided not pursue the matter.

"How was your night out?" Ian asked.

"Yeh, it was fine. It was good to meet up with Daniel again and to find out what's been happening to him."

"He's some sort of actor you say."

"Yes, struggling somewhat. But he's on tour like us at the moment with a one man show about a German priest who was executed for opposing Hitler."

"Sounds like a lot of laughs. I like musicals. " Tim added.

"So is he performing in Edinburgh as well at the moment?" Ian asked.

"No, he's between performances currently, but he will be performing during the festival later on this year. In fact, he and his par... friend are coming to see us play tonight, so you'll get the chance to meet him."

"Can't wait" added Siobhan, sounding as though she was lining up another conquest. I was just about to explain about his sexuality and then decided against it. They could find out for themselves.

After Siobhan and Tim had left in search of retail therapy, Ian started to explain what had happened the previous night. Apparently, he and Siobhan had gone out to a local bar together. Tim had met up with someone from the *Zoo Two* crew and they had decided to go to a local student bar and gig instead.

"Everything was going well between us." Ian explained. "You do know that Siobhan and I have become quite close don't you?"

"It hadn't escaped my attention."

"It's just that I know that sometimes you can be a bit slow to notice such things."

"Well this time, I was aware of your growing friendship."

"More than a friendship Kev. This woman is amazing in the sack," said Ian as he lowered his voice and spoke through clenched teeth so that no-one could see his lips move. It was obvious from the way that he was speaking, that Ian had no prior knowledge of my earlier liason with Siobhan and he felt the need to explain the sexual politics unfolding around the band's tour.

"Anyhow, we go out to this bar. She looks gorgeous as always. Spent ages getting ready and really put on a show, you know what I mean. Well of course she starts to attract a bit of attention from some of the blokes in the bar."

"Ian. Can I just remind you that you were the one who wanted some 'eye candy' in the band!"

"I know. I know. I guess that I just didn't think it all through. Normally a woman is flattered by that sort of attention and kinda takes the compliment without responding or else repels the interest in some way and remains aloof. But not Siobhan, she seemed to relish all the attention. Just kinda soaked it up and flirted with everyone she met. Well I didn't want to make a scene, so I just made a polite comment. More an observation or witticism about flirting and then she goes off her handle at me. Tells me that I don't own her. That she's a free agent and can do whatever she wants and that I'm totally pathetic because I'm getting all jealous. Next thing I know, she's off."

"You mean she left?"

"No, not straight away. She gets up on stage. They're doing some karaoke and she just grabs the microphone and takes the stage. It was like she was telling me, that she doesn't belong to anyone, but rather she belongs to everyone. Then she's on stage for song after song. Belting them out. Receiving free drinks from her adoring public. Enjoying the crack as she calls it. I try to give her a bit of space but after an hour or so she still hasn't come back to speak to me. So I suggest we leave and go on elsewhere and she just calls me a twat, says that she doesn't belong to any man and refuses to come along. So I leave."

"What happened after that?"

"Nothing, I came home. Watched the football on TV. Didn't see her again till the following morning. Tim said he saw her when he got in later. Said she looked a bit rough, like she was upset or something."

"Is he sure she wasn't just drunk."

"Maybe. You don't know with Tim do you. He isn't the most observant of people. All I know is that when I saw her again this morning she asked me how I was and said she was sorry for the way she reacted that evening, but when I asked her what happened to her afterwards, she just clamped up and didn't want to talk about it. But I could see that something wasn't right. Now I don't know what to do."

"Thanks for letting me know Ian. Siobhan is a bit of a mystery wrapped up inside an enigma. I'm sure that the details will come out one day. Do you want me to have a word with her?"

"No, let it lie for the moment. I just hope that this won't spoil things for the band. We need her contribution, especially now we've grown in confidence and have started to get used to each other's styles. I'd hate anything to disrupt the chemistry we have."

"Sure. So what's the agenda for the rest of the day?"

"Well we've still got some down time till this afternoon before we need to meet at the venue for rehearsal and a sound check. And you need to get your stuff out of the van. What are your plans for tonight?"

"I'm not sure. I'm not planning ahead a great deal these days."

"Only I don't think that Chaz has booked you a room at this place, so if you want to stay here you'll have to get something arranged this morning, or are you planning to stay with your friend again?"

"I don't know. I haven't arranged anything. I could give him a ring, but I don't know his home number."

"How about his mobile?"

"Oh yeh. I forgot about that. I've got that somewhere. I'll sort something out."

With that I left to make the various arrangements required for the recovery of my gear and overnight stay. I decided to spend my free time wandering around the streets of Edinburgh. I bought a Scottish newspaper. Examined the strange bank notes they gave me in my change, and wondered whether I would be able to use them freely back in England? Then I set out in search of a bookshop. I eventually found my way past various street artists, *Big Issue* sellers and people promoting ghost tours of the old streets of Edinburgh to find a branch of *Waterstones* that contained a decent coffee shop with comfortable chairs beckoning me to tarry awhile. Instinctively I scoured the shop for the religious books section, hoping to find some inspirational literature. When I finally located the appropriate section of shelving, all I could find were a few Bibles, some popular paperbacks introducing the Christian life, various books explaining the history and geography of the Holy Land and a number of glossy hardbacks on the historical churches and abbeys of Scotland. The three shelves that comprised the religious books section was swamped by other shelves on new age mysticism, alternative medicine and therapies, *Discovering your own Guardian Angel*, as well as books on psychology, psychotherapy and self help along with a travelling companion, *The De Vinci Code and Scotland* and a whole section of Richard Dawkins rants pointing out where God made his biggest mistakes. Moving on I decided to explore the sections on popular culture instead and bought a biography of Eric Clapton. I had long admired the technical abilities of Jack Bruce, the bass player in the sixties super group *Cream* and through my interest in the musical journey of *Cream* I had grown to admire the tormented genius that was Eric Clapton. I became fascinated by his troubled life and triumphs over adversity. This story would therefore provide a good holiday read.

Having decided to read my book over an in-store cup of coffee I was confronted by a bewildering array of caffeine choices: espresso, latte, cappuccino, americano, mocha, cafetiere, organic, fair trade, de-caffeinated. In the end I settled for my usual cappuccino, but decided to go for the fair-traded option. I had been committed to the cause of fair-traded coffee ever since what I refer to as 'the pioneering days' when the only choice for many Christians who felt strongly about the injustices of the coffee trade was a blended form of instant coffee trading under the name of 'campaign coffee'. Unfortunately it tasted disgusting and cost significantly more than the 'antichrist' of *Nescafe*, a situation which had stirred many stoic Christians to persist in buying fair trade coffee as a way of embracing the principle of personal sacrifice. Therefore I felt that I had served my time making sacrifices to taste in the cause of fair traded coffee. Now that the cause had been embraced more widely by a well-informed choice driven market, I nevertheless wanted to continue to support fair traded goods, and was constantly relieved that the quality of the coffee had now improved immeasurably.

"Do you vant a small, vedium or a large?" A small dark haired girl with a pierced eyebrow and strong Eastern European accent asked throwing me into another state of panic over making more choices.

"Umm. Umm. Don't know. I'll try a large." I panicked, having seen other customers man handling large cups, I thought that I could manage a similar challenge. Besides that I had plenty of time to kill. So why not?

What eventually arrived resembled a tureen more than a cup. I had baptised babies in smaller bowls than the two handled cauldron that was deposited on my tray along with one of those macaroon like biscuits. It transpired that what I had assumed was a large cup that I saw other customers handling was in fact only a small one and my resulting ambitious request immediately precipitated a surge in coffee prices on the international trading floor for coffee beans in the commodities market as scarce supplies struggled to keep up with increased demand created by the size of the cup that I was ceremoniously presented with. This was coffee for the seriously committed caffeine addict. Nevertheless I was up for the challenge and settled back into a fake leather armchair besides dog eared copies of yesterdays *Guardian* and *Daily Record*. Bring it on.

After reading the first three chapters of the story of old *slow hand*, I emerged into the streets of Edinburgh on a huge caffeine-fuelled high. I felt like I had springs inserted under my feet. Noise and colour appeared sharper than usual as I felt invigorated with enormous energy and vitality. I floated back to the hotel in time to meet up with Tim and Siobhan returning from their shopping trip.

"Hi. How goes it?" Suddenly I was aware I was perhaps talking louder than was strictly necessary, but found it difficult to curb my new found vigour.

"Yeh. Fine. Fine," said Tim. "I didn't buy anything but Siobhan did."

"Just a few girly bits and pieces," Siobhan explained, "some ciggys and a lotto ticket."

I hadn't realised that Siobhan smoked. Usually it is very easy to spot a smoker, even when they think they are being discreet or use body sprays to mask the smell of stale smoke, non-smokers can always tell when a smoker who has fed their habit enters the room. I had been up close and personal with Siobhan, but had never been alerted to the fact that she was nicotine dependant. Instead of dwelling on that subject I decided to steer the conversation in another direction.

"I didn't know you did the Lottery."

"Oh yeh. It's been going in Ireland for many years. Most weeks I get myself a ticket, though goodness knows why."

"Have you ever won anything?"

"Yeh. I won ten quid once a few years ago, but nothing since."

"Do you always use the same numbers?"

"Yeh, sort of significant dates, family birthdays and that."

"I see."

"What about you?" enquired Siobhan?

"No, I don't do the Lottery."

"Is that because you are opposed to gambling?"

"Sort of. I've certainly seen the damage that gambling can cause in people's lives, but also I guess that I feel that it is about putting your faith in fate, and I don't believe in that sort of fate."

"So you just believe that if you are a good Christian then God will look after you," said Siobhan mocking what she perceived as my self righteous piety.

"It's not quite that simple. Bad things still happen to good people, sometimes more so. But it is more a matter of trying to live by faith rather than luck or fortune or fate. I believe that we have freedom to choose our own path, but that faith and trust in God are part of the formula we use to make those decisions. Trusting in the Lottery to change our lives might be God's way of guiding us into something new and good, but generally it feels like we are placing our trust in another power."

"You can talk such sanctimonious crap at times Kevin. I'll tell you what. When's your birthday?"

I told her the date.

"I'll use that date instead of my sister's birthday. I'll see whether trusting in God is better than trusting in *Camelot*."

Later that day the band all assembled in the *Liquid Room* for a practice and sound check. It seemed like ages since I had last played and although my sore fingers were grateful for the rest, I appreciated the opportunity to get stuck into some songs and make some noise once again.

"There's an extra sequence I'd like to squeeze in if we can." Siobhan explained. "As we are in Scotland, I'd like to put a little Scottish folk sequence into one of our quieter numbers. There's this arrangement of *wild mountain thyme* I have been working on which could be worked into some of our own material if I can get the key sorted out."

"I didn't know you were into flower arranging Siobhan."

"Don't be such a smart arse Tim. *Wild mountain thyme* is a traditional Scottish folk tune. You'll recognise it when you hear it."

"Yeh that'd be cool," replied Ian, "we could fit it into one of our own songs. How about *Coming Home* in the middle section?"

Everyone seemed happy with the suggestion and it was good to keep introducing new ideas and improvisations into the set. It kept things fresh and alive. Given the effect of the huge caffeine shot that I was still living under I would have been up for any suggestion, no matter how demanding or unusual.

Whilst we were practicing, the *Zoo Two* musicians turned up with all their various equipment and started to set up around us. Ian had learnt not to be put off by such occurrences. After all it was their gig. The *Manic Tuesdays* were only the support band. Once we had finished our practice and agreed the new sequence with Siobhan's folksy interlude, Chris came across to speak with Ian.

"Ian, me old mate," Chris said putting his arm around Ian's shoulder in a manner which suggested that he was about to ask a favour of him.

"I wonder if I could beg on your kindness and borrow Siobhan for a couple of numbers tonight?"

"Yeh, I don't see why not."

"It's just that the lads in the band, really had fun when you and your crew joined us the other day in that jam session. And we thought it would be really cool if we could use Siobhan's sax on a couple of numbers. *Angel of Harlem* and *When love comes to town.*"

"Have you spoken to Siobhan?"

"Yeh. She's cool about it, but I wanted to have a word with you first."

"Well if she is OK about it, then no problem."

Ian and Chris continued speaking together before Ian broke away and came over to where I was practising on my own.

"They want Siobhan to join them for a couple of numbers."

"I'm not surprised. She made a big impression the other day when we jammed together. And a saxophone does add a certain something that you don't usually get with just guitar and vocals."

"Yeh, yeh. I know. I know. It's just that with the karaoke the other night, the extra bits she's adding to our set and now this, it's sort of turning into the Siobhan showcase. I was rather hoping that if they wanted to use anyone for a guest item, it might be me, after all I kinda helped them out when they needed a support band... perhaps I'm just being stupid or jealous or something... too sensitive I suppose?"

"It's just rock and roll Ian, not life and death. Also remember the reasons why you wanted Siobhan in our band apply for them as well. She does add a certain something."

"I know. I know."

With that Ian turned away, still appearing slightly troubled, but resigned to the situation.

That night the *Liquid Room* was packed with expectant fans. I managed to see Daniel and Clinton arrive and snatch a few words before going onto stage.

"Break a leg!" encouraged Daniel as I made to leave.

"Is that what all actors say, or is it just a myth?" I asked.

"It's certainly what this actor says." Daniel replied.

"I normally like to say a little prayer before I go out on stage," Clinton explained. "Would you like me to pray for you now?"

"Gosh, that's never happened before," I replied whilst trying to assess the situation. "Yes please. That would be good."

Then in the noise and general unruly disorder that surrounds large groups of people arriving at a rock music venue fuelled by copious amounts of expectation and alcohol, Clinton stretched out a hand over me and prayed that I would play to the best of my abilities, enjoy myself and entertain others with my gifts of music. This was proving to be quite a surreal moment and such a mood would continues throughout the evening.

The *Manic Tuesdays'* set went really well that night. We were starting to enjoy ourselves. During the new sequence in the middle when we played one of Ian's songs along with Siobhan's traditional Scottish folk riff, we stuttered initially, while Siobhan struggled to make the transition from a rock to a folk, but once she took hold of the melody line we managed to form around her and get a feel for where she was going, so that by the end, it finished in a way that felt appropriate as well as creative. The song even precipitated a whoop and yell from some appreciative punters in the audience. Hopefully it wasn't just Daniel and Clinton trying to be kind by whipping up the audience on our behalf.

As we came off stage, the band was greeted by a worried looking Chris in his 'Edge' persona.

"What's up Chris? Have you still not found what you were looking for?" Ian enquired, but Chris didn't get the joke and didn't appreciate the levity.

"Thanks Ian, but we're in the shit tonight. Steve's hurt himself and I'm not sure if he'll be OK to sing."

"What's happened?"

"He'd just got changed into his stage outfit and was wandering around in the wings when you were playing, and you know he's always bumping into things wearing those bloody shades of his, well he just caught himself on the lighting rig and gashed his head open. The first aider is with him now. He says he'll be fine, but I don't know. He looks kinda groggy to me."

"So what are you going to do?" asked Ian.

"I guess that the show must go on, but we'll be taking a bit of a risk."

Just then Steve appeared with a huge bandage on his head which he was trying to tuck under his thick dark haired wig which made up the on stage persona of Bono. A roadie was holding his wrap around shades and generally trying to help him to get into character and ready to go onto the stage.

"I'm all right. I'm all right." Steve insisted. "You can't keep Bono down. I'll be OK when I get onto stage. Just give me one of the swabs in case its starts bleeding again."

With that Steve and Chris got into a huddle with the rest of the band to discuss how they were going to handle the evening's event. Siobhan was hovering in the background, her red shiny outfit in sharp contrast to the dark colours of the *Zoo Two* brigade huddled in the gloom back stage. Then the volume of the PA began to rise as the backing track laid the foundations to their appearance on stage with their opening number - 'Where the streets have no name'. Chris reached for his favourite Fender strat, plugged himself into his effects pedal box and prepared to launch into the opening riff. The band indulged in some last minute back slapping and high fives, then they were live on stage and the magic began.

I decided that they would be OK, so I chose to go and find Daniel and Clinton to see what they thought of the *Manic Tuesdays* and join with them to watch how *Zoo Two* coped with a groggy Bono.

Daniel was propping up the bar at the back of the room, but there was no sign of Clinton. By now *Zoo Two* were well into their first number and so it was impossible to engage in conversation with him, nevertheless I joined him at the bar, nodding a greeting instead. Between tracks it was possible to snatch a few words with Daniel and the upshot of our conversation was that he was really impressed with the band and genuinely surprised by our musical range and professionalism.

Zoo Two were going down really well with the Edinburgh audience. Steve seemed to be performing like a man possessed with the spirit of Bono. Throwing himself into ever more demanding vocal forays and interactions with the audience. I felt that he must be on some sort of endorphin induced high as a result of the bump on the head and be over-compensating for the effect of the injury. Whatever the reason, it was an awesome performance.

"What do you think of Bono?" I mouthed to Daniel above the roar of Chris's reverberated wailing guitar.

"Bloody marvellous," I could just make out his response.

"He's had a bang on the head backstage. They didn't think he could go on stage." I spoke slowly and loudly to Daniel, trying to explain the background to the evening's events, but Daniel could barely make out every other word and so just nodded politely.

Eventually *Zoo Two* reached the part of their performance when Siobhan was invited on stage to perform with them. She sidled on rather sheepishly at first, joining in with the backing to *When love comes to town*. Having made a noticeable impact to enhancing the gospel feel of that song, she was then able to launch more confidently into the opening riff of *Angel of Harlem* causing the audience to clap along with rhythmic appreciation. Now she was obviously starting to relax and feel more at home, moving into the middle of the stage to brush up alongside Bono as he belted out the lyrics. After a some *Meatloaf*-like dramatized improvisation from Steve in which he used Siobhan as his foil to which he could address the lyrics of the song, Steve grew ever more confident, moving towards the audience with arms open wide in cruciform fashion to absorb their admiration and to demonstrate the self-giving energy of his performance. Just as he moved towards the edge of the stage he slipped and fell head first into the gyrating shadowy figures in front of him. Having disappeared from view for a few moments he eventually emerged rather unsteadily on his feet and unsuccessfully tried to climb back onto stage before collapsing in an undignified heap. Willing hands assisted in pushing him back onto stage, but he fell back once again, unable to regain his poise and balance. At that point Siobhan and Chris brought the song to a premature end and Chris put down his guitar desperately trying to see whether Steve was able to continue. After what seemed like an eternity of awkward silence and background cheering thinking it was all part of a body surfing act gone wrong, Chris eventually composed himself and stepped up to the microphone.

"I'm sorry but we're going to have to take a short break whilst we check out our singer here. He's been performing with a serious head injury and we'll have to see if he's OK to continue. So feel free to visit the bar and we'll see you soon."

By now I was making my way backstage, thinking I might have to administer the last rites or at least offer some pastoral care and sympathetic support to those involved. When I got backstage there was already a group of people huddled around Steve. Chris was panicking, swearing loudly and pacing around in circles only stopping briefly to kick a convenient speaker cabinet in frustration.

"Can I help at all?" I offered.

"No, not unless you can perform one of those miracles that your boss is known for!" barked Chris angrily, taking out his frustration on me.

In the meantime, Chaz had taken control and had called an ambulance. He resembled a pool of serene calmness amidst the exploding panic and undirected energy surrounding Steve.

"He's not carrying on. I'm sorry, but it just isn't worth the risk. We'll have to wrap it up here. If people aren't happy then perhaps we can give them a discount or something," Chaz explained to a couple of the *Liquid Room* management team who were trying to decide what to do next.

Just then a more focused Chris barged into their circle of deliberation as if possessed with some urgent news.

"Look fellas. I've got an idea."

"Forget it Chris. We'll have to call it off. There's no point in continuing." Chaz was trying to persuade him that the cause was hopeless.

"No, no listen to what I'm saying. We can complete the set. Ian can do it. He's already practised with the band and we ran through a couple of numbers together the other day."

"I don't know Chris... it's just that Steve is so closely identified with the part. They won't accept an understudy."

Chris was now beckoning Ian over towards him, still oblivious to his impending fate.

"No, we can do it. Come on Chaz trust me," Chris insisted.

By now the decibel level was starting to rise from the adjacent auditorium floor and clapping and stomping of feet could be heard as the audience started to lose patience with the lack of entertainment coming from the stage.

"Look Chaz, whatever we do, we haven't got a lot of time to debate it. What do you think mate?" Chris turned to one of *Liquid Room* managers who must have carried a degree of responsibility for taking decisions on behalf of the venue. There followed a nodding of heads and before Ian had a great deal of time to think about what he was doing, or even the opportunity to say 'No', he was led off to the dressing room to be squeezed into Steve's spare stage clothes whilst the required wig and shades were hastily put on Ian by willing roadies and band members.

Finally Ian was virtually carried from the dressing room by hands anxious to rescue a potentially ugly situation and restore something that resembled an evening's entertainment.

Ian approached me with a look of mild terror tinged with expectation which said, *'I did want more exposure, but didn't think that it would happen like this.'*

"Kev. You gotta help me out on this one. I'm not sure I can do this."

"Sure you can. You wanted an opportunity to join in with the *Zoo Two* crew didn't you? Well here it is."

"Yeh, but not like this. I wanted some time to prepare. Can you copy me out the lyrics for the last two songs? Chaz will tell you which ones. It's just that I don't think I can remember all the words."

"Yeh. No problem."

"We'll cover for you Ian," said Chris reassuringly. "I can fill for you if you get stuck."

"Thanks, but can I have some back up anyhow. I'd really appreciate it Kev. The drinks will be on me."

Siobhan then embraced Ian and kissed him so energetically on the mouth that it caused him to take a step back before she sent him out on stage with an encouraging smack on his backside. The barracking of the crowd started to subside when it became obvious that *Zoo Two* were going to reappear in some form. Chris made a short explanatory statement which produced huge cheers of appreciation and then whilst I chatted with Chaz and set about locating large sheets of paper and a marker pen, with which to copy out lyrics for an uncertain vocalist, *Zoo Two* launched into the opening bars of 'Bad' and Ian was on.

Considering what he had to cope with Ian did really well rising to the challenge of substituting for Steve. He didn't quite exude the same stage presence and engage with the audience like Steve did under his Bono persona, but lyrically he stood up well in comparison. By the time I had scribbled out the words to the next song and stuck them on Ian's fold back speaker, he was starting to relax more into the role and the audience appeared genuinely appreciative and understanding. When he got to the end of *One* he even allowed himself the freedom to spar with the audience offering them the opportunity to complete the creedal like lyrics for him. This was either a sign of growing confidence within Ian or else an indication that he had forgotten the words at that point or else couldn't read my hastily scribbled prompts. Whatever the reason, it went down a treat with the assembled crowd and as a result Ian and the band were loudly and sincerely called back onto stage to complete an encore of *Sunday Bloody Sunday* and *Vertigo*.

A much relieved Ian came off stage arm in arm with an even more relieved Chris. Siobhan embraced Ian once again in a genuine act of contrition and appreciation.

"You were fucking brilliant Ian. I'm so proud of you."

"Th..an..ks.. Siobhan" Ian tried to reply from beneath a sweaty embrace.

"I'm sorry for being such a shit the other night Ian. You didn't deserve it. I can be a real bitch at times."

Ian responded by pulling Siobhan towards him and whispering reassuring comments in her ear. Ian and Siobhan then went off together apparently reconciled and floating on an adrenalin fuelled high, leaving me and Tim to pack up the group's equipment and prepare to relocate for the night.

"That was certainly an interesting evening's entertainment," announced Clinton as he and Daniel joined me and Tim backstage. "I especially liked the physical comedy and the prat falls."

"Yeh it's all part of the act. We do this sort of thing most nights" said Tim ironically, "and if you don't mind me asking... but who are you?"

"I'm sorry Tim, this is Daniel and Clinton the guys I'm staying with."

"I see," said Tim, "Hi... I don't suppose you could possibly lend us a hand with this equipment could you as half of the band appears to have gone AWOL?"

"Yeh sure, where do you want it?"

"Over here would be great."

"That doesn't appear to be a very Scottish accent you've got."

"No, I'm a legal alien. An old fashioned southern American boy come over to *Scot-land* to improve his English." Clinton highlighted the word 'Scotland' in the manner that only Americans can, with a double emphasis both on the 'Scot' and 'land' parts of the word, that makes it almost unrecognisable to anybody from the UK. Fortunately Tim resisted the temptation to pass a comment or joke about it, probably because Daniel and Clinton proceeded to throw themselves so strenuously into the task of removing heavy equipment and generally making themselves useful to Tim and myself.

Later that evening I settled back into my box room at Daniel's flat. This time there was no late night theological discussion, but rather a few drams shared of a particularly fine 12 year old west coast malt whisky. Very smooth. Very peaty. Pure heaven!

I had left Tim somewhat bereft on his own at the hotel. There was still no sign of Ian and Siobhan and nothing was subsequently heard from either of them until the following morning.

Chapter Seventeen

Returning home

I awoke the following day to the noise of Daniel politely knocking on my bedroom door.

"I thought that you might like a cup of tea."

"Thanks. Brilliant. What's the time Dan?"

"Oh it's nearly half past nine."

"WHAT?" I exploded.

"Yes, I didn't want to disturb you earlier as you had such a busy night last night."

"I wish you had Dan. I need to be back with the band early today as we've got a lot of travelling to do. I hadn't realised it was that late. It's so dark."

"Well you are in the frozen north you know. We don't have that much sunlight up here, that's why we have to make so much of our own fun," said Daniel sounding rather unappreciated as he left the room.

I hastily downed a cup of rather stewed tea, dashed out on the landing only to be met by Clinton emerging from the bathroom. He was wearing a pair of shorts and a tight fitting white tee shirt emblazoned with a re-print of the publicity poster from *Gone with the Wind* with Scarlet O'Hara opposite Rhett Butler, under which was the slogan, 'After all, tomorrow is another gay!' I decided not to dwell on the picture or pass comment on the meaning.

"Hi Kev. How you doing buddy?" was Clinton's greeting.

"Fine, but I'm running a little late." I replied as I pushed passed him rather rudely seeking the sanctuary of the bathroom.

Fifteen minutes later and I was showered and dressed, although still unshaved. I suddenly noticed that the shirt I had been wearing the previous night had a rather noticeable blood stain down the front, presumably from Steve's head injury, although I hadn't realised that I had been in such close proximity with him during his unfortunate accident. I therefore turned up at breakfast looking as though I had taken part in a Glaswegian exchange of views the previous night.

"I don't suppose you've got anything to get blood out of a shirt have you?" I was hoping that Daniel wouldn't want to rip my shirt from my bare chest there and then in order to perform a heroic act of domestic laundry or else offer me one of Clinton's cheeky tee-shirts in exchange. I was still having some stereotyping issues and couldn't handle 'camp' so early in the morning.

"No problem. I've got just the thing for you to borrow." Daniel replied.

'Please God don't let it be pink or one of those camp tee-shirts, or anything that one of the Village People might have worn,' I thought.

Two minutes later Daniel emerged holding a blue sweatshirt with 'Edinburgh Fringe' written on it.

"I've got lots of these left over from a few years back. I had to sign one or two of them. Don't worry about returning it."

I gratefully received Daniel's gift, much relieved to discover my suspicions were not confirmed. After a hastily consumed breakfast I made to leave hoping that my departure would not be drawn out. I was already late and hated saying goodbye. It always evoked a very British sense of awkwardness within me as I never quite knew what convention to follow. Should we embrace, shake hands, kiss on both cheeks or just turn and wave goodbye or a combination of all those rituals. I was still feeling a little awkward in Daniel's flat and in the company of Daniel's partner. *'Hopefully they wouldn't want to do anything too touchy and feely – would they?'* Once again I needed to castigate myself for sexual stereotyping.

I stood facing Daniel and Clinton. A pause in conversation ensued, illustrating our shared uncertainty and awkwardness surrounding the social conventions of departing.

"Look Dan. I don't know when we will be able to meet up again, but I've really appreciated the way that you got in touch and seeing me play in the band and all that means a lot to me, especially after so many years. So... so don't be a stranger... I kinda appreciate your friendship, even though I guess we now live very different lives... it's just that..."

"Oh shut up you old fool and give us a hug!" Daniel blurted.

Then we embraced as friends. United by a common heritage and roots that neither time nor circumstances nor sexual orientation could ever erode.

"I thought that you were going to make some speech about how you didn't approve of my sexuality but nevertheless you were still my friend."

"Gosh, was it so obvious. I was thinking of saying something like that. It's not that I disapprove... it's just that I don't really want that to get in the way of our friendship. It makes me a bit unsure of myself I must admit, but I just want to reach out to you and to Clinton and say, 'I think you're great' and that God wants to reach out to you both as well and affirm you as people."

"I'm welling up....!" Clinton added sarcastically in a slightly camp manner reminiscent of the late John Inman from 'Are you being served?'

"Look let's keep in touch. Who knows what the future holds? You might be able to come and see me when I'm on tour with the old Bonhoeffer play."

With that valediction we embraced once again. I shook Clinton by the hand, displaying my English reserve, but then counterbalanced this by summoning up my best southern US drawl to encourage him to "Have a nice day," before departing walking briskly back towards the city centre and the location of the band's hotel.

Upon entering the hotel I was met by Chaz.

"Hi Kev. How's things?"

"Fine. How about with you? How is Steve? Is he feeling any better?"

"Well they decided to keep him in hospital overnight. Just for observation, but they discharged him this morning. He's actually here now, with Ian somewhere," said Chaz looking around the hotel foyer in an attempt to locate Steve and Ian for my benefit.

"Top of the morning to you." An exaggerated ironic Irish voice greeted me from behind him. It was Siobhan. "Where have YOU been?"

"I was going to ask you the same question. Tim and I had to do all the hard work clearing up on our own last night. Where did you and Ian go?"

"Oh that would be telling you wouldn't it. Suffice to say that you weren't the only ones getting hot, sweaty and breathless last night."

"Please spare me the details Siobhan. I just don't think that your disappearing act was fair on Tim and my friends as much as anything."

"Well, we're here now and ready to get under way…"

"Hi Kev." Ian approached putting a firm, but friendly arm around my shoulder in the manner he usually reserved for greeting acquaintances as long lost friends after a heavy night drinking session. "Where have you been?"

"Don't you start now? You know where I've been. I've been staying with my old school friend. He came to the gig last night and proved more helpful in packing up our equipment than you and Siobhan."

"OK. OK. I know. But last night was a bit mad all round. Did you see that reaction I got from the *Zoo Two* crowd and Chris is really impressed and reckons that this mixing up of band members could become some kind of permanent fixture. What do you reckon to that then?"

"Let's just remember that you were a second half sub for a butcher from Bolton who pretends to be an ageing Irish rock star for a living. We're all a bit long in the tooth to get too star stuck and X-factorish over what happened."

"Lighten up Kev. I know, but it felt real, like I never felt before... I guess it was just the rush of being out there, playing the role... it felt like I was someone at last, someone who mattered to other people, someone who was significant and valued."

"Look Ian. For what it's worth. I thought you were brilliant. I thought you did a great job under difficult circumstances and I'm sure that Chris and Steve and Chaz and all the lads are really grateful that you came through for them, so to speak, and saved their bacon. But we still need to take a walk down reality street and finish this tour off, so that we can all get back to what pays the bills for each of us... Right?"

"Yeh, yeh," said Ian in a grudging acceptance of my logic, before muttering under his breath, "Miserable old sod. It's like having Bryan back with us again."

An hour later we were heading down the A1 en route to the fair city of Leicester and to the *Y-Theatre*.

"So Ian, have you ever seen the real *U2* then?" asked Tim

"Yeh... just once, when they were in their early post-punk and bad hair cuts phase. It was the most awesome concert I've ever been to. Just blew me away. That's what got me into rock music."

"Where was that?"

"When I was at school in Leeds I saw them play in the YMCA. Bono even got to dance with the best looking girl, body surf the audience and climb all over the speaker stacks, but unlike Steve, without injuring himself in the process."

"That's interesting, there's a connection with the YMCA and the venue where we are playing tonight."

"How did you find out about that Tim?" I enquired. "Downloaded it all onto your WAP phone or your palm held Blackberry I suppose."

"No. Just read it in this leaflet that Chris gave me about the *Y-Theatre* – isn't there a dance about the YMCA or something?"

"Yes, but we are definitely not going there Tim," added Ian quickly drawing stumps on the direction of the conversation.

"Just making conversation," explained Tim before plugging in his iPod and game console. "Just passing the time of day."

The gig that night went fairly smoothly without the repeat of the drama of the previous night in Edinburgh. Siobhan was invited onto stage again to assist with a couple of *Zoo Two's* numbers that called for a brass backing section. This time Steve managed to negotiate his way through the entire set without falling off the stage or knocking himself out on any backstage fittings. Few people would have even noticed the black eye and bandaged cut on his forehead beneath the wig and wrap around shades that were now even more necessary to his stage persona, acting as a means to cover injuries as well as to create the character. Ian had looked on longingly from backstage as *Zoo Two* ran through their set without the need for an understudy this time.

That evening in the bar, the crew and band members from *Zoo Two* were in a happy and relaxed mood, grateful that normal service had been resumed and that further *Spinal Tap* moments had been avoided. I was looking forward to a relaxing drink with Ian and the *Zoo Two* crowd as an opportunity to touch base again following my two night stay with Daniel. I was also looking for an opportunity to make it up to Ian after I had been rather abrupt with him concerning his disappearance the previous evening. However, when I was on my way to the theatre bar, pushing my way unrecognized past a handful of committed *Zoo Two* fans anxious to get close to Steve and Chris in order to get their tour tee-shirts signed, I became aware of a strange bleeping noise. Looking around at the other people heading into the bar, no-one seemed to notice the bleeping noise. So I dismissed the sound as a feature of an overactive imagination or else the symptom of continuous exposure to loud rock music. However, once inside the bar, the noise started again.

"Tim can you hear that?"

"Hear what?....Oh yes, sounds like you've got a text Kev."

"A text? I don't do text. How can that happen?"

"It's y-o-u-r m-o-b-i-l-e g-r-a-n-d-a-d," said Tim deliberately slowing his words and increasing the volume as if I was going senile. "I can't believe you still haven't got the hang of it – it's not exactly rocket science you know… Someone is obviously trying to get hold of you."

I fumbled inside my jacket for my phone.

"I didn't realise it was switched on."

"Well it must have been. Probably when you put it in there. Have you locked the keypad?"

"Dunno. How do you do that?"

"Oh good grief. Give it here."

With that Tim snatched my mobile phone out of my hand in acute frustration borne out of a technological and generational chasm that separated the two of us.

"Yeh. It's from someone called Jonathan. He says, 'get in touch, urgently. Important developments.' Better do something about it Kev, sounds important. Who's Jonathan by the way?"

"Jonathan's my curate. He's in charge at church until I return. I'd better give him a ring. Probably just another funeral matter to deal with."

I made my way into a nearby stair well where it was quieter and returned Jonathan's call. Unfortunately, I just reached his voicemail instead, inviting me to leave a message. So now having sufficiently raised the level of my curiosity, I thought that it would be advisable to ring Barbara, one of my churchwardens. Fortunately Barbara was able to pick up her phone.

"Hello 4291"

"Barbara? It's Kevin. I've just received a text from Jonathan telling me to get in touch. Do you know what it's all about because I can't get hold of him?"

"Hi Kevin. Yes I do. Has no-one been in touch? A number of us have been trying to get hold of you for a day now."

"No, life's been pretty busy recently, and I must admit that I keep forgetting to leave my mobile on. So what's so important that you are all trying to get in touch?"

"It's your Dad Kevin, he's been taken ill. The nursing home has been trying to get hold of you for a while now and they ended up getting hold of us out of desperation. I'm terribly sorry Kevin, but it sounds rather serious, I think that you should get in touch with them as soon as possible."

Suddenly I started to feel rather light headed as my heart began to pound vigorously within my tightening chest. I was starting to panic whilst my mind raced over all sort of possible scenarios for what I might discover when I contacted Whiteview Nursing Home. I made my way into the bar to tell Ian what was happening.

Ian and Siobhan were happily joking with Steve and entwined with each other as I approached.

"Look Ian, I've got to return to our hotel to get things sorted out. My Dad has been taken ill and I need to contact the nursing home where he lives. I'll catch up with you later."

"Yeh, sure Kev," said Ian looking genuinely concerned and a little surprised. "Let me know if there's anything I can do."

"Well if you can leave your mobile on, then I'll let you know what's happening when I have some more information."

"Is there anyone else who could help with ya Daard?" enquired Siobhan, "have you got any brothers or sisters to ask?"

"No. There's just me. Look I'll be seeing you. I'll let you know."

With that I headed back at pace to the hotel room to locate my filofax in which all my useful phone numbers were stored. Having found the number, I immediately rang the nursing home.

"Hello Pro-Care Services. Viteview Nursing Home. How can I help you?" An eastern European accent greeted me.

"Yes, hello it's Kevin Birley. I'm ringing about my Dad. James Birley. I understand that he's not well."

"Please vait a moment sir," the voice replied. There followed a rather lengthy pause punctuated only by distant muffled voices and the sounds of slamming doors. Eventually the sound of approaching footsteps gave way to a woman's voice on the phone.

"Hello Mr Birley. This is Audrey White, Duty Manager here. I'm sorry to have to get hold of you like this, but your Father's been taken rather poorly I'm afraid. The doctor was with him earlier, but now he's gone home. He's stable at the moment, but the doctor feels that he's quite poorly and may be you might want to come and be with him."

The rest of the conversation with the nursing home was conducted through a fog of unreality. I remembered discussing details with them, but somehow I felt remote, as if floating above the whole situation and observing someone else having to deal with it. I put the phone down having promised the Duty Manager that I would come over as soon as possible. I now found myself returning to the experience of bereavement once again. It was like revisiting a familiar ledge on a high cliff face only to know that you must now throw yourself off into the darkness and uncertainty of a sudden drop. Experience tells you that the fall won't destroy you, yet nevertheless you are frightened of the impact and the inevitability of arriving at the bottom of the cliff face again. Memories of my former bereavement came surging back into my life with vivid clarity, even though I thought that I had already let go of Dad to the inevitable decline of Alzheimer's, but the process was kicking in once again and I had no choice other than to go and experience the full horror of it all.

I scrolled down my mobile's address book to find Ian's number. I couldn't face the noisy bar at the moment and decided to contact Ian by phone instead.

"Hi Ian. It's me. Look I'm going to have to go and see Dad. It sounds serious and I need to be there."

"Yeh, sure Kev. I understand. When are you going?"

"I need to go straight away, but realistically there's nothing that I can do tonight and Dad's sleeping right now. But the train station is close by and I think that I'll take the first train I can get tomorrow morning and return to Sheffield. Will that be OK with you?"

"Umm. Yeh. I'm sure it will be. It'll have to be. Look I don't know what we will do at the moment, but I'm sure that I can find another bass player. We are due in Gloucester tomorrow night, but we'll find a way to manage. Now you just do what you have to and we'll see you later. OK?"

"Thanks Ian."

Sometimes, during a crisis, you discover who you can rely upon. Ian sounded confident and assured on the phone although I suspected that he would secretly be panicking and making up his plans on the hoof to deal with the loss of a band member. The bottom line for me was that despite his faults, more than once Ian had demonstrated that he was a mate and I knew that I could rely upon him to deal with the fallout so that I could go and see Dad.

The following morning I arrived at Leicester railway station just after six. I had managed to secure information on train departures between Leicester and Lichfield courtesy of Tim's latest on-line gadget, demonstrating that they do have their uses at times. I just had time to grab a strong coffee from one of the track side franchise outlets before my train, full of commuters and bleary-eyed students, left for the north of England.

Once underway I found myself staring out of the carriage window into the gradually lightening gloom of the industrial scenery that faded into a grey rural dawn. More people crammed onto the train after each successive stop, gradually filling all the available seats and causing a few slightly irritable conversations between strangers. Condensation started to form on the carriage windows as more bodies were added and the world outside gradually disappeared from view, once again insulating the increasingly irritable passengers from the beauty of the countryside through a streaky damp mist.

On the whole I was mostly oblivious to the overcrowded commuting tension unfolding around me. My mind was engaged with re-visiting old childhood memories of my Dad before his descent into dementia. I remembered being helped to ride my bike without stabilizers for the first time. I remembered Dad playing catch with me in the family garden and how he had broken his glasses in an uncharacteristically energetic leap to catch a particularly wayward throw from an over enthusiastic nine year old. I remembered especially Dad's love of music. How he would delight in listening to classical music from Radio 3 much to my embarrassment when friends came to visit. How I had wished for a trendier Dad who was at least into the *The Police* or the *Dire Straits* or even *The Who*, rather than Greig or Verdi. I also recalled how Dad loved traditional New Orleans jazz and the pleasure he derived from listening to cassettes of such music bought for him on the occasion of his birthday or at Christmas time. One enduring memory fixed itself in my mind, recalling one Christmas Day when he had uncharacteristically indulged himself in one too many glasses of Liebfraumilch and sat in the back room wearing a Christmas hat and listening to his New Orleans jazz on his headphones. His rather loud and tuneless attempts to sing along caused such embarrassment to Mum yet provided great entertainment to me and my teenage girlfriend at the time. Then upon seeing how he had become the object of so much amusement, he resorted to calling everyone 'philistines' and 'fascists'. I also remembered how many years later Dad had invited me to a local pub to hear a favourite jazz band play, even though Dad didn't particularly enjoy pubs and got chesty as a result of all the cigarette smoke, yet his passion and enthusiasm for music shone through and had inspired me, even though my own musical tastes had taken me along a very different path.

Eventually a crowded and steamed up railway carriage pulled into Lichfield railway station and I made my way tentatively towards the taxi rank to try and arrange transport to Whiteview. I didn't normally travel by taxi, due to the expense, so that when I did it would often be as some sort of treat or special occasion, like a celebration or family holiday. The circumstances had now swung in another emotional direction entirely, however, it still seemed a fairly new and interesting experience even though my destination held so much uncertainty for me.

Early into the journey I managed to engage myself in conversation with the Asian taxi driver. Not only did he know the nursing home well, but I also found myself explaining the purpose of my visit and off loading all kinds of personal emotional baggage upon him during the journey. I guess I just needed someone to talk with.

Twenty minutes later, the taxi swept into the graveled entrance of Whiteview. Upon mastering the intricacies of the secure entry system I was greeted by another Duty Manager who introduced herself as Eileen and who led me up the stairs to the first floor bedroom where Dad was lying. Inside I was pleased to see a Caribbean lady in a nurse's uniform hunched over a frail and grey figure lying crumpled in the bed. I always gained confidence from seeing a uniform and generally found the no uniform policy of the nursing home somewhat bewildering preventing me from distinguishing carers from occupational therapists and activity coordinators. It was a lot simpler when visiting an NHS hospital when at least the staff were colour coded so that you could have a good guess at what they did and where they fitted into the managerial pecking order.

The nurse looked up at me and gave me a reassuringly broad smile.

"Hello Father, your Father is quite comfortable at the moment."

The absurdity of the patristic greeting struck me with a familiar resonance. I had been on the road and out of clerical uniform for so long, that it felt like coming into land on a strange runway marked 'professional carer' that I hadn't visited for some time.

"It's just Kevin. Call me Kevin. How is he doing? What sort of night did he have?"

"Oh fairly comfortable, like I said. But he's had this nasty chest infection for a few days now and just can't seem to shake it off. The doctor has given him some strong antibiotics but they don't seem to be having much affect. Also he keeps throwing his arms about and pulling out his drip. HE'S A NAUGHTY BOY, AREN'T YOU JIMMY. YOU KEEP PULLING YOUR TUBE OUT DON'T YOU," said the nurse addressing her comments to Dad whilst stroking his head in the manner of a concerned mother addressing a wayward child.

"Has anyone else been to see him?"

"Oh yes. I think there was a young priest that came yesterday."

"Jonathan perhaps?"

"Might have been. Can't recall his name. Very charming. Very well meaning and cheery."

"That would be Jonathan, my curate. He's a good man."

"And there was this older man this morning that turned up about half an hour ago. Gordon somebody or other. Said he was a friend. I'm afraid I asked him to wait downstairs in the day room. I thought it best that you see your father first and we knew you were on your way."

"Thanks. Yes that would probably be Gordon from the Bowls Club. He's been very kind to Dad over the years."

"Do you want me to ask him to come up?"

"Yes, but can you just give us five minutes together first."

"No problem Fath— Kevin." With that passing comment the nurse left the room and we were alone at last.

I knew what to do next. I had visited dying people many times in my capacity as a parish priest. Indeed, I had been invited into similar places to Whiteview in order to visit sick or dying parishioners. However, when you arrive as the vicar with a formal invitation and clear expectations as to why you are there and what you should do, it is easier to deal with the situation than it is when you are the remaining close relative of a resident and therefore emotionally engaged. Furthermore, pastoral visits were often mercifully short and business like. On such occasions I would talk with the relatives, try to engage the patient or resident, and then proceed to read scriptures, pray and often anoint with oil, a traditional sacramental sign of healing which is often used within the more catholic tradition of the Church as a commendation at the time of death, but which I happily embraced in my more evangelical style of ministry. However, sitting here as a family member I felt uneasy in offering any sort of pastoral or sacramental ministry. I just wanted to hug Dad, say I was sorry, although I didn't exactly know what for, tell him that I love him and that Jesus loves him as well and to not fear what lay ahead.

I looked around the room. It remained fairly bare and functional, devoid of personal items and furnishings despite the many years Dad had spent at Whiteview. So many personal belongings and symbols of Dad's former life and work had been sold or thrown away or passed on to other people following his coming into care and selling the family home. Dad had also given away many personal items during times of heightened confusion.

Several personal and idiosyncratic items remained however, including an early example of some of my art work such as a pot I made for an A level project and a pop art picture comprised of several brightly coloured silk screen prints of John Lennon in an Andy Warhol idiom that I produced at art school. The Lennon picture offered a strange accompaniment to the stark and clinical room in the nursing home. I often wondered just why Dad had held onto the picture and what other visitors had made of it over the years. In the corner of the room was an old fashioned 1960s *Decca* radiogram that Dad had refused to part with. He would often play old '78s and vinyls on it and even though it had become largely obsolete and useless over the years, he still hung onto it for some kind of sentimental reasons. On a cabinet next to his bed sat a radio cassette player attached to an old set of *Boss* headphones with which Dad still listened to Radio 3 along with a strange eclectic mix of classical music, light opera and traditional New Orleans jazz. I also noted an old cassette box open on the cabinet with *The Greatest Hits of Status Quo* tucked inside, along with a BBC recording of *The Best of Round the Horne.* I never did discover the reason for this strange addition to his music collection.

"Hi Dad. It's Kevin. I've come back to see you."

Dad seemed to shudder and move in recognition although he didn't speak and remained fairly still whilst sighing heavily and struggling to breathe through a rattling chest.

"I want you to know that…" I began choking up, put my head in my hands and once again wept like a baby, although no baby would recognise the place where my grief had came from.

After several minutes, I was able to compose myself and was suddenly gripped by a strong resolve to place my hand on Dad's head, sign him with the cross and pronounce a blessing. I looked around the room for some appropriate medium to use for the anointing, but all that I could find was some weak *Ribena* in a jug beside his bed. *Oh well if Ribena's good enough for the Methodists' and Baptists' Lord's Supper, then perhaps it's good enough for anointing as well.*

"Dad, I anoint you in the name of the Father who created you.

In the name of His Son Jesus Christ who
died for you.
In the name of the Holy Spirit poured out
for you…
Come now Lord Jesus and enter into Dad's
body, mind and spirit, bringing him your
love, hope and healing.
Dispel all fear, pain and sorrow and grant
him your peace I pray.
And may the Lord Jesus bless you and
keep you.
The Lord make his face shine upon and be
gracious to you.
The Lord lift up the light of His goodness
upon you and grant you His peace.
And the blessing of God Almighty, the
Father, the Son and the Holy Spirit, be
with you and remain with you always…
Amen."

Just as I offered the blessing, Dad suddenly coughed and said
'Amen' as clear as the day. At that precise point the picture of
John Lennon fell down the back of the radiogram on which it
had been delicately leaning on the other side of the room. I sat
back in my chair a gasp. I sat motionless in silence for several
minutes incredulous, trying to work out just what had happened
and whether I had imagined or dreamed it or had misinterpreted
its significance in some way. Whilst I was still trying to make
sense of what had just taken place, there was a knock on the door
and Gordon appeared.

"Hello Kevin," Gordon whispered.

"Come in Gordon. It's OK. Dad's sleeping… I think, kind
of?"

"How are you doing Kevin?"

"All right I suppose. A bit tired and shocked I guess."

"Shocked? Yes it had been a shock for all of us," continued
Gordon still in fairly hushed tones.

"No, not so much what has happened to Dad. But just now, I
felt that I should pray for Dad and even though he never seemed
to register with anything I was saying, when I finished my prayer,

he said 'Amen' as clear as anything, and then that picture over there just slid down the back of the cabinet. Look here it is." I went to retrieve the John Lennon print.

"Gosh Kevin. I hear what you are saying. Aren't you meant to expect the unexpected in your profession?"

"Yes, we are. But we don't. So when they happen you find me just as gob smacked as the next person."

"Oh right I see. Anyhow is there anything I can do?"

"Not really. Just being here is the most important thing anyone can do. Feel free to talk to him. He might not respond or say 'Amen' again, but that doesn't mean he can't hear. Often hearing is the last sense to go when people are in this state."

"Oh right I see." Gordon repeated himself.

"I'll leave you alone. I guess I may be here for a while, I'll go downstairs and try to get a cup of tea or something."

With that I left Dad with Gordon. Outside the room I was greeted by Eileen who offered me a cup of tea in their special 'family room' downstairs. I tried to make myself comfortable. I knew that such occasions could be very drawn out and tiring for those involved as well as mind numbingly boring and tedious. So I nestled myself into an armchair and started to flick through old copies of 'Hello' and 'Country Life' before dropping off into a surprisingly peaceful sleep.

"FATHER! FATHER! I mean Kevin…"

Familiar words penetrated my subconscious. I awoke to find the Caribbean nurse I had met earlier standing over me, shaking my arm gently.

"Kevin you need to come with me immediately."

She didn't look like the kind of person to be argued with. So I followed her upstairs not knowing what to think and asking no questions.

Upon entering the room, I saw Dad lying motionless in his bed.

"Where's Gordon?" I asked.

"Oh he went home some time ago. You've been asleep for a little while now. We didn't want to disturb you, but then we found him like this. I'm afraid he's passed away. I'm terribly sorry."

The words, 'I'm terribly sorry' seemed to hang in mid air.

I rushed to Dad's side and took hold of his dry, cold hand.

"I'm sorry Dad. I'm sorry. I should have been here for you."

"You were there for him," the nurse replied, "he just drifted off when you were downstairs. I'm sure he knew you were here for him."

"Yes. Yes. He did. He said 'Amen', when I prayed. He did."

"There you go sir."

"Did Gordon say anything?"

"No, I didn't see him leave. I don't know whether he would have been able to hold a conversation. I guess not."

"Thank you. Thank you. I understand."

"It must have been a great blessing to you, having prayed for your father and all that?"

"Yes it was. I never expected it to happen like this."

"Well God is full of surprises and His timing is always perfect isn't it?"

"I guess so."

"Was your father a believer?"

"I'm sorry?"

"Was he born again? Saved? Washed in the blood of the Lamb?.... Was he a practising Christian?"

"I don't think he would recognise any of those terms. But he was a good man... and he was my Dad." I started to well up.

"Ah that will be a great comfort. And I'm sure God has answered your prayer and he will have gone to be with Jesus now. Especially with you being a priest and all that."

"I don't know. I can't think about where he is now. I am just getting used to speaking of him in the past tense. As a priest all I can do is to help bring him into the presence of Jesus, after that it's over to Him as to what happens next. I've stopped believing in my ability to recognise the saved and unsaved. I think that's God's job, not mine."

"Well He certainly is a God of surprises isn't He? Remember those sheep and goats.[19] Surprises on both sides. So who can know?"

"I'll put my trust in the goodness of those surprises. That gives me hope and hope is all we have!"

"Well I'll leave you with your hope and with your father now. I'll be downstairs if you need anything."

"Thank you."

I felt that I should stay awhile with Dad. I looked around the room and noticed that a tape was still trying to play in the radio cassette besides his bed. I switched off the machine, the headphones lay dangling on the floor. I didn't remember seeing them there earlier so I picked them up wondering what had happened when Gordon was with Dad. Just then there was a knock on the door and Eileen, the Duty Manager came in.

"Hello Kevin. I've come to extend my deepest sympathies and say how sorry we all are for the death of your father. I've been reading his case notes and I gather that he is our longest serving resident. Even though I haven't been here for very long myself, I know what a special person he was and how all the staff and the residents are going to miss him terribly."

"Thank you that's very kind. I appreciate it. I wonder if you could just tell me something. I notice that these headphones were lying on the floor."

"Right... were they?"

"There's not a problem. It's just that I didn't see them there when I first arrived. Can you tell me whether they've been moved at all?"

"Well Mr Birley. I didn't really want to tell you this, because we usually don't discuss such details with relatives unless they ask. But it was me, rather than Isobel – she's the nurse you just met, who actually found your father. I came in about half an hour after his friend had left and found that he had passed away. Only he was still plugged in to his music, so I simply took the

19   Matthew 25.32-46.

headphones off before we came to tell you the news. I hope that you understand and you won't be offended."

"The old dog. Who'd have thought it?" I mused upon the significance of Dad listening to his favourite music as his passing shot at life. I removed the appropriate cassette from the machine and examined it in detail.

"I think I'll keep this. It had a special place in Dad's life and that makes it a rather special for me as well."

Then I left, pausing only to sign some paper work in Eileen's office. I felt I couldn't stay any longer, I wanted to remember Dad in ways other than as someone who occupied a bed in a nursing home.

Chapter Eighteen

Herbal medicine

Ten days later I was driving over the Derbyshire hills once again en route to Buxton and a meeting with Bridget, my spiritual director.

My well worn, battered Rover 45 diesel crunched over the gravel drive that marked the entrance to Bridget's rather impressive home. Rather unusually the front door opened marking my arrival to reveal Bridget waiting to meet me.

"Hello Kevin. I heard you arriving."

"Yes, that will be the old diesel engine I'm afraid."

"Come in, come in. It's good to see you again."

Bridget ushered me into her kitchen. She had been baking and invited me to help out by carrying the tray loaded up with cafetiere and her latest home made date and walnut cake into the living room. Bridget was capable of dispensing huge amounts of love, sympathy and understanding, but she also recognised that the people were capable of helping themselves and assisting with a simple household task, demonstrating they were more than simply victims. They were quite able to give and serve as well as receiving and being served. 'It never hurts to make those who feel vulnerable help out someone else once in a while.' She was heard to say.

"Come through here Kevin and put those things down for me if you could be a darling. Thank you so much."

I sat back in one of her large, well worn and slightly saggy armchairs in a huge bay window overlooking the majestic Derbyshire countryside. It was a slightly milder day than the last time I visited and so there was not roaring log fire to greet me this time. Pity.

"I'm so sorry to hear about your Dad, Kevin."

"Thank you. I appreciate it. I also appreciate you fitting me in like this. I know how busy you are."

"You see this wrist of mine?"

"Yes."

"Do you notice anything strange about it?"

"Not really. Have you not washed for a day or two?"

"Look again."

"It's bare, that's all."

"Precisely, no watch. No ticking timetable. In other words, I've always got time for you."

"That's very kind Bridget. This last week has been so hectic and I still need to return briefly to my travels to complete this tribute band commitment that I've got myself into."

"Oh yes, I remember. How's it going?"

"Yeh good. It's cool. Lots happening. Lots to take in. It seems that ever since I agreed to hit the road with the band my life has been spinning out of control, or rather moving in a whole set of different directions. But somehow recently it has all started to fall into a pattern of sorts. It's like the anarchy and messiness of it all has suddenly taken on a shape and meaning."

"Can you explain?"

"I'm not sure. I don't really understand myself. I just feel that it has all been part of me climbing that other peak we spoke about."

"Ah yes, the mountain of longing."

"That's right. The new beginning for me... I hope that I won't come to regret saying this, but I think that my life is finally starting to fall into place, like there's a new start for me. As if, at last, I can see the top of the mountain. I'm not quite there yet, but I'm finally leaving the valley bottom and the forest of undergrowth that was threatening to overwhelm me. I don't actually know where this journey is leading me; all I know is that I'm not returning to the place where I stood before. I've finally let go and left that place behind."

"That's wonderful Kevin. Really wonderful. I've been praying for you especially since our last meeting and I know that others have been praying for you as well. I'm so glad you feel you are moving on in your life. That's so good to hear. Perhaps you can tell me what has made you feel this way and what has changed in your life since last time we met?"

"Wow. So much to talk about. How long have you got Bridget?"

"Long enough. Remember: no watch!"

I then proceeded to tell Bridget all about the experience of being on the road, praying for Justin and Pippa, staying with Daniel and Clinton, the meeting with the Goths and joining up with Matt in Tewksbury and all that was happening back in Sheffield with Bill the Biker and the Friday evening pub group. I also described in some detail the incident with Siobhan, how she had come onto me so strongly and how my reaction surprised both myself and her.

"So how did you feel when Siobhan wanted to make love?"

"How do you think I felt? She's a gorgeous woman. Like one of the missing Corr sisters that the rest of them are jealous of."

"So why didn't you make love to her?"

"I can assure you that I wanted to. I may be a vicar, but I'm also a man, with the feelings and emotions of a man. I did want to make love. I guess there will never be such an easy lay for any bloke again, but that was the whole point. Siobhan was just too easy. It showed me that what I really wanted was significance not immediate gratification. I wanted my life to change, but I wasn't prepared to sell my soul in the process. She was a sort of catalyst that opened me up to the realisation of how truly lonely I was. I still had this huge chasm in my life that Julie had left me with. I guess that I was still kinda angry with her..."

"With Siobhan?"

"No, with Julie, for dying on me and making me feel so lonely, seeing Siobhan there made it all come back to me again. I've never been so intimate with anyone else since if you know what I mean?"

"Yes, I think I do." Bridget looked rather furtive and nodded.

"The whole episode sort of showed me that I have to move on. Julie is not coming back. She cannot be replaced. Siobhan would have just been a rag to wipe myself with."

"Oh... lovely image," said Bridget in apparent repulsion.

"Sorry, but you know what I mean, and – bless her – she might be a shallow sex kitten, but I would have been using her as much as she was using me and she did listen to me pour out my heart that night without exploiting my vulnerability in any way. I respect her for that."

"I can see why this trip has been so important for you. There's been a lot going on in your life recently."

"There certainly has, but that is only by way of introduction. The most significant events have taken place this last week."

"With the death of your father?"

"That's right."

"So tell me about it."

"Well I got this call to return home to see Dad; it came as a bit of a shock. I guess I hadn't really twigged just how poorly he was. Half of me reacted as his son, the other half as a priest. I found myself wanting to pray for Dad, just to let him know that everything was OK. Sort of let him know that I was there whilst giving him permission to go I suppose. Like I have done with lots of other people."

"Isn't that what priests are supposed to do?"

"Yes we are, but this was my Dad and it felt strange being a priest to him. So anyhow, I prayed, anointed and blessed him, in the same way that I would anyone else, but I wasn't expecting any particular reaction from him. He was deeply unconscious – not a flicker of recognition, but when I completed the blessing, he said 'Amen' as clear as anything, as if I needed confirmation that a special moment had been reached. Then at that exact moment, an old picture of mine that Dad had kept fell off the wall and slid down the back of his radiogram. The whole moment felt like we had crossed a rubicon, full of symbolism and significance. Like something had finally shifted or moved on."

"Like the picture falling?"

"I guess so."

"Was that the moment your father passed away?"

"No, it wasn't. You might have expected that. It's always like that in the movies, but never in real life. He died about an hour or so later while I was having a kip downstairs."

"So you weren't with him when he died?"

"No, but that didn't really matter as much as I thought it would, because his mate from the bowling club had been with him and had left him listening to some of his favourite music. It was whilst he was listening to the music that he must have died."

"Oh I see. And what was the music?"

"Just some of his 'trad jazz' stuff. A sort of compilation tape that he liked. But don't you see, what is connecting all these events?"

"Possibly? But it might be good if you can fill me in."

"Music, melody, symphony, song, rhythm. It's all in the music! Music is the one common factor. Music is the key to it all!"

"I see. And has this musical theme continued to be significant for you since your Dad died?"

"Yes, absolutely. Definitely. When I got back home, I started to listen to Dad's cassette. It had all sorts of tracks on there. A real eclectic mix. I just kept listening to it over the next few days in the car, at home whilst making the funeral arrangements. Then I had a few meetings with Jonathan, my curate and with deadly Doug..."

"I'm sorry...?"

"Oh yes, Douglas, the undertaker. We all call him 'Deadly Doug', but not to his face obviously."

"Obviously."

"Anyhow, I wanted Jonathan to take the funeral. He's a good chap and was kind enough to visit Dad when the nursing home couldn't get hold of me. I thought that the funeral should have a strong musical theme. Sort of celebrate his life and recognise the role music had played in his life."

"So did you have the funeral at your own church?"

"Yes, I couldn't stand the thought of one of those quickies down at the crem, and we had Julie's funeral at church and Dad had come to that. He wasn't much of a churchgoer; in fact Julie's funeral was probably the last time he had set foot inside a church building. So it just seemed right to do it there, but the problem was the music. Our regular organist is not really up to speed when it comes to musical contextualization. He's fine with 'Crimond' and 'All things bright and beautiful', but anything a bit left field throws him , so I thought, 'hello, who do I know who can play and do something a little bit different?' I decided to get in touch with the band. They actually had a gig on that evening, but they all wanted to come across from Bristol to play at Dad's funeral. How about that for good mates?"

"Very impressive. Look Kevin. I know that you might find this hard to accept, but you're OK you know. People like you. You're a decent chap and people love and respect you for that reason. I'm not surprised that they wanted to help out at such an important time for you."

"Tha..nk..s. Bridget. I appreciate that. Not only did the entire band come across but I also got in touch with Bryan."

"Remind me. Who's Bryan?"

"Bryan used to be in the band. He sort of still is, I think. There was a bit of a falling out between him and Ian, when Ian brought Siobhan onto the tour. But anyhow he came through for me as well. He and Siobhan got together to rehearse and actually started to get on OK with each other. So Bryan and Siobhan played mostly, with Ian joining in on guitar, Tim on the bodrhan and congos. I put the whole service together carefully with the band and Dad in mind. It just seemed like the perfect synthesis and collaboration."

Bridget's eyes were starting to glaze over, I was losing her attention and focus amidst all the technical details.

"Sorry for all this detail, but it's kind where I am at the moment and it's important to me."

"Please carry on," Bridget replied looking as if she had been found out.

"Well, it was a truly inspiring collaboration, despite the fact that none of the band were believers, they just felt their way through it instinctively and we experienced an unbelievably sacred moment."

"So the funeral service went well?"

"Yes it was wonderful. I thought I would feel kinda detached and wrapped up in my own thoughts, like I did when Julie died, but the music just spoke to me in a way that the words never could. Transported me to another place. We had Dad brought into church, carried by his old bowling club pals. They were brilliant, they couldn't do enough for me when I was arranging the funeral. When he was brought in, Siobhan and Bryan played this old gospel, trad jazz number, *Were you there when they crucified my Lord?*"

"The old Jonny Cash song?"

"Err yeh, I think so. I think a lot of folk have covered it. It was one of the tracks on Dad's cassette, played as an instrumental there wasn't a dry eye in the house. I had asked Siobhan to just go with the flow, to express herself and feel free to improvise if necessary, when the mood took her. So the whole number went on for quite a while, but it seemed appropriate somehow. Even Jonathan was moved and he's not really musical at all, not particularly emotional come to that. I kinda felt a little sorry for him. Having to be a rock in the midst of so much emotional turmoil is never easy and for someone in his position, he did brilliantly. Anyhow, we got through the whole service. Gordon did a wonderful tribute, complete with a few funny stories from Dad's bowling days. I never realised just how fond they all were of him.

Anyhow, the service went fine. No slip ups. Tim did an amazing job on the drums with 'Be thou my vision' but Ian didn't really join in all that well, for some reason. Then for the last number I wanted to play Dad out with something that I heard Siobhan do while we were on tour. I just thought that it was the most amazing, healing piece of music I had ever heard. It's called *Wild Mountain Thyme*"

"Mountain thyme... a sort of herbal medicine then?"

"Ye...s. You could say that. It certainly brought about some healing. Not only did Bryan play it beautifully on the piano and spark off Siobhan wonderfully with her haunting saxophone melody, they both sort of lost themselves in the music, cascading up and down and in and out of each other, building and fading, crescendo and diminuendo, evoking a sense of longing and... and presence."

"Presence? What sort of presence?"

"The presence of God I suppose. It just sounded so spiritual and evocative. I had to leave them to it and follow the coffin out of church, but afterwards at the reception Ian came up to me and started to tell me about how he had felt during the service."

"Did Ian know your Dad at all?" enquired Bridget whilst pouring me another cup of coffee and cutting me a slice of cake.

"Thank you... No. He never met him. Which is why I appreciate all that he did in coming over to play and that. But somehow the music and the occasion had spoken to Ian. We previously had this conversation about longing for something better, something significant, something 'other' in life, and we talked about God in kinda musical terms. You know like God is singing a song over us and just wants us to join in with his melody."

"Oh that's a lovely image Kevin."

"Yes, I know. Sadly not mine. But it really connected with Ian. He seems so full of himself at times, but he's really just an old softie and I think that he's been searching for direction for some time. This crazy dream and ambition he has to make it in the music industry is really all about that I think. He must know that his time has gone and that popular music is a young person's game these days. But the music and the whole funeral experience spoke really powerfully to him. He wasn't able to express himself all that clearly and I guess that I wasn't all that receptive to him as I was still having to deal with my own emotions, but from what he said, he sort of connected spiritually at last and was asking how he could get to know more about God and Church and Jesus and stuff."

"Wow. That's wonderful Kevin. So what did you say to him?"

"Well it's like I said, I wasn't a great deal of help, being so pre-occupied at the time, but I put him in touch with Matt, you know the one I got to know in the pub and gave Ian a couple of books to read. So hopefully something will develop out of that."

"Who would ever have thought that a friend could be brought close to God through the death of someone significant?"

"Bridget! Now YOU are being facetious. That is the sort of thing I usually say."

"So tell me what has happened since then?"

"Well Ian and the other band members had to go back to do a gig that night, so I haven't heard from them for a couple of days. I have been staying on just to smooth things out at the nursing home and to go and get probate sorted, see the bank manager and all that. The band has been really good about it. They said to take as much time off as I need, they've got someone else to play bass for them, but I am hoping to meet up with them all again tomorrow, because I want to finish the tour. It just feels like unfinished business. And I think that Dad would have wanted me to finish the gigs as well."

"I'm sure that your Dad would always want what was best for you. And he would want you to be happy as well. You deserve to be happy you know."

"I know. I know. People keep telling me that. I am happy some of the time. I am starting to find the happiness that has eluded me for so long. I can see the light at the end of the tunnel and this time it isn't another train coming in the opposite direction. What I haven't told you about is what happened later on at the funeral reception."

"Please carry on and please have some of my date and walnut cake. It will look better on your waistline than on mine."

"Thanks. Well during the funeral I hadn't taken a great deal of notice about who was there. You don't do you. You sort of get myopic and don't take in the details around the edges." I paused, realizing that I was now speaking with my mouth full in my enthusiasm and spitting date and walnut crumbs all over Bridget's carpet. "But anyhow, I hadn't realised that Melanie was there."

"Who's Melanie?"

"Melanie is this girl who used to come to our church. Julie was quite friendly with her and she was a great help during her illness. But she had this appalling husband and violent marriage and it all split up and got rather nasty and after Julie died she eventually stopped coming along to church and I kinda lost touch. Anyhow, I met up with her again the other night when Matt invited me to meet his friends around at the pub, but she just seemed distant and cold with me. I assumed it was because I had lost my rag with her when she started getting too close to Julie and then she had stopped coming to St Ebbs and it all became a bit difficult. So we kinda met up again at the reception over a vol-au-vent and sausage on a stick – even though she's a vegetarian. Did I tell you that? Well anyhow, it's not important. So we start to have a heart-to-heart and she is being really sweet and kind and sympathetic, but in a way thats goes beyond what most people express at such occasions. She just sort of looked directly into my eyes and kept going. You could say that we started to connect as people, more than friends. Does that make sense to you?"

"Do you mean that you connected as man and woman, rather than as priest and parishioner or as friends?"

"Y..e..h."

"Because I think I know what comes next."

"You do? Matt tried to tell me something about Melanie as well, but I just didn't get it. I thought that I had offended her. I even started wondering if she had held some sort of candle for Julie. Perhaps she was confused in her sexuality or lacking confidence as a woman because of the verbal abuse she had received from her ex-husband. I had no idea how she was feeling."

"So what DID happen next?"

"Melanie didn't want to go into any details at the reception, so we decided to meet up again the day after, yes, two days ago.

So we met in *Starbucks* in the middle of town during her lunch hour."

"And what did she want?"

"I think that it was a skinny latte if I recall, but it might have been an expresso."

"No. I mean what did she want to talk about?"

"Oh. Well that was the strangest part. Apparently she wanted to talk about us. All this time I thought that she had an issue with me when apparently, she did, but not the sort of issue I feared. Apparently she likes me. She has liked me for ages now and she just didn't know how to express it."

"She's not the only one. 'Likes me?' —what kind of language is that? You mean she is attracted to you, feels romantic affection, has the hots for you, is head over heels in love and passionately wants to have your babies! Come on Kevin… spit it out!" Bridget was plainly getting a little exasperated with my limited emotional vocabulary and long windedness.

"Yes, well maybe all those things, or some of them. I don't know. It's all come as a bit of a surprise to me. I'd never really noticed her in that way before. She's… she's very different from Julie. Not unattractive, but she is a little strange – bright red hair, tattoos, dock martins, weird clothes. She's also an actress by training and all 'out there' and touchy feely at times, whereas Julie was a little more self-contained and reserved. But anyhow, we chatted and then chatted some more and then last night we went out on a date."

"Oh that's wonderful Kevin. I'm so pleased for you."

"Oh and there's one more thing you should know about Melanie. She's got two children already. Twin boys. Three years old."

"Gosh there really has been a lot happening in your life recently. How does it all make you feel?"

"Feel? I guess it makes me feel really good. It's like I finally know that I am leaving my old life behind, not because it wasn't any good. In fact much of it was great, especially what Julie and I had together, but I can't live in that place any longer and I can't continue to honour the memory of that place by refusing to move on. I guess that I feel that I'm moving on now, that's what I feel. I still don't know where I'm going, all I know is that it will not be where I've been before... I've also arrived at a decision about my future: I will be leaving the ministry!"

"Gosh. That's a bit of a bombshell. What makes you say that?"

"I don't know. I just feel that I can't return to where I once was and that includes being a vicar living out a Christian ministry in the same old way."

"I see, but what you are talking about is very serious and you need to think it through thoroughly. You shouldn't be making too many important decisions so soon after losing your Dad and all that such an experience would have meant to you. Have you spoken with anyone else about this?"

"Oh yes, I spoke with the Bishop about losing my sense of vocation before I went away on the tour. He seemed to understand and thought that the time out of the parish might help to straighten out how I felt – and it has, strangely enough."

"Have you given any thought to how you might live? Do you have any savings or capital you can draw upon?"

"Yeh, I've thought about that. I still have some insurance money left from Julie's death and there's some money left over from my parent's estate, but not much. I'm not about to jack it all in immediately and go off back packing around Australia or anything. I'm not going menopausal. I'm just exploring a new future and making some decisions."

"But don't rush into anything at this stage Kevin."

"I'm not rushing into anything, but the status quo is not an option. I'm drowning where I am at the moment. It just isn't working. Tinkering around the edges only delays the inevitable change I must make."

"So what timescale are we talking about?"

"Weeks? Months? I don't know. The timing is not as important as the intention. One way or the other I am working my notice. Leaving full time Christian ministry is part of my journey of leaving behind the former mountain on which I stood and gazed with longing for another country. The only way to explore that new mountain peak is to completely leave behind my old familiar peak and set out without fully knowing where my journey will lead me. I've made up my mind, Bridget. I'm leaving!"

Epilogue

Being part of the band

The following night I was back on tour with the *Manic Tuesdays* and *Zoo Two*. We had two more musical commitments to honour. The first was at the *Corn Exchange* in Exeter, a large five hundred seater tiered auditorium, which could also be opened out onto the level to provide a better connection between the bands and their audience. It was somewhat reminiscent of the Durham venue where we had begun our tour some six weeks previously. After that we were due to finish at the *Picturedome* in Holmfirth, a recognised rock venue, where bands like *Wishbone Ash*, *Hawkwind*, *Magnum*, *Terrorvision* and *Focus* had all played recently. Strange bedfellows to the likes of Foggy, Compo and Cleggy that is usually associated with this place. This would be an appropriate place to bow out in style and to probably indulge in some sort of rock and roll celebrations.

By now there was a well rehearsed routine into which all members of both bands easily fell into. PA equipment, lighting rigs, musical instruments and personal effects were all unloaded at great speed and with little ceremony or direction. The size of the venue afforded the *Manics* their own dressing room and I was grateful of the space so that I could practise my bass lines and run through the pieces that the band had been performing for the last week or two with a stand in bass player from *Zoo Two*.

It felt really good to be back on the tour circuit again and I opened up the volume of my bass amp as loud as I dared in order to let rip and indulge in some reckless hedonistic rock and roll excess. Soon the room was vibrating with all the resonance and tonal range that my Rickenbacker could muster. In my mind I was Jack Bruce of *Cream*, John Entwistle of *The Who* or Chris Squire of *Yes*. In fact I lost myself so much in the excessive volume and freedom to make a noise that I didn't notice Ian enter the dressing room and so suddenly jumped, turning around in shock as he tapped me on the shoulder.

"KEVIN! KNOCK IT ON THE HEAD WILL YA?" He mouthed.

"Sorry Ian. Just trying to get back into the groove."

"Well you're in danger of flattening the groove at that volume. Have you turned it up to eleven again?"

"No, just letting off steam."

"It's OK. I understand. Have you seen Siobhan?"

"No, I thought that she was with you."

"I need to find her. Something amazing has happened and we've got to tell someone."

"Wow. What is it?" I asked, thinking that they might be announcing their engagement or something, even though I suspected that neither of them were particularly the marrying kind.

"I can't say. It's more Siobhan's good news than mine and I think that she should be the one to tell you."

'Great,' I thought, ironically. *'Ian's got her pregnant, I bet.'*

"OK Ian. I'll keep a look out for her."

I continued practising, although without the excessive volume and day dreams this time. Finally I put down the guitar in pursuit of the 'Gents' and a bottle of *Fanta* from a vending machine, only to meet Siobhan in the corridor outside, carrying her dressing bag slung over one shoulder which contained her show clothes.

"Hi. Ian's looking for you."

"So tell me sometink I don't already know. That limpet is harder to peel off than this dress."

This didn't sound like someone about to happily announce that they were expecting the joyful arrival of tiny pattering feet.

"Ian said that you had some good news. Is that true? Because good news would be most welcome, it has been a bit thin on the ground recently."

"Yuh. I have," replied Siobhan sounding as if she had just discovered that there was no such person as Father Christmas, rather than harbouring some wonderful news, "but I'll tell you later."

Later that evening when all the band were together in the dressing room and had decided on the running order for the evening, Ian straightened himself up and thrust out his chest in proud fashion, suggesting some important announcement was about to follow.

"Siobhan has got some good news to tell you. Haven't you luv?"

"Yuh that's right. I feel kinda embarrassed and I know that you aren't supposed to tell everyone straight away, that you're meant to wait or sometink. But I really feel I owe it to you all to tell you right now that I..."

'I'm pregnant... Go on tell us. We know already. We can see it in the blush of good health surrounding you and it's not just because you're wearing that red dress...'

"...I've—I've come into rather a lot of money. In fact I've had a win on the Lottery and I kinda owe it to you all, or in particular to Kev, as it was your numbers that came up for me."

"Bloody hell," I said.

"Fuck me," said Tim, adding, "Sorry Kev. But how much have you won?"

"Oh enough."

"What millions?"

"No, not mega bucks, there were eight jackpot winners and it was a quiet week, but without going into details, I have won enough to allow me – well maybe all of us – to follow our dreams a bit more in the future."

"Isn't that just brilliant," said Ian getting caught up in emotion of the moment, having no doubt already performed the mental calculations necessary to work out exactly what his own share might be in Siobhan's good fortune. "It's like everything is coming wonderfully together at the moment. The music. The band. The God thing. Siobhan and I. I just can't get over it."

"I'm very pleased for you," I added, "but I just don't know where this is leading us all. After all, it's your money…"

"Yeh, but since Edinburgh I've been using your birth date in my numbers as well as…"

Just then a bell rang backstage indicating that it was time to go on stage and begin the evening's entertainment.

"We'll have to continue with this later, but let's just have fun tonight and relax about what the future holds." Ian suggested whilst pulling all the band members together into a group huddle that had become part of our pre-concert routine.

"Kev, can you say a prayer or something?"

This was a new departure and clearly a sign that Ian had been deeply affected by his experiences at Dad's funeral. Once again, I wanted to pause and try to reflect upon the significance of all that was exploding around me, but time wouldn't allow, so once again recalling Tim's metaphor I decided to go with the flow. I blurted out a quick prayer, along the lines of thanking God for His goodness and provision towards the band and asking that we could all be drawn together into a tight unit whilst on stage and perform to the best of our abilities so that other people would be entertained and have fun also. Not exactly anything that the Liturgical Commission would be proud of, but it seemed to sum the situation up.

The gig went really well that night. Ian was in good form once again and even Tim was able to launch into an extended drum solo without cause to grab his inhaler. Siobhan rocked as usual and seemed more at ease alongside Ian on stage. She even lent him a hand with the vocals. Ian was on such a high that he started to get chatty with the audience. Never a good idea for a band whose sole mission in life is to warm up an audience who have paid to see someone else perform. He tried saying how we had all gone through some ups and downs recently, but none so much as our bass player, who had given them all so much help and encouragement despite his own troubles. Ian tried to draw me into a bass solo and pull me towards the front of the stage to be recognised and to receive warm applause, but the audience didn't really seem bothered and I just wanted a hole to open in order to swallow me up. I had no desire to seek the spotlight that Ian cherished so dearly.

Afterwards in the dressing room, Ian challenged me as to why I hadn't been willing to step forward more enthusiastically.

"It's just not me Ian," I explained.

"What do you mean? I was trying to big you up a little."

"I know and I appreciate it, but I've learnt many things whilst being on tour with the band, and one of the most important is that I enjoy occupying the back of the stage. I've spent many years at the front, directing operations, now I just want to be part of the team. I want to be part of a community, not form it. I want to belong to it, not to be in charge of it. I want it to shape me, not me to shape it. Does any of that make sense to you, Ian?"

"Not really... but I guess it makes sense to you."

"Yes...it does." I said quietly.

****

Ms Danny Short
14 Redwood Terrace
Heaton Mersey
Greater Manchester

Dear Danny

Thank you for getting in touch again. I'm sorry you lost my email and it has therefore taken so long to report back on what has been happening since last time we met. I thought that I would write back by snail mail for a change and then if you can use any of my thoughts to provide the 'reflective narrative' that your editor requires you can chop it about as necessary. Also, I always tend to rush when sending an email – great way to arrange meetings and share information, bad way to convey sensitive information and personal feelings.

I hadn't realized that it was over two years since all those crazy and surreal events took place on my sojourn with *Zoo Two* and the *Manic Tuesdays*, it seems like looking back on a dream. Since then so much has changed but the character who has changed most is me.

I am no longer vicar. I finally made the break with full time christian ministry, having realised just how unhappy I had become within my role. Leaving wasn't easy though. I thought that I would quickly find another job and role for myself. I had this vain and unrealistic idea that as soon as I put myself on the job market offers would pile up and I would be beating off future employers with a stick. But it wasn't like that. I guess that I had become institiutionalised and the stumbling block of 'transferable skills' reared its ugly head. What else can a vicar do if they no longer wish to be a vicar? Then there was the stigma of being labelled a deserting soldier – a caring professional who appears to have stopped caring about what he is doing, or as a salesman who has lost faith in the product he is meant to be selling.

However I tried to justify it to myself or explain it to others, I couldn't escape the feeling of having fallen short in some way. When who you are and what you do are so closely linked – a career change looks and feels more personal than professional. It just felt like failure. Even though many people regard what a priest does as serving a failing institution. I guess that the bottom line for many people is found in what value the Church and christian ministry add to our society? Many want the Church to be there when they feel that they need it, but for the rest of the time, it's regarded as something of an irrelevance – a sideshow, a bit player, a historical anomaly in a much bigger secular story that is being played out elsewhere. Nevertheless I didn't sign up to fail, nor did I set out in order to turn back or abandon a sinking ship.

In the meantime, those who choose that way of life are not meant to notice or to complain. They are expected to remain stoically whole hearted and dedicated, upholding a concept of vocation or calling abandoned by other professions generations ago. Once God calls you into the Church, that's it. It's a life sentence. You are married to the Church for better or for worse until death or retirement do you part. If anything interrupts that path then either you weren't genuinely called in the first place or else you heard the call wrongly. Breaking the covenant of that original lifelong call must therefore be a symptom of my failing priesthood or leadership. I obviously couldn't take the heat or stand the pace or cope with the role. Take your pick from any of the above.

But if God can call someone like me into something, then surely He can also call someone like me out as well. It is not a case of falling down, turning back or jumping ship, but rather a case of turning aside in order to explore another path.

As I look back, I see myself as having been led into a period of exile. Called out of my familiar territory into a foreign and alien culture. A time for personal reflection, but also a time for repentance, not necessarily for any moral failure, but rather for a change of mind and direction. My ministry is now being expressed in dispersion, rather than through the cipher of God's chosen people and God's chosen place. I am a work in progress. I am living in a place of continual transition. Moving from the old and familiar towards the new and uncertain.

I guess this all sounds rather trite, but what does that mean practically? Well in my case, it meant hanging on as vicar at St Ebb's for a very awkward and painful waiting time in which I sorted out my future options and explored new avenues. During that six month period I was like a dead man walking – a hollow shell from which my passion had departed whilst I explored various career paths. Finally, I was accepted onto a place at a teaching training college to do a PGCE. Fortunately, I had my life assurance money and a small inheritance from Dad to draw upon. I didn't qualify for one of those 'golden hellos' that students in priority subjects such as science or mathematics attract. I just want to help people to love art and the teaching of art doesn't really come that far up the utilitarian pecking order in terms of a government skills and training agenda. What's the point in promoting art? What do we need artists for other than to describe the past and dream the future?

So now I teach bolshie teenagers the virtues of Rembrandt, Turner, Tracey Emin and Banksy at an inner city state school who can only raise their profile in the community by becoming a centre of excellence for the performing arts. And you know what…even though it can be tough at times, I love it. I've never felt so alive, so free and so at home.

In the meantime, Matt and friends have continued to meet in the pub every Friday night in order to sort the church out and to change the world. Others have begun to join them and I've now become part of their group. Ian and Siobhan have even joined us in what is becoming something of a faith-based community for lost sheep and spiritual seekers, although I sense that Siobhan hasn't really bought into the faith part as much as Ian has. Ruth the doctor has become a regular and she along with Bill, Matt and Andrea now appear to be wrestling with some kind of vision and strategy for the group, to discover a new way of being…being a church, I suppose, but hopefully not the kind you knew in Manchester.

It's all very exciting and very scary. Not only have I now become part of their community but they have even asked me to be their pastor. A sort of spiritual mentor or elder, but I just keep delaying any decision. I don't know if I'm ready for such a role all over again. I'm not unwilling to lead; I just don't want to lead in the same old way.

Siobhan's Lottery money still remains largely unspent. She made a very generous offer to subsidise my teacher training, but I felt awkward in accepting it. I'm still not clear exactly how much she won, she remains very coy on the subject, but it appears to have provided a very pleasant house for her and Ian to share, whilst the rest remains set aside for what Siobhan calls her 'nest egg' and what Ian calls his 'next BIG project'. Ian still harbours all sort of ambitions and dreams for performing, making music and developing a creative business of some kind. I only hope that he doesn't over extend himself or sink too much money into a crazy new venture.

I still hear from some old colleagues. Justin and Pippa keep in touch. Apparently the Buenos Aires blessing has petered out, but I'm sure that a new one will appear soon. On the other hand their church continues to go from strength to strength and provides one of the few good news or success stories in a local church scene which continues to struggle and reluctantly adapt to change. He continues to be very supportive of what he calls my 'church in the pub thing', but still can't find the time to *do* lunch or come along to any of our get togethers.

Nowadays my priorities are located elsewhere - upon teaching, and also upon music. The *Manics* still perform, although Tim has finally gone off to university. We have even managed to get a regular booking at the *Irish Club* courtesy of Siobhan, whereas at school I am hoping to do some extra curricular work with some of the less engaged students by forming a 'rock school' for them, but without Jack Black or Gene Symmonds and all the rock and roll clichés.

So life is generally good, although not without its challenges. And Melanie? Oh yes, Melanie is right here with me. She's now got a part time job as a drama therapist and loves working with challenging kids, helping them to express their feelings. Last year I managed to persuade her to perform in a new play I'd been working on for some time by saying "I will" to me in the presence of God and many witnesses. So, there's a new drama being played out now, called "Kevin and Melanie Birley – the pub church years." We have a supporting cast of two small and energetic twin boys and many friends…many good friends.

I hope that some of this helps you on your faith journey Danny.

Best wishes